A Lady's Temptation

Tracey Devlyn

TEAM DEVLYN
2022 Remastered Edition
Edited by Martha Trachtenberg
Cover Design by Elizabeth Mackey
Author Photo by Lisa Kaman Kenning, Mezzaluna Photography

A Lady's Temptation
First published in 2013 as Checkmate, My Lord. This remastered edition
published in 2022.
Copyright © 2013 by Tracey Devlyn

Remastered Print Edition, April 2022
ISBN: 978-1-940677-15-6

www.TraceyDevlyn.com

ALSO BY TRACEY DEVLYN

Nexus Spymaster Series

A Lady's Revenge

A Lady's Temptation

A Lady's Secret

A Lord's Redemption

A Lord's Bargain

Tea Time Shorts and Novellas

His Secret Desire

Steele Ridge: The Steeles

Co-authored w/Adrienne Giordano & Kelsey Browning

The Beginning

Going Hard

Living Fast

Loving Deep

Breaking Free

Roaming Wild

Stripping Bare

Enduring Love

Vowing Love

Steele Ridge: The Kingstons

Co-authored w/Adrienne Giordano & Kelsey Browning

Craving Heat

Tasting Fire

Searing Need

Striking Edge

Burning Ache

Steele Ridge: Christmas Capers

Co-authored w/Adrienne Giordano & Kelsey Browning

The Most Wonderful Gift of All

A Sign of the Season

His Holiday Miracle

A Holly Jolly Homecoming

Hope for the Holidays

All She Wants for Christmas

Jingle Bell Rock Tonight

Not So Silent Night

A Rogue Santa

The Puppy Present

For the Love of Santa

Beneath the Mistletoe

To Helene,
Thank you for always celebrating my accomplishments, no
matter small or large, with hugs and kisses.

AUTHOR'S NOTE

First published in 2013, Catherine and Sebastian's story was originally titled *Checkmate, My Lord.*

This remastered edition includes a new title—*A Lady's Temptation*—and a new cover. I also tightened up the story to deliver a more immersive experience.

Enjoy the adventure!
Tracey

ONE

August 6, 1804
London, Somerton House

"Please, my lord," Catherine Ashcroft said. "If you would only read my husband's letters." She indicated the small packet she had placed on the Earl of Somerton's clutter-free desk moments ago, willing him to pick it up. Despite her personal misgivings about her humorless neighbor, she had made this godforsaken trip to the city to beg his assistance, hoping her late husband's friend would know what to do.

With trembling fingers, she pushed the tattered, black beribboned packet closer to him. "These two mention you," she said. "I have more at Winter's Hollow. Could you please read them and tell me if anything seems amiss?"

The earl cast her a level stare. "Aren't you in a better position to judge such things, Mrs. Ashcroft?"

From the moment she had entered his study ten minutes ago, he had treated her with courtesy and respect, but she had yet to witness a single emotion crease his strong brow or bend his full lips.

It had always been so with him. Unlike her late husband, Geoffrey, she had never enjoyed a companionable relationship with the earl. Their acquaintance had always been one of distance and wary glances. A situation she now regretted, for Lord Somerton might be the only person who could help her locate her husband's murderer.

Catherine took in the earl's wide shoulders and six-foot-something frame, both a formidable contrast to Geoffrey's slighter build. Not for the first time, she noted his calm strength and an almost imperceptible aura of danger penetrating the air around him.

"Indeed, sir." Her fingers curled until her nails dug into the tender flesh of her palms. "I have already determined something's wrong, but what, exactly, I do not know." Had there been any other way of determining Geoffrey's state of mind, she would have followed it. Being in the earl's company made her body hum with restlessness and her mind waver with doubt—a state that would have her father, a highly decorated naval officer, convulsing in his grave.

There had been no avoiding this meeting, though. Geoffrey's abandonment three years ago had ensured she knew little of her husband's activities and even less of his desires. Lord Somerton was the one person who could enlighten her on both.

"What makes these letters different from the rest of Ashcroft's correspondence?" he asked.

Dread filled her chest. How could she explain the tenor of desperation that had penetrated Geoffrey's every word? Or how his words of love were nothing more than a farce? Could Lord Somerton, a man known for his cold logic and intolerance for theatrics, detect the nuanced message beyond Geoffrey's protestations?

"I'm not sure I can supply you with a satisfactory explanation, my lord," she said. "It's complicated, to say the least."

He tapped an impatient fingertip against the letters several times. "I'll be sure to listen very closely, Mrs. Ashcroft."

Emotion, at last. But it came with a cost. His scrutiny intensified and the space between them turned thick and suffocating. Catherine smoothed her damp palms down her black pelisse. A sudden urge to flee scraped against her nerves.

What if she was the one wrong about the character of Geoffrey's letters? Maybe he really had wanted to reconcile and happened to be in the wrong place at the wrong time. If that were the case, her entire trip to London was nothing more than a humiliating waste of time.

"Mrs. Ashcroft," he said, "I don't mean to press you, but I have another appointment at the top of the hour."

Catherine drew in a slow, steadying breath while allowing her attention to sweep around the room. The austere quality of his lordship's study made her itch to return to Winter's Hollow. Every room in her country manor was decorated with cheerful colors and warm, inviting furniture to make her guests feel at ease and welcome. But more than that, she ached to return to her six-year-old daughter. Sophie's limitless curiosity and boundless energy always soothed Catherine's nerves.

London held nothing for her but pain and loneliness and an acute sense of inadequacy.

She forced the tightness from her chest and the doubts from her mind. She had not been wrong in her assessment of her husband's letters. She might not know what their disjointed nature meant, but it was something besides undying love.

Meeting the earl's gaze, she said, "I don't know that I can explain how they're different, my lord." She nodded toward the stack of letters. "In those words, I do not recognize the voice of my husband."

When his features flattened, revealing the smallest hint of skepticism, Catherine knew she had failed. Disappointment darkened the edges of her vision before she gathered what was left of her pride and stood. She would find another way to decipher Geoffrey's final scribblings. "I'm sorry for wasting your time, sir. I thought my word on the odd nature of my husband's correspondence would be enough for you to at least read them, especially since your name appears more than once, but I can see that I was wrong." She held out her hand. "If you'd be so kind as to return my property?"

He scooped up the letters and strode around his desk. The closer he came, the smaller, more insignificant she felt. When he stopped before her, the heat from his body penetrated the layers of her clothing, heating her flesh.

Slowly, reluctantly, she lifted her gaze to meet his. Awareness stabbed through her center, splintering her mask of sophistication. Always, she had sensed a volatile power lurking behind his cool facade. One that drew her, one that resisted all arguments of morality and honor and "until death do us part."

When Geoffrey still visited her bed, their intimate relations had been sweet and calming, beautiful in their perfection. Not primal or compelling. Not hot and wanting.

No matter how much she resisted, the earl's big body

and his I-can-see-into-your-soul eyes made her yearn for a night of mindless, unrestrained lovemaking.

With him.

She tore her attention away from his luminescent eyes and focused on the letters. Focused on her reason for being in London.

To find Geoffrey's murderer.

Lord Somerton stepped closer. "Are you unwell?"

Yes.

She gestured again toward the packet. "My lord?"

"You no longer require my help, Mrs. Ashcroft?"

Catherine's pulse jumped. Something unpredictable and menacing prowled behind his words. Dropping her arm to her side, she said, "Of course I do. But I sense your hesitance and I have no more time to persuade you to my cause."

Her plain speaking caused both his eyebrows to arch high, and his eyes, a light blue mixed with steel gray, appeared to glow and pulse with an inner life. She had never seen such a startling eye color on anyone else and had always thought the uncommon hue haunting and beautiful.

And impossible to forget.

"No more time?" he asked. "Why the hurry? Your husband was killed a month ago."

Guilt slammed against her chest. Her love for Geoffrey might have vanished long ago, but she still cared enough to mourn his death, for her loss and for Sophie's. Between gritted teeth, she said, "My reasons don't concern you."

"Help me understand the situation. I don't often have a dead man's wife sitting in my study asking me to read her private correspondence." He waved the packet in the air. "I must ask once again—what makes these letters any different from the others you had received from Ashcroft?" His features returned to their placid position. "I cannot assist you if you refuse to communicate the full extent of your concerns."

"Please, my lord." Not thinking, she gripped his arm. "Won't you read his letters and tell me what you make of them?" She had come prepared to divulge the full scope of Geoffrey's transformation and to confess the appalling circumstances of her marriage before his death, but now embarrassment trapped the shameful words in the back of her throat.

He studied her face for several seconds before shifting his attention to her hand. Catherine freed his arm, discomfited and shocked by her rash action.

Releasing a breath, he waved toward her chair. "Please, won't you sit?"

Not until that moment had Catherine noticed the dark patches beneath his eyes and the deep grooves bracketing his mouth. Fatigue pulled at his handsome features, and Catherine experienced an answering tug of empathy.

What would cause the Earl of Somerton to lose sleep? A family crisis? He had no close living relatives, only his two wards. Former wards, for they were both adults now.

She found it hard to reconcile that the detached man before her was the same individual who had taken in two young children after their parents were brutally slain by thieves. All in the name of friendship.

"If I've come at an inconvenient time, my lord," she said in a gentler tone, "I apologize. Would you prefer that I return tomorrow?"

"That won't be necessary. I am persuaded to read your husband's letters, madam." He indicated her chair again. "Please."

Catherine resumed her seat, and the earl followed suit. "Thank you—"

"Before I begin," he said, interrupting her. "I must know what about their contents compelled you to travel all the way to London to seek me out."

"You are quite persistent, my lord."

"I could say the same of you."

Just get it over with, Catherine.

Pulling in a fortifying breath, she said, "Not long after my daughter was born, Geoffrey became involved in several reformation issues that required him to spend a good deal of time away from us." She plucked at the soft fabric of her reticule. "At first, I applauded his passionate belief that he could make a real difference and even encouraged him to build political relationships that would aid his many causes."

The earl nodded. "Ashcroft was well respected among his peers. He had distinguished himself as a man of honor and principle."

"Yes, well," she said, "during the first year, he wrote to us at the end of every week and came home as often as his schedule would allow. By the second year, his correspondence dwindled to once a month and his visits to three or four times a year. After the third year, he no longer bothered to make an appearance, not even for our daughter's birthday or for Christmas, preferring to send gifts instead."

"And his correspondence?"

"Nothing more than beautifully written instructions on estate management."

"I see," he said in a low voice. "Go on."

Catherine forced herself to hold the earl's gaze. "Before my husband's funeral, my daughter had not seen her father in three years, and I hadn't received a letter from him for the same length of time." She glanced away then, swallowing back the bitterness that rose to the top of her throat. "My husband's unexplained silence came to an abrupt end a month before his death."

He glanced at the packet. "Are you saying Ashcroft sent these, and the ones you have at home, all within the last month of his life?"

"Yes, my lord." Her throat closed around the damning words.

"You are only now reading them?"

"They arrived while I was away, attending my father's funeral." She swallowed around her tight throat. "I had no reason to expect any communication from Geoffrey, so I failed to instruct my staff to forward his correspondence. The day before I was scheduled to return home, I received word that my husband had been stabbed to death by footpads."

"I am sorry for your loss, Mrs. Ashcroft. On both accounts."

The sincerity in his voice helped ease some of the tension in her shoulders. "Thank you."

The unending ache in her heart was not for her husband, or even her father who had forsaken his family for his career, but for her daughter, who would live the rest of her days without a father.

"I regret the lengthy delay," she said. "However, once you read Geoffrey's odd ramblings, you will see I was right to bring them to your attention." She pressed on, knowing he would indeed think her a featherbrain after her next words. "My husband was in some kind of trouble before he died, sir. I can feel it in the depths of my soul. I no longer believe a random criminal killed Geoffrey. This situation has the stamp of something far more deliberate."

Her declaration did nothing to disrupt the earl's pensive expression. What was he thinking? Was he devising ways to get her out of his study? Was he measuring her words and wondering if he could trust her judgment? Or did he worry he was dealing with the illogical thought patterns of a woman scorned? Her knee bounced beneath her skirts.

"A rather sensational view of the matter, Mrs. Ashcroft."

Catherine's teeth gnashed together. She had prepared herself for his mockery, but that did not stop the sting of his words. "Read the letters and see if you still think so."

He studied her for an interminable amount of time before he finally asked, "How long will you be in London?"

"Not long," she said. "I must get back to my daughter."

Nodding, he rose to his full height, and Catherine experienced the same sensation of smallness—no, delicacy—when his large frame towered over her. On one level, his presence was disconcerting, but on another, he calmed her, made her feel—she shook the words from her head. She *did not* feel safe and secure in this man's presence.

"I have another pressing matter I must attend to first, Mrs. Ashcroft." His crystalline gaze roamed her face with a thoroughness that sucked the breath from her lungs. "Go home to your daughter. I will join you in a few days to review the rest of Ashcroft's correspondence."

Her shoulders sagged, heavy with relief. "Thank you, my lord. I appreciate your assistance. Grayson and Mrs. Fox will be happy to hear of your return."

"Do not bother informing my staff of my imminent arrival," he said. "I don't plan on staying long."

TWO

"Chief, we need the other letters."

The Earl of Helsford's pronouncement pulled Sebastian Danvers, Lord Somerton, out of his dark musings. Musings that had occupied more of his time of late.

Sebastian shifted his attention from the black ribbon wound around his finger to his secret service agent, Guy Trevelyan, who stood near the library window. "You're sure?"

"As sure as one can be when deciphering the words of what appears to be a desperate man."

If anyone could piece together Geoffrey Ashcroft's message, Helsford could. As a master cryptographer for the Alien Office, the earl's talent at cracking complex codes was unmatched. A talent Sebastian had used well over the years to thwart Napoleon Bonaparte's hunger for domination.

"Perhaps Ashcroft's widow held the others back to lure you away," Ethan deBeau, Viscount Danforth, interjected with his normal lack of finesse. His former ward sank farther into the cushioned chair, propping his booted foot over the opposite knee. "After the failed attempt on your life, we must rule out nothing."

As they were wont to do since yesterday afternoon, Sebastian's thoughts turned to the widow, and his thumb pressed into the black ribbon. She had changed little in the last four years. Blond, petite, and so stunningly beautiful that not even her ever-present fichu and scuffed leather boots could diminish her effect.

What had changed in the intervening years, and to his mind for the better, was her confident tone and direct gaze. No longer did she hover behind a man's protective shoulder or avoid lengthy eye contact. The woman he had spoken to yesterday exuded self-assurance and vibrated with purpose.

She had come to him for answers, alone and unprotected. Had left her daughter behind to venture to a city she detested to seek assistance from a man she barely knew. What would it feel like to have such a champion?

Sebastian pulled in a shallow breath. Dark, unproductive musings, indeed.

"He's right," Helsford said into the silence. "You are a direct threat to Napoleon's success. We cannot be too cautious."

Sebastian nodded, recalling the recent assassination plot Helsford had uncovered in time to save his life. "I will keep your words of warning in mind."

During his time with the Nexus, an elite group of international spies sworn to stop Napoleon Bonaparte's conquering tempest across Europe, he had learned many things, often the hard way. But the one lesson he would never forget was that one can never know another's true heart.

A beautiful face could mask the blackest soul, and the most horrific mien could protect the purest heart. In his experience, people were not wholly evil nor wholly good, but something infinitely more dangerous and unpredictable—a little of both.

He glanced between the two men who had been friends since childhood, men he had helped raise, train, mold. Helsford, silent and thoughtful; Danforth, vocal and volatile. Both lethal when the moment called for such actions. The only one missing from this reunion was Cora deBeau, Danforth's younger sister, and one of Sebastian's best intelligence gatherers.

Over the years, he had wondered what their lives would have been like had Ethan and Cora's parents not been murdered. The incident had set off a chain of events that turned the trio of friends into the brilliant spies they were today. Many thought that Lord and Lady Danforth's deaths resulted from an interrupted theft, but those close to the family knew otherwise.

Predicting the coming storm between England and France, his former mentor, Roland deBeau, the late Viscount Danforth, had introduced unusual skill sets to his two children to test their interest and aptitude. Of the deBeau children, Cora had always been more focused, more levelheaded.

During a rather humorous pickpocket training session, his mentor had extracted a promise from twenty-three-year-old Sebastian to watch over his children should something happen to him. Three weeks later, Danforth and his wife were brutally murdered by a French assassin, and Sebastian became the guardian of two grieving children, Cora, age ten, and Ethan, age fourteen.

Although he had little experience with children, he

had been overseeing his vast estates since the age of twelve —which made him a perfect guardian for Ethan. He understood the young man's grief and fear and lack of confidence. His resentment and his restlessness. For it was Sebastian's restlessness and determination that had caught the attention of Roland deBeau, the former chief of the Nexus.

Sebastian honored his mentor's wishes, becoming Ethan and Cora's guardian and continuing their father's unique training, shaping them into instruments of the Crown.

"Shall I pay Mrs. Ashcroft a visit?" Danforth asked in a low, silky tone, a voice he had used to great effect in boudoirs across two countries.

"No."

The viscount raised a dark brow and shared a glance with Helsford.

Sebastian understood their confusion. He was rather surprised by his immediate, almost visceral, response, too. Any other time, he would have ordered Danforth to employ his special skills. Women loved him. They happily revealed their husbands' or lovers' secrets for a few hours in his bed, where he made them feel special and desirable.

A vision of Catherine Ashcroft surrendering to the agent's well-honed touch tightened his chest. The widow's gentle beauty had always drawn his eye, and for that reason alone, he had kept her at a distance.

He never dallied with his agents' women. Never. Which made his reaction to Danforth's query both surprising and confusing.

He shoved the ribbon into his coat pocket and pushed away the disturbing image of Danforth and the widow. Removing the image from his mind took far longer than it should. He forced his thoughts toward a conversation he'd had earlier that morning with the Superintendent of Aliens. "According to Reeves, the Alien Office is investigating my part in the traitor's deception."

Danforth shot up from his chair, and Helsford turned his back on the window.

"Are they mad?" Danforth demanded.

"What's this?" Helsford asked.

Sebastian rose to refill his glass from the sideboard. He took a healthy, fortifying swallow of the brandy. "It is nothing I would not do if I were in his place."

"That's absurd and you know it, Chief," Danforth said. "No one is more loyal to the Crown than you."

Sebastian stared into his now empty glass, debating whether to replenish it or not. "Ah, but it was my friend and my watch."

"The traitor was also your superior. You can't be expected to know his every move." Danforth strode the length of the library. "Bloody nonsense, if you ask me."

"What now?" Helsford's calm question was a stark contrast to the viscount's fierceness.

"Now I retire to Bellamere Park while the office determines the extent of my commitment."

The viscount stopped pacing. "They're exiling you?"

Sebastian resumed his spot at the sideboard. "Reeves suggested a holiday away from the city."

"Who the hell does Reeves think he is, banishing the chief of the Nexus?" Danforth continued his defense. "The man's been in charge of the Alien Office scarcely a year."

"Precisely," Sebastian said. "Reeves has not been in his position long enough to develop a solid opinion of me one way or another. Who knows what nonsense has been spewed in his ear." He had intended to stop pouring at the two-finger mark, but the amber liquid kept rising. "I am inclined to follow his suggestion. It's long past time I visit my country estate."

"By removing you, he's putting England at risk."

Sebastian studied Danforth, growing more worried for the viscount's peace of mind by the day. In the last year or so, his temper and volatility had grown. "I will not be gone so long as that." He kept his voice calm and even. To Helsford, he said, "Did Ashcroft's letters divulge anything else, besides whispers of a faction seeking to destroy the Nexus?"

"Only a personal message to you, sir."

Dread stirred in his gut. "Go on."

"He asked that you look after his family."

Sebastian tossed back half the glass's contents.

"Doesn't Ashcroft's property abut Bellamere?" asked the ever-sensible Earl of Helsford.

His jaw turned to stone. "Yes."

A new light entered Danforth's eyes. "Brilliant," he said, oblivious to Sebastian's mental turmoil.

Helsford understood, though. Empathy softened the man's normally fathomless black eyes.

Danforth continued, "You can see to your estate, retrieve the other letters, and watch over Ashcroft's family." He smacked Helsford's shoulder. "We'll keep an eye on Reeves and his Inquisition from here."

Such a neat bow tied around such an untidy package. "Yes. Brilliant."

"What are you going to tell Mrs. Ashcroft about her husband?" Helsford's soft query reminded him that the worst was yet to come. "We are still investigating the situation."

Danforth's expression flattened as understanding dawned. "I'll do it."

Sebastian sent him a grateful yet pained smile. "Thank you, but no."

"There is no reason for you to deal with this alone, Chief."

"My watch, remember?" The brandy in Sebastian's stomach churned. "You both can help by keeping me informed of Reeves's activities and finishing those ciphers." He glanced from one man to the next. "There can be no announcement as of yet. Our agents need more time to find those responsible."

They all fell silent. Helsford and Danforth were no doubt reflecting on the scarcity of information they had collected since finding Ashcroft in a filthy alley, lying in a pool of his own blood. Sebastian's thoughts, however, had turned to his unavoidable meeting with Ashcroft's widow and what lies he would devise about her husband.

THREE

The moment Catherine exited Grillon's Hotel, a fierce midday sun stabbed her already burning eyes. She paused in the shade of the building until the white spots overwhelming her vision disappeared.

Not for the first time, she smoothed a hand over her quivering middle. A putrid stomach had interrupted her departure from this blasted city. All morning, she had either been scrambling for the chamber pot or reliving her torturous conversation with Lord Somerton.

Even now, a faint roiling deep in her midsection made her question the wisdom of embarking on a long carriage ride. But her parental instinct pushed her onward, despite the potential consequences to her pride. It was just her bad luck to have selected the pork instead of the fish.

"Excuse me, ma'am." A young man motioned to the door behind her.

Vision restored, Catherine gave up her shadowed spot. "My apologies, sir." She continued on to where her maid, Mary, watched over her trunks while waiting for their carriage to arrive.

Lord Somerton's delay continued to chafe her nerves. So much of her life had been wrapped around the act of waiting. Waiting for her father, waiting for her husband, waiting for the denizens of Showbury to lower their pompous noses. And now she must anticipate Lord Somerton's arrival and pray he could help assuage her terrible guilt by tracking down Geoffrey's killer.

Once she solved the mystery of her husband's death, she could begin anew with her daughter and hope her guilt would ease in time.

A large cat with matted once-white fur darted across Albemarle Street, chasing a smaller scruffy black dog, whose short legs were nothing more than a dark blur.

"Oh!" Mary exclaimed, scurrying out of the way when the two creatures streaked by, ruffling Catherine's skirts.

Catherine followed their zigzag path, hoping the little dog would make it to safety. She glanced at Mary, and they shared a smile. But the disappearing animals made Catherine consider her own departure. Was she doing the right thing by leaving the city? The restless energy thrumming through her veins begged her to stay and search for clues. Whatever they might be.

"Good day, Mrs. Ashcroft," a man called from the street.

A blond-haired gentleman dismounted from a rather expensive piece of horseflesh and handed the reins to a young hostler. He advanced upon her with a sure stride.

Catherine raised a brow a brow at the stranger. Society had strict rules about men approaching women without a proper introduction. She was never one for rules. "Do I know you, sir?"

He removed his beaver hat, revealing an array of handsome curls, and bowed. "I am so glad to have caught you.

Allow me to introduce myself. My name is Frederick Cochran." Sorrowful blue eyes gazed at her. "A good friend to your husband, or was, I should say."

Mary backed away to a discreet distance.

Cochran, Cochran, Cochran. The name was familiar, yet she could not recall meeting him at her husband's funeral. Then again, much of that day was a blur.

She opened her mouth to apologize, when a thought struck her. Geoffrey's correspondence? She had a vague recollection of him referring to someone named Cochran. Or had it been Corbin? Collins? Cook?

"Mr. Cochran? Your name is somewhat familiar, sir."

"Indeed? Did your husband speak of me?"

"To be honest, I'm not sure how I recognize your name," she said. "You were looking for me?"

He inclined his head. "Due to circumstances beyond my control, I was unable to attend your husband's services. When I heard you were in the area, I rushed over to offer my condolences."

"I had not thought my arrival was widely known."

"When one works at the Foreign Office, one hears all sorts of chatter."

"Foreign Office?"

"Why, yes," he said in a curious tone. "That's how I came to know your husband."

Catherine's world narrowed to a small circle of vision, one that centered on Cochran's mouth. She stared hard, waiting for more words to emerge. Words that would clarify his ridiculous statement. None arrived.

"Pardon, sir? Are you implying my husband was also employed by the Foreign Office?"

He searched her face. "You didn't know."

Time slowed, and Catherine's heart slammed once,

twice, three times against her rib cage. The crowd, the carriages, the squabbling vendors disappeared. Only silence remained. Punishing, unrelenting silence. Deafening, suffocating silence. "How long?"

He glanced around. "Is this your carriage approaching?"

She nodded, unable to take her eyes off his face.

Observing her small cache of luggage stacked behind her, he asked, "You are returning home?"

"Yes, Mr. Cochran," she said with growing impatience. "Please answer my question."

The carriage rocked to a halt, and Cochran motioned her inside. "Let me explain in a more private setting."

Catherine considered the propriety of allowing a stranger into her carriage, especially while in mourning. But this was London, not Showbury. No one knew her here, and she had learned long ago to take matters into her own hands if she wished for a particular result.

"Very well, Mr. Cochran. Mary," she called.

"Yes, ma'am?" The maid eyed Cochran.

"Would you mind riding with the driver for a short time?" Catherine asked.

"No, ma'am."

While the hotel staff busied themselves loading her trunks, Cochran assisted her into the carriage and made arrangements to have his horse tied to the back. When Mary was seated and all was in readiness, he bounded inside and settled across from her.

They rumbled down the street in silence for what felt like hours. Her pulse pounded hard within her ears and sweat trickled down her right side. "Please do not torture me with your silence any longer, Mr. Cochran. How long did my husband work for the government and in what capacity?"

"I believe Lord Somerton brought him into the fold about four years ago."

Catherine ignored the sharp clenching pain around her heart. "And his capacity?"

He brushed a few specks of dust from his coat sleeve. "Since Ashcroft is gone, I suppose telling you won't do any harm. But I must ask you to keep what I'm about to impart to yourself. Discussing Foreign Office affairs, even old affairs, could have an ill effect on current initiatives—and my career."

"You have my word." She would have promised him anything at the moment. "I will not repeat your confidence."

"Ashcroft was in the business of collecting sensitive information."

"What sort of information?"

"I can't go so far as to tell you specifics, but he sought any type of intelligence that would protect England's shores."

"Do you mean he was a spy?"

He paused a moment. "The preferable term is agent."

Geoffrey was a spy. For years. Under Lord Somerton's tutelage. *Dear God.*

How could she be ignorant of something so important and dangerous? Could Geoffrey's work for the government be the reason he had all but abandoned his family? The timing could not be more perfect.

"He wasn't always an agent, mind you," Mr. Cochran said. "Somerton started him out as a messenger. Your husband made many forays across the Channel retrieving vital intelligence on Napoleon's movements."

Gut-churning dread washed over her for the danger her husband had faced. On the heels of her dread came white-hot anger for the role Lord Somerton had played in Geoffrey's activities and his decision to keep this knowledge from her. How amused he must have been yesterday. "Are you aware of the details surrounding my husband's death?"

"He was set upon by footpads, as I recall."

"That is what was reported to me." She studied him. "However, I have reason to believe something far more nefarious occurred."

"What do you mean?"

"Based upon what you've disclosed and the nature of the letters I delivered to Lord Somerton, I can't imagine any other outcome at the moment."

"Letters?" A new intensity entered his tone.

"Geoffrey sent me several pieces of correspondence before he died. They made little sense to me, but a few of them mentioned Lord Somerton, so I thought they might be of use to him."

"Interesting, to be sure." He stared out the carriage window. "Did your husband mention anyone else in his correspondence?"

Catherine hesitated, still unable to recall where she'd come across the man's name, though the letters seemed the most likely source. "I'm afraid I don't recall offhand. Once I receive the letters back from his lordship, I'll review them again and let you know."

"Very well," he said. "Since we are developing a temporary partnership, I will say that I share your view on Ashcroft's means of death."

"You think he was murdered, too?"

"In a manner of speaking."

"What manner, exactly?"

"One that is quiet and effective."

Catherine stared at him, uncomprehending.

"Assassination, Mrs. Ashcroft."

Catherine closed her eyes and drew in a deep breath. When she had her stomach under control again, she asked, "Why didn't Lord Somerton explain this to me when we met yesterday?"

"It is difficult to say why his lordship does anything. However, in this instance, I suspect he was more concerned about the investigation."

"Investigation?"

Cochran grimaced, as if realizing he'd said too much. "The Foreign Office is investigating a few of its staff for aiding the French, and I'm afraid Lord Somerton has not escaped their notice."

She thought back to her brief audience with the earl and recalled the dark circles beneath his eyes. "That is unwelcome news, sir."

"Indeed, it is for all of us, ma'am. Lord Somerton is known for his loyalty and willingness to defend those under his command. If he is found guilty, the trust he spent years building will be broken and I'm afraid the Foreign Office shall never be the same."

"Well, let us hope the investigation proves Lord Somerton's innocence rather than his guilt." Why she hoped so after the earl's subterfuge she did not know. But her husband had believed him to be a man of honor and so would she—for now.

"Let us hope." He cocked his head to the side. "Am I correct in that you share a border with Lord Somerton's country estate?"

Something about the way he asked the question made

her sour stomach take a turn for the worse. "Yes."

"Very good. Superintendent Reeves is a cautious man and will require Lord Somerton to leave the city while the investigation is under way. No undue influence, you understand?"

"Of course. But why is it good that we share a border?"

"Because you can help us keep watch over his lordship while he's away from the city."

"Pardon?" she asked, incredulous. "Are you asking me to spy on the earl?"

"Goodness, no, dear lady. I would not put you and Sophie into such a dangerous position. All I ask is that you share with me any unusual activity you might witness and, in exchange, I will keep you apprised of our inquiry into your husband's murder."

Catherine stilled. "You know of my daughter?"

He smiled. "Ashcroft spoke of his *redheaded moppet* often. So much so, that I think of her as a treasured niece." He rubbed the side of his forefinger along his full bottom lip. Thoughtful, silent. His blue gaze conveyed a secret message she could not decipher. "Perhaps one day I shall meet her."

Redheaded? Geoffrey hated his red hair and often bemoaned the fact that Sophie's blond curls were interlaced with the atrocious color. This conversation had ventured down a path that made Catherine unaccountably ill at ease. She strove for a noncommittal answer. "Perhaps."

"Splendid." He rapped on the small sliding door behind his head. The carriage slowed. "I shall call on you in a few days. It will be a most productive visit."

The black jet beads dug into the flesh of her fingers. "Productive for whom, Mr. Cochran?"

He hopped down from the carriage and turned to give her a knowing smile. "For us both, of course." Once Mary climbed in and settled on the seat opposite her, he shut the door. Through the window, he held Catherine's gaze as he accepted the reins of his horse. "*Adieu,* Mrs. Ashcroft."

The carriage jerked forward, jostling Catherine as it regained a more even rhythm. She hardly noticed. Her mind spun so fast it felt like the large terrestrial globe that used to take up a good deal of space in her father's study.

Around and around, her thoughts revolved, but they failed to land on anything that would help her understand the events of the last few days. What she had hoped would be an investigative bid for justice had turned into an unwelcome introduction to a world of spies and intrigue.

One thing was for certain, though. Her rather mundane country existence was about to become a good deal more interesting.

FOUR

S ebastian's chest rose high as the gray stone walls of his childhood home came into view. Unlike him, Bellamere Park, with its clusters of square chimneys and expansive gardens, had changed little in the four years he had been away.

Closing his eyes, he inhaled the earthy scent of newly shorn grass and crisp air, never realizing until that moment how much he had missed spending time in the country, where a man concerned himself with putting food on the table, rather than preventing the next attempt on his life.

The last few months had challenged his intellect, his endurance, and his long-held beliefs on a level that frightened even him, a man jaded by intrigue and ruthless in his pursuit to protect English interests. Never before had he wondered if all his sacrifices, and those of his agents, had been worth the price.

Not until recently.

A biting afternoon breeze swept away his disturbing thought. He opened his eyes and kicked Reaper into a trot for the final quarter mile of their journey.

As he descended the low rise, he glanced to the east, toward the Ashcroft estate, and a sense of foreboding filled his chest. Dealing with death, in all its many forms, had become part of his life. Although he could still experience remorse, pity, and sympathy, he never allowed himself to linger in the emotions for long. He could not afford to.

But the Ashcroft situation was different, more complex. More gray than black or white. His duty, first and foremost, was to England, to the security of its borders and the safety of its people. The needs of one woman and one little girl were secondary. They could not factor into his decisions.

He released a steadying breath.

Not at all.

Reaper tossed his big black head and broke into a gallop. The powerful thrust forward pulled Sebastian out of his ruminations, and he tightened his grip on the reins again and loosened his thighs. His mount obeyed, slowing his gait back to a trot.

Not for the first time, an image of his hands around Geoffrey Ashcroft's neck surfaced before his eyes. He should never have involved his wife in government affairs. However, Sebastian understood the man's caution and, in less bloodthirsty moments, appreciated his genius.

Who would ever suspect an agent of sending his wife coded messages intended for the Nexus chief? Ashcroft had known his wife well. Had known it would only be a matter of time before she brought the letters, dotted with Sebastian's title, to him.

The too-intelligent fool's only mistake had been in not keeping abreast of his wife's activities, or he would have realized she wasn't at Winter's Hollow to receive his correspondence. The delay had likely cost the young agent his life.

Another secret to keep.

But as Geoffrey had known she would, his wife had traveled to London with the damned letters, and Sebastian had been forced to pretend nothing was amiss. It was a role he had played a hundred times before, though this time proved far more difficult.

Every instant Catherine turned those big brown eyes on him, he had come close to telling her everything. She had always had a disturbing effect on his control. When her husband was alive, he had found the wherewithal to fight her pull. Now that Ashcroft was dead, no more physical obstacles stood in his way.

Only a damned ghost.

He shoved aside his pointless musings and halted Reaper outside of Bellamere's wide double doors. An instant later, a liveried footman emerged to hold his master's exhausted mount. After several hours in the saddle, Sebastian's endurance had also waned. He wished now that he had sent word ahead to warn his staff of his arrival. Waiting for his chambers to be aired and linens to be laid would feel like an eternity.

By the time his foot hit the top step, though, his aging butler materialized. "Good afternoon, my lord."

"Grayson." Sebastian smiled at his former accomplice to unspoken crimes, taking in the stooped quality of his shoulders and the deep grooves in his forehead. The man appeared to have aged a score of years since his last visit. "You don't seem surprised to see me."

"Indeed not, sir. Rucker sent word ahead."

"Of course he did." He must remember to give his London butler an extra day off for his welcome, albeit insubordinate, forethought. "Then you know Parker is following behind with my luggage."

"Indeed, sir. We'll be on the watch for your valet." Grayson waved his age-spotted hand toward the open door. "Per your preference, my lord, I did not assemble the staff." His butler did an admirable job of keeping his displeasure out of his tone. "However, they are ready to serve you as needed."

Nodding, he said, "Well done, Grayson." He had never favored the custom of pulling the servants from their duties to line up in neat rows to bow and dip toward their employer as he majestically strolled down their center. A bunch of useless rot, as Danforth would say.

Entering the spacious Great Hall, he found it as much unchanged as the exterior of the manor. Built during the virgin queen's reign, the Great Hall was designed to leave its visitors speechless. And it did. Whether in awe or horror depended on one's fondness for ostentatious trimmings.

Even though he had spent much of his childhood here, his gaze still roamed over the twin marble columns stretching three stories high. Wide Flemish tapestries lined both sides of the room, covering the upper portion of the walls, and a twenty-foot trellis table sat center-stage before a fireplace large enough to harbor a small family.

His ancestors had a flair for the dramatic—not really to his taste, but he held fond memories of Bellamere Park and would always consider this his true home. A home he had been away from for far too long, he realized with some regret.

Raised, muffled voices down the corridor drew his attention.

"That would be Mr. Blake, my lord," Grayson said, noticing where his attention had strayed.

"In my study?"

"Yes, sir."

"Is he with a tenant?"

"No, my lord." Grayson's pale blue gaze shifted to the distant closed door. "Mr. Blake is speaking with your neighbor."

"My neigh—" Sebastian's heart jolted. "Ashcroft's widow?"

"I'm afraid so, sir."

His fatigue evaporated. As he removed his gloves, he strove for calm. He had not expected to see her this soon, and he certainly had not wanted to be covered in road dust at their first meeting. "What business does Mrs. Ashcroft have with my steward?"

"More of the same, I suspect."

He stared at his butler, wondering how he was supposed to decipher the man's remark when he had not set foot on his estate in years. Pulling in a fortifying breath, he turned to find out and did his damnedest to keep his pace even, unhurried. "Thank you, Grayson. That will be all."

As he neared his study, the agitated conversation from within wafted through the slightly ajar door.

"The railing is completely missing, Mr. Blake," a female voice said. "Garry Lucas came close to tumbling through the small opening and falling into the river."

"But he didn't, Mrs. Ashcroft," the steward said. "Had Garry's mother kept a better eye on her son, we would not be having this conversation."

"You know as well as I that the northern bridge is a favorite thoroughfare to the village for the children."

Sebastian leaned closer to the opening.

"Mmm-hmm."

"You said the bridge railing would be fixed a fortnight ago."

"Mmm-hmm."

"When might we expect its repair, Mr. Blake?"

"Mmm...soon."

"Could you please put down your brush and honor me with your full attention, sir?" Her voice held a warning edge.

The steward answered with a deep sigh, and the clattering of wood against wood followed. "I have heard your every word, Mrs. Ashcroft, and have responded accordingly. What else do you want from me?"

"Action, Mr. Blake. I want you to care for his lordship's tenants as is your responsibility."

"I know my responsibility."

"Then why do you ignore it?"

Sebastian's eyebrows rose. The side of his cheek pressed against the door frame, bringing his ear closer to the conversation. He hoped Grayson or one of the other servants did not happen by and see him eavesdropping in his own home.

"I do not ignore my duties, but I refuse to cater to the tenants' every complaint."

"Is that not for his lordship to determine?"

"Lord Somerton is not here. In his absence, he trusts me to do what's best for the estate."

"You've determined that broken bridges are best for the estate?" Incredulity sharpened her tone.

"Of course not—"

Sebastian pushed open the door, having heard enough of the steward's feeble explanation. The moment he entered the study, his nostrils flared, assaulted by the thick, cloying smell of linseed oil and turpentine. His gaze swept across the room, taking in the dozens of amateurish oil paintings leaning against every viable surface. And some not so viable surfaces, like his mother's two-hundred-and-fifty-year-old Cassone chest.

Then he found her, standing five feet away from his steward, wearing all black as custom dictated, her blond hair knotted at the back of her head. Her appearance seemed more somber, more severe than when she had visited him in London. Instead of repelling him, however, her look drew forth several questions, intriguing his analytical side and capturing his attention much longer than was proper.

"Excuse me, sir." Indignation lined the steward's brow. "What do you do here? We are in the middle of an important meeting."

Sebastian tensed at the younger man's tone until he realized Blake had no idea to whom he was speaking. Two years ago, he had hired the steward, sight unseen, on the recommendation of an acquaintance. Even though they had never met, Sebastian had corresponded frequently with the gentleman and never had cause to be concerned about the steward's management of Bellamere.

Sparing Mrs. Ashcroft another long look, Sebastian caught the glint of righteousness sparkling in her eyes. When she realized she had become the focus of his attention, the sparkle dimmed until it was extinguished altogether.

An odd pang of disappointment gripped his chest.

"Sir? I must insist on an answer."

Blake's shrill command interrupted his contemplation of the widow. "A better question is," his attention slowly settled on the steward, "what are you doing here? The last I recall, this was my study, not your studio."

The steward's face lost all color. "Lord Somerton?"

Sebastian gave him a mocking bow. "At your service." His gaze cut back to the widow. "Mrs. Ashcroft."

"My lord," she said with a curtsy. "Welcome back."

The neutral tone of her voice gave Sebastian pause. What had he expected upon seeing her for the first time? A bright smile? A glimmer of warmth? Another slow perusal of his body, as she had done in London?

The answer did not come to mind. Whatever he had expected, it was not impassivity.

"My apologies for the mess, my lord." The steward jumped off his high stool. "Had I known you were coming, I would have removed my collection."

"Perhaps you might do so now while I speak to Mrs. Ashcroft."

"Of course." The steward began scurrying about the room, gathering as many canvases and frames as he could carry. "Right away. I'll call for a footman to fetch the rest."

"I'm afraid that won't be possible." He moved to the door and held it open. "The staff are busy preparing my rooms." He had no intention of making this easy for the man.

Blake attempted an awkward bow. "As you wish, my lord."

"Mrs. Ashcroft, please join me."

She pulled her reticule close and glanced away as if bolstering her courage. The action was reminiscent of how she used to respond to his presence. Where had the confident and determined woman from London gone? Then he recalled her impassioned defense of Showbury's children and determined the London widow had not gone far.

Setting aside her bewildering behavior for now, he addressed Blake. "Open the windows once you've cleared out your possessions. Once you're finished here, I should like to speak with you in the library."

Blake knocked over a jar of brushes. "Yes, sir."

He closed the door against the steward's fumbling attempts to clean up his mess. Of all the places the man could have set up his studio, why had he picked Sebastian's study? It would take weeks to rid the room of such strong odors.

Dismissing the problem from his mind, he guided the widow down the corridor. "Do you have a moment? I thought perhaps we could step outside to clear our heads."

"Certainly," she said.

He studied her profile, trying to divine her thoughts, but it was no use. Somewhere along the way she had crafted an impenetrable mask, one with perfect neutral symmetry. It was a tactic he knew all too well.

They strode through the Great Hall and exited one of the double doors leading out to a large terrace at the rear of the house. Sebastian guided her to the stone balustrade that separated the small table and chairs from the formal gardens and parkland beyond. His lungs expanded with a deep, purifying inhalation while he scanned the area for potential threats, an act as natural to him as breathing. When he finished his search, he took in his first glimpse of Bellamere's gardens in years.

Row after row of flawlessly groomed hedges and precisely placed flowers greeted his eye. Winding gravel paths connected each unique section to the last. Statuary, ponds, and iron trellises dotted the landscape, providing secluded nooks to soothe one's soul.

The sunken garden was a particular favorite of his. Many times, as a boy, he would take refuge in the far corner of the deep-set rectangle, where a small fountain gurgled and splattered water over its low basin. There, he had dreamed of a different life, filled with laughter and family... filled with love.

Even then, his responsibilities had threatened to over-whelm him. As heir to a thriving earldom, he'd had much to learn. Which meant long days of study with his tutor and intense sessions on estate management with his father, who was more concerned with creating a replica of himself than nurturing a motherless boy.

His rigid schedule left little time for being a child and, when he became the seventh Earl of Somerton at the age of twelve, his childhood disappeared. Not until years later had Sebastian understood his father's obsessive need to ready him for the management of his inheritance. Knowledge that he was dying and fear of leaving his son alone had driven his father to push Sebastian. Sometimes to the point of damaging their relationship.

It had been Sebastian's first lesson in sacrifice.

Movement to his right pulled him from his bitter-sweet contemplations. He transferred his attention to the widow and found her studying him. For the first time, he noticed the fatigue pulling at her pretty eyes and wondered what, besides Mr. Blake's oils, might be plaguing her.

Ashcroft. The muscles in his neck clenched tight. Of course, she would be worried about the circumstances surrounding her husband's death. Sebastian regretted not being able to set her mind at ease—though learning the truth behind her husband's brutal murder might have the opposite effect.

Ignoring her evident signs of strain, he focused on a matter he could control. "Better?"

She blinked two times in quick succession. "Pardon?"

"You are rubbing your temple," he said. "Did Mr. Blake's painting supplies leave you with a headache?"

"I've never understood how he could stay cooped up in that room for hours." She lowered her arm. "Every time I meet with him, my head begins to pound within minutes."

"Shall I have Mrs. Fox bring you something for the pain?"

"Thank you, no. The fresh air will do." She paused as if waiting for him to speak. When he did not, she asked, "You needed to speak with me, my lord?"

"May I call on you Sunday, after services? I thought we could further discuss the letters Ashcroft sent. Given what I just witnessed inside, I fear tomorrow will prove too busy a day."

Her mask slipped, just enough for him to witness the disappointment that flashed across her face.

Again, she leveled her dark gaze on him. Intent. Probing. And somehow, seductive as hell. "Have you nothing to share with me now, my lord?"

"I believe it might be best to discuss the matter once I've had an opportunity to wash the road off and rest for a few hours." Talking to her now, with exhaustion beating against his mind, could open the door for mistakes, and that was something he must guard against around this observant widow.

"Yes, of course." She drew her reticule close. "I will leave you to it."

He stepped closer, resting his hand on the balustrade near her hip. Before he realized what he was doing, he pulled in an exploratory breath, searching for her scent and finding only a subtle essence unique to her. Nothing artificial, no expensive perfumes or aromatic soaps. No, this was pure woman.

Sebastian's chest expanded and he had to swallow hard before he could speak again. "I take it Mr. Blake's antics are the reason Grayson urged me to return in his last update."

She nodded. "He did not want to bother you, knowing you were needed in London. But, after Mr. Blake attended a local art exhibit last autumn, his disinterest in managing your estate affairs magnified to an alarming rate."

He waved his arm toward Bellamere's vast gardens. "Everything here seems to be in order."

"Your steward likes his comforts."

"And the tenants? How have they fared?" He suspected he knew the answer already, given the conversation he had overheard.

"They grow increasingly disgruntled, my lord."

"Why do I get the feeling I've placed you in an untenable situation?"

"I don't mind confronting Mr. Blake. I actually look forward to our tête-à-têtes. My household all but runs itself these days, so championing your tenants' concerns has given me something else to focus my mind on."

"How do I respond to such a statement? *You're welcome* doesn't seem quite right."

A small smile appeared. "What I have done is of little concern. Grayson, on the other hand, has to work with the man and try to keep the peace within the household."

Sebastian had a deep affection for the old retainer and did not like hearing about the butler's undue frustration. "I take it Mr. Blake not only absconded with my study but a suite of rooms as well."

Her eyes flared wide. "How did you know?"

"It's obvious the steward's cottage would not be sufficient for his needs." He released a sigh. "It appears I have much to rectify in my short visit."

"A man in your position should be able to trust those in his employ to see to his interests."

Caught off guard by her defense, his grip tightened on the balustrade. "You are much too kind, I assure you. We both know I have duties to the sound management of this estate, one of which is placing qualified individuals into positions of importance." He paused a moment. "But I thank you for the encouragement, all the same, and appreciate your intervention with Mr. Blake."

"You're welcome, my lord."

She took a step back, and that's when Sebastian realized the gap between their bodies was achingly small. He straightened.

"I've been keeping a list of items needing your steward's attention." She retrieved a folded piece of paper from the depths of her beaded reticule. "You might find this of use as you move forward."

Taken aback, he stared at her offering with a mixture of wariness and wonder.

"My lord?"

He reached for the list. "Thank you." He studied her neat writing and counted twenty-seven items. "You are quite organized, Mrs. Ashcroft. An admirable trait."

She had structured the information into a series of columns, noting the item in need of repair, the tenant's name, when Mr. Blake was notified, dates she had checked on the projects' progress—

His gaze narrowed on the last column labeled *Date Completed*. The column was empty. Not a single date had been entered. "Mr. Blake has failed to address all of these repairs?"

"I'm afraid so, my lord."

"Some of these items are more than a year old."

She held his gaze, her silence ringing louder than a death knell. Then she said, "Thankfully the older repairs are more aesthetic in nature. As you can see, the bridge repair occupies the first slot. The farther you go down the list, the lower the priority."

Frustration coiled inside his muscles. *Damn Blake's incompetence.*

The relaxation he had experienced upon seeing his estate was nothing more than a vague memory now. "I'm grateful for your attention to my tenants' needs, Mrs. Ashcroft. Is there anything I might do for you in return?"

A look of bewilderment crossed her face. "N-no, sir. Attending to those items is more than enough."

"You are rather easy to please, Mrs. Ashcroft."

She chuckled low, but the sound held little humor. "On the contrary, my lord. I'm told I'm quite difficult to please."

"Then it is their failure, not yours, madam." He experienced an ungovernable need to ask for the name of anyone who had made such a callous statement, so he could drag him back here by the scruff of his miserable neck to apologize.

She sent him an appreciative smile before fixing her gaze on the horizon, toward her home. "I must be off. I promised my daughter a stroll to the lake before dinner."

Mention of her daughter had the same effect as sleet rolling down his spine. Somehow, he had to find a way to honor Ashcroft's request of watching over his family without becoming personally involved. For their safety and his sanity.

"She fares well, I hope."

"More than well, my lord." The somber edges of her features transformed into glowing angles. "Sophie is a sweet-hearted girl, full of life, and rather horse-mad, I'm afraid. She turns seven next Saturday."

"From the sound of it, your daughter keeps you busy."

"Indeed, she does. Her old nurse, too. The poor woman can do little more than watch her flit from one distraction to the next."

"No matter how hard they might be, enjoy these years while you can. Children grow up all too soon."

The widow studied him with a peculiar look that made heat gather around his neckcloth. He broke eye contact and scanned the gardens and tree line again. "I should not keep you any longer. May I escort you home?"

"Is anything amiss, sir?"

He jerked his attention back to his companion. Her gaze flicked up from his hands, where he toyed with his signet ring. "No, why?"

"You appeared distracted." She waved toward the wooded area. "Searching for something?"

Surprised by her perception and irritated by his lack of finesse, he emptied his expression of all emotion, stopped twirling his ring, and forced his voice into an even tone. "I'm merely enjoying the view, madam."

"Ah, I see," she said, clearly not fooled.

He bit back a curse. His transition from protective agent to bored aristocrat had been too abrupt, too jarring. This mess with Latymer and Reeves was affecting him more than he realized.

He settled what he hoped was a pleasant smile on his lips. "May I provide an escort, Mrs. Ashcroft?"

"No need, my lord. I have navigated the path connecting our two properties many times. If you have nothing more for me, I shall retrieve my horse and head back to Winter's Hollow."

Sebastian gritted his teeth, bowing. "Thank you again for your assistance. I shall see you Sunday."

She curtsied and set off for the stables.

He tapped the folded list against the stone ledge while he followed the widow's route through the garden until she disappeared behind the small maze of tall green hedges.

The sensual awareness that had been present during their meeting in London was all but nonexistent today. In fact, she seemed a wholly different woman. Her wardrobe, her hair, her openness—it was all... suppressed. What had changed in the last four days?

He glimpsed her again when she turned toward the stables. One thing that had remained the same from their previous meeting was the layer of underlying loneliness he sensed in her. This she could not mask. At least not from him, a man who had lived in emotional isolation for years. Too many years for him to change now, but the widow made him yearn for something closer, something more meaningful.

Paper crackled between his stiff fingers. Once again, his responsibilities had closed in on him. What he had viewed as a sanctuary a mere half hour ago now felt like another beautiful, unwanted burden.

FIVE

Catherine did her best to retreat from Lord Somerton's presence in a calm, there's-nothing-wrong-with-me manner. But there *was* something wrong. Very wrong. It was all she could do not to run, not to flee from the chaos crowding her mind and the unholy sensations invading her body.

How does one run from oneself? She closed her eyes and allowed her lungs to expand on a long breath. The exercise did not help. She suspected nothing would. Squaring her shoulders, she refocused on the path.

The man on the terrace differed vastly from the one she had encountered in London. His anger over Mr. Blake's inaction, his concern for his butler, and his appreciation of her efforts were the reactions of someone who cared. Not someone who could not be bothered with a grieving widow's request.

Today's Lord Somerton had created a compulsion within her. A compulsion to lean closer as he spoke, to inhale his intoxicating scent, to lift a hand and trail a finger along his stubbled chin.

But what disturbed Catherine the most were his eyes—a piercing blue-gray flecked with an unholy silver. The striking colors bore right through to her soul, laying open all the raw pain she tried to hide from the world.

She felt wary around him. Exposed. Yet drawn to the strength chiseled into his lean features.

Catherine veered toward the stables. Why had he been so surprised when she had defended his decision to leave Bellamere in the hands of his steward?

Making her way down a small hill, she allowed her thoughts to circle back to his stunned reaction. One would believe he was unaccustomed to such defense. Perhaps for the same reason she had been unprepared for his offer to return a favor. In her experience, few men offered such things without expecting something in return. But his expression reflected only sincerity and gratitude.

She shook her head, unwilling to contemplate the earl's motivations any longer. All she knew in that moment was that she had given him an opportunity to tell her the truth about Geoffrey's murder, and he had chosen once again to remain silent. Not one flicker of regret had crossed his handsome face.

She had been watching.

Closely.

"Good afternoon, Mrs. Ashcroft."

Catherine halted mid-stride, startled by the grooms-man's greeting. "Hello, Jasper. Could I trouble you to bring out Gypsy?"

"Ain't no trouble at all, ma'am." He leaned the pitch-fork against the side of Lord Somerton's enormous barn before disappearing into its depths. Two minutes later, he led a sweet chestnut mare to the mounting block and rubbed her nose until Catherine was settled onto the saddle.

Jasper handed the reins up to her. "Did you see his lordship, ma'am?"

She patted Gypsy's neck. "Indeed I did, Jasper."

"Do you think his lordship will see to things?"

Known for his gentle nature, the groomsman rarely spoke his mind. That he did so now confirmed the deplorable state of Mr. Blake's management.

"I believe so."

He nodded. "Some folks have it in their heads that his lordship agreed with Mr. Blake's way of taking care of concerns."

"But you know better. Isn't that correct, Jasper?"

"Aye, ma'am." He scratched the back of his head, making his hat go askew. "Though some folks wonder why it took his lordship so long to return."

Damn men and their infernal habit of being absent. "Lord Somerton is a busy man, with many responsibilities. If he had known what was happening here, I'm certain he would have returned posthaste. His lordship hires individuals, like yourself, to care for his properties, because he cannot be in more than one place. Unfortunately, not every member of his staff has the same love of their job as you do."

The barrage of words had barely left her lips before Catherine cursed her wayward tongue. If she could have done so without an excessive amount of blood, she would have bit the troublesome appendage off.

What on earth was she doing defending the earl yet again? She did not even know if he deserved such support. For all she knew, the man was an excellent candidate for a cell in Newgate.

The groomsman smiled. "I knew it had to be something like that, ma'am. My uncle used to be his lordship's head gardener. You'd never meet a surlier, more hard-to-please man than Uncle Henry, but he often spoke well of his lordship." He tipped his hat in her direction. "Thank you for setting my mind at ease. I'll let the others know."

Catherine nearly groaned. The earl had better have been sincere in his outrage over Mr. Blake's lack of attention. If he wasn't, she would have a lot of explaining to do. "Be sure to say hello to your wife."

He released Gypsy and stepped back. "That I will, Mrs. Ashcroft."

The ride back to Winter's Hollow gave her time to wrestle her tumultuous thoughts back into their proper place. She rather liked Mr. Cochran's idea of keeping an eye on Lord Somerton, even though the process was clearly spying. But her mind seemed willing to overlook that fact for two simple reasons. One, if the earl was found innocent of treason, he—along with Cochran—might be able to solve the mystery of her husband's death; and two, just being near the earl made her feel sensations she had not felt in a long time. And God forgive her, she did not want to give that up yet.

Why she was drawn to a man who had made a sport of avoiding finer feelings was a mystery. But it had always been so with him, even while Geoffrey was still alive, much to her shame. She had never acted on the deep yearnings of her body, nor had she given the earl reason to suspect she carried them.

They had troubled her, all the same.

In two days, she could begin her first—no, second—observation of him when they met after church to discuss

Geoffrey's correspondence. A thrill of anticipation brightened her mood.

Outside her small barn, she reined in Gypsy. Her toes had barely touched the ground before a small body plowed into her skirts and thin arms encircled her waist. "Mama, you're home!"

Catherine laughed, as she always did when around her precocious daughter. She twisted around to smooth her hand over Sophie's soft red-blond curls. "What's all this? Surely I was not gone long enough to warrant such an enthusiastic welcome."

Big, sorrowful blue eyes peered up at her. "You were gone foreeever. I thought that mean Mr. Blake gobbled you up."

In her nine and twenty years, Catherine had few things she could boast about, her daughter being the one exception. Sophie amazed her each and every day with her infectious laugh, insatiable curiosity, and uncanny ability to recall the smallest of details.

She pried open her daughter's clasped hands and found one held a wooden warrior brandishing a sword. From her earliest days, Sophie had been fascinated with anything that had to do with knights, castles, war, and horses. Catherine suspected part of her interest had to do with her desire to hold her father's attention.

Every time Geoffrey had visited, he and Sophie would add a new figure, weapon, animal, or piece of furniture to her miniature castle. In recent years, it had been left to Catherine to continue their tradition of bringing Castle Dragonthorpe to life. The experience was not the same for Sophie, but her sweet daughter had been careful not to show it.

"Don't be silly, young lady," she said. "If anyone was

going to do the gobbling, it was I." She emphasized her pronouncement by tickling her daughter's middle, under-arms, and neck.

The girl's laughter echoed through the stable yard. The joyous sound delighted Catherine's aching heart.

"Stop, Mama! Stop." Another wave of uncontrollable giggles followed.

A boy emerged from the barn, and Sophie's laughter broke off, replaced by a sunbeam smile. "Teddy, we're going to the lake. Want to come?"

He glanced at Catherine, then into the stables. "Can't, Miss Sophie. I've chores to finish."

Her daughter's face fell. "Can't they wait until later?"

"No, Miss Sophie. I'm still trying to catch up from this morning. Mama wasn't feeling well and—" He swallowed hard. "Maybe tomorrow."

When her daughter started to protest, Catherine set a hand on the girl's narrow shoulder. "Teddy, sounds like your mother could use a big bowl of Cook's chicken soup. I'll drop some off later this afternoon."

"Thank you, ma'am." He shuffled his feet. "She'll take to Cook's soup much better than what Papa and I have been fixing." His gaze shifted to Sophie, then back to Catherine. "Should I see to Gypsy now?"

She nodded. "Thank you, Teddy."

He tugged on the mare's reins. "Come on, girl. I've a nice big carrot waiting for you." Gypsy's ears perked up, and she followed him inside with a bit more prance to her step.

Sophie sighed and leaned into Catherine's hip. "He never wants to play with me."

Catherine kissed the top of her daughter's head and nudged her toward the house. "We've talked about this."

"I know," she said in a beleaguered voice. "He's working to help his family. But boys need to play, too."

Smiling, she said, "Yes, they do. Let me see if Carson can spare Teddy for a few hours tomorrow."

Her daughter spun around with her hands clasped together in a prayer-like fashion. "Truly, Mama?"

She tapped her daughter's nose. "I'm making no promises. Carson has the final say."

Sophie bounced on her toes. "Oh, thank you, thank you."

Catherine laughed. She hoped her daughter would always be this easy to please. "You're welcome. Now let's collect our poles and see if we can catch some fish for dinner."

Hand in hand, they set off. "Can I go with you to see Teddy's mama? She's always nice to me at church."

"Of course, dear. But I want you to wait in the gig until I know what's ailing Mrs. Taylor. I don't want you getting sick."

"What about you?"

"I'll be fine, pumpkin. There's no need to worry about me."

Her daughter nodded, having no reason to doubt Catherine's word. "Grandmama said I must 'temper my enthusiasm' on Saturday. Does that mean I can't have fun on my birthday?"

Catherine knew her mother was being cautious about appearances. Society observed a strict set of customs when it came to mourning one's father and grandfather. However, Catherine would be damned if she allowed Geoffrey's absence—even in death—to cast a black cloud over another of her daughter's birthdays.

"Normally, I would agree with your grandmother. But

I have taken special care to invite only our closest friends and relatives." She tweaked one of her daughter's curls. "We can laugh until our bellies hurt."

Sophie's eyes twinkled. "And dance until our feet fall off."

Catherine laughed. "And sing until the dogs howl."

"And eat sweets until we cast up our accounts."

"What are you two going on about?" a new voice demanded.

Swiping the tears from her cheeks, Catherine smiled at the newcomer. "Good afternoon, Mother." The same height as Catherine, Evelyn Shaw commanded attention wherever she went. Her slender beauty, keen wit, and approachable nature made her a much sought-after companion in any social gathering. However, few would recognize her mother in all her current disheveled and dirt-dusted glory.

Sophie bolted forward. "Grandmama, we're going to have such a grand time on Saturday."

The older woman transferred her basket of cut flowers to her opposite arm and hugged her granddaughter to her middle. "From the sound of it, the festivities have already begun." She peered up at Catherine. "Do you think that's a good idea?"

Catherine winked at her daughter. "What is a party without laughter?"

Giggling, Sophie asked, "Will you dance with us, Grandmama?"

"Certainly not." Grandmama looked aghast. "I will be much too busy using my fan to beat back all the young men who will be vying for your attention."

"Young men? I do not want to dance with *men*."

"Then I'll turn my fan onto the grubby boys who will no doubt be scampering about."

Frowning, Sophie asked, "Who will be left to dance with me?"

"Don't you have any female friends?"

Sophie chortled. "No, Grandmama. You can't be serious."

"Indeed, I am, young lady."

"But I'll be seven."

"So you will."

Sophie rounded on Catherine. "Mama, tell her I'm much too old to pair up with girls."

Turning her hands up in a helpless gesture, Catherine said, "Sorry, sweetheart. I have yet to sway your grandmama to my side once she has her mind set."

Sophie glanced at her grandmama, then back to Catherine. Her eyes narrowed, suspicion making her scowl. "Grandmama, is this another one of your *inducements*?"

Evelyn sniffed. "You make the notion sound positively criminal."

Shifting her weight to one foot, Sophie propped her little hands on her hips. "What must I do for you not to scare off my dance partners?"

"The rose bushes could use a bit of snipping."

Sophie started to protest until her grandmama's eyebrow arched. "Perhaps you would rather weed the herb garden?"

Her daughter's curls jounced with a violent shake of her head. "No, ma'am. I love snipping off dead things."

"It's settled then." Catherine placed her hands on Sophie's shoulders and kissed the back of her head. "Run along and locate our fishing gear. I have something I need to discuss with your grandmama."

With her shoulders bent forward and her head hanging low, Sophie trudged up the path as if she towed a great load.

Evelyn said, "I shall see you at seven tomorrow morning, young lady."

Sophie's mouth dropped open, but she quickly closed it again. Instead of protesting, she made for the garden gate and released her frustration with a solid stomp of her foot and a low growl from her throat.

As soon as she was out of hearing range, Evelyn chuckled. "Such a little spitfire. Not unlike you at that age."

Catherine stared at the garden's arched entrance long after her daughter had disappeared around the corner. "She will not be pleasant company at the lake now, thanks to you."

"Nonsense. One bite from a fish and her sunny disposition will resurface. You know as well as I do that Sophie does not sulk for long."

"True." Catherine's response ended on a long sigh. "Let us hope she gets a bite."

"What's wrong, daughter?" Warm fingers closed over Catherine's arm.

The simple touch replenished her faltering courage and, at the same time, splayed open her terrified heart. "Lord Somerton has returned."

Her mother's hold tightened. "Did you speak with him?"

"He came upon me at Bellamere while I was admonishing Mr. Blake about the bridge repair."

"What did he do?"

"He threw the steward out of his study."

"No." Her mother's eyes rounded. "You jest."

"Not at all. I wouldn't be surprised if Mr. Blake finds

himself searching for employment elsewhere. Quite soon, in fact."

"I do like a decisive man. Months of turmoil resolved in a single afternoon. Makes you wonder why wars are fought."

"Greed causes wars, Mother. Not broken bridges."

"Enough about that now." Her mother waved the subject away as one would a pesky insect. "Did he say anything about Ashcroft's letters?"

She shook her head. "He did ask to call on me after Sunday services, though."

"Why not tomorrow?"

Catherine recalled his haggard features, even more pronounced than when she had seen him in London. "He has much to attend to at Bellamere."

"Indeed," her mother said. "Given his current coil, I suspect Lord Somerton will want to confirm the contents of your husband's letters. Probably wants to make sure Ashcroft did not implicate him in any way."

"Implicate him in what?"

"I have no notion. This situation has grown so complicated that I wouldn't be surprised if a French spy were to appear before this was all over."

"Oh, Mother," she said. "Do not let that active mind of yours run amok. As much as I hate to consider this, I suspect Geoffrey attached himself to the wrong woman and Mr. Cochran and Lord Somerton are somehow involved."

"I must say I like my theory better. Yours is just so...common."

"Indeed, it is."

They stared at the garden gate, both steeped in their

own musings, then Catherine shattered the silence. "I am thinking of offering Lord Somerton my help."

"Help with what, dear?"

Swallowing back her apprehension, she said, "He's been away for a long while. It will take him days to meet with the tenants, hear their grievances, locate the appropriate craftsmen, and monitor their work. All while he searches for a new steward."

"Don't you have a list of what needs to be done?"

"I gave what I had to him, but I'm sure he will wish to visit each site."

"What are you thinking, daughter? Why this?"

She braced herself. "Working with the earl on the repairs will give me an opportunity to observe his activities."

Her mother's lips thinned into a firm line. "I do not understand what this Mr. Cochran thinks you will see. It's not likely that his lordship will reveal anything of value. One does not carry on about one's treasonous exploits in front of a neighbor."

"You are no doubt right." She found herself unable to confess that she had another reason for spending time in the earl's presence. "However, according to Mr. Cochran, Lord Somerton knew more about Geoffrey's death than he let on during our conversation. Perhaps I will see or hear something of relevance."

"I can't be comfortable with this situation. Lord Somerton is no fool."

"Nor am I. I will remain vigilant."

"Promise me that you will cease this charade the moment you detect danger."

"Promise." She kissed her mother's forehead, then sighed. "Even in death, my husband keeps us in a constant state of anticipation. Always waiting for some sign of him—a letter, a gift, a visit. Why did I not put an end to this half-life years ago after he missed Sophie's fourth birthday?"

"What would you have done? Gone to London and dragged your husband home?"

"Why not? It's what a husband would have done to a wife in similar circumstances."

"I can think of two reasons." Evelyn anchored the basket around both her forearms. "One, if you had managed to force your husband home—and that's a rather large if—society would have labeled you a termagant and your husband a gelding."

"Mother, I don't think—"

"And two, any man who must be led home by his ear would not have made a happy addition to this household." Her chin lifted. "I daresay if you had not been moved to stick a knitting needle in his eye, I would have."

Catherine's lips twitched. Would not the infamous Isaac Cruikshank have had a jolly time drawing a continuity scene with Catherine dragging her husband home by his oversized ears in one drawing and her mother chasing after her wayward son-in-law with a sharp, gleaming knitting needle in another? She could even see the title of the caricature: *The Gelding*.

The humorous scene faded to the back of her mind and an image of her daughter's hopeful, yet guarded, expression surfaced. An expression she had seen so many times over the years, one that usually diminished into disappointment, then resignation.

"A daughter should know the security and strength of her father."

"Yes," her mother said. "But so few do when competing with the *ton*'s entertainments or the Crown's business."

Catherine's throat clenched at the note of regret tingeing her mother's voice. For years, she had resented her mother's passive attitude toward her father's long absences while an officer in His Majesty's Royal Navy. Not until she found herself standing in her mother's shoes had she been able to put aside old resentments—and exchange them for new ones.

"Sophie will survive the void left behind by her father," Evelyn said. "She will come out of it stronger, more self-reliant, and more considerate of others' feelings." She paused, her determined gaze boring into Catherine's. "As you did."

Catherine bent to kiss her mother's garden-stained hand. "As *we* did, Mother."

Evelyn's fingers squeezed hers. "Yes. As *we* did."

They stayed that way for several seconds until her mother pulled away, wiping moisture from her cheeks. "We cannot let this business with Lord Somerton and Mr. Cochran carry on too long. Not only is it dangerous, you and Sophie must move on with your lives. No more wallowing around in this senseless guilt."

"Mother, I—"

Voices from within the garden interrupted Catherine's rebuttal. A young girl's high-pitched voice intermingled with a man's low baritone. Before long, Sophie and their manservant, Edward, passed beneath the arch, toting rods, creel baskets, and a container full of worms.

"I'm ready, Mama." Sophie ran the short distance, her creel sliding off her shoulder. She displayed none of her earlier ill humors.

Catherine ignored her mother's gloating look. "Here, let me help you with that, dear." She lifted the long strap supporting the creel and hooked it around her daughter's neck, so that it rested diagonally across her small body. Made for adults, the basket still bounced low against the girl's knee. "Is that better?"

"Oh, yes," Sophie said. "Now I won't have to worry about losing my fish."

Catherine gestured to the rods Edward held. "I'll take those."

"You sure, ma'am? I can carry them down to the lake so you don't soil your fine dress."

She glanced down at her black merino riding habit. "Thank you, Edward." To Sophie, she said, "Run along with Edward to the lake while I change into something more appropriate."

"Yes, Mama." Her small frame nearly vibrated with its need to run free.

"Listen to Edward," she warned. "Do not go into the water and be careful with the hook."

"Yes, Mama." Her acknowledgment came faster this time, more impatient.

"Don't you worry none about us, ma'am," Edward said. "I'll take good care of Miss Sophie until you arrive."

"I know you will, Edward. I'll see you both in a little while."

"Come, Miss Sophie," the manservant said. "Have you ever played Ducks and Drakes?"

"No," Sophie said, beaming. "But I'm sure I'd like to."

"Oh, you'll love this game. You take a nice flat rock, you see, and throw it across the lake's surface..."

While the two gabbled on about the best angle for skipping rocks, Catherine strode to the house, with her mother at her side. "He's always so patient with her."

"You probably worry about her antics more than the rest of us," Evelyn said. "It's a mother's lot, but try not to stifle her exuberance too much, daughter. I always feel much younger when in her presence."

"This coming from the woman who told my daughter to 'temper her enthusiasm' on Saturday?"

Her mother sent her a cross look. "Most of our guests understand the situation here, but I thought she needed a gentle reminder about appearances."

"You were quite right, as always." She patted the older woman's arm. "I must go change."

"Enjoy your time at the lake, dear."

Catherine climbed the stairs to her bedchamber, but instead of ringing for a maid to assist her with her dress, she went to her writing box, one of the few presents hand-delivered by her husband. He had taken great delight in showing her the box's hidden compartment, thinking it a clever contraption. She thought back to when she had shown Sophie how the mechanism worked. Her daughter had been spellbound for an entire week, constantly asking Catherine to open the secret compartment. When this business with Cochran and Lord Somerton was behind them, she would present the writing box to Sophie. Her daughter would cherish it far more than Catherine.

She tapped the edge of one panel and another clicked open. Lifting the panel wider, she retrieved a stack of five letters. Although no one else knew of her hiding spot, she wanted to make sure the letters were where she had left them, knowing she would have to deliver them to the earl on Sunday.

The moment she had returned home from London, she had sifted through her final stash of missives for any mention of a Mr. Cochran. She had not come across his name until the final letter. Though she knew it would be fruitless, she pulled the folded missive from the beribboned packet and attempted to decipher Geoffrey's words. But like the last hundred times, chunks of legible phrases were broken up by a series of meaningless words.

With impatient fingers, she refolded the note and jammed it on top of the others. She tossed the packet into the secret compartment and moved to close it.

"Mama, are you ready?"

Catherine pivoted to find Sophie standing in her bedchamber's doorway, flushed and unkempt.

"Not yet, dear," she said. "I thought you were headed down to the lake with Edward."

"I wanted to bring my little wooden boat." She held up one of the first figures Geoffrey had carved for Castle Dragonthorpe.

"Be careful not to lose it."

"Yes, Mama." Sophie's blue eyes settled on the writing box before lifting to meet Catherine's gaze again. "I'll see you at the lake."

"I won't be but ten minutes behind you."

Sophie smiled. "Enough time for me to catch the biggest fish." Then she was gone.

Catherine laughed and turned to close the secret compartment. She smoothed her fingers over the fine grain, contemplating her upcoming meeting with the earl. Once she handed the letters over to him, she hoped he would soon be able to answer all of her questions.

An exhilarating trepidation coursed through her blood. And God help her, she looked forward to seeing him again. She became *aware* while near him. Aware of her heartbeat, aware of her flushed cheeks. And aware of the ache between her legs. All of these sensations had been denied her for so long, she had nearly forgotten they existed.

Her fingers began unfastening the buttons on her

riding jacket. Geoffrey might not have desired her, but she had not mistaken the glimmer of interest in the earl's eyes.

Remembrance alone was enough to send a pulse of heat through her body. She would hold on to the heat and the memory of the earl's silvery eyes until Sunday, the day she would become a spy.

SIX

Sebastian tipped back the last of his brandy, his mood blacker than the cheerless moon outside his library window. Alone with his own thoughts, his mind had inevitably focused on the French's recent infiltration of the Nexus and their subsequent assassination attempts.

The depraved Frenchman, Valère, had nearly succeeded. Had nearly destroyed England's greatest spy, Raven, and severed the head of the one organization that could put an end to Napoleon's dictatorship from the shadows.

Instead of ending the usurper's reign, Sebastian's well-crafted plans had splintered, crippling the Nexus almost beyond redemption. Had Valère's plan succeeded a fortnight ago, Sebastian's agents would have been operating blind, placing them and England in jeopardy. The safeguards Sebastian had put in place long ago would have bought them all a little time, but not much.

All his attention to detail had failed to protect those he loved. Valère had come close, so close, to killing—

He poured himself another brandy and drained half

the glass in one smooth motion. But no matter how much alcohol he consumed, he could not hold back the avalanche of emotions at the mere thought of how close he had come to losing his wards, Cora and Ethan.

As he had sworn off marriage, the deBeau siblings were the closest he would ever come to being a father. They meant everything to him.

Eyes burning, he swore, "I will not fail you again."

Unfortunately, the Nexus traitor was not the worst complication of Sebastian's last mission. The traitor's rather convenient escape had forced the Alien Office to turn its suspicious eye on Sebastian. He was officially *unofficially* placed on leave. Relegated to the country like some recalcitrant child while the new Superintendent of Aliens sifted through his confidential files for signs of sedition.

Gritting his teeth, he grabbed the decanter, filled his glass, and turned away. A man in his position did not surrender over a decade's worth of clandestine operation files without experiencing a degree of gut-churning dread.

He stared at the single sheet of paper resting on the small writing desk. The damned thing had kept him pacing long into the night. Before he had left London, Superintendent Reeves had demanded a list of names, precious names. His agents' names.

Sebastian had protected his operatives for years by never revealing their identities. Not to his superiors, nor to other operatives. Everyone used code names to protect them and their families.

Thank God for his foresight. Had he made their identities and missions available within the Alien Office, the traitor would have handed the information to Valère and they would all be dead by now. But the combination of Reeves's investigation and Sebastian's brush with death gnawed at his conscience. For the first time, he questioned his decision to not share his agents' information with a select few at the Alien Office.

What if his safeguards failed? What would become of those he had protected with his silence? Who would take command of the Nexus and lead his agents through their next mission?

He had only to recall Cora's captivity in an enemy dungeon for that particular point to be driven home. If the madman who had kidnapped her had not carried a distorted version of love for her, he would have killed her long before her rescuers had arrived.

Still, he hesitated. If the request had come from his previous superintendent, William Wickham, Sebastian would have had fewer qualms about handing over such deadly information to a man he knew and trusted.

In the year since Reeves's appointment, he had allowed Sebastian to run the Nexus as he saw fit. Sebastian was certain a gentleman with Reeves's credentials—Oxford education, learned lawyer, King's Printer—would look into the backgrounds of those closest to him. The same as Sebastian had done when Reeves accepted the appointment. If the traitor had whispered lies into Reeves's ear, Sebastian would have to trust that the superintendent would use that clever mind of his to untangle the lies from the truth.

Tearing his gaze away from the blank sheet of paper, he strode to the window and pressed his forehead against a cool pane, savoring the contrast to his heated skin. He looked to the east, toward the widow's estate. From this vantage point, he could just make out...nothing. With a new moon riding high in the sky, he could barely see the large urn-shaped flowerpots marking the entrance to the sunken garden.

Thoughts of the widow brought him back to his blunder on the terrace earlier in the day. Unobtrusively scanning an area for potential threats was one of the first tasks he had mastered after joining the Alien Office. How was it that a widow from the country had noticed his preoccupation, but skilled international spies could not?

From what little he had gleaned from his butler, Mrs. Ashcroft made a habit of detecting people's failures. His steward's in particular. Her keen observation skills were not the only reason for him to remain vigilant in her presence. While speaking with her earlier in the day, he'd had an annoying tendency to compare her honey-colored hair to that of a soft winter's sun and her petite, yet perfectly proportioned figure to sculptures he had seen of the Roman goddess Venus.

With Superintendent Reeves searching his private files and the widow distracting his thoughts, it was no wonder he had bungled his surveillance. He closed his eyes and forced the tension from his neck, shoulders, and arms. He worked his way down his body until his knees unlocked, and he leaned his full weight against the windowsill.

Damnation, he was tired. Intrigue had ruled his thoughts for so long that he could not recall a time when the Realm's safety had not commanded his daily schedule. Long hours, sleepless nights, and extended trips away from home. Add in a liberal dose of lies, deceptions, and countermeasures, and one had a recipe for growing older far faster than the body was designed to handle. His three and a half decades suddenly held the weight of a man twenty years his senior.

Pushing away from the window, he liberated his glass

of its amber contents. The expensive liquor slid down his throat with practiced ease but refused to dull his disquieting thoughts. He lifted the decanter from the sideboard and sat down at his desk with an uncharacteristic *plop*.

A glass in one hand and the decanter in the other, he rested his forearms on his desk, framing the sheet of paper. The emptiness mocked him. Burned his eyes with its challenging glare.

Why hadn't he thrown the bothersome thing back in the drawer and said to hell with Reeves and his debilitating demands? Because he could not answer one simple question: Should he?

His heart began the familiar, painful tattoo while he watched ghostly vowels and consonants weave together to create forbidden links. Links that could one day force a power-driven ruler to his conquering knees.

It was not lost on him that Cora had faced a similar decision while in a French dungeon. She had not betrayed her country, even under torture.

Would complying with his superior's request be a form of betrayal?

He had sworn never to write down such valuable intelligence. If the information fell into the wrong hands, dozens of lives he was responsible for would be forfeited, and by extension, hundreds would perish.

Should he?

Dear God, he did not know. Never in his life had he been so indecisive. But this decision could have ramifications far beyond his comprehension. And yet, if he did not give Reeves the list of secret service agents and something happened to him *and* his safeguards collapsed, the Nexus would suffer. England would suffer.

How could he not?

If Reeves stripped him of the chief's position, he would lose access to not only intelligence within the Alien Office but the Foreign Office. Such information was vital to his mission planning.

He tipped the heavy crystal decanter toward his glass again, not stopping until the liquid threatened to spill over the side. He stared at the trembling contents for a long contemplative moment before raising the drink to his lips and indulging in an uncivilized gulp, and waited.

Ah, there it was. Finally.

The first stirrings of numbness penetrated the deep recesses of his mind like a slow, thick fog pushing through the streets of London. Sebastian inhaled a cooling breath, encouraging the numbness to greater depths.

He took another sip for good measure before exchanging his half-empty tumbler for an ink-dipped quill, steeling himself against the inevitable bout of sickness. Because no matter how potent the spirit, he would never feel at ease with what he was about to do.

Dabbing the pen's nib against the inkwell, he considered his first entry. None of them would be easy, but the first—the first name would start an unpredictable series of events that scared the hell out of him. He tightened his hold on the pen. Who would be his first sacrifice?

Images flashed before his eyes with blinding speed, making his head spin and his world tilt to the left. That's when he saw it.

A missive propped against the table lamp. He recalled Grayson handing it to him hours ago, but he had paid it no mind for he had already crossed the threshold into the darkness that engulfed him more and more these days. Why he noticed it now, he could not be sure. But he welcomed the distraction.

Replacing the quill, he picked up the letter and regarded the neat script. Beautifully formed letters made by a confident hand. He lifted the parchment to his nose and detected a faint feminine scent that managed to calm his raging imagination in a way the alcohol had not.

Breaking the seal, he pressed open the folds and skimmed the contents. Warmth flooded his chest.

Dear Lord Somerton,

I do hope you are settling in at Bellamere Park. After giving your situation additional consideration, I would like to extend an offer of my services. I have come to know the craftsmen in the area quite well and can make recommendations based on that knowledge.

Should you wish to go it alone, however, I have taken the top three pressing issues from my previous list and indicated an appropriate craftsman for the task. Grayson will know how to contact them. This abbreviated list will get you started while you are sorting through the circumstances at Bellamere.

Please let me know if I can be of further assistance.

Your faithful neighbor,
Catherine Ashcroft

His thumb traced over the widow's signature. Like her handwriting, her name exuded quiet confidence, warmth, and invitation. The room shifted again, righting itself, and the darkness surrounding him ebbed away.

She wanted to help him.

He could not recall the last time someone wanted to be of service to him without an outstretched hand in return or, in less favorable circumstances, using the service as a mask for something a great deal more diabolical. He supposed the widow could be pandering to him in the hopes of snagging a new husband.

But that scheme did not ring true. With a difficult marriage behind her, she would not be keen on taking vows again. Unlike the aristocracy, Ashcroft had had no qualms about investing his money in the Stock Exchange. As a result, his widow and daughter were set for the foreseeable future. However, she was nothing if not practical and would want what was best for her daughter. Which meant she might be father-shopping rather than husband-hunting.

He pressed the tips of his fingers into his pounding temples. Agents shackled with families could be compromised by the enemy and distracted from their purpose. He had known this when recruiting Ashcroft. Given his distancing himself from his family, Ashcroft had known it, too. But the young man had shown such promise that Sebastian had ignored the greatest—and last—lesson his murdered mentor had ever taught him: *Families do not survive the spy business.*

Sebastian would have to live with the knowledge that, given the same situation, he would have recruited Ashcroft all over again. England had needed the clever young man as much as, if not more than, his family did.

The sight of Geoffrey Ashcroft slouched against the side of a soot-covered building, blood spreading across his filched peasant's shirt, surfaced with aching clarity. Slamming his eyes shut, he squeezed the bridge of his nose in a feeble attempt to block the memories of that disastrous night. When pressure failed to provide the desired results, he retrieved his glass and belted back the last of his drink.

Once he retrieved the rest of Ashcroft's letters, and

Helsford deciphered them, he would come up with a believable story for the widow. One that would identify a murderer and provide Catherine and her daughter with a measure of justice.

From the tone of Ashcroft's previous correspondence, Sebastian suspected the agent had stumbled across something significant. Something he had not wanted to reveal through their normal channels of communication. Which meant they could be dealing with one or more prominent figures in the government or the *ton*.

Again.

They were still trying to assess the damage done by the previous traitor's scheming. If the Foreign Office was housing another high-level double spy, the repercussions could be disastrous. Sebastian prayed Ashcroft's last batch of correspondence held the vital clue they needed in order to circumvent another threat.

He stared hard at Catherine's signature. All thoughts of Ashcroft, danger, and missives faded to the background. The widow, with her generous heart, staunch support, and perfect English body, sliced through his troubled musings.

What would it be like to share the company of an attractive woman who wished him no ill will? Just a few stolen hours. Hours in which he debated nothing more complicated than overseeing a series of repairs or the welcome of a stolen kiss.

Could he spend time with Catherine and keep the details of her husband's death a secret? Could he watch over his agent's family while enticing the man's widow into his bed? He released a cynical half-snort. Of course, he could. It was what he did best.

Deception, lies, and secrets.

SEVEN

The intruder stared at the sleeping form well into the predawn hours for the simple pleasure of knowing he could. The widow's locking mechanisms were good, but they were no deterrent for a man who had spent years accessing forbidden places.

The bed creaked and its inhabitant shifted onto her side, facing him. Feminine perfection. Innocence personified. A weapon of destruction.

All she had to do was open those long-lashed eyelids and the serenity of the moment would be lost, transformed into precipitous violence. But her eyes remained shut and her soft, even breaths pierced the air with their gentleness.

Disappointment settled in his chest. Even though he enjoyed the power of undetected observation, he loved the thrill of discovery more. Loved witnessing his victim's first moment of awareness, that paralyzing second when she senses danger lurking within her haven of safety. The ensuing gasping, pleading, and crying for mercy all added to his pleasure. The longer his victim lived in a world of anticipatory terror, the greater his excitement.

Fear stimulated him in a way no other sentiment could. He craved its power, sought its bliss. He looked forward to the moment when he could blend his secret passion with his driving ambition.

Soon.

Everything was falling into place. Before long, he alone would hold the power of the greatest minds in England, and beyond. Lions taken down by their beloved lambs.

Bored by his companion's idleness, he bent at the waist and smoothed back a lock of red-gold hair from her unlined forehead. Her skin was warm against his lips, her scent fresh, exciting.

Soon.

Straightening, he pivoted to leave and stepped on something small and hard. He waited for the ensuing crack, the telltale sound that would signal his presence.

But nothing cracked or shattered or snapped beneath the pressure of his weight. He carefully lifted his boot and knelt down to retrieve the object. Holding it up to the faint light filtering in from the window, he made out the wooden shape of a kilted man holding a long two-handed claymore.

He glanced back at the sleeping form and smiled.

Dropping the warrior into his coat pocket, he slipped out the nursery door.

EIGHT

S ebastian made his way down the grand staircase with a crushing headache and bleary eyes. If he had not had a full day planned, he would have shot Parker the instant he disturbed his sleep. Instead of murdering his valet, he had scraped his body off the sweat-cooled sheets and made his way downstairs.

Within seconds of gaining the entrance hall, his butler appeared. "My lord, there is something you should know—"

"In a moment, Grayson. Please bring a strong pot of coffee to my study. Then we can discuss what's troubling you."

"But sir—"

"Coffee, then talk." He headed toward his study, hoping the noxious fumes caused by Blake's singular passion had dissipated. The last thing his aching head needed was an immersion in turpentine and linseed oil. Turning the handle, he braced himself against an olfactory assault and was gratified when only the merest of fumes reached his nose. He drew a deeper breath and received the same not-so-unpleasant result.

A sound from the opposite end of the room drew his attention. A growl crept up his throat at the pleasure-pain of finding the widow in his sanctuary. The sight did much to improve his sour mood, but he now regretted not allowing Grayson to perform his duties. If he had, Sebastian would have detoured to the kitchen for a restorative cup of coffee and another splash of cold water over his face. Perhaps then he would have been prepared for this keen-witted woman.

Nothing for it, he closed the door and braced himself. "Mrs. Ashcroft."

She jerked into an upright position, her cheeks a deep, becoming red, whether from bending over the metal bucket on the floor or from being startled, Sebastian could not be certain.

"Good morning, my lord."

Feeling disoriented, he nodded toward the bucket. "What have you there?"

"An old family recipe for neutralizing unwanted aromas." Her flush deepened. "I decided to make myself useful while awaiting your arrival."

Sebastian glanced around, finding three more buckets. "Your family appears to be very wise, Mrs. Ashcroft. I can barely detect Mr. Blake's oils."

"It is amazing what charcoal, soda ash, and dampened cloths can do."

"Have you been waiting long?"

Confusion clouded her pretty eyes. "I arrived a few minutes before the appointed time."

Caution gripped his stomach. Habit forced his gaze to make a thorough sweep of the room, looking for anything peculiar, out of place, or that did not belong. If anything, the room appeared a good deal tidier than it had yesterday. But Sebastian could not shake the feeling that he was missing something vital.

He returned his attention to the widow—*Catherine.* "Forgive me, Mrs. Ashcroft, but I seem to have forgotten our appointment."

She stilled. "Shall I come back at a more convenient time?"

The room became blistering hot, and he tried to loosen his too-tight cravat. A vague recollection hovered at the periphery of his mind. "That won't be necessary. Perhaps you could remind me of the nature of our meeting."

She strode toward a small octagonal table and picked up her reticule. Digging inside, she produced a note and offered it to him. "This might help your memory, sir. I received your summons quite early this morning."

Even from this distance, he could see her name scrawled across the outside of the dispatch, the writing both familiar and somehow wrong. What had he done in his inebriated state last night?

The churning mass in his stomach curdled and swept into the back of his throat with unexpected vigor. He raised his fist to his mouth, fighting back the foul taste. What had possessed him to send a dispatch to her at such an absurd hour?

Once he had his body under control, he said, "Last night, I was...not myself and fear I might have written that note at an awkward moment." He flicked his fingers toward the missive. "Would you be so kind?"

She peered at him with wide, owlish eyes. "You want me to read your note to you?"

"Please."

Her gaze flicked down to where his fingers toyed with his signet ring. He locked his jaw and clasped his hands behind his back. "Mrs. Ashcroft?"

"This is rather awkward, my lord. Are you certain you do not wish to look at it yourself?"

"Quite, madam."

The command in his tone caused her lips to compress, but she smoothed her fingers over the creases and began reading.

My dear Catherine,

I accept your kind offer of assistance. Please attend me tomorrow morning at ten.

Your forever grateful neighbor,
Sebastian

She hesitated over his Christian name, a subtle confirmation of the message's too-familiar address. Although not appropriate, the contents were not as bad as he had feared. Snippets of last night crystallized and took shape. Much to his shame, the volatile mix of fatigue, frustration, and doubt that had become harder for him to master had spilled onto the paper in the form of a dangerous yearning.

Even now, hours later, he craved the companionship of this woman. Why? There were hundreds of widows in London who would provide such solace and would come to him with far fewer complications. Knowing all of this did not stop him from wanting to sink his hands into the mass of gold silk piled atop her head.

But she had done so much for him already, during a

time when she should have been concentrating on her own difficult circumstances. How could he ask for more?

"I am sorry to have inconvenienced you, Mrs. Ashcroft. My summons was a regrettable mistake."

"Mistake?" A shot of dismay skittered across her features. "You have not inconvenienced me, sir. I would be grateful for the opportunity to help."

The tendons in his neck pulled tight. "You have already provided more assistance than I deserve, madam."

"The process would go much smoother and quicker with my aid." She tilted her head to the side. "I assure you, this task would be a welcome diversion. You do recall that I offered to help?"

"I recall. But I also know you likely did so because it is in your nature to set things aright."

She started to protest, but he held up a staying finger. "Within the last three months, you have lost your father, your husband, and you have dueled with my steward. I will not add to your burden."

Dropping her gaze, she said nothing for several seconds. He followed her line of sight, to where her hands clutched the drawstrings of her reticule with crushing force.

Finally, she lifted her chin and straightened her back. "Very well, my lord. Please feel free to call upon me should you change your mind."

"Do not fret, Mrs. Ashcroft," he said, driving the point home. "If I find myself in need of counsel, Grayson is more than up for the task."

Nodding, she regarded the door behind him. "Grayson would make an admirable attempt at seeing to your needs."

Against his will, he asked, "Attempt?"

He could see the topic made her ill at ease, but she

eventually answered. "When Mr. Blake began refusing to meet with your tenants, Grayson tried to resolve their issues without the steward's knowledge, but then his knee started bothering him and he could no longer move about the estate."

Sebastian had noticed a subtle limp in his butler's gait. "Go on."

"Mr. Blake realized what was going on and made a terrible scene, embarrassing Grayson and infuriating some of your tenants." Indignation strengthened her voice, her gaze steadied. "This is the main reason why I became involved in your estate affairs. Not only did I keep the issues in front of Mr. Blake, I relayed information between Grayson and your tenants."

Few people distinguished themselves enough to warrant Sebastian's notice or garner his admiration. Somehow the widow had managed to do both. "How unfortunate that I did not know any of this before sacking the man."

His attention veered toward the sideboard, with its stoppered decanters of various colored liquors. Lifting his watch fob, he confirmed the hour. Bare minutes before eleven. *Eleven.* Much too early to indulge and much too late for her to have lingered for an absentee earl.

Had she really waited an hour for him to arrive? If any of his agents learned he had been late for a meeting that he had set, they would never let him live it down. At least those who dared to tease him would not. Most did not.

Unlike many members of the *ton,* he never slept past seven, even when he stayed up into the wee hours of the morning. His body needed little sleep to function properly. Inebriation being the obvious exception to the rule, of course.

"It would take me no time to turn the list of repairs I gave you into an actual work schedule," she pressed.

If she were a man, he would swear that God had finally thrown a kindness his way. But she was a woman. An intelligent, beautiful, far too perceptive woman. God had nothing to do with the temptress before him. The Devil had brought her into Sebastian's world, and the fiend had his trident pointing straight at Sebastian's heart.

Why else would he be experiencing this overwhelming desire to feel her bare body wrapped around his, to tangle his fingers in the loose skeins of her silken hair, to free his mind of everything but her, while her husband's dying plea still echoed in his soul?

"Watch over my family."

As much as his body would like to ignore the fact, seducing a woman he was supposed to protect was wrong. Even for a ruthless bastard like him.

Stepping toward the bellpull, he gave it two hard yanks. "Mrs. Ashcroft, I can see that you have a genuine need to set things to rights around here. However, I have managed my family's affairs for over twenty years. Fear not, I will remedy this situation."

As rebuffs go, it was not the harshest he had ever delivered, but it was by far the hardest. Especially when hurt pulled at her features.

"Yes," she said at last. "Yes, of course, you can. How silly of me to have thought otherwise." She waved her hand toward the buckets. "You will have no further need of those by tomorrow." She dropped into a curtsy. "When you are ready to discuss Geoffrey's letters, please send for me. Good day, my lord."

The finality of her farewell cut into the steel surrounding his heart. But he did not try to stop her.

Instead, he bowed. "Again, my apologies for the disruption—"

The click of the door closing cut off his apology. He did not blame her. Not one bit. Although he had spent a lifetime perfecting the art of lying, nothing felt perfect about this situation.

In fact, a sense of deep wrongness slammed in his gut with a pugilist's precision.

NINE

"No, m'lord," the farmer said, propping his shovel against the back wall of a small lean-to. "I explained what needs to be done to Mrs. Ashcroft. Haven't the time to go into it again."

Sebastian clenched his teeth around a curse. He had met with the same resistance all afternoon. Most of his tenants were not as vocal about their displeasure as Mr. Hayton, but all made sure he understood he had a lot to make up for. The effects of Blake's mismanagement cut deep in their minds, and they were not ready to forgive Sebastian.

"Mr. Hayton," he tried again. "I mean to have men working on the repairs as early as next week. If you would take a few minutes to show me what needs attending, I'll be able to provide a detailed list for the tradesmen."

The last time he had seen Hayton, a few strands of gray had striped the area above the old man's ears. But the farmer had always tackled each day with admirable enthusiasm, putting many men younger than he to shame. Now, Hayton sported a full head of gray hair and his normally square shoulders slumped forward as if they were too heavy for his frail body to carry.

"The roof needs fixing now." Mr. Hayton retrieved his pitchfork. "Rain's coming. Waiting till next week'll do me no good."

Sebastian gathered Reaper's reins. "I'll do what I can to get someone here sooner."

"Mrs. Ashcroft knows who to contact," Mr. Hayton said, combing the pitchfork through a pile of soiled straw.

He set his jaw, not used to such willfulness and in no mood to hear yet another tenant touting the widow's accomplishments. Mounting Reaper, he set off for home. He'd had enough for one day. He had let them down by not ensuring the steward was performing his duties. However, being flogged in the face at every turn would not make him regret his inaction any more than he did already, or fix the damage already done.

Over the course of the next fortnight, he would show them that he remembered how to be a competent landlord and pray they would allow him to repair the many wrongs done by Blake. As he rounded the farmer's small cottage, he observed the thinning thatch on the northeast corner of the roof. At least he had persuaded the stubborn old goat to mention that much.

"Good afternoon, Lord Somerton," a man's voice hailed from the road.

Sebastian turned to find Showbury's vicar sitting astride a large bay, a welcoming smile on his face. "Mr. Foster." He joined the other man on the rutted drive, making note of the deep tracks and adding them to his growing list of tasks. "What brings you out this far?"

"I'm meeting Mrs. Ashcroft at the McCarthys' to check on the eldest daughter." The vicar guided his horse around a large hole in the middle of the road. "All of sixteen and on her way to becoming a new mother." He shook his head. "And the father nowhere to be found."

Sebastian's lips thinned at the mention of the widow. "Does the girl have anyone to help when the babe arrives?"

The vicar sent him an approving smile. "Indeed, my lord. Despite her current predicament, Meghan's a fine young lady and the McCarthys are good people."

"Do you and Mrs. Ashcroft work together often?"

"Quite often, my lord." Warmth seeped into the vicar's voice. "I find Mrs. Ashcroft's assistance and practical nature invaluable. Showbury's residents admire and respect her, which makes visits like today's go much smoother."

Something about the vicar's praise of the widow unsettled him. He eyed his riding companion, who appeared a few years younger than he and sported masculine features some women might find attractive.

"Are you married, Mr. Foster?" Sebastian heard himself ask.

"No, sir. Not at present. But I have been thinking on the subject of late."

Rather than calming the odd swirling sensation in Sebastian's stomach, the vicar's answer made the feeling grow stronger. Before he could decide whether to inquire further, Mr. Foster waved toward a cottage.

"Ah, here we are, my lord."

Sebastian's gaze swept over the homestead. He expected to find the same age-worn buildings and unkempt prospects that he had encountered on his other inspections. Instead, the cottage and outbuildings appeared well-maintained, plucked free of weeds and devoid of clutter. Yellow and white flowers lined the footpath leading up to the cottage.

The vicar pulled his mount to a halt. "Declan McCarthy moved his family here a little over a year ago. He's hardworking and a skilled carpenter, but I'm afraid the residents of Showbury have never welcomed the family as they should."

"Irish?"

"Yes, sir." The vicar's lips firmed, his back straightening. "They're honest folks and don't deserve suspicious treatment. If not for Mrs. Ashcroft, I fear the family would've been forced to move on by now."

For the love of God.

Did the woman have her hands in everything? "How did Mrs. Ashcroft help the family?"

A flush spread across the younger man's cheeks. "Well, she, um—" The vicar's eyes widened a moment before he waved at someone behind Sebastian. "Hello, Mr. McCarthy."

He eyed the vicar, waiting for the man to finish his sentence. But the vicar dismounted, avoiding his gaze.

With no other choice, Sebastian followed suit.

Declan McCarthy held out his hand. "Good day, Vicar."

"It is that, Mr. McCarthy." The vicar shook the man's hand and turned to Sebastian. "I'd like you to meet Lord Somerton. Just returned from London."

The carpenter's friendly mien leeched away. "M'lord."

"McCarthy."

The Irishman turned to the vicar. "Are you here to see my Meghan?"

"Yes, sir, I am." Foster glanced around, frowning. "Has Mrs. Ashcroft not arrived?"

McCarthy rubbed the stubble across his chin. "Not yet. I expect her any minute."

"I've never known Mrs. Ashcroft to be late for an appointment," the vicar mused after checking his timepiece.

"I'm visiting with each of my tenants," Sebastian said. "Is there anything you need, Mr. McCarthy?"

Declan thick eyebrows drew together. He looked to the vicar, who gave him an encouraging smile. "The gate leading into the south paddock needs some mending. I was going to take care of it myself once I finished repairing the molding on the door leading to your gallery."

"My gallery?"

"Declan," the vicar said in a rush. "Is Mrs. McCarthy inside?"

The carpenter nodded, his gaze shooting between Sebastian and Mr. Foster.

Sebastian studied the vicar's flushed face. "Mrs. Ashcroft hired McCarthy to repair the molding, I presume?"

"At the request of Grayson, I believe." Foster swallowed hard. "Declan, I'll go pay my respects to your wife before checking on Meghan. Perhaps Mrs. Ashcroft will have arrived by then."

Catherine had mentioned that she had operated as Grayson's liaison, but he had not imagined her assistance extended to Bellamere.

"Would you care for a refreshment, m'lord?" McCarthy asked.

He glanced at the carpenter's cottage and found three curious faces in a window. A young boy and girl craned their neck, this way and that to see the stranger outside, and a pretty brunette, who looked to be on the verge of womanhood, stood sentinel behind them, watchful and unmoving. He guessed the eldest of the three to be the enceinte Meghan.

Wanting no part in the upcoming discussion, he turned back to his tenant. "Thank you, no. I must be on my way."

After mounting Reaper, he said, "When you've repaired the molding, come see me. I have additional work, if you're interested."

McCarthy's eyes widened in surprise. "Thank you, m'lord."

He nodded before wheeling Reaper about.

As leaving the McCarthy residence, he found himself scanning the country lane for a blond head. Foster's concern for her absence replayed through his mind for nearly two miles before he shut out the vicar's voice. A decade of deciphering men's words and their true intent had him imagining calamity where none existed.

Showbury was not London. Men did not go around terrorizing innocent women in this sleepy village. He had to let his mind rest, to suppress the uneasy feeling eating at his stomach. His special talents were not needed here. He would save those for when he returned to the city.

While in Showbury, he would need to employ patience and charm. Patience to break through barriers of mistrust erected by his tenants and charm to convince the widow he needed her help after all. Because without her, making the necessary repairs around his estate would be a study in frustration and inefficiency.

He kicked Reaper into a faster pace, one to match the anticipation thundering through his blood.

TEN

Catherine made her way down the staircase, going over in her mind what she would say to Meghan McCarthy. Such an inauspicious beginning for a shy young girl, especially since she refused to reveal the identity of her babe's father. The vicar was an optimist, though, and had asked her to join him one more time at the McCarthy cottage to see if they could coax a name from her.

This venture would no doubt be as unsuccessful as the last. Every time someone broached the subject with Meghan, she became agitated and withdrawn. At first, Catherine thought the girl protected the father because of some misplaced loyalty. But during their last unfruitful conversation, she suspected the girl feared her beau.

This time, she would find an opportunity to speak with Meghan alone. See if the girl would confide in her. Reveal her secret, if she harbored one.

Deep in her own thoughts, she missed the low exchange of voices at the entry door.

"Good day, Mrs. Ashcroft."

She glanced up to find a gentleman handing off his hat and gloves to her butler.

"Mr. Cochran," she said, at a loss for words. "This is quite unexpected. What brings you to Showbury?"

"Why, you, of course." He combed his fingers through his hair. "Do you not recall my promise to see you in a few days?"

"Indeed, I do." The stiffness in her muscles relaxed from their initial shock. "You simply caught me by surprise."

"Shall I return at a more convenient time? You appear to be on your way out."

"I have a few minutes to spare before I must be off to an important meeting." She motioned toward the drawing room. "Shall we?"

"By all means."

Still stinging from Lord Somerton's rebuff, she had a difficult time piecing together information she could share. "If you've come for a report on my observations, I'm afraid I have little to convey." She sat on the edge of the high-back chair, leaving the lemon-and-mint-striped sofa for her visitor.

He eased himself onto the sofa with a languidness that bespoke of someone settling in for a nice long chat. Folding one leg over the other, he asked, "Why is that, Mrs. Ashcroft?" The smoothness of his voice cut through the air like a saber slicing through its victim.

"His lordship returned only yesterday. I gained a short audience with him, but that was only because I was already there when he arrived."

"Yes, I see what you mean." He drummed his fingers on the cushion beside him. "How did Lord Somerton appear?"

She searched her memory. "Tired. Somewhat preoccupied." *Incredibly compelling, satisfyingly disgusted with his steward. Achingly grateful.* "But his condition might have had more to do with his long journey and the disturbing news he received about his estate than with his troubles in the city."

"Disturbing news, you say?"

My dear Catherine.

The earl's salutation raced through her mind. Not for the first time, she wondered what it would be like to hear those words leave his lips. Would they carry the same reverent quality she had conjured? Or would they be nothing more than three everyday words?

Either way, she could not forget the look of acute vulnerability his handsome features bore upon entering his study. What had he been thinking? What burdens did he carry?

"Mrs. Ashcroft?"

"A steward who took advantage of his position." She rose, suddenly uncomfortable with their conversation. "I'm sorry, but I really must go if I'm to make my appointment."

Instead of following suit, he smiled and indicated her seat. "Another moment of your time, please."

"I don't have another moment." Every instinct she possessed urged her to be quit of this man. "I will send word if and when I learn something of substance."

"I, myself, am under time constraints." His smile turned brittle. "Please. Sit."

Gritting her teeth, she sat.

"Thank you." His blue eyes bore into hers. "Have you ever heard of the Alien Office, madam?"

"No, sir."

"I'm not surprised. Few have," he said. "The Alien

Office operates under the auspice of the Home Office, although some members of the office report directly to the Foreign Office."

He paused, seeming to wait for her acknowledgment. "I'm listening," she said.

"Simply put, the Alien Office was established to gather intelligence, both at home and abroad, of any potential threat against England."

"I suspect they have their hands full at the moment." She noticed her knee bouncing, a sign that her already thin patience was coming to an end. "Interesting, but I don't understand what this has to do with me."

"You soon will. It's important that you understand the full scope of the situation in which we find ourselves."

"Very well. Go on."

"As I mentioned, a small number of the agents in the Alien Office report their activities to the Foreign Office. These individuals comprise an even lesser-known group called the Nexus. The Nexus's reach spans many countries —England, Germany, Austria, Italy, America, and more— and the agents' identities are a carefully guarded secret, even within the Alien Office."

Dread settled over her. "Perhaps I've heard enough of this secret organization."

"It's not so easy as that. You and I, we have an agreement. One I shared with my superior, who now has certain expectations."

"Why did you do such a thing? We were just talking, sharing confidences."

"You thought participating in the Foreign Office's investigation a lark, madam?"

"No! No," she said in a calmer voice. "I merely agreed to observe Lord Somerton during his stay at Bellamere in exchange for news about my husband's murder investigation."

"This is true, but we have come by new information. Information that raises the stakes."

She made a valiant effort to close off her hearing. All she had wanted was for someone to help her confirm her husband's means of death. By doing so, those who killed him would be brought to justice and she might be able to begin the process of forgiveness—of Geoffrey and of herself.

"As it turns out, Somerton commands this elite group of international agents."

"Agents? Spies, do you mean?"

"Both terms apply, yes."

The earl did not appear the dashing type, nor could she see him gallivanting about as a footman or gardener or whatever disguises a spy uses.

"Lord Somerton? You're sure?"

"Oh, yes."

"That's good then, even heroic."

"For many years, Somerton's actions were quite heroic." He glanced out the window, revealing the line of his jaw where a muscle beat. "But he became greedy, as many men do in his position."

"Surely you are mistaken. He's an earl, for goodness' sake."

"Greed afflicts all men, no matter their rank, wealth, or personal convictions."

She did not believe such rubbish. Over the years, she had witnessed many acts of kindness from individuals who had little to spare. Not all men were greedy, just the bad ones.

Which was Lord Somerton?

"What immoral path has greed led the earl down?"

"Espionage."

"Yes, we've already established that he is a spy."

Cochran's features hardened. "Against his country."

"A double spy, you mean?"

"Correct," he said. "The Foreign Office has reason to suspect that he is using intelligence received from his agents to aid Napoleon's bid to become emperor of Europe, of all the world, if left unrestrained."

The idea was so fantastical as to be ludicrous. "If you believe his lordship to be guilty of seditious behavior, why not arrest him?" Her eyes narrowed. "You did say you worked for the Foreign Office, did you not?"

"Indeed, Mrs. Ashcroft. However, this situation takes a little more finesse than slapping him in irons. Somerton might not be the only agent in the Nexus involved in this unfortunate scheme."

She clasped her hands together in her lap to stop their trembling. "I assume you have some reason for telling me all of this?"

"You're quite perceptive." The smile he sent her lacked the admiration of his words. "We cannot arrest Lord Somerton, because he alone knows the identities of the agents comprising the Nexus. The moment we apprehend him, they will disappear, and we cannot allow that to happen. Until we confirm the guilt or innocence of each person, we must be careful not to draw attention to our suspicions."

"Because you fear a French invasion and believe the traitorous members of the Nexus will continue their efforts, with or without their leader?"

"Bravo, Mrs. Ashcroft. You have summed up our concerns precisely."

Sickness filled her stomach. "What is it you would have me do?"

"The Foreign Office has directed Somerton to compile a list of his agents while in the country."

"After protecting them for so long, will he comply? Especially in light of your accusations?"

"Hard to say with any certainty. Knowing Somerton, I wouldn't doubt that he'd create the list, then conveniently misplace it."

"I'll be interested in seeing how his lordship faces this challenge."

"Glad to hear it, Mrs. Ashcroft, because this is where we need your assistance." His gaze caught hers, held her immobile with feral claws. "I want you to copy the list of names and deliver them to me within the next sennight."

"*What?*" She bolted from her chair and paced the confines of the drawing room. "You can't be serious. What you're asking me to do goes far beyond our arrangement of reporting suspicious activities."

He did not flinch at her outburst, simply followed her about the room. "Indeed, it does."

"What if his lordship catches me? If he's as ruthless as you say, I'm putting not only myself in danger but also my daughter."

"That is an unfortunate side effect to this request, but my superiors are concerned about Somerton's ability to complete his task."

"Unfortunate side effect?"

"You do understand now that the Nexus might be the ones responsible for your husband's death, don't you?"

She stilled. "What does my husband have to do with the Nexus?"

Cochran settled deeper into the sofa. A knowing smile creased his right cheek.

"Geoffrey was a spy?"

"Well done, Mrs. Ashcroft. He was recruited by none other than the earl himself."

Based on Lord Somerton's unwillingness to discuss her husband's murder, she had convinced herself that a jealous spouse or lover had killed Geoffrey. All of the years he had spent away from them, all of the special moments he had missed, were not a result of his indifference, but a necessity of his work.

Somehow, the knowledge both lessened the sting of his abandonment and made it hurt worse.

"You must also now realize," Cochran continued, "that the letters Ashcroft sent you were coded messages, warning the intended recipient of Somerton's perfidy. Are you certain Ashcroft did not mention my name anywhere in his correspondence?"

Every drop of blood drain from her face. "This can't be happening."

"Ashcroft did mention me."

She nodded. "It's how I recognized your name."

"You lied to me." Ice chips ringed his eyes. "This revelation complicates matters."

"How so? If the letters were meant for you, shouldn't that knowledge clarify, rather than complicate?"

He waved off her comment. "I must think on this more. In the meantime, keep an eye out for a list of names. It will go a long way to repairing the damage you've wrought and bring you one step closer to the justice you seek."

Her jaw tightened. "How on earth do you expect me to locate something so important?" Especially after Lord

Somerton rebuffed her earlier. "If he compiles it at all, he'll likely keep it in a secure spot in the family wing."

"Mama, are you still here?"

At the sound of her daughter's muffled voice, terror ripped through Catherine. She glanced at Cochran, whose gaze slithered from the closed door behind her. She did not like the calculating gleam pulsing in his eyes.

"In whatever manner you deem necessary and expedient, madam." He nodded toward the door. "Invite her in."

"Are we finished? I am late for my appointment."

He stood, the action so abrupt that she stepped back, even though several feet separated them.

"Indeed, we are." Before she could stop him, he strode to the door and opened it.

Her daughter, who obviously had her ear plastered to the wood panel, tumbled inside. She popped up with the speed of a rabbit, looking from Cochran to Catherine with wide-eyed curiosity. "Hello," she said.

"Miss Sophie," he said. "It is nice to finally meet you."

"It is?"

Catherine angled her body between them. "Sophie, run along. I believe you have lessons to finish."

She did not budge. "I heard your voices. Aren't you going to see Meghan McCarthy?"

"Yes," she said, disturbed by the way Cochran continued to stare at her daughter. "I'm leaving for the McCarthys' now."

In a stage whisper to Cochran, Sophie said, "She's insane."

"Sophie, we do not discuss such things in front of visitors."

Cochran glanced at Catherine.

"She means enceinte. In the family way," she provided.

"McCarthy," he said. "This Meghan is Irish?"

Her daughter nodded. "Mama's going to try to find out who the father is."

"Sophia Adele, enough." Catherine was mortified. How had her six-year-old daughter come by such information? She recalled Sophie's recent penchant for eavesdropping and bit back a curse. "Back to the nursery. Now."

Not used to Catherine's sharp tone, Sophie dropped her head. "Sorry, Mama." She ran from the room.

With her daughter no longer under Cochran's sharp attention, she managed a full breath. "My apologies, sir. Sophie does not meet many strangers."

"Like her mother, she has made this a most productive visit."

She stared at him in confusion until she recalled his comment in London about wanting to meet Geoffrey's daughter.

"Now I will leave you to your appointment. Sounds like you have a challenge ahead of you." He cast her a knowing smile. "In more ways than one."

She did not need the reminder of the terrible task ahead of her. Either of them. How had she become entrenched in espionage? She prayed Lord Somerton cooperated with the Foreign Office's edict, and soon.

After collecting Cochran's hat and gloves, she led the official to his sleek black curricle. "If I locate the item, how will I notify you?"

He settled onto the high bench and accepted the reins from Teddy. "You won't. I'll be in touch. Good day, Mrs. Ashcroft."

She followed his curricle's progress down the lane, while smoothing her fingers over her aching throat.

"Gypsy's saddled and ready for a nice trot, Mrs. Ashcroft."

"Thank you, Teddy." Using the mounting block, she settled onto the saddle and arranged her skirts before taking the reins. "I'll be back in a few hours."

"Aye, ma'am."

She kicked Gypsy into motion, her mind a constant stream of *ifs*, *buts*, *hows*, and *whens*. She must set aside this issue of Lord Somerton's list of agents for the next couple hours and focus on Meghan McCarthy. The girl's situation needed her full attention.

But her good intentions ground to a halt the moment her gaze swept westward. On a low rise separating their two properties, the Earl of Somerton—*Sebastian*—sat astride a monstrous black horse.

Wind caught in his mount's tail, whipping it back and forth. The black's rider sat as calm as a morning lake. Something about his utter stillness sent a shiver of apprehension down her spine.

Had he seen her speaking with Cochran? She peered down the lane and was relieved to find it empty.

Gypsy shuffled on her feet, and Catherine patted her sleek neck. "It's all right, girl."

Once she had regained control of Gypsy, she squinted up at the hill and found nothing but undulating grass.

ELEVEN

"Mama, I have to *go*."

Sophie's indelicate whisper took a moment to penetrate the dark layer of Catherine's thoughts. She had not been able to focus on anything since her disturbing discussion with Cochran yesterday and her brief glimpse of Lord Somerton.

As a result, her talk with Meghan McCarthy had the same dismal results as previous attempts they had made to discover her lover's identity.

"Mama?" Sophie squirmed at her side.

"Five more minutes, dear."

"*You shall love your neighbor as yourself,*" the vicar quoted to the congregation. "Jesus went on to say that we should love one another as he loves us."

Her brows rose, and she wondered if Mr. Foster's sermon had anything to do with Lord Somerton's return or Mr. Blake's mismanagement.

Sophie crowded into her side and tugged at her sleeve. "Mama, I can't wait."

Catching the note of panic in her daughter's voice, she

glanced down and found Sophie's big blue eyes round with alarm. She sighed and started collecting their personal belongings. In her severest voice, she whispered a warning in her daughter's ear. "You will follow me from the church like a civilized young lady. Is that understood?"

Her six-year-old nodded and scooted to the edge of her seat. "Yes, Mama."

They marched toward the open entrance door, and Catherine smiled apologetically to the other parishioners as they passed. When she neared the last pew, the Earl of Somerton's penetrating gaze caught hers. He neither smiled nor nodded, simply followed her approach with gray eyes that glowed with a moonlit iridescence.

Her determined stride faltered, and an embarrassing staccato of anticipation vibrated through her veins, warming her skin. Dressed in his London finery, his tailored coat and dazzling white neckcloth stood out in stark contrast to the more loose-fitting and well-worn Sunday garments of the other gentlemen present.

Why Lord Somerton chose to sit on a hard wooden pew in the back of the church when his family's cushioned seat sat empty at the front, she did not know.

She would have to mull over his lordship's seating arrangements another time. Because at that precise moment, her daughter's small hand pressed against Catherine's lower back, propelling her forward in a frantic attempt to get outside. Her toe stubbed against the doorsill, causing her to stumble down the two front steps. In a drunken dance of cartwheeling arms and churning feet, she somehow regained her footing at the last minute and skidded to an undignified halt.

For several disbelieving seconds, she heard nothing except the thundering of her heart. She pulled in a calming breath and tapped her hand against her chest in a feeble attempt to soothe her nerves. Even though she had saved her backside, the same could not be said of her pride.

"Sorry, Mama," Sophie yelled over her shoulder. Her little feet tore across the churchyard until she reached the privy, the door slamming shut behind her.

If she did not know her daughter any better, she would be tempted to thrash the little vixen for breaking her promise. Her temper did not last long, though. It never did when it came to her wild child. Although rash at times, Sophie had a heart that was sweet and pure, especially when compared to other children her age. Rather than pull the legs off a grasshopper, Sophie would rather place the creature in Castle Dragonthorpe, replete with turrets, drawbridge, and a straw bed.

"Are you injured, madam?"

She closed her eyes against Lord Somerton's soft inquiry, her reluctant smile disappearing in an instant. It had been too much to hope that he would have turned a blind eye to her ignoble exit. Given his obvious desire to be quit of her presence the previous day, she was rather surprised by his current solicitude. With reluctance, she turned and checked the church's entrance before settling on his handsome face.

"Do not fret, Mrs. Ashcroft," he said. "No one else observed your near mishap."

The news should have cheered her, it really should. But all she could think about was that *he* had observed her. "That is good to know, my lord. I'm sorry to have disturbed you."

"You didn't." He glanced back at the church. "In fact, you saved me from Mr. Foster's well-intended but rather pointed sermon."

His comment confirmed what she had already suspected. "You think the vicar was trying to mend the rift of Mr. Blake's neglect?"

The right side of the earl's mouth curled into a self-deprecating smile. "Without a doubt."

She considered asking him to expound, but his expression hardened before her eyes.

"Your daughter's hasty departure has proven fortuitous, however."

A shot of chagrin heated her cheeks. "My daughter is lively—"

"There's no need to explain. I'm sure neither one of us has forgotten what it was like to sit through church at such a restless age."

His understanding acted as a balm, and the pressure around her chest relented. So few days passed by that did not challenge her belief in her ability to raise her daughter without the anchoring presence of a husband. Was she being too strict about Sophie's studies? Not strict enough? Was she giving her enough guidance? Too much? The questions revolved around her mind in limitless patterns, often painful, and generally without answers.

"Indeed, I have not, sir." She regarded the privy, wondering what was taking her daughter so long. Had she missed Sophie's exit? She scanned the area for a mop of blond and red curls.

With most of Showbury attending Mr. Foster's peacemaking sermon, the road and footpaths were deserted. Even the shops were closed up tight, the anomalies being Mr. Littleton, the general store owner, and Mr. Baggert, the butcher. Both men claimed to have their own connection to God and did not need to sit through the vicar's ramblings to know right from wrong. At times, she agreed with them.

And other times, she simply needed to hear Mr. Foster's reassuring words.

Her search produced no little girl and the privy door remained closed.

Catherine's stomach quivered with a familiar uneasiness. Ever since Cochran's revelations about double spies and coded messages, she had experienced a strange compulsion to glance over her shoulder and had difficulty letting Sophie out of her sight for any length of time.

Over the last year, she had often prayed for deliverance from her boring, well-ordered life. Had she known a perilous game of espionage would be the answer to her request, she would have kept her yearnings to herself. She stared at the privy's weather-worn door. Sophie was safe, she told herself. The girl's needs were simply taking longer than normal.

"Mrs. Ashcroft?" Lord Somerton prodded.

Startled from her introspection, she shot a quick glance at the earl. "Yes, my lord?"

"Is something wrong?" He looked toward the small outbuilding, where her daughter was taking her merry-sweet time.

She forced a nervous laugh. "I'm sure everything's fine, sir. I fear my daughter might be delaying a tongue-lashing."

"I found this on one of the church steps." He held out a small carving of a destrier, a knight's warhorse. "Does it belong to your daughter?"

"Yes, thank you." She made to reach for it, but a movement on the opposite side of the street snagged her attention. Between the millinery and butcher shops, half-hidden by the building's shadow, stood a man. A short man with a skeletal build eating something tucked inside wrapping used by Mr. Baggert.

Bile bubbled up inside her throat. There were few things that came out of the butcher's shop that could be eaten right from the package. However, at that moment, Catherine could not think of a single one of them.

When the stranger noticed her scrutiny, he stopped chewing. His hooded eyes locked with hers for a tension-filled moment. Then he began the slow mastication of whatever he had tucked inside the butcher's paper.

The pressure in her chest returned.

"Do you know him?" The earl touched the center of her back, a featherlight connection from which she drew much-needed calm.

"I've never seen him before." She moved toward the small outbuilding sheltering her daughter. The disgusting little man was far too close, and she could not stop the niggling suspicion that something was wrong. "Please excuse me. I must check on my daughter."

"Mrs. Ashcroft, allow me to assist."

She hastened across the churchyard. Something propelled her forward with an inexplicable drive to put her body between that of her daughter and the terrible little man.

Please be in the privy, please be in the privy. I swear if you're not I'm going to lash your behind.

The fact she had never laid a disciplining hand on her daughter was immaterial. Simply making the threat gave her overactive mind something to center on rather than dredging up horrifying images.

"Sophie," she called from a carriage length away.

No answer.

"Sophie—"

A large hand clamped around her elbow. She whirled about, her reticule arcing out to bash her assailant's head.

Lord Somerton blocked her swing with his forearm. "Easy," he said in a calm, not-the-least-bit-perturbed voice.

"My lord, release me." She pulled at her arm, her gaze returning to the small outbuilding. "Something's amiss with my daughter."

"Stay here." He marched ahead and tested the privy door. *Locked.* He knocked on the door. "Miss Sophie?"

Never one to take orders where her daughter was concerned, Catherine joined him at the privy's entrance, garnering her a sharp look.

"Sophie, is everything all right?" she asked.

Silence.

Fear sent her heart racing. "Sophie, sweetheart—" She made to yank on the bolted door.

He caught her hand, and his thumb smoothed over the backs of her fingers. "A moment, Mrs. Ashcroft."

He knocked again, louder this time. "Miss Sophie, this is your neighbor, Lord Somerton, and I'm here with your mother. If you do not come out in five seconds, I'll be forced to kick down the door."

Nothing but an unearthly silence met his warning.

"Five. Four..."

"Sophie dear, please come out." Each number tightened the fist clutching her heart. "I'm not hurt or upset, so you needn't hide in there."

"Two. One." The earl grabbed the latch. "I'm coming in, Miss Sophie."

"No!" shrieked a strangled voice from within.

Catherine shared a quick look with the earl. "Sophie, are you well?"

"No," her daughter cried. Muffled sobs penetrated the privy's oak-planked door.

"Ask if she's injured," the earl whispered.

"Sweetheart, are you injured?"

"No." Her voice sounded small, defeated.

The oppressive tension diminished to a trickle of apprehension.

Lord Somerton stepped back several feet. "Perhaps she needs her mother."

Catherine nodded. "Unlatch the door, dear."

The telltale slide of wood against wood reached her. A moment later, Catherine slid through the small opening, holding her breath against the stench of a well-used facility. A fly landed on her nose.

Swatting it away, she located her daughter wedged in the corner of the small building, her face wet with tears.

"What's wrong?" she asked, though she already had a good idea of why her daughter refused to leave.

Her normally brave little girl bit her bottom lip and stared at the floor.

Wishing she could take this conversation out of this stinking, fly-infested closet, but knowing it was impossible, Catherine did what any good mother would do. She kneeled on the filthy floor before her embarrassed daughter. "Sweetheart, did you have an accident?"

A small nod. "I'm s-sorry, Mama."

She cradled her daughter's small chin and forced her head up until their eyes met. "No need to apologize, pumpkin. You tried to tell me."

"How am I to leave here without all my friends knowing what I've done?"

"Let me worry about that." She rose. "Stay here a moment."

Sophie grasped her sleeve. "Mama, don't leave me."

"Have I ever broken a promise to you?"

"No."

She kissed her daughter's forehead. "I promise to return in two minutes."

Sophie swallowed, glancing between the door and the open pit full of winged insects. "Two minutes?"

"Two minutes." Once outside, she drew in a cleansing breath.

"How does she fare?" Lord Somerton asked in a low voice.

Surprised to find the earl where she had left him, she spoke without thinking. "She had an accident, my lord."

He nodded as if having already guessed the answer.

"With such fine weather," she said, "we walked to church today, so I must request use of Mr. Foster's carriage."

"There's no need." He motioned to someone behind her. "Mine's waiting."

She peered over her shoulder and found his driver steering a well-matched team of horses their way. "Oh, no, my lord, we couldn't."

"Why not?"

She lowered her voice, even more. "She might soil your seats."

"No need to worry." He threw open the carriage door. To the coachman, he said, "Miggs, hand me one of the carriage blankets, then lay out another on the bench."

"Yes, m'lord."

Without another word, the earl accepted the proffered item and strode into the privy, eliciting a startled shriek from within. Everything happened so fast that Catherine barely had time to widen her eyes before the earl marched back outside with a blanket-covered bundle in his arms.

As he passed, Catherine glimpsed her daughter's watery blue eyes peering out, her small fingers wrapped around the warhorse she had dropped on the church steps. Her throat closed, grateful for his thoughtful gesture. How long had it been since a man had carried her daughter in such a protective way? When an answer did not readily come to mind, her vision blurred.

He placed Sophie inside his carriage before turning to offer his hand to Catherine. "Mrs. Ashcroft."

She glanced from his hand to his strategically placed carriage to the church beyond. No one milling around outside could have seen past his conveyance and restless horses. Had the earl known before she had ever stepped foot inside the privy what she would find? Could he have arranged such a masterful escape in the short time she was inside?

"Madam?" he said, with an encouraging curl of his fingers. "Shall we go?"

She glanced at her daughter, who sat bundled in his carriage, enduring a bout of embarrassment but oddly content inside her thick blanket. What if Cochran was telling the truth about the earl's involvement with the French? Placing herself in danger was one thing, but allowing Sophie to come in contact with a potential murderer—possibly her father's killer—smacked of foolhardy behavior.

Speaking of foolhardy, she searched the area near the butcher's shop for the skeletal man. She cursed her ridiculous imagination. Had she really charged across the churchyard, determined to save her daughter from the odd-acting stranger? In front of a gentleman she was supposed to somehow impress long enough to obtain his list?

So much for her motherly instincts.

"He disappeared while we were trying to coax your

daughter outside," Lord Somerton said, his arm returning to his side.

Surprised, she shifted her attention back to the earl—and his probing eyes.

"Are you sure you don't know him from somewhere?"

"Quite sure. One does not forget such a face."

"True." He held out his hand again. "Ready?"

"Mrs. Ashcroft," the vicar called, rounding the corner of the carriage.

"Mr. Foster. I see services are over." Behind her, she heard a muffled squeal and a masculine sigh.

"Indeed, they are, ma'am." The vicar stopped a few feet away and bowed. "Lord Somerton."

"Vicar."

Catherine's attention slid to the earl, expecting to find an expression of annoyance, given his curt greeting. Instead, she found him looking as serious and sophisticated as ever. If not for the small cleft in his chin, one might liken him to one of the somber marble statues in the British Museum. But the cleft saved him from being too unapproachable.

"My apologies for missing the end of your sermon," she said.

"I'm sure you had a good reason." The vicar glanced at the earl's carriage. "Are you off so soon?"

"I'm afraid Sophie's not feeling well."

"I am sorry to hear that. Shall we postpone our ride?"

"That won't be necessary. I'll have Sophie back to rights in no time. Besides, I'm rather looking forward to our visit."

"Vicar," Lord Somerton said. "It is past time we get the child home."

"Of course. Forgive me for keeping you. I'll see you later, Mrs. Ashcroft."

"Until later, Mr. Foster."

This time, when Lord Somerton held out his hand, Catherine experienced no compunction about accepting his escort. With the vicar seeing them off and expecting her to accompany him later, she doubted the earl would indulge in any villainous behavior. Once again, she had allowed her imagination to run amok. Unless Lord Somerton knew about the content of her meeting with Cochran, he would have no reason to harm her or her daughter.

"Thank you, my lord." She laid her fingers in his palm as she ascended the carriage steps. Heat tingled its way up her arm and across her shoulder, spreading until her ears felt like they were on fire.

The moment she settled next to a lump of squirming blanket, he shut the door behind her.

She sat forward. "You're not joining us, my lord?"

He glanced at Sophie. "I think it best if I ride up top with Miggs."

"Please ride inside with us, where you'll be more comfortable. I don't like that we're dislocating you from your own carriage."

"I don't mind. I rather like riding with old Miggs and his flamboyant stories." He stepped away. "Pull the curtain, Mrs. Ashcroft."

Then he was gone. She stared out the window for several seconds. His considerate nature didn't match Cochran's description of the Nexus's leader. How could a man show so much care for one small girl and also conspire against his country? An act that could kill hundreds?

The carriage rocked to the side with the earl's weight,

the movement snapping her out of her musings. She closed the curtain and sat back as they lurched into motion. A few seconds later, her intrepid daughter emerged from her cocoon of wool.

Blowing a gold-red curl out of her eye, Sophie asked, "Do you think anyone saw me, Mama?"

She wrapped her arm around the girl's narrow shoulders. "No, pumpkin. Lord Somerton provided a clever disguise."

"Not even Mr. Foster?"

"Not even Mr. Foster. Lord Somerton made sure of it."

"The earl smelled nice."

"Did he?"

Sophie nodded. "Like a tree."

Catherine smiled. "Lord Somerton smelled like a tree? Was it a beech?"

"More like an oak. Sprinkled with cinnamon."

She pulled her daughter's head toward her and kissed her mop of curls. "Sounds lovely, dear." She adored the innocence of Sophie's imagination. Somehow, she had birthed a perfect little girl from her less-than-perfect womb.

Sophie galloped her destrier across Catherine's lap. "Do you think the earl will come on Saturday?"

Catherine's pulse quickened. "Why do you ask, sweetheart?"

Her daughter shrugged. "I don't know."

"Are you sure you don't?" She smoothed her hand over her daughter's curls. "You can tell me."

Sophie picked at the black ribbon on her dress. "I know we're supposed to keep my birthday to just family and close friends, because we're mourning Papa and Grandpapa. But I thought the earl could help me add a piece to Castle Dragonthorpe."

Tears stung the backs of Catherine's eyes, and the destrier swam in her lap. More and more of late, her daughter craved the attention of a masculine figure. Edward, the vicar, the Walkers' father—it didn't matter, as long as the man showed an interest in her. And now, she wanted to share their special castle-building custom with the Earl of Somerton.

"Mama, please don't cry," Sophie said, her voice cracking. "You can still help. No one decorates the chambers better than you."

"Thank you, pumpkin." Catherine hugged her daughter to her side. "I'm sorry your father can't be here to celebrate with you."

Sophie shrugged her shoulders again before casting Catherine an agonized, sidelong look. "Mama, please don't be cross."

"What's this?" She lifted her daughter's chin. "Sophie, you can ask whomever you wish to help build your castle. I would never be upset with you for such a thing."

Her daughter swiped a skinny arm underneath her nose, leaving a liquid trail behind. "I thought the earl could help me set up the torture devices Edward carved for me. I know how you dislike blood and violence." Watery rivulets streaked down her smooth cheeks. "But that's not what I meant."

"Tell me, Sophie," she said with growing concern. "I promise not to be upset."

"Papa's face." Her little knuckles whitened as they squeezed the wooden horse. "I don't see it anymore."

Like the ends of a knot being pulled swiftly in opposite directions, Catherine's throat closed again, cutting off her air. Her head swam, her heart broke. "Oh, sweet pumpkin. You do not have to see your papa's face to love him with your heart." She laid her hand over her daughter's thundering chest. "He lives here. Always will."

Sophie snuggled against Catherine's breast, clutching the destrier and sniffing back her sadness. They both said nothing for a long while, simply sat immersed in their own thoughts. Then, in a voice thick with tears, her daughter asked, "Will you invite the earl, Mama?"

She closed her eyes. "Yes, sweetheart."

In the quiet that followed, Catherine's mind settled back onto the earl. Somehow, she must learn more about his lordship. If she could somehow burrow her way into his good graces, she could play a small part in fixing Mr. Blake's disastrous stewardship while tracking down Cochran's information, plus bring an end to the mystery of her husband's death.

And for a short period of time, she wouldn't be alone.

Perhaps she could invent an excuse to visit him at Bellamere. The contrivance made her cringe. Women such as she, especially while in mourning, did not call on aristocratic gentlemen. When she had visited him in London, she had reasoned that no one knew her there, so the risk had been minimal. That was until Frederick Cochran showed up.

Not only would Lord Somerton see through her desperation, he might come to believe she had designs on his person. The notion mortified her less now than it would have an hour ago. His management of her daughter's embarrassment had been nothing short of heroic.

One of the carriage wheels found a rut in the road, jolting her back to the present. She forced back thoughts of the earl's heroism. Romanticizing a privy escape would do nothing to further her mission to uncover Geoffrey's murderer.

Observe the earl, locate the list. Those were the things she needed to concentrate on. Not the way his eyes had softened as he carried her daughter.

"Can we open the curtain now, Mama?"

Catherine drew back the heavy material, only to find towering black clouds in the distance.

"Looks like rain."

"Indeed, it does, pumpkin." She tilted her head back to rest against the cushioned seat. She stared at the dark panel above her and tried to ignore the dread seeping into her bones.

TWELVE

Sebastian studied the small collection of books in the widow's library, his impatience growing with each passing minute. He had escaped the vicar's pointed sermon about forgiving one's neighbor only to be met with Mrs. Ashcroft's domestic issue.

He did not know what was worse—the vicar publicly challenging the residents of Showbury not to cast judgment on their landlord for hiring Blake or getting himself involved in the welfare of yet another child.

A girl, no less.

He gritted his teeth against the pain of remembrance, of Cora's imprisonment. Of the helplessness that followed. But he did not dwell there for long. Recriminations about the past were useless in the present. The decisions he made today, this minute, were all that mattered. If previous mistakes helped guide him down a better path now, all the better.

Shrugging off images of dungeons and pain-filled eyes, he stared at the door. Where the hell was she? The longer he idled in her library, the more restless he became.

She had implored him to stay before shuffling her blanket-draped daughter upstairs and issuing a full gamut of orders to her staff. He had thought she was going upstairs to retrieve the letters, but too much time had elapsed for so simple a task.

Why hadn't he disappeared when he'd had the chance? Their discussion regarding Ashcroft's letters would be better held at Bellamere, away from the distracting presence of a child. He needed to concentrate and he could not afford to care.

Not again.

Why had he allowed the widow's beseeching eyes to win out against his better judgment?

Disgusted with his weakness, he released a harsh breath. Through all the bustle, he had admired Catherine's ability to direct her household with a firm hand and genuine gratitude. All signs of a good mistress.

He focused on her bookshelves again. They, too, carried her stamp of authority. Every shelf contained its own category, and every category was alphabetized. Only in the finest libraries had he ever seen such an exacting system.

With her delicate beauty as a distraction, one could easily underestimate the widow's fortitude. His gaze surveyed the room at large. Took in the aged, yet comfortable, leather chairs, the white and yellow roses on the side table, and the floral draperies protecting the room from draughts.

She had made a home here, despite her husband's preoccupation in London. If Sebastian were not so anxious to leave, this would be a room where he could spend many comfortable hours reading in front of the fireplace.

A disturbance in the air drew his attention to the doorway. With pink cheeks, tamed hair, and a radiant smile, the little girl entered the room on limbs more buoyant than a mere quarter hour ago.

The muscles in his neck tautened.

Her mother appeared behind her. "Thank you for waiting, my lord. Sophie has something she'd like to say."

The girl dipped into a commendable curtsy. "Thank you for bringing me home, my lord."

A vision of Cora greeting him after her parents' deaths surfaced. She had been only a few years older than Sophie when she and her brother had barreled into his life. Cora had been blessed with the same sweet manners and impish curiosity. He had loved her as a father would a daughter from the moment she lifted her uncertain blue-green eyes to meet his.

Sebastian inclined his head, ignoring the clenching pain in his throat. "You're most welcome, Miss Sophie."

Mrs. Ashcroft placed a hand on her daughter's shoulder. "Run down to the stables, dear, and ask Carson to saddle Guinevere and Gypsy. I'll be there in a few minutes."

The girl didn't budge. "Is the earl joining us?"

"Lord Somerton," her mother corrected. "No, pumpkin. His lordship has attended us long enough."

Relief spread through his limbs at the possibility of escape, but the imp's crestfallen expression wreaked havoc on his conscience.

Glancing at his timepiece, he said, "I must be on my way, I'm afraid."

The widow nudged her daughter toward the door, but Sophie wheeled around after only a few feet. "Can we ask him now, Mama?"

"Now is not the time."

Sebastian noticed the widow kept her gaze averted.

Unperturbed, the girl tried a different tactic. "Do you have horses, sir?"

"I have a great many horses."

"A white one?"

"Yes."

"A black one?"

"Of course," he said, amused despite his best efforts.

"A brown one?"

"Sophie," her mother scolded, eyeing him.

"Well, Mama. If the earl has a black and white horse, he must have a brown one."

Mrs. Ashcroft turned her daughter toward the door. "No, *Lord Somerton* mustn't."

"May I come see your horses, sir?" the girl asked over her shoulder while being ushered out of the room.

He said nothing. The last thing he needed was a curious girl running around his estate, no matter how enchanting.

"Sophie, I told you," Mrs. Ashcroft said in exasperation. "Lord Somerton's a busy man. He can't set his duties aside to play nursemaid to you. Now run along."

"But Mama—"

The widow's glare cut her daughter's complaint short.

The girl dipped into a hurried curtsy. "Good day to you, Earl."

Her mother sighed. "Sophie."

The vixen smiled, and Sebastian knew she cared not a whit about such formalities.

"Good day, Lord Somerton."

He inclined his head. "Enjoy your ride with the vicar."

Once the sound of her daughter's running feet faded,

the widow turned to him. "I'm sorry, my lord. Sophie's horse-obsessed and begs an introduction wherever we go."

"Quite understandable."

"I believe you wanted to see these." She held out a packet of letters, tied together with a black ribbon. The ribbon trembled.

"Thank you." He studied her face as he accepted the bundle, but her even features gave nothing away. "I know how hard it must be to share your private correspondence."

"Yes, but worth it if they help you find my husband's murderer." She swallowed. "Did you learn anything from the others I gave you?" She turned the full force of those beautiful eyes on him.

"Unfortunately, no," he lied, holding up the new stash. "We need to decipher these in order to fully understand Ashcroft's message."

"I see."

"Tell me, Mrs. Ashcroft." He stepped closer, his gaze sliding over the contours of her face. "What will you do if it's decided that your husband's death was an unfortunate case of being in the wrong place at the wrong time?"

Her eyes widened a fraction, but her answer came swift and determined. "I'll get a second opinion."

Sebastian's body went hard. Desire like nothing he had ever felt before rushed through his veins. Not for the first time, he wondered what it would be like to have such a fierce champion. "Are you this loyal to everyone you care about?"

"What can you mean, sir? Would you not do the same for a wife?"

"I have never been married, madam. Therefore, I cannot answer your question." Closer now, he drew in a long, slow breath until her scent drenched his senses.

Tantalizing and fresh. Understated, yet feminine. His chest expanded around another deep inhalation. "But I find I like the idea of a wife defending my cause. No matter the obstacles placed in her path."

"You make me sound heroic." She folded her hands in front of her. "I assure you, I'm not. Merely practical."

He studied the pulse point on her slender throat, noted its frantic rhythm. Blood pounded into his extremities. "My tenants provided several testimonials yesterday that would make you eligible for sainthood."

"Don't be ridiculous." Her voice was breathless. "Unlike your tenants, I had nothing to lose by holding Mr. Blake accountable for his actions."

He raised his hand and brushed the backs of his fingers along the curve of her neck. "Unlike *you*, not everyone in your situation would have bothered to right the injustice."

"M-my, lord, what are you doing?"

Engaging in a monumental mistake.

But he could not take his eyes off her lush full lips. Lips that would mold to his in an exquisite embrace. His insides curled into a tight knot of anticipation. He should not want her, his agent's widow, but he did, with staggering force.

All of his earlier misgivings faded behind his fevered desire.

It was then he realized she was in danger. And perhaps so was he.

He settled a hand on her waist, bringing their bodies closer together. "I'm going to kiss you now."

"My lord—"

Soft flesh, luscious warmth, and an inexplicable rightness assailed his senses the moment he covered her mouth with his. He deepened the kiss and pulled her unresisting body into the cradle of his arms. Her delicate frame was a flawless fit, made for him alone.

The small hands resting on his chest inched their way around his torso and squeezed with a force that verged on desperation. He cradled her sweet face with unsteady hands. His breaths came more rapidly and his body sought a closer contact. He was losing control, and the realization cut through the fog of desire clouding his mind. Ending the kiss, he buried his face in the crook of her neck and fought to temper his erratic heartbeat.

Think, Somerton!

Catherine was under his protection and in mourning. Two inviolable conditions. Until a year and a day, her marriage vows still breathed life, a condition she would honor even though her marriage died years ago. That she had accepted his kiss was unexpected and more than a little stirring.

"I believe it best if you release me now, my lord."

Removing his arms and backing away proved surprisingly difficult. She took a moment to smooth out the creases in her dress and tuck a few stray hairs back in place. Sebastian watched her slow retreat with a heavy, suffocating dread.

He did not want to lose this. Not yet.

He could not remember the last time he had gone against his better judgment, or the last time a woman had compelled him to lose control. Both situations would normally cause him to pause, to step away and not look back. Maintaining control kept those around him safe.

For the first time, he did not—could not—turn away. This attraction was different. Tangible. Invigorating. *Consuming.*

She felt it, too. Any time they were in proximity, the air pulsed with awareness.

Could he submerse himself in raw, unadulterated pleasure for a few short days? Could he set aside his honor? Could he ignore her potential ruination?

Yes.

Once he got her out of his system, he would be able to return to his cold, passionless existence. If he did not seize this rare gift, he would regret it, always. He was damned tired of regrets. The guilt, he would deal with later.

"Should I apologize?" he asked.

She sent him a wistful smile. "No more so than I, my lord."

"Good, because I'm not sure I could have managed it with any real sincerity."

"You do not mince words, do you?"

"On the contrary, I have done so on many occasions, but with you I don't think it necessary. Or was I wrong?"

"No."

Her quiet confirmation seared his blood. "I have need of your services, after all."

"E-excuse me?"

"Thanks to Mr. Blake, my tenants have become rather suspicious of my commitment."

"In time, they will see the truth of the matter."

"I agree. With your help."

"Rest assured. I will do what I can to spread the word of your steward's perfidy. A casual word in Mrs. Walker's ear should set things into motion."

"If you are willing, I should like more from you than a whispered word to Showbury's most dedicated gossip."

Pink crept into her cheeks. "I'm not sure what else I

can offer, my lord. You weren't interested in my knowledge of the local craftsmen."

He slid the letters into an inner pocket of his coat. Using the back of his forefinger, he caressed the line of her jaw. "That was not a lack of interest you witnessed."

The color in her cheeks deepened, and her uneven breaths peppered his wrist. "What was it, then?"

All-consuming desire.

"Pride."

"Pride?"

He removed his hand. "I believed I could take care of this without your assistance. However, my tenants have shown me the error in my logic."

"What would you have me do?"

"Everyone I spoke to yesterday was rather content to continue working with you."

She frowned. "You would have me act as your steward?"

"Only until I hire a replacement. If you're willing, I could use your help in creating a schedule of repairs."

Her eyes brightened at the suggestion, and he was struck again by her conventional beauty. Beauty that became less common every time she smiled.

"What of Grayson?"

"He has offered his support, should you need it."

"You don't wish for him to take on the responsibility?"

"I have already given Grayson the short list of repairs you provided. He's content to assist rather than direct."

She considered him for a moment. "You appear quite capable of organizing the tenants' complaints yourself."

"As it happens, I have other issues requiring my attention while in Showbury."

Her gaze dulled, and he wondered at its source.

"When might you begin preparing a schedule?" he asked.

"I'll start on it tonight."

"You're certain?"

"Yes, my lord. The less time I spend on the schedule, the faster the repairs can commence."

Again, her thoughtfulness had a warming effect on his starving emotions. Gratitude manifested into a ball of heat. Heat spiraled into yearning. Of its own accord, his voice dropped. "Are you an early riser, Mrs. Ashcroft?"

Her feminine instincts could not miss the latent need underlining his words. Instead of retreating, her attention dipped to his lips. "Generally, my lord."

An image of her lithe body, aching for release and tangled in his sheets, flashed before his eyes, sharp and clear. His cock hardened, pulsed with near painful intensity.

A whoop of girlish laughter outside penetrated the intimate confines of the library. Familiar reality iced his heated blood. His spine straightened. "I'll send my carriage around to collect you at eight, then. You can show me what you have over breakfast."

She turned toward the window, to where her daughter chased something too small to be seen from this distance. He watched her cautious enthusiasm for her new project leech away. The upturned crinkles around her eyes fell into joyless slants and her lips thinned into a line of resignation.

"No need to bother your staff, sir. As I mentioned before, my horse knows the way."

"Very well." He bowed a farewell. "If you'll excuse me, Mrs. Ashcroft? I really must be going."

"Yes, of course."

She guided him through the house, out the front door, and stopped to await his approaching carriage. A heavy silence hovered between them as they watched his restless team of horses advance. The black geldings tossed back their sleek heads and dug their massive hooves into the ground until his driver Miggs drew them to a halt before them.

Sebastian had an unnerving need to throw back his own head to release the tension thrumming through his body.

"Thank you again for seeing to my daughter's welfare," she said. "Sophie will be retelling the tale of her rescue to the servants for days. I would not have been as successful in keeping her secret." She glanced up at him, revealing a feminine vulnerability few men could ignore.

As it happened, he was one of the few.

He had not earned a reputation as a cold bastard for no reason. The brutal slaying of his mentor over a decade ago served as a constant reminder of how one's enemies will use every tool at their disposal to get what they want. Even murdering a man's wife. And torturing a spymaster's ward.

"Excuse me, my lord?" A footman appeared at his side, holding out Sebastian's hat and gloves. He welcomed the distraction and accepted the servant's offering.

He needed to establish a few boundaries for their new partnership, though. The last thing he wanted was her daughter skipping around Bellamere Park, getting into God knew what, and reminding him of everything he had set aside for the welfare of his country.

"Mrs. Ashcroft, it's been a long time since I had a child in the house. I find that I work best in a less spirited atmosphere."

Her chin lifted a notch. "I hadn't considered bringing

my daughter along, my lord, but I thank you for the warning."

Her chiding retort bit into his conscience. Before he did something ridiculous like apologize or kiss her again, he tipped his hat in her direction. "Good day, madam."

She produced an abbreviated curtsy. "My lord."

Sebastian settled against the carriage bench, calling upon his notorious control not to acknowledge the intriguing widow as he rumbled by. No matter what occurred between the two of them, he could not allow sentiment to enter the picture.

Because emotion was a weakness, and weakness killed loved ones.

THIRTEEN

Sebastian stood at the window of the sunny breakfast room, holding a steaming cup of coffee while awaiting Catherine's arrival. Yesterday's kiss fired through his mind at unexpected intervals, tying his stomach into an uncomfortable mass of need.

After forcing himself to eat a late evening meal, he had closeted himself off in the study until the wee hours of the morning. In that time, he had added only one more name to his list of agents. His progress was slow, painful. No matter how much he reasoned this was the right course of action, each consonant and vowel ripped through him like a stab of betrayal.

Including each agent's code name and current location would come next. The thought of having such damaging information in one place nauseated him all over again. But the more he thought about it, the more he reasoned having a visual map of everyone's whereabouts might help him spot missed opportunities, like identifying a potential ally or redirecting his enemy's efforts.

He would transfer everything he knew to paper, study

it, then burn the record, rather than hand it over to Reeves. The strategy steadied his stomach, somewhat. Having an alternative plan—an escape route, of sorts—removed some of the pressure he had been carrying around since receiving Reeves's demand.

A low rumbling disturbance near the entry hall caught his attention.

"Lord Somerton can finish his damned breakfast while I speak my mind," a man said. "Stand aside, Grayson, or I shall have to..." The intruder's voice lowered to a conspiratorial whisper, no doubt promising all sorts of retribution.

Sebastian's former ward, Viscount Danforth, was a master of collecting secrets—of the personal variety. Even poor Grayson would not be immune to Ethan deBeau's machinations.

Taking his seat at the table, Sebastian snapped open a copy of the *Times* and waited for the oncoming storm. He did not have long to wait.

Within seconds, heavy footsteps pounded down the corridor, then a tall, disheveled rascal entered the breakfast room. "Somerton."

"Danforth." He continued scanning the newspaper, waiting. Ethan's restless energy reminded him of a warship's 32-pounder long gun, with its dark, cavernous muzzle staring out a square gunport, primed and ready for ignition. "What brings you to Bellamere? I thought you were tracking down your mystery savior."

"Trail went cold," Danforth grumbled, making himself a plate from the sideboard.

An anonymous, cloaked savior had pulled Danforth from a London alleyway and transported him to an abandoned building, where his injuries had been looked after until he was able to walk away on his own.

"Your savior is going to great pains to avoid discovery. I wonder why."

He felt, more than saw, Danforth's aggrieved glance. "When I find the hooded bastard, I'll be sure to pose your question." His plate clattered against the table. "How are you doing?"

Sebastian raised a brow. "Well enough. And you?"

"I spent four and a half hours in Superintendent Reeves's office, answering questions about our last mission." Danforth leveled his gaze on Sebastian. "He was inordinately interested in your role."

Sebastian settled back in his chair, projecting a calm he did not feel. "We discussed this in London. I'm here so the Foreign Office can conduct a thorough investigation into the matter without my interference." He rubbed his fingertips over the newspaper. "The Nexus traitor's scheming ran deep in the organization. Reeves is no doubt wondering why I did not detect the man's treachery. I certainly would in his shoes." The question of why he had not discerned his colleague's double spying had weighed on his thoughts since the day they discovered Danforth's sister, Cora—also known as the Raven—in the man's dungeon.

"That's all well and good. But I've already given them an accounting of those events. To have to relive it a second time was not how I had hoped to spend yesterday afternoon."

"No, I suspect not. Did you come here only to inform me of your deposition? Or do you have some other grievance you wish to vent?"

Danforth sent him a cross look. "Helsford's busy with the Littleton case, so Cora asked me to retrieve Ashcroft's remaining letters. Did the widow hand them over yet?"

"Yes, four more."

"All is well in that regard, I take it."

"She is nothing more than a wife trying to make sense of a heinous crime. I detect no ill intent."

"Finally, a piece of good news."

"Where's Cora?"

"With Helsford, of course." The viscount lifted a forkful of sausage to his mouth, pausing. "After surviving their recent nightmare, I doubt Helsford's going to allow my sister to stray more than a dozen feet from his side ever again."

Not that anyone could prevent Cora from doing anything she set her mind to. However, they had all underestimated her gaoler. A condition Sebastian had no desire to repeat. "A day or two more, and I would have delivered the letters myself. There was no reason to make a special trip."

"That's what I said, but my sister had other ideas."

"Falling into bad habits again?"

"Cora's been through so much. Directing me and Helsford around takes her mind off other things."

Like being tortured for a fortnight. Sebastian pushed the thought away. He had already spent hours punishing himself. Right now, he needed to focus on the restless man in front of him.

"Helsford asked me to deliver this." Danforth tossed a sealed missive onto the table. "So I can't blame my presence entirely on Cora." A corner of his mouth quirked up. "Although it's a great deal more fun making the runt take responsibility."

Sebastian smiled, his gaze sliding over the nondescript black seal. It was good to hear Danforth's aggrieved tone. He knew when Ethan and Cora were forecasting doom upon one another that the world had somehow righted itself.

No matter how hard he had tried to keep an emotional distance between him and his two former wards, they had paid no attention. They did not fear his quelling looks or stony silences, nor his sharp rebukes. That was not to say they did not respect him or give him a wide berth at times. They simply kept coming around, invading his home at unexpected times—like now—and spoke to him as they would any intimate colleague. It was maddening and, if he were honest, comforting.

"There is no need for you to stay," he said. "I have a few ends to tie up here over the next sennight, then I'll return to London."

"What of the Foreign Office's investigation?"

"Their inquiry should be completed, by then. I've nothing to hide. It's my agents' identities I'm most concerned about, but I'm questioning my decision on that score."

A stunned expression crossed Danforth's face. "You can't allow them access to our identities, Chief." The viscount reverted to the form of address most of the Nexus agents used. "It would make us all vulnerable."

"It's also dangerous to have all that knowledge stored in one man's memory."

"Nothing's going to happen to you."

"That's a naïve perspective, Danforth, and you know it."

The younger man stared down at his plate, his hands gripping his utensils with bruising force. "Everything is changing."

"Yes."

"Well, I don't bloody like it."

"Few of us do."

The viscount crammed half a piece of toast into his mouth, chewing with such vigor that Sebastian was certain the man's jaw would ache later.

"What now, sir?"

Sebastian toyed with the stem of his glass. "Return to London and continue to keep an eye on Reeves. Let me know if you perceive a significant shift in the superintendent's intentions." He dropped the sealed missive on the table. "I have the letters for Helsford, too."

The tension visibly eased from Danforth's shoulders. "Consider it done, Chief." He began stuffing his mouth full of Cook's famous hotcakes.

"Pardon, my lord," Grayson said, entering the breakfast room. "Mrs. Ashcroft has arrived."

Danforth transferred his attention from the hotcakes to Grayson, a rogue's grin spreading across his handsome face.

Sebastian's muscles stiffened at the sight. "Behave."

The bastard's smile grew brighter.

"Grayson, show her into the study. I'll be there in a few minutes."

The butler bowed. "Yes, sir."

"Having breakfast with Ashcroft's widow," Danforth said. "No wonder you wanted me to rush back to London." His expression turned thoughtful. "Have you told her about the circumstances surrounding her husband's death?"

He shook his head. "Nor do I plan to until we know what we're up against."

"Do you think that's wise? No one disputes the fact that Ashcroft was killed for the content of those letters. She could be in danger."

"All the more reason for you to hightail it back to

London." He rose. "Concentrate on Reeves's movements and deciphering Ashcroft's missives. I'll take care of the rest."

"I hope you know what you're doing."

"We'll soon find out. Godspeed, Danforth."

The viscount pushed out of his seat. "At least introduce me to your new friend."

"Not a chance." He pivoted toward his study, his pulse picking up speed with every step.

"Come now, Chief. Not even a quick hello?"

"There would be nothing *quick* about your greeting. Now, off with you." He grasped the drawing room's door handle and nodded to his butler, who dutifully offered the viscount his hat and gloves. "Grayson, please see Lord Danforth out."

"Of course, my lord."

Sebastian opened the door, saw the widow leaning against the far side of his desk, and felt a frisson of warmth settle into his chest.

A low whistle sounded behind him. Sebastian stepped inside and shut the door in Danforth's face.

The abrupt noise startled her, and she straightened. "My lord?"

"Forgive me, a draught caught the door." She looked even lovelier today than yesterday. Wisps of blond hair curled against her flushed cheeks, and her graceful neck rose above a round neckline that hinted at a full bosom any man would admire.

"Good morning." She tapped her finger against a sheet of a paper. "Here is the schedule."

He joined her at the desk, his chest inches from her shoulder while he studied her well-organized itinerary. The moment he caught her delicate fragrance, the page blurred and the room dimmed. Heat raced across his flesh, and his muscles contracted with the strength of his need.

He turned his head a fraction. "Did you sleep well, Mrs. Ashcroft?"

She did not look up from the schedule. "W-well—" She cleared her throat. "Well enough."

"I did not." Instead of focusing on his task for Reeves and solving the mystery of Ashcroft's death, he had created inventive ways to entice the fair widow into his bed. When he had finally fallen asleep, he awoke not long after, sweating and aching and cock in hand.

She was dangerous—to his peace of mind and to his mission. And he could not force himself to care. For the first time since becoming the leader of the Nexus, he would put his own selfish needs before England's and damn the consequences.

He caressed her cheek, needing the contact and yearning for the connection that could only be had while looking into another's eyes. She lifted her face and her fathomless brown eyes, soft with budding desire and an enchanting trepidation, met his gaze. The need to possess burned through his veins. He wanted this woman like none other.

"Perhaps tonight," he said, "I might enjoy a more pleasurable slumber."

Confusion lit her features a moment before her eyes flared wide. She might not have a courtesan's polish, but she was experienced enough in the ways of men to glean his invitation.

A sharp rap at the door shattered the moment. "Chief, I believe you had something you wanted me to deliver."

Sebastian cursed beneath his breath and thought of the

many ways in which he would make Danforth pay for this intrusion. Ashcroft's letters lay on his desk.

"Chief?" she asked.

He waved off the viscount's careless comment. "Lord Danforth's humor. Ignore it. Or at least, try." He placed a kiss at the corner of her mouth while pocketing the letters. "I'll be back in a moment to take you to breakfast. Make yourself comfortable."

FOURTEEN

Catherine followed the earl's determined strides, fighting the violent urge to halt his retreat and beg him to continue with his gentle assault on her senses. She released a low, shuddering breath. Like the day before, his touch awakened stirrings that had lain dormant for years. Years in which her blood had moved through her veins with boring efficiency.

But not yesterday, nor a few minutes ago. She smoothed her hand over her tight chest, recalling their passionate kiss in the library. Never had she been so consumed by the press of a man's lips. Had he not pulled away, she was ashamed to think of what might have happened in the light of day. With her daughter playing just outside.

She had trouble reconciling this new, unexpected side of the earl. He had always treated her with cool reserve. Had even done so during her most recent visit to London.

Where had the warmth come from? The passion? The need?

The earl jerked the study door open, and she caught

the attractive visage of a gentleman in his late twenties. He flashed her an appreciative smile.

"Good morning, Mrs. Ashcroft." He pushed his way past a scowling Lord Somerton and bowed before her. As he lifted her hand to his mouth, he paused to raise an inquiring brow toward the earl.

Lord Somerton sighed. "Viscount Danforth, may I present Mrs. Ashcroft."

The gentleman smiled and kissed the back of her fingers. "Enchanted."

She needed no introduction. No one in Showbury did, least of all the female denizens. With his charm and striking features, he was assured a spot in every young girl's heart. Even Catherine had grinned at his antics. Although she had only seen him from afar, he was as hand-some as she remembered. "A pleasure to meet you, Lord Danforth."

He released her hand and glanced around. "What brings you to Somerton's lair this morning?"

"None of your business." Lord Somerton indicated the door. "Don't you have somewhere you need to be?"

Danforth glanced between her and the earl, a devilish look in his eye. "But the company is so much more pleasant here."

"A situation easily remedied."

"Our host is in a singular mood." The viscount sent her a knowing smile. "I wonder what has come over him."

"Enough, Danforth." Lord Somerton's crystalline eyes glowed with an unearthly foreboding.

The viscount blew out a beleaguered breath. "The package?"

The two seemed to be engaged in a silent battle of wills that made no sense to her. They obviously held each other in affection, but the earl's reaction to Lord Danforth's playfulness seemed cold, even for him.

To Catherine, Lord Somerton said, "I will return in a few minutes. With any luck, your breakfast will still be warm."

Danforth bowed. "My apologies, dear lady. I didn't mean to keep you from your morning meal. I look forward to the time when our paths cross again."

She curtsied. "As do I."

"Come, Danforth." Lord Somerton did not wait to see if the viscount would do as commanded. He simply turned and left the room.

Danforth winked at her and followed the earl at a more languid pace. Once the viscount closed the door behind him, he let out the first notes of a merry whistle.

Catherine shook her head. The Language of Men had always been an enigma to her, and she did not believe her expertise would grow any time soon.

Her mind cast about for something familiar and solid. Something safe. The schedule of repairs she had developed lay in the center of his desk.

Desk.

A place where men sometimes secreted things. Like valuable lists?

The reddish-brown grains gleamed invitingly, tauntingly. They seemed to eddy down toward the nearest drawer handle, tempting her. Fear seared her heart.

She glanced at the closed study door. Would he really keep sensitive information in such an accessible location? Surely, he would not be so trusting, even in the country. Doubtful, but passing up such a rare opportunity like this would be foolhardy. Cochran would return soon, and he would expect something tangible to pass on to his superior.

She rushed to open the first drawer. A stack of pristine paper, with his family's seal emblazoned at the top, sticks of red sealing wax, and several uncut quill nibs met her hurried inspection.

Even as she tried the second drawer, her conscience screamed with guilt. She could not stop wondering at the veracity of Cochran's assertions about the earl. Leading a secret group of agents did not make him a murderer, or even a double spy. There could be any number of reasons why the viscount called Lord Somerton by that unusual epithet—*Chief*—though none came to mind.

But more importantly, the more she spoke to Cochran, the more he aroused her suspicions. Something about the tenor of their last discussion made her feel unclean and off-center. His demeanor seemed more predatory during their second meeting, far less congenial than their first. But maybe her insistence they postpone their conversation simply put him in a foul mood.

Despite her concerns, she pressed on, inspecting drawer after drawer. If she could find one thing that would either prove the earl's innocence or point to those responsible for Geoffrey's death, all this subterfuge would be worth the risk.

A noise from the far end of the corridor caught her attention. She angled her head, listening. Then came the distinctive sound of a man's heavy tread. She considered the last drawer. Every muscle in her body was at odds with the voice in her head.

Hurry, you still have time.

Her muscles remained locked in place, while the footsteps grew louder, closer.

The last of her courage disappeared. *Another time. Please, let there be another time.*

She leaned forward to grab a quill, and the ink blotter shifted, sliding to the right a few inches and nearly knocking a stack of ledgers off the desk. It was then she noticed Geoffrey's letters were gone. The batch she had given him yesterday had been sitting on top of the ledgers, but now they were missing.

More footfalls penetrated her confusion, and she hurried to right the ledgers and straighten the blotter. When she did the latter, she revealed the corner of a sheet of paper hidden beneath.

The list?

The footsteps stopped outside the door.

Out of time.

Her heart pushed into her throat, and she hurried to dip the pen into the inkwell. She scribbled a word into one of the columns, praying the frantic beating of her heart was noticeable only to her ears.

The study door swung open, and Lord Somerton filled the frame. Once again, his big body held her spellbound and made her feel achingly feminine. She followed the path of his penetrating gaze—over her body, the desk, and the surrounding area. A flush burned its way up her neck and fanned out over her cheeks.

Setting the pen aside, she rose. "I hope you don't mind, my lord. You did say to make myself comfortable, and I had an overwhelming urge to sit behind this massive desk."

"My grandfather had it commissioned years ago. It's a great heap of wood that takes up far too much space."

She stepped away to give the desk a better look. "The craftsmanship is quite stunning."

"So it is."

When she glanced back at him, she found his attention was no longer on his grandfather's desk, but on her. A hint of sensual awareness still softened his features, though his eyes no longer gleamed with erotic hunger. They penetrated, as if searching for answers.

"Shall we discuss your schedule while working our way through a cold plate of food?" he asked.

"By all means." She scooped up the schedule. "I'm ready."

While they strode toward the breakfast room, she considered the hidden sheet of paper. Did it contain the list of possible traitors? Was he done compiling the list? Or still writing it? If so, how would she copy it? She could not think of a scenario that would leave her alone in his study long enough to get the deed done.

So many questions with too few answers. All this subterfuge made her head hurt.

"Another headache?"

She stopped the circular motion of her fingers against her temple and gripped the schedule with both hands. "No, my lord. I simply have much on my mind."

They entered the breakfast room, and he held out a chair for her. "Would you care to share your thoughts? Perhaps I could help."

Indeed, you could.

"Thank you, but no. You have enough to worry about without adding my concerns."

At the sideboard, he lifted silver domes and began filling their plates. The sight struck her as odd. Never had she expected to be served breakfast by an earl.

"It would relieve my mind to think on something else for a while, Mrs. Ashcroft." He placed a mounding plateful of food in front of her. "What taxes you so?"

Telling him the truth was out of the question, so she settled on a topic close to her heart. One in which he could find little fault. She spooned a dollop of jam onto her toast. "Geoffrey's letters, my lord. I confess I am more than anxious to hear of your assessment."

Silence. Under the cover of her lashes, she chanced a peek at the earl. He appeared inordinately focused on cutting up his food—all of his food—into bite-size pieces.

Finally, he said, "You were right."

She raised an eyebrow. "About what?"

"As you said in London, there was something peculiar about his messages." He stabbed several pieces of mutilated sausage with his fork. "Now that I have the rest of Ashcroft's correspondence, I'm hoping some of the questions that arose in the first batch will be answered in the second."

"What if they're not?"

"It's best not to speculate," he said, without looking up. "Allow me to analyze the lot and we shall go from there."

He was keeping something from her. Anger coiled in her heart like an asp getting ready to strike. Her reaction was ridiculous, especially after all that Cochran had conveyed about him. But she had revealed details about her marriage to this man that she had never discussed with another. Not even her mother.

In the same carefully modulated tone he had used with her, she said, "Perhaps it is time for me to journey back to London."

"Why is that?" His utensils clattered against his plate.

She ignored the undercurrent of danger lurking beneath his words. "Sitting idle, waiting for news, goes against my nature. I must do something. Maybe I can call upon Geoffrey's friend from the city to escort me to my husband's various haunts. Someone must have seen something of note the night he was murdered." The thought of calling upon Cochran made her stomach sour.

"Is this the same gentleman I saw leaving your home the other morning?"

For some inexplicable reason, she felt a modicum of relief that the earl had not been able to identify his colleague from such a distance.

She nodded, barely able to hold his gaze. "Yes."

"His name, Mrs. Ashcroft?"

Every question he threw at her carried the sting of authority. Even though his features revealed nothing of his thoughts, his watchful eyes sharpened while awaiting her answer. Catherine's inexperience with prevarication left her indecisive. However, everything inside her rebelled against revealing Cochran's name to this man.

"John Chambers," she said, relying on her instincts. "Do you know him?"

"I'm afraid not."

Her bravado returned enough for her to prod him. "He mentioned something about my husband working with the Foreign Office. Have you heard anything of the sort, my lord?"

His eyes flared for an instant before he severed the connection long enough to drain the last of his coffee. "Mrs. Ashcroft, we do not yet know what we are up against regarding your husband's death. Any sleuthing on your part will only redirect our attention and slow the process down."

She dropped her untouched toast onto her plate and rubbed the bread crumbs between her fingers. "I am sorry to hear that, because I must do something besides this incessant waiting."

He indicated her schedule. "You will be."

"It's not the same, my lord, and you know it."

"You are set on this course, I see."

"Yes."

Using a serviette, he wiped his mouth. She could almost hear his keen mind searching for a way to stop her.

"Then there is something I must tell you."

Apprehension cut through her anger. Would he finally reveal all? In a show of nonchalance, she followed the earl's lead and dabbed her mouth. "Oh?"

"Danforth brought some disturbing news from London."

Her pulse pounded so hard that she could actually feel the skin on her neck rising and lowering. "Does this have something to do with my husband?"

"I'm afraid so."

With uncharacteristic fervor, she bent forward and placed her fingers on the back of his hand. "Please tell me, my lord. No matter how difficult. Not knowing is worse than any news you could deliver."

He stared at her hand for a long time before the bones of his fingers curled into a fist, and his lips thinned into a hard line. He shifted his arm, breaking their contact. The room's temperature plummeted, as did her hopes.

"With any luck, Mrs. Ashcroft," he gathered his utensils again, "you will be spared from ever experiencing the innocence of your statement." He layered food onto the tines of his fork, his movements careful, precise. "As to your husband, I've received word that he was being followed, which might explain some of the comments he made in his correspondence."

For several agonizing seconds, she waited for him to expound, but he seemed disinclined to further discussion.

In fact, he appeared the portrait of a man who often dined alone and was quite content with his state.

Except for his glowing eyes. Although he did an admirable job keeping them downcast, disconnected, she glimpsed the fire burning in their frigid depths. She shivered, unsure what to make of this complicated man.

"Why would anyone be following Geoffrey? Do you think it has something to do with his Foreign Office connection?"

"I have told you all I know, madam."

"Why would I not make the trip then? The answers lie in London, not Showbury."

He stabbed his fork into a slice of bacon and conveniently stuffed it into his stubborn mouth. "As are Ashcroft's pursuers, madam."

"Your reticence is due to your fear for my safety?"

He lowered his utensils and leaned back in his chair. "Did you trust your husband, Mrs. Ashcroft?"

"Pardon?"

"Your husband," he repeated. "Did you trust him?"

Before the last few years, she could have answered the earl with an unequivocal "yes." Now, however, she was less certain of her answer. Trust had as many facets as a superbly cut diamond. Depending on the light, the gemstone's aspect either sparkled and gleamed or appeared gray and almost colorless.

She saw a lot of grays in Geoffrey's actions. He had provided for them and made sure they had wanted for nothing. But emotionally, her husband had long ago left their world colorless and empty. How does one trust a spouse capable of such callous disregard?

"There was a time when I trusted him implicitly, my lord."

He studied her with an intensity that rattled her nerves. "During that time, did Ashcroft ever mention me?" When she raised her eyebrows, he clarified. "Or more specifically, my character?"

Numerous times, in fact. Her husband's fascination with the earl was one of those areas she never comprehended. Lord Somerton had always been cordial and pleasant to her at gatherings, but no one besides Geoffrey had ever penetrated the thick, immovable barrier that surrounded him.

"My husband held great admiration for you."

His gaze became even more piercing. "Try to hold on to that knowledge as we maneuver through the next several days."

Catherine was torn. She wanted to bring about a resolution to this whole intolerable affair. Yet the earl's request carried a note of calming sincerity she could not ignore. "You know more about my husband's death than you're willing to share, don't you, my lord?"

His gaze did not flicker, nor did he answer her question.

"How much longer do you need to sort out whatever it is that needs sorting?"

"A few days."

A few days. They would be the most interminable of her life.

"Perhaps your daughter might like a tour of my stables."

His change of topic left her speechless for several awkward seconds. "You are inviting Sophie into your stables?"

"Consider it a birthday gift."

"A rather generous one, given your aversion to children."

"I don't dislike children. I simply prefer them not to be underfoot." He tossed his serviette onto the table. "I'll make an exception for Sophie's birthday."

She was not convinced. "This feels like a rather masterful bit of redirection, my lord."

"Not so masterful if you saw through my ploy."

"For my daughter's happiness. I'm inclined to allow it. But only for *a few days*."

He nodded, accepting her challenge.

She recalled the request Sophie had made on the way home from church. "This might be a good time to extend my daughter's invitation."

He straightened. "To what?"

"To her birthday celebration. Your daring rescue the other day has secured you an introduction to Castle Dragonthorpe."

"Castle Dragonthorpe?"

"A project she started with her father," she said around a lump in her throat. "All you have to do is dutifully place any new pieces—warriors, farm animals, torture devices—where she points. The furniture, I'm told, is my responsibility."

His features softened, and she wondered about his insistence to keep Sophie away from his estate.

"I thank you and Sophie for the kind invitation." He indicated the schedule. "Shall we?"

Not exactly a refusal or acceptance. He was rather adept at avoidance and redirection. "Of course." She spent the next ten minutes detailing her recommendations and offering possible solutions. Every once in a while, she would send the earl a sideways glance to gauge his reaction. He remained as impassive as ever, but attentive.

"Well done, Mrs. Ashcroft." He folded the sheet of paper and slid it into his coat pocket.

"Once you meet with the craftsmen and discuss time frames and repair costs, I can fill in those columns," she said.

"Then all that would be left is the Date Completed column."

"Thus ending our partnership."

His eyelids lowered. "Would you accompany me to meet with the men?"

There was no dearth of surprises when she was around this man. "I'm not opposed to doing so, but may I ask why?"

"A good question." His lips tilted into a faint, self-deprecating smile. "Two reasons come to mind. First, the people respect and trust you. If I arrive on their doorstep with you in tow, my reception will be much more pleasant than my last attempt to mend relations."

His cutthroat logic made the situation feel mechanical, rather than a genuine wish to win over the craftsmen. Then there was her role in the matter. He had relegated her to an adornment, there to bring respectability to his visit. "It is good to be useful, I suppose."

"I have offended you."

"No." She searched for the appropriate words. "Your logic is sound, as always."

"But?"

"Showbury's residents are a hard-working, somewhat suspicious, and always prideful bunch. If you approach them as Lord of the Manor, my presence will have no effect."

"What do you suggest I do, Mrs. Ashcroft?"

"Act as though you care, my lord."

"You think I don't?"

His swift dealings with Mr. Blake indicated, if not a care for his tenants, a belief in doing his duty by them. He had also saved Sophie from a great embarrassment. However, this issue of keeping vital information about her husband from her pointed to a more calculating side of his character. "I really couldn't say. You have a way of muddling one's perception of you."

"Do I?"

Fire trailed up the back of her neck as she cleared her throat. "Your second reason?"

"One I should probably not share with you, given our previous discussion." With his elbow resting on the arm of the chair, his fingers idly rubbed along his lower lip. "But I will. It is best if you understand."

A tremor started down deep in the center of her body and worked its way to the very tips of her extremities. She curled her fingers and waited. "Understand what?"

"The danger you're in."

FIFTEEN

Sebastian took a certain amount of pleasure in watching Catherine's shock transform into wariness. The woman was twisting his insides into an inconvenient mass of wanting. And her daughter's invitation sparked a powerful yearning that nearly suffocated all his good intentions.

She squared her shoulders. "What sort of danger?"

He rose from his seat and moved to stand behind her chair. For a brief second, he considered sparing her. But the man inside him, the one who had given up moments like this to ensure England's safety, bent forward until his lips were but a hairsbreadth from her ear and whispered, "Me."

Her lips parted on a quivering breath. "I've never shared a bed with any man but my husband."

"Are you amenable now?" He brushed his fingers along her hair, where it lifted away from her nape.

"You would not think me uncaring?"

Sebastian knelt at her side, one hand gripping the back of her chair, the other resting on the table before her. "I suspect you finished mourning your husband long ago."

She bit her full bottom lip and averted her gaze, blinking in quick succession. Empathy twisted his heart. He covered her clenched hands with his. "Am I wrong?"

Her attention remained fixed upon the floor. "No."

Placing his finger on her chin, he urged her to face him. "Why the sorrow?"

"I don't know," she said in a broken whisper. "So many years wasted."

A sentiment he knew well. He could have spent the last score of years cherishing a wife and producing a bevy of children who would comfort him in his old age. Instead, his elder days would be spent haunting the corridors of Bellamere Park alone and, he hoped, reliving hours of stimulating interludes with his beautiful neighbor.

He splayed his fingers, cradling her cheek. "We shall waste no more." Until the moment their lips met, he'd had their *affaire* carefully planned from beginning to end. But he had not counted on her degree of passion or her skillful mouth.

She trembled beneath his touch. Pulsed with a pent-up need that fed his barely controlled desire. His hand shook.

In one fluid movement, he drew her up and deposited her on the dining room table. The fine china clattered, the crystal tinkled.

The widow squeaked.

"My lord." She glanced about the room. "What of the servants?"

"They have been instructed to make themselves useful elsewhere." He discarded his coat and leaned one hip against the edge of the table. Unable to resist, he caressed the delicate curve of her jaw and the smooth skin along her throat. Her pulse pounded, and his need grew. He nuzzled the sensitive hollow hidden behind her earlobe. "Brace yourself."

Eyes wide with wariness, she planted her palms on the white table cover. Her vulnerable expression sent a surge of liquid power through his veins.

He pushed away from the table and slid his hand over the soft leather of her boot-covered ankle, beneath the folds of her riding habit, along the soft profile of her slender leg. Leaning closer, he captured her earlobe between his lips and gently suckled. A seductive rasp of pleasure erupted from her arched throat, persuading him to linger, to kiss his way down her neck until he reached the swell of her breast.

"Oh, dear Lord."

Lifting his head, he followed the play of emotions as they streaked across her face. Desire suited her far more than worry or wariness. Desire transformed her into unadulterated temptation. And Sebastian was tempted. His conquering instincts clamored for control. Screamed for release. Ached for surcease. All of which made his next action nearly unbearable.

He waited for her to open her eyes. "Second thoughts?"

She blinked hard twice, as if to cast off a deep fog. "God, yes."

Sebastian's muscles hardened, instantly regretting his decision. Of all the cork-brained things to do—

"But not enough to stop," she whispered.

He stilled. Flames resumed their trek through his veins, his chest grew taut. "Be very sure, Catherine."

From the way her eyes widened, he knew he had been unsuccessful in keeping the rough edge from his voice. He also knew the moment he slid into her welcoming body that the devil himself would not be able to rip him from her warmth until he'd had his fill.

She trailed her fingers along his cheek and eased back onto the table. The leg he had bared with his roaming hand rose to an inviting angle, and she hooked her dainty black boot around his backside.

Something inside his chest unhinged and a blast of heat encircled his heart. She was not the only one in danger. The realization should have had him backing away, retreating to the far side of the world. Instead, he placed ravenous kisses up her throat and along the delicate ridge of her jaw. The faint scent of a lavender-filled meadow reached his nose. He wanted to pause for a deeper inhalation, wanted to draw her essence into his very center. But the craving to taste her lips one more time won out.

She must have sensed his intention, for in the next instant she turned her head until their mouths touched. The dam broke, and Sebastian plunged into a watery abyss for which there were no handholds.

SIXTEEN

Catherine could not breathe, and she did not care. The earl's demanding mouth angled first one way, then the other, stealing her breath and rattling her wits. Never before had she been *overwhelmed* by her lover. Geoffrey had always taken his time and ensured her comfort. She did not even know one could do *this* on a table.

She loved this mindless seeking of pleasure, this chaotic grasping for gratification. This demonstration of their mutual desire. How long had it been since she had experienced the simple joy of being wanted by a man? She clasped his head tighter and arched her back, needing to feel the weight of him along every inch of her body.

Cool air swirled around her calf, her knee, her naked thigh. With her voluminous skirts now bunched around her waist, the lower half of her body was exposed for the household's delectation. She prayed his staff followed his instructions and stayed away. Knowing what they were doing was one thing. Catching them doing it was quite another.

Ending their kiss, he straightened away, curving his palms over her breasts and stomach, up her raised legs, and down her inner thighs. He did not stop until both thumbs reached her aching cleft. She groaned and thrust her hips, sending sharp needles of pleasure-pain up her spine.

His thumbs never moved from the crest of her opening, tantalizingly close, frustratingly far away.

She lifted her head. "My lord, please."

"I can feel your heat," he said in a low, rough voice. "See your need."

Her inner muscles clenched, and he moaned like a man on the brink of salvation.

In that moment, she would be whatever he wanted her to be. *If only*—she lifted her hips—*he would*—she grasped the tablecloth—*relieve her*—she tilted her head back and squeezed her eyes shut—*agony*. "Pleeease."

Instead of touching her, he attacked the falls of his breeches, unfastening the placard with inhuman speed.

As he took his member into his hand and pressed the thick head against her silky cleft, he said, "Need to feel you. Now."

"Yes. *Now*."

He entered her slick passage. The heated friction more delicious than anything she had ever experienced. Even with her shoulder blades digging into the table, she was swimming in decadence and thrilling at her boldness. But at the halfway point, her muscles tensed and the exquisite contact transformed into a dull, intrusive pain.

She grimaced, and he stopped. When she opened her eyes, she found his luminescent gaze—now filled with concern—raking her features.

"Did I hurt you with my impatience?"

Catherine's heart slammed into her chest. If she

confirmed their lovemaking had caused her some discomfort, he would become considerate and gentle. *Boring.*

She wanted to live his every emotion, thought, and hunger in full, vivid detail. Now that she had tasted the Bordeaux, she would never settle for the ratafia again.

Cradling his face, she gave him a reassuring kiss. "No, you did not hurt me." A different kind of heat spread across her cheeks. "It's been a long time, is all."

He covered one of her hands, lifting it enough to kiss her palm. "You needn't be brave. Allow me to share your burden, so that we may both enjoy the moment."

The ache in her throat returned. But not for long. He transferred those decadent lips to hers while he eased his shaft back a few inches, then he pushed forward until her muscles tautened around him again.

Lifting his head, he locked his gaze with hers, repeating the action of his lower body over and over until finally he settled fully between her hips. "Ready?" he whispered.

She nodded, wrapping her arms around him. The first three long strokes were more exploratory than passionate. By the sixth stroke, she stopped breathing. The twelfth stroke started an avalanche of sensations that had them both burying their faces in the other's shoulder to muffle their cries of pleasure.

For several heart-pounding seconds, they stayed locked in each other's embrace, enjoying the aftershocks of their lovemaking. He lifted his head and kissed her with a reverence that surprised her before drawing away. After an expert flick of her skirts, he pressed a clean handkerchief into her palm.

Giving her some privacy, he swiveled away to refasten his breeches.

"Thank you," she said, heat suffusing her cheeks.

Without a word, he held out his hand to assist her off the table and waited until her legs regained their strength. The process took much longer than it should have. "Perhaps I should sit for a minute."

He did not leave her side, and she found it impossible to meet his eyes as she settled into a nearby chair. She stared down at the wrinkles in her black skirts, at what both represented—the wrinkles and the color—and experienced a moment of conscience. What was she doing having intimate relations with the man who might have ordered her husband's death? What wickedness had invaded her soul to make her crave the ecstasy of his caress? How could she both honor her husband and yearn for this man's touch?

If word got out about their indiscretion, she would be ruined and her daughter would be mocked. The home they had made for themselves at Winter's Hollow would be destroyed by a single act of idiocy.

He traced a finger down her cheek. "How do you fare?"

She made to cover his hand and lean into his caress, but stopped herself. Even now, her body hungered for him again. But she could not allow herself to fall under his spell. Not now. Maybe not ever. From this point forward, she had to consider how her actions would affect her daughter. No more mindless pleasure.

Smiling up at him, she said, "I'm very well."

He kissed her again, and Catherine closed her eyes. She would be strong next time.

When he finally pulled away, he tapped her nose. "I did warn you."

His arrogant comment penetrated the mist of pleasure he had cast around her. She eyed him with displeasure a moment before she raked her chair back and clipped his toe. He grunted, his leather Hessians providing little protection against a stout oak leg. Rising, she glanced at his injured foot. "Pardon, my lord. I should have warned you."

His grimace turned to an appreciative grin. "*Touché,* madam." He waved his hand toward the door. "Shall we go meet with your army of craftsmen? I vow to *act* like I care."

"See that you do, my lord." As she rounded the chair, she ground the heel of her boot into his injured toe. In a flash, he grabbed her waist, twirled her around, and kissed her hard before setting her away.

Indicating the door again, he said, "After you, my dear."

She stared, surprised by his playfulness. Then her eyes narrowed.

"Your retribution shall have to wait," he said. "We have repairs to see to. You don't want Mr. Hayton's cottage to flood again, do you?"

The tenants. She had to focus on the tenants, but not before imparting her own warning. "I have a long memory, my lord. You would do well to remember that fact."

She tucked a stray hair behind her ear and strode from the room, wishing for a looking glass and delighting in the earl's uneven gait.

SEVENTEEN

"You had an urgent matter you wished to discuss, my lord?" Frederick Cochran eyed his companion with thinly veiled hatred. The man's negligent facade masked a cunning mind and a merciless soul, not unlike Cochran's, but Lord Latymer had betrayed his country, which made him a desperate man. One he would not underestimate, even while he exploited the source of the baron's misery.

Summoning him to this wretched gin shop in the middle of St. Giles, rather than communicating by messenger, spoke volumes of Latymer's daring and of his desire to be quit of his current circumstances. The authorities rarely entered the rookery, which made it an ideal location for a high-level fugitive to have a meeting. A bit of dirt on one's face and a layer of tattered peasant's clothing provided a believable cover in this den of despair.

"Lose the formal address," Latymer commanded, accepting a mug from a barmaid who could not be more than twelve years old. The drink sat untouched. "You have not reported in for several days, a condition not to my liking. What progress have you made?"

As always, when in the baron's presence, a dark shadow drifted through Cochran's consciousness like the silent, inevitable approach of death. "I paid the lovely widow a visit a few days ago and impressed upon her the importance of obtaining the earl's list." He recalled the widow's initial confusion and her dawning wariness. He had achieved the right balance between conveying the severity of the situation and not completely losing her trust. Not everyone could have achieved such a delicate task. "If Somerton has compiled the list, I have no doubt the widow will deliver it before week's end."

"No doubt." Latymer stared at him over his steepled fingers. "Tell me, on the small chance your abilities have missed their mark and the widow disappoints, what is your plan?"

His neckcloth became too tight and the room too warm. "She's an intelligent woman. I am confident she will do as she's told."

"Of course, you are." The baron's expression did not alter. "But what if she does not?"

The retribution Cochran had planned for the widow if she failed him glided through his mind in vivid detail. A familiar, exciting fever simmered beneath his skin, causing beads of sweat to form on his brow. He shifted in his seat, becoming more uncomfortable with each pulse of his heart-beat. "I assure you, sir. She is not without weaknesses."

"Don't wait long." The baron rose. "Every second I'm without that list is another second of your dream lost. Our destinies are entwined, Mr. Cochran. You would do well to remember that fact."

He watched the baron stride from the overcrowded

room, knocking into prostitutes and footpads and defending his person against pickpocket after pickpocket.

After a fair bit of digging, he now knew why Latymer wanted the list so badly. The French were of course involved, but the baron had a more personal reason for betraying his country—and his friend. Now Cochran had to figure out how to best exploit the situation, so that the French got what they wanted and so did he. As for Latymer, the man was nothing more than a bothersome extra step that could be struck from the process.

Even in his borrowed clothes and soot-covered face, Latymer could be picked out of this crowd by a discerning eye. Not Cochran, though. He melded with the filth and vermin inhabiting the warren of interconnected buildings and overcrowded houses. Here, no one paid attention to a child's screams from the next chamber or a woman's whimper in a nearby passage.

Because this was a godless lot, and the devil could roam here unheeded. Cochran smiled and grabbed Latymer's untouched drink. He belted back the watered-down brew, then crooked his finger at the young barmaid.

EIGHTEEN

For the hundredth time, Sebastian glanced at Catherine's profile, wondering what machinations cluttered her brilliant mind while she put the finishing touches on The Plan. On their way back from meeting with the craftsmen—a journey completed in relative silence—they had returned to Bellamere so she could assign a workman to each of the repairs and make adjustments to her schedule.

Even knowing she was here at his request, something about her eagerness to be of service gnawed at him. Why would a woman who had her own estate to manage take on the extra burden? What possible benefit could she derive from this partnership?

Given her history of reticence in his company, what would lure her to his home? To spend days in his company? Hours coordinating his repairs?

Why would she risk the good opinion of Showbury's residents by sharing his bed?

An image of Catherine spread out on his breakfast room table, her head tossed back with one leg locked around his waist, materialized with a clarity that astounded him. In that moment, she had been an angel and a temptress. And tight. So tight that he had nearly lost the few wits he had left.

"My lord?"

He shut out the seductive image and focused his fevered eyes on Catherine. She sat at his mother's writing desk, brought into his study by the servants a quarter hour ago, looking comfortable and intent.

What was it about her that compelled him to want to be with her, when he knew they must part ways in a few short days? Having her nearby brought an unusual contentment to his life, something he did not fully comprehend and, at that particular moment, decided not to analyze.

"Yes," he said finally. The word emerged harsh, uneven.

She searched his features. "Did you make promises to anyone besides Mr. Hayton?"

"Not that I recall." He dropped his gaze to his desk and shuffled papers around. "Why?"

She bent over The Plan again. "Just making sure I'm prioritizing everything correctly."

"When might the men you hired begin the repairs?"

Her quill pen scratched across the paper. "We still need to speak with Mr. McCarthy. He's a competent carpenter in need of work."

"I've met him."

The scratching stopped. "You have?"

"Yes, Saturday afternoon, when I attempted to catalog all the repairs myself."

"Is that why we circumvented the McCarthy residence?"

He nodded. "You should add a gate repair to your list."

She looked down at her chart, her lips thinned in disapproval. "You might have mentioned that a tad earlier."

"But I only just now recalled the fact."

"Any others you're only now recollecting?"

She was adorable when annoyed. "Not that I recall."

Pulling a clean piece of paper in front of her, she dipped her pen into the inkwell with a little more force than necessary. "Tomorrow, I will present an individual task list to each of the craftsmen. In the meantime, please don't feel as though you need to entertain me. I'm sure you have more pressing matters to attend."

She had provided him with a perfect opportunity to escape, but he remained rooted in his chair, yearning for her in torturous silence.

Did she not think about their time together in the breakfast room? Did she not grow wet with wanting, with imagining them joined together again?

Paper crackled, and he looked down to find the report he had been trying to read in ruins. He had hoped making love to her would soothe the hunger burning in his loins. But one loving was not enough. His body felt more starved than ever, depleted of an essential element he could not long go without.

Standing, he strode toward her, keeping a tight rein on the conflicting emotions roiling inside him. Dammit, he did not want to want her. A young widow with a small child would come to expect more of him than he could give. Keeping his agents alive and England free from invasion was all he could manage.

Getting involved with Catherine would not be the simple dalliance he had hoped. The need to be with her, near her, already blinded him to his other duties. Would his priorities still be compromised after a few days of pleasurable indulgence?

If so, this *affaire* could put them all in danger.

So why wasn't his body listening to the warning bells of logic?

Hearing his approach, she turned to look at him, and her eyes grew wide. Was her reaction due to his determined advancement, or had his mask slipped? Sebastian feared the latter, which did nothing to improve his disposition.

She rose and shimmied around her chair, as if that meager piece of furniture would provide adequate protection. He wanted to witness one glimmer of remembrance in those beautiful eyes, one sign that she had not forgotten their passionate interlude this morning.

"M-my lord," she said in a shaky voice. "Did I say something to upset you?"

"Hardly, Mrs. Ashcroft. You've barely said anything at all."

Her brows furrowed in confusion. "I don't understand. We discussed Mr. McCarthy at length."

Sebastian pressed beyond the warning bells and physical blockades. "Ah, but I'm not talking about the Irishman. I refer to this morning." He stopped a few feet in front of her, the chair between them. "You do remember this morning, don't you?"

"Of course."

"Do you not wish to discuss what happened?"

"No. Not really."

"Why not?"

"To what end, my lord? We indulged the demands of our bodies, a circumstance I hope we can repeat before you return to London. But to talk about what happened gives the event more significance than it truly carries." She raised her chin. "Don't you think?"

He could do little more than stare at her. Words, logic, arguments—they all failed him. Because she was right. He had delivered the same reminder countless times to mistresses who had placed too much meaning on their sexual encounters.

Being on the receiving end of such a reminder escalated his frustration, causing him to lash out. "Indeed, Mrs. Ashcroft." He pushed the chair beneath the desk. "Perhaps I did not make my intentions clear enough."

She clasped her empty hands in front of her. "Oh?"

He stepped closer. "Since you are receptive to furthering our morning activities, I propose an *affaire*."

"*Affaire?*" After a moment, the confusion vanished and her features cleared of all expression. "Kind of you, my lord. But I have no need of your money."

The muscles in his neck grew taut and a vein in his temple pounded. "I'm not suggesting that you become my mistress, but rather my lover."

She thought about that for a second. "I see."

Did she? To be sure, he pressed his point home. "A pleasurable interlude with a definite beginning and end, an association without expectation. The only exchange of payment would be the slaking of our mutual desire."

A satisfactory flush blanketed her throat and covered her cheeks. She might be well versed in negotiating domestic affairs, but Sebastian was a master at more intimate arrangements.

"What of my reputation, my lord? And my daughter's future? One or two encounters could be...managed. More than that would draw unwanted attention. This will remain my home long after you return to London."

"There are a few options. We do what we can to quell the rumors, or, if you prefer, we can find you and Sophie a nice place away from Showbury. Somewhere you can start fresh, free from unpleasant memories."

"You have given this some thought."

More than you will ever know. "Like you, I prefer to have a plan."

"What if I don't wish to leave our home? What then, my lord?"

"Then I find a way to persuade you, Mrs. Ashcroft."

She took a small step back. "I don't think this is the right time—"

"When would?" he asked more sharply than he intended. "After we find Ashcroft's killer? When you're out of mourning? Once Sophie is older?"

"I don't know," she admitted. "But I don't want my selfish act to hurt Sophie. She deserves better."

"I will protect your daughter from any consequences of our *affaire*. You have my word. I'm offering you a few days of pleasure, something I believe we both need. Trust me to see to Sophie's welfare. And yours."

She moved toward the window and stared at something in the distance. Sebastian's hands balled at his sides, waiting for her answer. His pulse grew thick in his ears and sweat gathered between his shoulder blades.

"Well then," she said quietly, turning to face him again. "I suppose the business of when our *affaire* will begin has already been decided. We need only to determine when will it end."

Never. The reply shot through his mind with blinding speed, surprising him with its savagery. Ever since their exchange with Danforth this morning, he had been hounded by an animalistic need to possess her, to protect her from other appreciative male eyes. He also had an over-powering desire to thrash Danforth.

The viscount's talent for charming vital information from the mistresses and wives of powerful men had been quite useful over the years. But the thought of his agent employing those skills on Catherine had stirred a primitive need in him to rip the young rogue's head off.

"I plan on returning to London by the middle of the following week," he said. "Does that suit for an end date?"

An odd mixture of relief and exasperation crossed her face. He wondered about the reasons for both.

"Yes, my lord. Quite definitive."

"Perhaps, it's time for us to dispense with the formalities, Catherine." He slid his palm against the soft skin of her neck. "Catherine."

She inhaled a shaky breath, but did not reciprocate.

"Say my name." He stared at her beautiful mouth. "Please."

"Sebastian," she whispered.

His heart wanted to pound free of his chest. Clear thought was near impossible with her this close to him. Placing his fingers on her cheek, he smoothed his thumb over her bottom lip. "Now that we have the business side of our arrangement settled, I propose a sampling of the pleasurable side."

She nodded, sucking in her bottom lip. When it reappeared moist and red from her ministrations, his control snapped. He covered her mouth, drawing her lip between his teeth to savor its texture, toy with its softness. Tease and test its plumpness.

He slid a hand around her waist, drawing her in closer until their bodies became one. Her small hand smoothed its way up his chest, along his neck. Not stopping until her warm palm rested on his cheek. When he deepened the kiss, her sweet, adventurous tongue swept into his mouth.

Desire fired through his veins, sleek and hot. He wanted her again. A sampling was not enough. "Never enough."

"Pardon?" she asked on a shaky breath.

He stilled.

"What's not enough?"

Unable to free himself of the hunger numbing his mind, his attention remained fixed on her swollen mouth. Had he been so far gone in the sensation of her kiss as to reveal his hidden desires?

"My lord?"

He swallowed back a stab of agitation and retreated a step. The evidence of his possession glistened on her lips, making him regret his withdrawal. What was it about this woman that made him forget time and place? Why did she now haunt his dreams and plague his waking hours?

He lifted her hand and kissed the delicate blue veins running along the inside of her wrist. "Forgive the intrusion. I know you're most eager to get the repairs under way, which cannot happen until the men have their task list." He released her and gripped his hands behind his back. "Are you free for dinner?"

She checked the timepiece hanging around her neck. "I'm afraid not. Mr. Foster will be here any moment."

Every muscle in his body locked in place. "The vicar is coming here?"

"Yes, I hope you don't mind. We are to check on Mrs. Taylor before dinner. Knowing we would have a long day, I suggested that he collect me from here."

"So that's why you walked over today."

"Yes."

"Always planning, aren't you, Catherine?" he asked with more bite than necessary. "Why must you accompany the vicar to check on Mrs. Taylor?"

She cast him a perplexed look. "Because he asked me to and we have things to discuss."

Things to discuss. He did not care for the sound of that, especially after the vicar's comments about marriage. "Did you tell him that we have work to do?"

"I don't understand, my lord—Sebastian. We've done all that we can do here today."

He moved to the window, needing a moment to grapple with the sensations pounding through his body. Where had this need to throttle every man who came within an arm's length of her come from?

He did not want her spending time with the good vicar when she could be having dinner with him. Did she not feel the same yearning that nearly overwhelmed him every second they were in the same room?

His control was slipping, something he could not let happen. She was nothing more than a diversion. Sweet and charming and so different from the pampered ladies of the *ton*. But a diversion, nothing more.

The memory of her splayed out on the breakfast room table resurfaced, and he amended his assessment. Seductive and tempting. Beautiful and thrilling.

His cock stirred and his stomach clenched. He wanted her. In his bed, with her golden tresses fanning over her body like an angel's cape. Her desire-filled eyes on him, and no other.

He bit back a curse. *Control, Somerton!*

"Sebastian?" she said in a soft voice as if sensing the war that raged inside him. "Was there something you needed me to do before I left?"

Closing his eyes, he forced himself to recall Ashcroft's lifeless body lying in the middle of a filthy alley, his clothes soaked with blood and God only knew what else. The awful scene had the desired effect. His erection withered in record time, leaving him with the sour mood of an unfulfilled man.

"I assume I'll have your undivided attention tomorrow, Mrs. Ashcroft?"

Her spine straightened. "Of course."

"No midweek jaunts through the countryside while I'm here dealing with the repairs?"

"What is this about, my lord?"

"We had an agreement, madam."

"What is your point, sir?"

"For the next several days, you're working for me, and I expect your full attention on the repairs."

The tips of her ears turned scarlet. "First of all, I'm working *with* you, not for you. And second, my attention has been on the repairs for *months*."

He opened his mouth to argue, but she held up a staying hand.

"After my husband turned his back on us, the residents of Showbury blamed me for Geoffrey's absence." She swallowed hard. "I constantly battled greedy shopkeepers, disapproving matrons, and small-minded men. If the vicar had not stepped in and befriended me, I'm not sure what I would have done."

The tension thrumming through his body ebbed away.

"I owe much to Mr. Foster," she continued, "and will happily accept any of his requests for assistance. Now, if you will excuse me, my lord." She gathered her things, and he watched it all through a narrow, slightly blurry lens. He felt like a fool, and offering his apology seemed inadequate.

He had no sooner finished the thought when he found himself standing before her, aching to pull her into his arms and kiss away the angry lines scoring her forehead.

Instead, in the softest voice he could manage, he asked, "Will I see you tomorrow?"

She glanced away as if to give the question considerable thought. He held his breath, afraid to make the slightest move that would push her toward a decision that would rip away a vital piece of his sanity.

"Might you behave yourself?"

"It is my dearest wish to do so."

Pounding footfalls sounded down the corridor. Within seconds, his butler knocked on the door before sticking his harassed face through the opening. "My lord," Grayson panted. "Mr. Foster to see you."

The vicar squeezed by Grayson. "I'm sorry for barging in, my lord. Mrs. Ashcroft. But I've received some unsettling news about Meghan McCarthy."

Catherine rushed forward and placed her hand on the vicar's sleeve. Sebastian's hands knotted into fists.

"What's happened?" she asked. "Please don't tell me something is wrong with the baby."

"No, ma'am. Well, yes. I mean—"

She grasped his hand in both of hers. "Take a deep breath, Mr. Foster."

He sent her a sad smile. "You're always so strong." He pulled in a long breath. "Yes, something is wrong. Very wrong. Meghan McCarthy has gone missing."

NINETEEN

After sending word to her mother at Winter's Hollow, Catherine and Sebastian accompanied the vicar to the McCarthys' to help search for the missing girl. According to Mr. Foster, Meghan had gone for a walk with a friend after their meeting with her on Saturday and never returned home. Figuring their daughter had decided to stay the night at her friend's house, something she often did, the family did not begin to worry until she failed to return home the following afternoon.

When they entered the McCarthy cottage, Catherine noted Meghan's younger sister and brother huddled in a corner, watching their father shove items into a satchel. Both Declan and his wife looked as though they had not slept in days, and Mrs. McCarthy's eyes were red-rimmed and sunken with grief.

"What is the latest, Declan?" the vicar asked.

"Still no sign. We've pounded on every door and traveled down every lane. Sally Porter said she parted ways with my Meghan near the woods about a mile from here.

I'm going to search the woodland and waterfall she liked to visit."

Sebastian asked, "Do you think she left with the baby's father?"

Mrs. McCarthy shook her head. "My daughter's refusal to provide the man's name was not because she wanted to protect him, but rather to protect her and the babe."

Catherine recalled her suspicions about Meghan's reticence. "She was afraid of the father?"

Mrs. McCarthy shared a look with her husband. "We think so, although the stubborn girl would not admit it."

When everyone fell silent, Sebastian asked, "Is no one else assisting with the search?"

Declan's features hardened. "No."

The earl didn't react, but she sensed his anger. Her own temper and disappointment bubbled to the surface. "No one?"

"The people around here have never welcomed us." Mrs. McCarthy blotted her nose. "If not for your assistance, ma'am, we would have left months ago."

"I did little more than nudge a few customers in your husband's direction. Mr. McCarthy's work speaks for itself."

"The vicar and I will help search the woodlands." Sebastian's pronouncement held an age-old ring of authority that the other two men responded to without question.

"Thank you, m'lord," Declan said. "I welcome the extra eyes."

Mr. Foster nodded. "I'm ready."

"As am I," she said.

Sebastian assessed her for a moment. "Your skills would be better employed elsewhere, madam."

"Don't think to exclude me. Meghan's my friend, and I will not leave until she's found."

"I thought as much."

His mood confused her. She detected none of his earlier pique in his expression or voice, but something was churning in his brilliant brain.

"Then define 'elsewhere,' if you please."

"Are you up for a few social calls?"

"Social calls? Now?"

"We need more people to assist with the search."

His meaning became clear, and something inside her warmed at the knowledge that he trusted her to help. The one thing she had mastered over the years was the fine art of prodding people to do what they would not otherwise do, if left to their own devices. "Of course." Turning to the vicar, she asked, "May I borrow your gig, sir?"

"By all means, Mrs. Ashcroft."

"What of me, m'lord?" Mrs. McCarthy asked. "How can I help?"

"Stay here, in case your daughter returns." He laid his hand on the woman's shoulder. "It's also best to prepare for the worst. Do you have clean linens you can tear into strips?"

She nodded.

"Have several ready along with hot water and whatever medical supplies you have. Also, keep an eye out for any recruits Mrs. Ashcroft sends our way. Let them know where to find us. Can you manage it all?"

"Yes, m'lord. Keeping busy will keep my mind from straying down dark paths."

When Sebastian nodded, Catherine knew the tasks he

had given the young mother had not been random or without intent. Warmth gripped her heart at his thoughtfulness.

Sebastian pointed at Declan's bag. "Do you have any weapons stashed in there?"

The carpenter hesitated a moment, his lips firming into a grim line. "Yes."

"Good. Shall we go?"

Declan glanced at the vicar, who smiled.

They left the cottage en masse. She made her way to the vicar's gig, while the men set off for the wooded area. When she prepared to climb into the conveyance, Sebastian's hand materialized in front of her.

Startled, she glanced at him, accepting his assistance. "Did you need something, my lord?"

"See if you can locate a cart." He unraveled his cravat and shrugged out of his coat. "And do something with these, if you will."

Without thought, she draped his garments over her lap as if she had performed the same act a hundred times before. The mindless deed gave her a brief opportunity to admire the bit of flesh revealed by his open neckline—until his words sank in. "A cart? Do you think Meghan's injured?"

"I don't know. As I mentioned to Mrs. McCarthy, it is best to prepare for the worst."

"Be careful."

His attention dropped to her mouth, brushed it softly with a single sweep of his gaze before lifting again.

The visual kiss had nearly the same impact as the stunning press of his lips. Her stomach clenched around a surge of longing so powerful she came close to reaching for him.

He stepped back. Had he sensed her temptation? Had he shared it?

"Coerce as many as you can to come, Mrs. Ashcroft. Promise them whatever you must."

The gravity of his tone told her he was more concerned with Meghan's welfare than he cared to share.

A fresh wave of anger washed over her. How could Showbury's residents turn their backs on the McCarthys at a time like this? To do so was reprehensible.

She would enjoy this opportunity to remind her neighbors of the many times Mr. and Mrs. McCarthy had set aside their own duties to harvest a crop or protect a home from high waters. She narrowed her eyes on the lane ahead. Yes, indeed.

"Promises will not be necessary, my lord." She flicked the reins. "Be prepared for my return."

Two hours later, she stood with a large group of chagrined neighbors in a small meadow near the woods. Not long after their arrival, Lord Somerton emerged from the tree line, looking disheveled but no less determined.

She rushed to greet him.

He glanced over her shoulder, appreciation lighting his blue-gray eyes. "You did well."

An unexpected shyness made it difficult to meet his gaze. "Some had already come to their senses and were making their way here."

"Others needed a few not-so-subtle reminders, I take it." Although his expression did not change, his voice carried a teasing quality.

"No sign of Meghan yet?"

He shook his head. "We've combed the wooded area as best we can with the three of us. I'll have your troops sweep through again, while McCarthy, Foster, you, and I search the streambed that leads to her waterfall."

Declan and the vicar joined them, and the earl explained his plan. The carpenter nodded his understanding, but his gaze was on the assembly behind Catherine.

"They want to help," she said.

"Why now?"

"I suspect they had time to consider how it would feel if their circumstances were reversed."

Sebastian placed a hand on Declan's shoulder. "Allow me to set up a search line and provide the group with some instructions, then we can set upon the stream."

She could tell the carpenter wanted nothing more than to continue his sweep of the area. But in a short period of time, the earl had won Declan's respect to the point of deferral.

"Your wife said you have not eaten anything since yesterday," Catherine said. "She sent a small basket of foodstuff along, as did many of the women from the village."

"Thank you, ma'am," Declan said. "But I'm not hungry."

"You soon will be and probably at a most inconvenient time." She motioned him toward the gig. "Eat, please. Keep up your strength until we find Meghan. You, too, Mr. Foster."

"Did the ladies by chance send refreshment?" the vicar asked.

"We have water and ale in the back."

Declan pulled a sandwich from an overflowing basket. "I should never have let her out of my sight. She was always so trusting of strangers."

"Meghan's disappearance was not your fault," Mr.

Foster said. "You can't always know another's mind, no matter how much you love them."

"Ready?" Sebastian strode toward them and did not stop. He simply wrapped his long fingers around her elbow and pulled her gently, yet firmly, along. "Mrs. Ashcroft and I will head north a quarter mile and work our way down. You two gentlemen head upstream from the south. We will meet in the middle, or until we find Meghan. Agreed?

"Yes, my lord," came their reply.

"Good luck, gentlemen."

They walked in tense silence until the men were out of earshot.

"You think something has happened to Meghan, don't you?" she asked.

"I can't be sure."

"What do your instincts tell you?"

"That this day is going to end badly."

She bit her lip, trapping the grief welling up in the back of her throat. "Who would want to harm such a sweet girl?"

"Bad people do bad things. Sometimes for personal gratification, other times out of fear."

She sent him a sideways glance. "You sound as if you know firsthand."

"I do."

"Did my husband also know?"

His fingers tightened around her arm. "Yes."

"You won't share his travails with me?"

He released her arm to grasp her hand, guiding her through a thicket of shrubbery. "Start scanning for anything out of the ordinary. Discarded clothing, a disturbed area...anything."

His mention of discarded clothing had the desired effect, for her line of thought reverted to Meghan. They traipsed through the thicket for several more minutes until the underbrush gave way to a twenty-foot bluff overlooking a stream.

Under different circumstances, she would have stopped to enjoy the gently rolling hill, the fluttering leaves, and the twittering birds. But the earl paused only long enough to determine the best path downward. Every unsteady step they made toward the stream increased her trepidation, her certainty that they would find Meghan in an unwelcome situation.

She shrugged off the vile images. Meghan was alive. This business with the unnamed father had everyone suspicious and on edge. Perhaps the girl ran away with her lover, knowing her parents would not approve of the match.

Then again, Meghan could have taken a nasty tumble and now she lay injured somewhere, awaiting rescue. So many possibilities. So many unknowns. She glanced around. So much ground to cover.

"Hold on." He did his best to keep their descent steady and sure, but the steepness and decaying leaf litter made it impossible. Every few steps, her foothold would give way and she would slide several inches until he steadied her again. Three-quarters of the way down, they gave up the fight. She lifted the hem of her skirts, and they barreled down the hill.

The moment they hit firm, even ground, he turned south. "We will stay to this side. The stream is wide enough and deep enough here that it's unlikely the girl crossed over." He scanned in front of them. "Are you able to keep to within five feet of the water without my assistance? I would like to increase our efforts by moving up the hill a bit."

Because she had walked to the earl's, rather than take Gypsy, she had her sturdy boots on. "I'll manage quite well."

He rested his hand on her cheek. "You're being very brave, Catherine."

She nodded, unable to speak. His unexpected gentleness and praise threw her off balance. "Thank you for not insisting I keep Mrs. McCarthy company."

He cradled her other cheek, studying every nuance of her face. Before her eyes, his features grew stormy, almost savage in their intensity.

"Be careful," he said in a rough whisper. Then he kissed her. Not a quick, hard, possessive kiss. But a hot, I'm-fighting-against-my-natural-instincts kiss. The pads of her fingers had barely grazed his back when he pulled away, almost as if he feared her touch.

"Remember, do not discount anything you see, no matter how small."

"I won't."

They continued in a southerly direction, often in concentrated silence and sometimes stopping to investigate. As they closed in on the small waterfall, she could not decide if she was relieved or disappointed. She mentioned as much to him as they picked their way along a rocky edge that led down to a small pool of water.

"If she's not here," he said, "we will continue until we find her."

His calm assurance amazed her. "Have you even met Meghan?"

"I caught a glimpse of her once." He eyed her. "Why do you ask?"

"Simply trying to understand your willingness to help the McCarthys, when others who knew them were not."

He held out his hand to assist her around a particularly difficult area. "Despite my absence these last few years, I take my responsibility to my estate and those who care for it seriously."

"Yes, I can see that you do." She hopped from one rock to the next. "But that does not account for your insistence that I do whatever it took to bring additional help."

"Perhaps I can empathize with the McCarthys on some level."

She halted. "Did you lose someone, my lord?"

He set his hands on his hips, staring out over the area below. He nodded to someone, and the vicar and Declan meandered their way toward their location.

"Sebastian?"

Through tight lips, he said, "I lost someone quite dear to me. It's not a feeling I would wish on anyone else."

She stepped closer. "Did you find him or her?"

"Her." He swallowed hard and gave her a short nod. "I found her, but not soon enough. She will never fully recover from the trials of her ordeal."

"I'm sorry to hear that."

"As am I. Come." He grasped her hand again. "Let us join the others. I fear the weather has taken a turn."

It was then she noticed the two men below were cast in deep shadows. She chanced a glance to the west, above the treetops, and found a line of ominous dark clouds rolling their way. Was this Mother Nature's way of sending them a sign?

Once they reached the other men, Declan asked, "Any sign of my Meghan?"

Sebastian shook his head. "Not even a set of tracks. Let us do a thorough search of this area before the storm hits."

The temperature dropped and the air grew thick with

moisture. She shivered, wishing she had worn her warm wool cape, rather than her nankeen pelisse.

A man's coat enfolded her in blessed warmth. She opened her mouth to thank the earl, but found Mr. Foster's smiling face. "You looked chilled."

"Thank you. I'm afraid I wasn't prepared for such a drastic shift in the weather."

"Nor could you have been. None of us expected all of this."

"Vicar," Sebastian called. "Perhaps you should take Mrs. Ashcroft back to the gig and see her home. McCarthy and I will finish up here. Once the storm passes, we can resume our efforts."

She wanted to argue, but the men would be concentrating on her comfort, rather than on looking for signs of Meghan. "I will check on things at Winter's Hollow, then return to sit with Mrs. McCarthy."

"And I will see how the other searches progress," the vicar said.

The wind picked up, freeing locks of her hair and whipping them into her eyes. She trapped her escaped tresses with one hand at her temple, gazing back at the earl. A sudden reluctance to leave him behind kept her rooted in place.

Standing in his shirtsleeves and waistcoat, he resembled a gentleman pirate with the wind molding fabric over his muscles, outlining the hidden strength beneath.

He nodded toward the woodland behind her. "Go."

His soft command carried a note of tenderness that tangled with her heart. What would she do if she found out this man was responsible for Geoffrey's murder? She feared the answer became more complicated with every minute she spent in his presence.

She turned and followed the vicar from the clearing. Within seconds, the rain started. Sharp, driving nails of water stabbed her face. She tucked in her chin and squinted her eyes. As she stepped under the canopy of trees, the rain eased but the wind kept up its relentless pace.

Unable to ignore the nagging voice in her head, she peered over her shoulder to check on the earl while keeping pace with the vicar. He stood alone, with his hand shielding his eyes, watching her.

She held up a hand, letting him know she was fine. Only then did he turn to resume his search.

As she faced forward again, she stumbled over a rut. Her shin connected with something hard, and her world tilted downward. She braced herself for the impact. Rather than hitting hard soil, her hands sank into rich, pungent earth made soupy by the downpour.

Everything happened so fast, she did not think to call out or even shriek her alarm. She glanced up to see the vicar had veered to the left to avoid a low-hanging branch. Had she not been preoccupied with Sebastian, she would have followed him on the safer route.

As it was, she was literally elbow deep in mud. "Mr. Foster, I need your assistance."

She clambered to her knees, or at least tried to. Her hands plunged deeper and deeper into the wet soil. Then her hand connected with something firm and round. A log, perhaps. When she made to push off, she realized it could not be a log. The surface beneath her hand was too pliable. Too smooth.

Too familiar.

She stared down at her arm, where it disappeared inside a mound of too-fresh earth. "Oh, God." Water rolled down her temples and streamed into her eyes. She blinked to clear her vision, only to have them fill up again.

"Mrs. Ashcroft, are you injured?"

She ignored the vicar, keeping her full attention on her exploratory fingers. She did not speak. She daren't breathe. Her fingers and her heart were the only things that moved.

When she came across an object that had the distinctive features of a hand, she could no longer hold back her scream.

TWENTY

At the sound of Catherine's scream, Sebastian launched himself through the relentless sheet of rain. He knew what that sound meant. Had heard that type of scream too many times to count. But once was enough to have it seared onto one's brain like a brand scorching one's flesh.

Painful. Memorable. Permanent.

It was the sound of horror.

A sound dredged up from one's most primitive core, when the sight before one is so heinous, so unexpected, as to terrify one's soul.

Catherine had found death.

"Mrs. Ashcroft, what are you doing?" the vicar cried.

"Help me!" she commanded.

Sebastian broke through the underbrush and took in the macabre scene with one glance. Catherine and the vicar were bent over a mound, scooping up handfuls of mud and throwing them to the side. Their frenzied movements told him all he needed to know.

He hauled her up and set her behind him, nudging her

toward the meadow. "Do what you can to keep McCarthy away from here. He will likely have heard you." He dropped to his knees and focused on what he hoped was the upper end. "Vicar, start praying."

Neither Catherine nor the girl's father should see death in such a horrendous form. No one should. He had feared this ending, though he had held out hope for something more palatable, like an elopement. But his instincts could not ignore the signs of foul play any more than a sailor could ignore a red sky in the morning.

A man's roar of pain sounded from behind him. "Faster, Vicar."

No sooner did he give the command than the side of his hand glided over flesh. He stilled, as did the vicar. More carefully, he scraped away the mud. Section by section, they revealed parts of the girl's face. First, her mouth, open and full of wet dirt. Then her nose, cheeks, and, finally, her eyes.

They stared straight ahead, the rain rinsing them clean to reveal the vacant gray irises of death.

Too late. *Too damned late.*

"Mr. McCarthy, please don't!"

Catherine's entreaty was the only warning he had before the distraught father pushed him aside.

"Oh, Jesus, no." Declan stared down at his dead daughter. Anguish like nothing Sebastian had ever seen crumpled the rugged man's face. "No. Not my Meghan. Not my baby girl." He dropped to his knees and picked up where Sebastian left off, removing great heaps of mud, apologizing and promising retribution in the same heaving breath.

"Catherine, stay back," Sebastian ordered when she made to move to his side. "McCarthy, allow me to do this for you."

The brawny carpenter ignored him, shoveling away layers of mud and dirt until finally his daughter's body was revealed. Meghan lay squeezed inside a shallow grave, with no visible wounds or signs of trauma. Only a slight bump on her stomach, marking a second, much smaller grave.

"Sweet Jesus." The scene was so horrific that even Sebastian had to avert his eyes. He looked for Catherine and found her several feet away, her mud-slicked hands covering her silent sobs. He wanted to go to her, wanted to wrap her small frame within the safety of his arms. But he knew in these situations that those involved needed to stay occupied in order to hold back the shock. He noticed she no longer wore the vicar's coat.

"Catherine." He drew her hands from her face, but she continued to stare straight ahead. He bent to peer into her eyes. "Catherine, I need Mr. Foster's coat."

She blinked once, then several more times in quick succession before her gaze cleared.

"Did you hear me? Please find where you dropped the vicar's coat."

She nodded and swiveled to find the fallen garment.

"Vicar, please relieve Mrs. Ashcroft of your coat once she finds it and bring it to me."

"Yes, my lord."

McCarthy bent to lift his daughter from her watery grave, and Sebastian laid a hand on the man's shoulder. "I'll help you."

The carpenter nodded and moved to grab Meghan's legs.

Sebastian braced his boot on the opposite side of the hole and burrowed his hands under the girl's shoulders. "Ready."

Together, they hauled her up, the action creating an

awful sucking noise as the pit released the girl from its inky grip. That's when Sebastian noticed the deep purple bruises circling her throat.

The vicar appeared at Sebastian's side, using his coat to protect McCarthy's memories as much as possible. They laid her on the ground and everyone stared at her ragged form in appalled silence. Sebastian broke the spell, intending to carry the girl to the cart, but McCarthy shook his head.

"I'll be doing that, m'lord. I failed to protect her as I should. This will be my penance."

Catherine opened her mouth to reassure the grieving father, but Sebastian shook his head. Words would not cut through the man's grief and recriminations. Only time would do that. A good deal of time.

He held his hand out to her, needing the contact. She came to him and wrapped her arms around his waist, burrowing her face in his chest. He kissed her sodden head, giving McCarthy time to cradle his daughter in his arms and set off for the meadow, with the vicar leading the way.

He framed her sweet face, thankful the rain had gentled to a light patter. "I'm sorry you had to witness such evil."

She grasped his wrists, turning tearful eyes up to his. "Who would do such a thing?"

He scanned the area. "I don't know, but I vow to find out." He shifted her to his side, though he did not let go. "Come, let us be quit of this place."

Several hours later, Sebastian drew Reaper to a halt outside Bellamere's thick double doors, with Catherine snuggled in his arms. He had not the heart to take her home, where her daughter would see her mother in such a disheveled state and would no doubt shower her with diffi-cult questions.

Although the driving rain had rinsed off most of the mud, their skin and clothes were still stained with bits of silt. Her blond hair hung in long, lanky clumps down her back, and her boots carried deep, ruinous gashes.

Grayson and two footmen appeared, rushing to their aid. "My lord," Grayson said. "Is Mrs. Ashcroft injured? Should I prepare a room?"

"No and yes. Please send word to Winter's Hollow that Mrs. Ashcroft is fine, but will be staying the evening here. Leave two footmen over there as a precaution. Have Mrs. Fox draw us hot baths."

He could not wait to be rid of his damp, abrasive clothes. He was certain Catherine felt the same, although she had not spoken a word since leaving McCarthy's cottage.

"What are we doing here?" she stirred, her voice raw. "I must make sure Sophie and my mother are well."

"I sent two footmen to stay with them. They will see that clean clothes are sent over." He skimmed the backs of his fingers over her cheek. "It's best you stay here tonight. You're in no condition to see your daughter."

"But the killer—"

"He's accomplished what he wanted and is likely long gone."

The tension in her body drained away, replaced by a racking shiver.

"Here, let us get you out of the elements." With Grayson's support, Sebastian set her down. "Steady."

He dismounted, handing the reins to his butler and offering an arm to the widow. "Grayson, please see what

Mrs. Fox can find in the way of food. Mrs. Ashcroft has not eaten all day."

"Nor have you." She snaked her hand into the crook of his arm, leaning on him as they made their way inside. "Bath first, food later."

Another footman arrived to relieve Grayson of his hostler duties.

"My lord." Grayson entered the entry hall behind them. "I'm told the countess's bedchamber is the only aired-out room. The maids are working on the rose room."

"No need. Mrs. Ashcroft can use the countess's chamber."

"Oh, no," she said. "I am happy to wait for the rose room."

"You would have the maids go through all that extra work for no reason?" He knew she worried about the impropriety of sleeping in a bedchamber next to his, but he could not bring himself to care. He wanted her close.

She glanced from him to Grayson, as if the butler would help plead her case. Grayson, like most seasoned servants, had learned long ago not to get involved in his employer's business.

"No, I suppose not," she said.

"Is there a fire in the drawing room?" Sebastian asked.

"Yes, my lord."

"We will wait there while Mrs. Ashcroft's bathwater is drawn."

Grayson bowed. "Very well, sir."

They made their way to the drawing room, and he settled her near the fire. Flickering red-gold light reflected off her face, revealing a classic profile but for the dark hollows beneath her eyes.

"What a horrible end to what would otherwise have been a grand day," she said.

Given they had started the day off by making love on his table, he had to agree with her.

"You knew all along, didn't you?" she whispered.

"Knew what?"

"That we would find her dead."

"Not with any great certainty."

She snorted. "That's what my husband would have called a clanker."

His jaw clenched. How did this woman continually see through his mask? "She could have eloped."

"But you suspected otherwise." She sent him a sidelong glance. "Instinct? Or something else?"

Ice trailed down his spine. "Do you have an accusation you would like to share, madam?"

She shifted her attention back to the fire. "Of course not, my lord."

He grappled with his temper. In his line of work, he was used to being an object of suspicion. But to have her question his integrity, especially over the murder of an enceinte girl, burned every nerve ending in his body.

Outside of withholding her husband's role in the Nexus and the facts around his murder, he had been careful not to lie to her. Very careful.

"By your own admission," she said, "you have enjoyed an interesting past. One that has more than a passing familiarity with the insidious side of mankind. I thought perhaps this incident reminded you of something that occurred in London."

His nostrils flared around a deep breath. When he released it, a great weight drifted away as well. "Only one other occasion comes close to matching what I saw today.

Neither image will lose its grip any time soon." He swept the room for something to drink. "But you were right in that my past has prepared me for days like today."

"A past involving my husband?"

All the weight came crashing down on him again. "You are nothing if not relentless, madam."

A shadow crossed her face. "I suppose I am. Without the protection of a husband, it's how I've survived living in Showbury all these years."

He tried to swallow back the guilt that clawed its way up his throat, but his mouth had gone completely dry. Not a single drop of saliva to soothe the sensation of his throat being ripped apart. He grasped the mantel to hold himself in place.

"Won't you tell me what you know about Geoffrey?" she asked, driving the pain deeper.

"I cannot."

"Why can't you? Do you think I don't deserve to know the truth?"

He closed his eyes. "Of course, I do."

"Then why, my lord—Sebastian? I don't understand."

"I know you don't." He pushed away from the fireplace and paced the small room. "And I can't enlighten you."

"Can't?"

He whipped around. No one in the last decade had challenged him in the way this woman dared. Not his subordinates or his superiors. She poked and prodded and pried into places that could get them all killed. Did she not understand his silence protected her? And her daughter?

No, because he could not tell her. Not even that much.

But he could reveal the circumstances surrounding Ashcroft's death. At least some of them. "You win, Catherine."

"I-I do?"

"I doubt your victory will be as satisfactory as you believe, however."

"You might be wrong."

A knock sounded at the door.

The widow's eyes narrowed.

He sent up a prayer of thanks. "Enter."

"Pardon, my lord," the housekeeper said, peering around the door.

"Yes, Mrs. Fox?"

"Mrs. Ashcroft's bathwater is ready."

He looked to Catherine. "After you."

She stopped in front of him. Fierce brown eyes ablaze with defiance. "I intend to hear more about this victory."

TWENTY-ONE

Catherine sat on the hearth rug in front of a low-burning fire, attempting to untangle the mass of knots that was her hair. It was not going well.

Each time she tried to pull the tortoiseshell comb through a snarl, her wet tresses slapped against her bare arms and dampened her cotton chemise. Mrs. Fox had offered to assist Catherine herself, but all she had wanted after stepping into the countess's bedchamber was to be alone.

Thank goodness her dear mother had thought to send along a few items to get her through the evening as well as a change of clothes for tomorrow. Everything she had worn today was beyond salvaging. Even if the maids managed to clean her tattered dress, she could not have borne to wear it again.

Each rip and stain would be an awful reminder of today's events. God forgive her, all she wanted to do was forget.

Her stomach took that opportunity to remind her of how little she had eaten. Mrs. Fox had prepared a small tray of cheese and fruit for her to nibble on while in the tub. Instead of filling the hollow in her stomach, Catherine had concentrated on digging the dirt out from beneath her nails and picking the flecks of decaying leaves from her hair.

Abandoning her futile effort with the knots, she scrambled to her feet and padded over to the tray. Balancing it on one hand, she gobbled down two squares of cheese and four grapes before heading back to her place by the fire.

For what felt like the hundredth time, she flicked a glance at the door connecting her bedchamber to the earl's. She had not seen him since he had nudged her inside the room with a pithy comment not to fall asleep in the tub. As if she could sleep with him lurking in the next chamber.

At times, she thought she heard him pacing back and forth, with intermittent pauses at her door. But the handle never turned and the door never opened. She put two more pieces of cheese in her mouth and willed him to check on her.

She wanted to finish their conversation. He had been about to reveal something important. Something that might put an end to this intolerable anticipation, this constant waiting for resolution. She was so tired of waiting.

Setting the tray on the floor next to her, she grabbed the comb again and attacked her hair with renewed vigor. She would conquer her tangles, finish her food, and climb into bed for some much-needed sleep. She would not think of the earl again.

He could pace his bedchamber until the New Year dawned for all she cared. Whatever bothered him had nothing to do with her. If he was haunted by images of Meghan's broken body, there was nothing she could do to alleviate his burden.

She swallowed. Nothing.

A low knock reached her ears.

Her hand stilled, and she choked down her cheese. Or at least, she tried to. A bit of it stuck to the roof of her mouth, refusing to budge. "Yeth?" She looked around for something to drink.

The connecting door cracked open. "May I come in?"

All she could do was eke out an *mmm-hmm,* for her attempt to force the cheese down without the aid of a beverage only lodged it deeper in the back of her throat.

A halo of light fanned across the floor, broken only by his large silhouette. Sapphire silk clung to his large frame, outlining every hill and dale of his torso with exotic splendor. His dark hair glistened in the candlelight, revealing his own attempt to be free of the day's tragedy.

Cheese forgotten, she met his eyes. They glowed blue-silver. Even more so after they trailed over her thin chemise, made nearly transparent by her wet hair. She fought the urge to cover herself, unused to such heated scrutiny.

Especially from a man like Lord Somerton, whose passion smoldered beneath the surface like a field of peat gone to flame. Aboveground, all looked normal but for the occasional plume of smoke. However, if one peered below the surface, one would spot the silent advancement of a devastating, all-consuming blaze.

He held out a glass filled with red liquid. "Care to join me?"

"I would love th-o."

Six slow strides later, he bent and offered her refreshment. Fragrant, humid air trailed into the chamber after him. She lifted her nose and inhaled.

"Musk," he said. "A special blend."

She hid her mortification behind the rim of her wine-glass and was relieved when the bothersome piece of cheese washed away without further incident. "With violets, I believe."

"You have a keen sense of smell." His fingers brushed over an untamed portion of her hair. "Do you need help with the tangles?"

Embarrassed by her dishabille, she said, "Are you applying for the part of lady's maid, my lord?"

"If you'll allow it."

Good Lord, he was serious. She stared at him, unsure what to say. *Why, thank you, sir. Most kind.* Or better yet, *Splendid!*

In the end, he took her silence for approval and plucked the comb from her hand. He set his drink on her tray, then made himself comfortable behind her. A bit of rustling occurred before she felt the first tentative tug on her hair.

Heat burned the tips of her ears and cheeks. Her heart thundered so hard that she was certain he must hear it.

After a few experimental strokes, he asked, "Am I hurting you?"

She forced herself to breathe, to close her eyes and sink into the ecstasy of his ministrations. "Not in the least."

He started at the bottom and worked his way up with a patience and dedication to the task that surprised her. When he finished one section, he would begin the process all over again. His big hands were so deliciously gentle, always soothing a hurt, rare though they were.

Once he had dispatched all the knots, he replaced the comb with a soft brush. Long, even strokes, followed by long, gentle caresses. The rhythmic action lulled her into a semiconscious state, easing away her tension. Soon, her body sagged into a more natural curve.

"Better?" He draped her hair over one shoulder, leaving the other one exposed and vulnerable and aching for attention.

"I've never enjoyed a hair brushing more. Thank you."

He kissed the side of her head and rested his cheek there while his arms snaked around her middle. The movement brought her back flush against his chest. Warmth, security, and a desire-filled serenity flooded her body. Today, she had walked in the footsteps of evil. Tonight, she sat in a halo of heaven. Heaven suited her so much better.

She rolled her head to one side, as if she could snuggle farther into the cocoon of his embrace. "I understand you enjoy the sunken garden."

"Of all Bellamere's gardens, the sunken is my favorite." He tipped his head to the side to see her face. "What exactly did Grayson tell you?"

"Who said I received my information from Grayson?"

His arms tautened.

"*Someone* might have mentioned you would hide in the garden to evade your father."

"Someone should not be telling such tales."

Steel underlined his words. "Please don't be upset. It was an idle comment, nothing more."

"I'm not angry." His hold loosened. "Where my father is concerned, I have many conflicting feelings."

"As do I. Many times, as a child, I wondered why my father bothered having a family at all. The Navy seemed to be all he ever needed. Or wanted."

The rhythmic brush of his thumb against her bare arm helped smooth the jagged edges of her memories.

"Mine was bent on turning me into the perfect earl."

"How old were you when your father died?"

"Twelve."

"A child."

"One who grew up rather fast." He released a long breath. "My father knew he was dying and wanted to make sure I was ready to take over the earldom. Had he explained that in the beginning—no matter how difficult—I would have spent far less time in the garden and more time at my desk."

She covered his hand. "He would be proud of the man you are today."

"Perhaps."

"Disappointing my daughter is one of my greatest fears," she whispered.

With a finger to her chin, he nudged her head around until they faced each other. "You're a good mother. No, a wonderful mother. You might get it wrong a few times along the way, but Sophie will never doubt she is loved. That's a mistake you will never make."

She pressed her lips against his. He did not push for a more intimate kiss, but seemed to enjoy the slow exploration, the affirmation of their past hurts, as much as she.

Ending the kiss, she said, "Thank you."

"If that is how you express your gratitude, I will try to come up with nice things to say more often."

They lapsed into a companionable silence for several long minutes.

"Are you thinking of Meghan?" he asked.

"Not at this precise moment, but she is not long from my thoughts."

"I should have forbidden you to join us on the search. It was no place for a woman."

"Nor a man. Besides, I am not so easily commanded, my lord."

In a slow, deliberate motion, he smoothed his hand up her stomach and between her breasts, his fingers skimming across her left nipple. Her back arched and she pressed her head against his shoulder. His hand continued its erotic journey, not stopping until his devilish fingers cradled the exposed side of her neck. "I am forewarned."

As was she. His thumb urged her chin up, and she came to the uncomfortable realization that this man could command her with little effort if he set his mind to it.

He took her lips in a full, melting kiss. For the next several minutes, time held no sway, discovery gave no pause. When he lifted his head, he asked, "Did I manage to take your mind off whatever is troubling you?"

"Yes," she whispered. "But not for long, I'm afraid." She made to sit up, though her boneless body refused to cooperate.

Without a word, he supported her next effort. "I suppose you've recalled your earlier victory and wish to collect."

"With some things, you'll find I am not a patient woman." She rolled to her feet and retrieved her rose-colored wrap from the foot of the bed.

He sighed, grabbing their wineglasses as he stood. "Let us move to my bedchamber, where there is a chair that won't crumble beneath my weight."

She glanced at the feminine chairs dotting the room and smiled at the image of the earl perched on the edge of such dainty furniture. "By all means, my lord."

Guiding her to his suite of rooms, he set their drinks on a small side table separating two large wingback chairs, then strode to the bellpull, giving it two tugs. "I much prefer your use of my name."

Sebastian. A strong name, yet gentle around the edges. Much like its bearer.

He indicated one of the chairs. "Please sit."

After taking the opposite chair, he said, "What I'm about to tell you mustn't leave this room."

She clasped her hands together. "I understand."

"Not good enough, Catherine. I must ask for your word."

"You have it."

"You were right to question the reasons behind your husband's murder."

"He wasn't killed by footpads?"

"No."

"Who killed him?"

"We don't know. I'm hoping the correspondence he sent you will shed some light on the killer's identity."

Even though she had expected foul play, she still had a hard time understanding. "Why would anyone want to harm Geoffrey?"

"Until we know for sure who killed him, I can't answer that question."

"Who is 'we'?"

A muscle jumped in his right cheek. "The Foreign Office."

On some level, she had hoped Mr. Cochran was wrong about the earl's connection to the government. But so far, everything the government official had told her had proven true. "Doesn't that branch of the government handle foreign affairs, rather than domestic?"

He began twirling his signet ring. "I believe we have veered off our original topic, madam."

"Madam, is it?" Her spine straightened. "I disagree. Everything we've discussed is intricately woven together. Tell me, my lord," she said, matching his formality. "Are the facts behind my husband's death a recent revelation, or have you known it wasn't footpads all along?" When he remained silent, she prodded harder. "Were you aware of this when I came to London? When I begged you to read his letters?"

The twirling stopped. "Catherine, it's complicated—"

A knock echoed through the room, making her jump. Although his expression did not change, she sensed the earl's relief at the interruption.

He strode to the door and accepted a covered tray from one of the maids. "After you turn back Mrs. Ashcroft's bed, that will be all tonight."

"Yes, m'lord."

Once the maid was gone, he slid the tray onto the table separating their chairs. "I asked Mrs. Fox to prepare something a little more substantial than fruit and cheese once we finished our baths." He lifted the cover and inhaled. "Smoked salmon and steamed asparagus. I hope you don't mind the casual setting."

With the truth of his deception echoing in her ears, food was anathema. One bite of the delicious-smelling meal and she would spew all over his expensive carpet. "Not at all. But I am no longer desirous of eating."

He re-covered Mrs. Fox's hard work and stood staring at the silver dome, silent and contemplative. "Many times over the years, I have held back information that could bring comfort to the recipient." He impaled her with his gaze. "None have preyed upon my conscience. Until now."

Her heart constricted, for she understood the cost of such an admission. The knowledge did little to soothe the sting of her humiliation, but she was heartened to hear he took no pleasure in his deception.

"I don't understand your silence. Are you trying to protect Geoffrey in some way? Do you fear for my safety? Or is there some other reason?"

"Yes."

She waited for him to expound, to deliver a more satisfying answer. He did not.

Frustrated and suddenly, overwhelmingly tired, she rose. "Since our conversation has all but ground to a halt, I'm for bed. I find I don't have the stamina for this kind of verbal swordplay. It's been a long day."

When she made to walk around him, he blocked her path. "Please stay."

"Will you answer my questions?"

"Isn't it enough to know the true nature of Ashcroft's death and that we're doing everything we can to track down his killer?"

She rubbed her arms. "Believe me, Sebastian, I wish it was enough. I'll be quite happy to have this business behind me."

He laid his palm against her cheek and kissed her with a sweet reverence that made her eyes prickle. "This won't allay your current disappointment," he whispered against her lips, "but I want you to know, all the same."

Surprised to find her hand on his chest, she registered the rhythmic beat of his heart. Too fast, much too fast. "I'm listening."

"If I could tell you more, I would. I swear it."

God help her, she believed him. Believed the struggle he could not quite mask behind his carefully controlled features. She pressed her lips to his palm but said nothing. Something he'd said earlier simply did not make sense. "You work for the Foreign Office in some capacity?"

The muscles beneath her hand flexed. "Yes."

"Then you know whether my husband worked there?"

"I do."

She arched a brow, waiting.

His chest expanded on a deep breath. "He did."

"How could I not know my husband was a spy?"

He moved away. "Who said he was? John Chambers?"

She shrugged. "It seemed a logical conclusion given all that's happened." Cochran's name was on the tip of her tongue, but instinct cautioned her to keep his identity secret for a little while longer.

"Tell me, Sebastian. Once you find Geoffrey's killer, will you then share the full details?"

He picked up his wine. "No."

Her heart plummeted, but she was unsurprised by his answer. She had held on to the tiniest bit of hope that he would eventually provide her with a sense of resolution. Unfortunately, she was still no closer to understanding his involvement with Geoffrey and this Nexus.

The earl might have developed an ephemeral *tendre* for her and might wish to convey the circumstances around her husband's death, but that did not mean he was not the one responsible. Hopefully, Cochran would come through for her in a way Lord Somerton was determined not to.

"I see." Because of his bone-chilling honesty, she managed to send him a polite smile. "In that case, I guess there's nothing left to say but good night."

His lips thinned. "I will see you in the morning."

She strode across the room and entered the connecting chamber, closing the door behind her. She leaned against the solid oak panel and tipped her head back, willing the war inside her body to abate.

Part of her wanted to ignore all the warning signs surrounding Sebastian—the danger, the prevarication, the single-mindedness. Another part of her wanted to pack Sophie up and head to the coast for a much-needed holiday. His actions with her daughter, his tenants, and Meghan McCarthy all pointed to a caring and considerate man. Grayson admired him and Mrs. Fox adored him. Lord Danforth had an easy relationship with him.

All of this still could not account for the secrets he kept or the isolation he lived under. He guarded his emotions with a small infantry. Any tiny chink to his defenses was swiftly replaced by another shield.

She pushed away from the door. A sudden sense of loss blackened her already somber mood. His reticence to confide in her had now forced her to act in a way not to her liking. She must now find her own answers. In doing so, she must violate his trust and set aside her moral principles.

Lowering herself into one of the dainty chairs, she waited.

TWENTY-TWO

With one hand anchored on his hip and the other clutched around a near-empty glass, Sebastian paused in the midst of the sunken garden. Where was that blasted bench?

He squinted into the darkness, twisting this way, then that way. No bench. He took another lurching step, his body listing to the left.

If only this bloody garden would stop moving.

The widow was to blame for his current predicament. Had she not harangued him with question after question, he was certain they would be more agreeably engaged.

In his bed. Naked and sweaty.

Not in a garden cracking his shins on every earthenware container he owned.

He tipped back the rest of his brandy, and this time the amber liquid slid down his throat like liquid silk. His gaze settled on the second floor, on the long balcony framing two sets of double doors. To the right, the countess's bedchamber sat in forbidding darkness, its occupant fast asleep, making his current state all the more laughable.

For nearly two hours, he had tried to find surcease from the image of the McCarthy girl lying in a vat of mud, her mouth agape and her eyes deadened.

He had seen death many times and in various forms. Men, women, sick, poor, elderly, young—no one was immune, all could be sacrificed. Children were the worst, though. Their innocence made them easy targets. Their defenses laughable to predators.

He lifted his glass for another healthy swallow, only to be met with a single drop. He eased his arm back down, the empty glass dangling from his fingertips. Unbidden, his gaze rose to the countess's chamber again. How he wished he could have confided in her. His jaw actually hurt from the strain of keeping his tongue behind his teeth.

One detailed explanation would have been enough to set her mind at ease until the Nexus located Ashcroft's killer. One detailed explanation would have removed the wariness from her eyes and kept her in his bed. One detailed explanation would have exposed an organization whose success depended entirely upon its anonymity.

He rubbed his aching temples, hating his role as chief of the Nexus in a way he never had before. He lifted his glass again and remembered it was empty. Time for a refill.

Shuffling his feet, he made his way up the four steps that led down to his favorite section of the garden. Once there, he could see well enough that he did not have to walk like an old man anymore, although his balance continued to favor one side of his body.

He entered through his study door, banging his shoulder into the frame. Someone cursed at the opposite end of the room. Instinct took over. He dropped into a crouch, away from the open door.

His rapid change in position made his head spin, and

he took precious seconds to shake off his alcohol-induced fog. Once he regained a modicum of clarity, he peered hard into the gloom, searching for shifting shadows and subtle sprays of light. But all remained eerily still. Too still. The air became rife with the intruder's fear.

Setting his glass down, he removed the knife from a hidden sheath on his right arm. Even in his inebriated state, he knew better than to leave the house without protection. With more determination than finesse, he slid from one piece of furniture to the next, closing in on the intruder's location.

Or at least, where he hoped the intruder was hiding. With nothing more than a sliver of moon riding high in the sky, he was operating on instinct alone. His inner guide led him to the darkened corner behind his desk.

Keeping to the shadows, he peered around his desk and listened for the distinctive sounds of life—shuffling feet, shuddering breaths, shaking furniture—while searching the darkness for movement. Nothing. He mentally retraced his steps to the moment he entered the study.

Had he really heard a harsh exclamation? Or was it perhaps his own noisy entrance that he mistook for another? When the possibility gathered merit in his mind, a flush heated his already dampened skin. He straightened from his concealed position, disgusted by his overreaction.

And that's when he caught a familiar scent. A scent that, only a few hours ago, had drenched his senses and made him yearn for a life not his own. A scent that was hers, and hers alone.

Catherine.

Lowering his blade, he sheathed the weapon and moved toward the gloom-filled corner. What had brought her to his study so late at night? Could she not banish the day's events, same as he, and sought solace elsewhere?

His heart slammed against the wall of his chest when he considered another more pleasant reason for coming here. Had she been looking for him? If so, why did she remain quiet?

Then he realized she might not know it was him. He had stumbled into the room from the outside and immediately ducked out of sight. Maybe she thought *he* was the intruder.

At the sound of her faint rasping breaths, he stopped a few feet away. "Care to tell me why you're lurking in the shadows, my dear?"

A cudgel sliced through the space between them, connecting with the side of his knee. He went down on all fours and had only enough time to raise his forearm to protect his head. But his assailant was not interested in bashing his skull.

The cudgel rammed into his lower back. Pain, sharp and debilitating, shot up his spine, arching his vertebrae and throwing him off-balance. He crashed to the floor, incapacitated.

His assailant shuffled closer but was careful to stay out of reach. A low, raspy voice said, "Why, I'm waiting for you, my lord."

Sebastian tried to scramble away, tried to get to his knife. But exhaustion, alcohol, and excruciating pain made him clumsy and slow. A boot slammed into his head, and his face slammed into the rough carpet. His last thought before the night claimed him was of her.

Catherine.

Or, more specifically, her scent.

TWENTY-THREE

Sebastian woke to low murmurings behind him.

"Is he alive, Grayson?" Ethan deBeau asked.

"I believe so, my lord," his butler said. "The doctor is on his way. I dared not move him with such a head injury."

He tried to push himself upright, but his arm would not move and his leg hurt like bloody hell. Images of the brutal attack rushed in. He clenched his jaw. How could he have been caught so unawares?

"Wise decision," Danforth said. "Any idea who did this?"

"None, sir."

"Have you noticed any unusual activity in the area?"

"We did have a peculiar event occur yesterday. A local girl was killed. Lord Somerton and Mrs. Ashcroft found her in the woodland not far from here."

"How did she die?"

"Strangulation. The poor thing was also *enceinte.*"

Opening his eyes, he saw nothing save the bottom of his bookshelf. The more conscious he became, the more aware he became of his body. His right arm was trapped beneath his weight and his neck ached from its twisted position.

"Looks like he's waking, sir."

"Chief." Danforth shook his shoulder. "Can you hear me? Can you get up?"

He winced at the sudden jarring of his arm. "Yes and no," he said through clenched teeth. "My arm."

The viscount eased him onto his back, taking care of Sebastian's useless arm. Blood rushed into his fingertips, releasing angry needles of retribution into his flesh. He flexed his hand, the action clunky and awkward, until feeling returned.

"Grayson, can you fetch his lordship some water?"

Said water materialized in front of Danforth's face. He accepted the butler's offering with a wry look. "Thank you, old chap." To Sebastian, he said, "I'm going to lift your head a little so you can drink. If I hurt you, grunt or something."

The cool liquid soothed his parched throat, and he drank until Danforth forced him to pause for breath. His mouth must have been a big, open, yawning hole while he was unconscious. Not a pleasant image.

"Is everyone else unharmed?" he asked, his thoughts going to Catherine.

"Indeed, sir," Grayson said.

He tried to sit up, but a sharp pain sliced through his lower back.

"Careful," Danforth warned. "You have a nasty bump on the head."

"Your hand," he commanded, ignoring the viscount's warning. Once he was upright, he probed the gash above his temple. Nasty, indeed. "What time is it?"

Danforth checked his timepiece. "A little past eight."

Combing his fingers through his hair, he asked, "Where's Mrs. Ashcroft?"

"She left about an hour ago, my lord," Grayson said. "She mentioned that she'd knocked on your door to relay her plans for the day. When you did not answer, she thought you were overtired from the previous day's events and insisted I leave you be. Your valet reported you missing not long ago."

Danforth whistled low. "You have packed a good deal of activity in the last twenty-four hours. Did you see who assaulted you?"

"No," he said. "The study was dark, the attack swift."

"You recall nothing else? The chap's height, his smell, what he wore, anything?"

"A raspy voice."

"He spoke to you? What'd he say?"

"Something about waiting for me."

"That's it? That's all you remember?"

Another memory niggled at the edge of his addled mind. What was it? Something he noted right before the attack.

A scent.

Not just any scent, but Catherine's.

A pure feminine fragrance he would recognize anywhere. Even inebriated. Had she been meeting with his assailant, or had she been in his study minutes before? If so, why?

"As I said, everything happened so fast." He would not share anything more until he spoke to Catherine. "When did you arrive?"

"Only just." Danforth handed him the rest of the water. "I have news."

The doctor picked that moment to arrive, and Sebastian spent the next hour enduring his ministrations. After the doctor left and the drapes were drawn, he lowered himself into the chair behind his desk and tried to pretend his head was not splitting in two. "What do you have to report?"

"Helsford's informant made mention of a conversation between two gentlemen yesterday in St. Giles." Danforth poured them both a drink before lowering himself into a chair. "Although both wore disguises, they could not completely 'shuck off the stench of quality,' or so his informant said."

"The rookeries are bulging at the seams, but they're still a close-knit community and would be wary of strangers." He pressed a hand against his throbbing thigh. "I take it the meeting had some significance to our present situation."

"The informant believes Lord Latymer was one of the gentlemen. He had the same unusual height, lean build, and straight black hair as the undersuperintendent."

His jaw tightened at the mention of his former friend and superior at the Alien Office. Latymer had plotted with the French to kill him in order to cripple the Nexus in a desperate attempt to protect Napoleon. He still did not understand why Latymer would turn his back on his countrymen or on such a promising career within the Foreign Office.

"Do we have his location?"

"No. He put his training to good use and lost his tail within ten minutes."

"And the other gentleman?"

"Identity unknown. We have only a description—English, blond, and a peculiar tendency toward violence. If not for Helsford's informant, the barmaid he took a liking to would no doubt be dead now, or wishing for death."

He gritted his teeth, sending an arrow of pain through his skull. Men who preyed upon those weaker than they sank below the level of vermin in his estimation. They were nothing more than scavengers, afraid of their own shadow, though always trying to convince the world they were gods.

"Did the informant hear anything of note?"

The viscount's gaze slid toward the door, his look pensive. When he turned back, he asked, "What do you know of your pretty neighbor?"

Dread slammed into his chest. "Little, besides the fact that she was Ashcroft's wife and has a six-year-old daughter." *And she frees my soul with a single touch of her lips.*

"The men spoke in low tones, so the informant was unable to glean the entire conversation. However, one of spoke of 'the widow' several times and there appeared to be a sense of urgency in their conversation."

"Do you know how many widows there are in England?" He could not keep the derision from his tone. The pressure inside his skull increased with each passing second, making it hard for him to concentrate and even harder to curb his impatience.

"Quite a few, I imagine," Danforth said, unperturbed. "But not so many associated with you."

"My name was mentioned?"

Danforth nodded, cocking his head to the side. "This is the second time Helsford's informant has come to your rescue. Anything I should know?"

At a critical moment during their last mission, he had received an anonymous note of caution. Had the warning come ten minutes later, he would have made a terrible mistake.

"Your question is better put to Helsford. I have no notion as to the identity of his informant or why the individual would want to help me." He considered his next words carefully. "But I am questioning Superintendent Reeves's sudden interest in our agents and his decision to banish me to the country."

"You think Reeves is in league with Latymer?"

"Coincidences do occur, but I can't ignore the logic linking the two men together."

"Might explain some of what Helsford deciphered from Ashcroft's letters."

"How so?"

"Ashcroft spoke of his suspicions about a double spy in the superintendent's office. In the last letter of the second packet you delivered, Ashcroft believed he had isolated the traitor and that the man was a liaison to Latymer."

"Did he provide a name?"

"Not in the letters we have."

"You think there are more?"

"It's possible, or the traitors learned what Ashcroft was up to and killed him before he had the chance to identify the double spy in a final letter."

"Or a combination of both."

"There is that." Danforth angled his neck one way, then the other. "Who else at the Foreign Office knew of Reeves's request?"

"No one, as far as I know. Reeves gave me his word that he would be the only other official to see the list of operatives."

"Damn me." Danforth bolted back a drink.

"Find Latymer and expand your investigation to include Reeves. Be careful, Danforth. Reeves is a spy among spies, dangerous and cunning."

"Yes, sir." The viscount flicked something off his coat sleeve. "Does it not disturb you?"

"A great many things disturb me. What exactly are you referring to?"

"Knowing powerful people are plotting your death."

"Of course, it does." He lifted his own spirits to his lips, then recalled his inability to subdue his enemy last night, with Catherine in the house. He set the drink aside. "But it's a circumstance I've operated under since becoming chief more than a decade ago."

"Allow me to send for a few guards. As a precaution."

The viscount, along with Cora and Helsford, had argued long and hard against his refusal to bring guards to Bellamere, but he wanted to spend his time in the country in relative peace and isolation.

He had not counted on Bellamere being in disarray, and he certainly had not counted on Catherine.

"The addition of guards would alert anyone who might be watching that I suspect something's amiss. Get me something to work with—find Latymer, identify his companion, and increase your efforts where Reeves is concerned. Rule nothing out."

He thought back to the afternoon when he saw a blond-haired man leaving Winter's Hollow. A friend of Ashcroft's—John Chambers—or so Catherine had said. But something in her tone, possibly the slight hesitation before she answered, made him question the veracity of her answer. What possible reason would she have for lying to him?

"Do me a favor," he said. "See if you can track down any information on a John Chambers."

"Where does he fit into all this?"

"Unknown, at the moment. He might be somehow acquainted with Ashcroft."

"Anything else?"

He rubbed his forehead and squeezed the bridge of his nose, not liking what he was about to do but knowing he would do it anyway. He clasped his hands together on his desk. "Find out if Mrs. Ashcroft met with anyone besides me while in London and see if you can identify the gentleman who paid her a visit three days ago."

"John Chambers, I take it?" Danforth asked.

"Yes." He sagged back in his chair, feeling more tired than he could ever remember being. If he could just close his eyes for a few minutes, perhaps the pain in his head would ease. "Notify me once you've learned more."

"Somerton, about you and Mrs. Ashcroft—"

"Don't."

Danforth's mouth clamped shut.

"Your concern is appreciated. Let us continue to act, rather than react." He considered Danforth's tendency for rash action. "Keep a level head about this."

The viscount nodded, no doubt recalling the time he had not followed orders and had placed his loved ones in danger. "What if the trail leads back to Ashcroft's widow?"

"Tell me, but leave her to me." Sparks of white light flashed across his vision, and he fought to clear them away.

Danforth stood. "I'll report back once I have more information." He strode toward the door, but his steps slowed until he finally stopped.

He knew what his agent was about before he ever turned around. Danforth never backed down from a fight, especially when the skirmish involved someone he cared for.

"Listen, about the widow—"

"Save it, Danforth. I will keep my wits about me. Now, be gone." He fought to keep his eyelids open. "And be careful. I have no wish to feel your sister's wrath."

Danforth stood his ground, revealing a hint of his legendary stubbornness. "Grayson mentioned a dead girl at your doorstep."

"A domestic issue, nothing more," he lied. "Besides, she was hardly found at my doorstep."

The viscount snorted. "I have never known you to be so blind to your surroundings."

He pressed a hand against his roiling stomach and shook his head in a vain attempt to focus his blurred vision. "Mind who you are speaking to, Danforth..." His eyes rolled back in his head and he pitched forward.

TWENTY-FOUR

The pleasant breeze blowing across the lake did nothing to alleviate Catherine's concern for Sebastian. This morning, after failing to rouse him from slumber, she had gone on to meet with each of the craftsmen and returned to report her progress. That's when she had received the unwelcome news from Lord Danforth that Sebastian was unwell.

Not considering the impropriety of her request, she had asked to see him. The viscount refused, and her angry reaction ignited an argument that continued to ring in her ears, even hours later.

"Mama, you have that funny look again."

She glanced down at her daughter. They sat on a large flat rock at the lake's edge, their bare feet dangling in the murky water below. "What look is that, dear?"

Sophie shrugged. "I don't know. It's the same one Papa used to get when he sat alone in the library."

An image of Geoffrey's faraway expression materialized. She knew it well. In the beginning, she had wondered about it, had often asked him about its source. But after so many evasions and insulting quips, she had stopped wondering and asking.

"I'm sorry, Sophie. I learned this morning that Lord Somerton was not feeling well, so my thoughts had turned toward his recovery."

"May we take him some of the biscuits Cook and I made last night?"

How she loved this little girl. "That's very thoughtful. We'll send them along with a note, inquiring about his lordship's welfare." She kissed the top of her daughter's head. "I have a surprise for you."

Sophie lit with delight. "A surprise for me?" She tore off a piece of bread and tossed it into the water.

"Smaller bits, pumpkin. You don't want the fish to mistake our toes for your bread."

"Yes, Mama." She followed words to action. "Do I have to wait until Saturday?"

"I'm afraid so."

Her little face fell. "Oh, I wish you hadn't told me. I will go *mad* thinking about my surprise."

"In that case, I probably shouldn't tell you that it has to do with Bellamere's stables." She still found Sebastian's change of heart amazing. One day he did not want her daughter underfoot, and the next he was inviting Sophie into his inner sanctum.

"The *earl's* stables?" Sophie dropped the whole slice of bread in the lake and clambered up on her knees to squeeze Catherine's face between her grubby hands. "Tell me about the stables, Mama. Please, oh, please, oh, please."

She laughed, hugging her daughter to her, but the horse-crazed girl was having none of it.

"Mama, this is *serious*." Her daughter's breath caught and her eyes widened in excitement. "Am I going inside?"

Nodding, she said, "At Lord Somerton's personal invitation."

"You mean I don't have to sneak in?"

"Have you?"

"No, but Teddy and I have been plotting ways to see the earl's horses."

She bit her lip and forced her features into stern lines. "No, young lady." She gave her daughter a little shake to emphasize her point. "There will be no sneaking in anywhere. Lord Somerton will personally introduce you to his horses."

Sophie whooped as she threw her arms around Catherine's neck and pressed a dozen smacking kisses on her face. "Must I wait until Saturday? I will *die* with antishipation."

"Yes, you do." She tweaked her daughter's nose. "And where is all this drama coming from?"

"What do you mean, 'drama'?"

She settled her daughter more comfortably across her lap and pulled a cucumber sandwich from the nearby basket. "You are experiencing some extreme emotions, my dear. *Mad, serious, die.* Quite unlike you." More than normal, she amended.

"Oh, that," she said around a mouthful. "Eloisa Walker's older sister is very sophishticated. She knows all the important words."

"Well, if you're going to mimic your elders, you must listen carefully. You will die with *anticipation* and Eloisa's older sister is very *sophisticated*."

She nodded her head. "Yes, exactly."

Although the Walkers had a penchant for gossip, they treated Sophie as one of their own. With four girls and three boys, the Walkers provided her daughter something she never could—brothers and sisters.

She had always wanted a large family, not as large as the Walkers', but three or four children would have brought her immense joy and, when the time came, many grandchildren. Being an only child herself, she understood the challenges Sophie faced.

"Mama, who is that man?"

She jerked her head up, her thoughts going to Sebastian. Even though they had been apart for less than a day, she looked forward to seeing him again and feeling his strong arms wrapped around her. She examined one side of the lake to the other, but saw no familiar—or otherwise— masculine figure. "I don't see anyone, dear."

Sophie pointed her half-eaten sandwich at a cluster of trees and tall bushes to their right. Pushing her daughter's hand down, she tried to piece together greens and browns and pale yellows into a recognizable form. When she was on the verge of giving up, something stirred, and she realized she was looking too high.

She concentrated harder until finally a face emerged. Bulbous, watery eyes, wide forehead, thin, greasy hair, and yellow, neglected teeth. Her blood froze in her veins.

The disgusting little man from the butcher's shop had visited her thoughts often since their first encounter. Each time, her uneasiness grew. And now, he was in their private sanctuary, observing them with an unholy gleam in his eyes. But who was he and why was he following them?

With a surreptitious sweep of the area, she considered their options. He had picked his location well. In order to return to the house, she would have to pass his hiding spot. She could take the southern footpath, but that would lead them through a dense woodland before turning back east. The isolated nature of the route troubled her more than walking by the man.

She could head west, to Sebastian's estate, even though that way lay an uncertain welcome. But, like the southern route, the west footpath would still take them past the stranger.

"Do you see him, Mama?"

"Yes, pumpkin." She set her daughter away. "Put on your stockings and shoes, please."

"Must we go? I want to hear more about my surprise."

"Do as I say, and we will discuss it all you want. Up at the house."

Catching the note of authority in Catherine's voice, her daughter ended her protest and hurried to comply. Catherine picked up her own discarded footwear. When they were ready to go, she knelt down in front of her daughter. "Listen closely, sweetheart, but do not be alarmed." She waited for her daughter's nod. "We're going to walk past that man, but I do not want you to speak with him or acknowledge him in any way. Is that understood?"

"Uh-huh," Sophie said, looking toward the man's location.

"That includes staring."

Sophie's eyes flashed to Catherine's. In a stage whisper, she said, "Is he a bad man? Papa warned me about them."

"I don't know." Why were the men in her life never around when she needed them? "And I don't intend to find out today." She glanced around the area to make sure they had retrieved all of their belongings. "Ready?"

Her daughter tunneled her hand into Catherine's. "Ready."

She kept their pace steady and sure, chatting along the way to help keep Sophie's attention on other things, rather than the man who followed their every move. It didn't help. Curious by nature, her daughter could not stop glancing toward the clump of shrubbery protecting the man from her inquisitive eyes.

"What did I tell you, young lady?" She followed the query with a gentle pull-squeeze of her daughter's hand.

Sophie whipped her head around so fast that Catherine was surprised she didn't hear it snap.

"Don't talk to him or gape at him."

Sophie peeked over her shoulder. "But, Mama, he's following us now."

Catherine halted mid-stride. Her heart plummeted all the way down to her toes. When it started the slow, sluggish ride back up to her chest, a wave of murderous rage licked through her veins. She stashed Sophie behind her and met the man's eerie gaze.

He stood thirty feet away, watchful and patient. He neither spoke, nor indicated chagrin for having been caught. Nor did he move.

"What do you want, sir?"

His head tilted to the side like a dog's did when considering the best way to pounce on a cat. He didn't respond, only pointed toward her house.

She glanced between Winter's Hollow and the dreadful man, trying to understand his unspoken message. The attempt only confused her more.

Grabbing her daughter's hand, she resumed their march to Bellamere, but at a much faster pace. She nudged her daughter in front of her, aiming to keep herself between Sophie and the silent man.

He cut them off.

"Stand aside, sir," she said. "We're on our way to meet with Lord Somerton."

Shaking his head, he once again indicated the path leading them to Winter's Hollow.

As her grip tightened around Sophie's small hand, a keen sense of vulnerability shook her to the core. She had no options. Though he was a small man, she detected a wiry strength about him. If they tried to run, he would catch them.

"Mama," Sophie whispered.

The strange man's eyes narrowed, and he stepped forward.

Making up her mind, she gave her daughter's hand a reassuring squeeze and trudged toward Winter's Hollow, praying she had not sentenced them to a terrible fate. An image of Meghan McCarthy's broken body surfaced, and her terror knew no bounds. Had this man killed the girl? Was he the elusive father? She shoved aside the repulsive thought.

When they reached the garden, she glanced back and found their tormentor gone. She hurried them through the gate and into the back door of the house. Once she clicked the lock in place, she felt a measure of relief until her maid Mary entered and announced that she had a visitor. "A Mr. Cochran to see you, ma'am."

She kissed Sophie's forehead. "All is well now, sweetheart. Run along upstairs and change your clothes while I speak to our guest. I'll be up in a little while to check on you." She turned her daughter around and nudged her toward the servants' staircase.

Her daughter pinched the sides of her frock, looking for splats of dirt and bits of grime. "Mama, there's nothing wrong with this dress."

"No, there's not. But it's your play dress, not your house dress. Up you go."

Sophie groaned. Her progress up the narrow stairs had all the signs of a convict headed to the gallows.

"Mary, please see Miss Sophie to the nursery."

"*Oh, Mama.*"

Catherine allowed herself a small smile as she watched the two make their way up to the first landing. Once they turned the corner, she rushed to the window to peer outside. She searched tree to tree, building to building, shadow to shadow. But nothing moved or appeared out of place. Everything seemed oddly untouched, yet frightfully violated.

She checked the lock on the kitchen door again and made her way to the drawing room. When she entered, she found the Foreign Office official lounging on her sofa, an easy expression on his handsome face. "Mr. Cochran, this is an unexpected surprise." *Again.* After their last meeting, she had not looked forward to their next.

He did not rise to greet her. "Good afternoon, Mrs. Ashcroft. I'm afraid our former timeline has been compromised. Have you the list?"

She strode farther into the room. "There is no list, sir."

"What do you mean?"

"I had occasion last evening to search his lordship's library, study, and even his bedchamber, and none contained a list of secret agents." The only names she found were the two tucked under the earl's ink blotter— Sebastian Danvers and Geoffrey Ashcroft. Hardly a list.

"Yes," he said with a slight curl to his upper lip. "I heard you spent the night with Somerton."

She squared her shoulders. "Perhaps the intelligence you received regarding Lord Somerton's involvement with the Nexus was wrong."

"I can assure you, the information I shared with you is quite accurate."

"Maybe his lordship has not compiled the list yet."

"Could it be that you have not looked well enough?"

"Where else would I search, sir? Based on what I have witnessed, Lord Somerton is not a threat to anyone. Quite the contrary, actually. He's been nothing but helpful to those in need. What you are accusing him of simply makes no sense."

"All men, even those with evil intent, have a weakness. It is how governments do business, madam. They find the other's weakness and exploit it." Clasping his hands together, he steepled his two forefingers and tapped them against his lips, considering her for a moment. "The better question here is which one of the Ashcroft women is Lord Somerton's greatest weakness?"

His considering look sent a rush of wary tingles down her spine. Why had she never noticed his piglet eyes before? "What can you mean, sir?"

A pregnant pause, then the official's face split into an affable smile. "I mean nothing at all. My mind tends to venture off course at the most inconvenient times."

Drawing in a deep breath, she said, "Sir, I have made a gross miscalculation in my eagerness to bring my husband's killer to justice. I can no longer assist you in this endeavor."

"That is not good news, my dear. Is there nothing I can do to change your mind?"

She shook her head. "I'm sorry to have wasted your time."

Cochran rose from his chair, pulling at the sleeves of his forest green coat to smooth out the wrinkles. "This exercise wasn't a waste of time, madam." He strode toward the door. "It's always best to attempt the path of least resistance, don't you agree?"

She stared at him, not understanding his cryptic remark. "Excuse me?"

His eyes crinkled at the corners. "Give me but a moment and I'll explain." He turned and disappeared down the corridor.

When the front door opened, she made her way to the window overlooking the small circular drive. Outside Cochran's carriage stood a short, wiry man with a balding pate interspersed with clumps of stringy brown hair.

Recognition crashed into her chest like an angry bull trying to breach a fence. Cochran joined the stranger, jabbing a thumb over his shoulder as he spoke. While the little man listened, his gaze rose to meet hers.

She stepped back, her throat closing around a string of questions. What was going on? What was Cochran doing with this man? Was it all coincidental? Or was there something more sinister afoot?

Craning her head around the drapery, she watched Cochran open the carriage door and reach inside—

A door slammed, then the sound of pounding boots running up the stairs stopped her heart cold.

Sophie.

She flew across the drawing room and into the corridor while her mind frantically attempted to understand what was going on. When she reached the staircase, it was empty.

Lifting the hem of her dress, she ran after the intruder.

"Not so fast, Mrs. Ashcroft."

She whipped around to find Cochran reentering her house with a pretty sable-haired woman on his arm. The woman's expression indicated she was not pleased with the situation any more than Catherine.

"What is going on?" She inched her way up one step, then another. "Mr. Cochran, who are these people? Why have you brought them into my home?"

He passed her, up the stairs. "In due time, madam."

She followed his gaze. Nothing.

A feminine screech sounded from above.

Mary.

Her fear—barely controlled—unleashed, and she bolted up the stairs.

"Stop," Cochran ordered. "Silas won't hurt them. No guarantees, though, if you charge up there."

She halted, gasping for air. Every instinct she owned urged her onward, but Cochran's threat kept her pinned in place, helpless in a way she had never experienced before. She heard Sophie's furious voice a moment before the little man—Silas—appeared, dragging her resisting daughter down the corridor.

"*Sophie.*" She started after her daughter, but a large hand grasped her arm.

Cochran's cold gaze met hers. "I told you. My man has everything under control."

"Mama!"

Silas slung Sophie over his shoulder. Her small hands pounded against his back, shoulders, head, anything she could reach. "Let me down, you rabbity beast."

Catherine jerked hard on her arm and winced when pain shot up to her shoulder. She clawed at Cochran's restraining grip, and his other hand grasped her throat, forcing her chin into an unnatural angle.

"I said stay."

"Mama!"

Unable to move her head, her eyes found her daughter. "Be still, Sophie." Her fear for her daughter's safety was as palpable as the hands restraining her. "Mama will take care of everything."

Cochran chuckled, his thumb raking across her lips. "Will you, indeed?"

"Release me at once." Her sight was becoming blurrier by the second.

His nails bit into her neck for a long moment before he pushed her down the stairs.

Sophie yelled.

She scrambled for purchase, her world a whirl of images until she caught the balustrade. Cochran came up behind her, grasping her arm and towing her the rest of the way down, giving her no time to catch her breath. She tried to keep her daughter in sight, but failed.

"Mama!"

"Be strong, Sophie." She twisted around to meet her daughter's frightened gaze. "It will be all right."

"Do you promise?"

When she hesitated a moment too long, her perceptive daughter struggled in earnest, kicking and pounding on her captor.

"Say it, Mama. Say it."

"Quiet," Silas ordered with a hard shake.

"Leave her alone," she demanded, fighting Cochran's grip.

Silas's scold did nothing more than stun her daughter into speechlessness for a half second. Enough time for Cochran to yank hard on Catherine's arm, making her cry out and forcing her toward the drawing room.

Away from Sophie.

TWENTY-FIVE

Catherine stared into her daughter's wary blue eyes as her six-year-old scooted her small frame back into the chair's cushioned seat.

"That's a good girl, Sophie." Cochran patted her narrow shoulder, acting as though she had been invited down to the drawing room, rather than packed down like a sack of potatoes. "Thank you for joining us."

His sly smile made Catherine's stomach cramp.

"Now then, where were we, Mrs. Ashcroft? Oh, yes, I remember. You wished to discontinue your involvement in our little investigation." He smoothed his hand over her daughter's blond curls. "I hope I've provided sufficient inducement for you to press on."

"*Inducement?*" Her daughter spat out the word, no doubt recalling her grandmama's various incentives.

"Not now, Sophie." Her gaze returned to Cochran. "Yes, more than sufficient. Now may my daughter return to the nursery?"

His hands folded over her daughter's tiny shoulders,

looking more like manacles of death than objects of comfort. "But I'm enjoying her company."

His threat could not have been clearer. Because of Catherine's moment of conscience, Sophie would now be used as a tool to ensure her mother's good behavior.

"All men, even those with evil intent, have a weakness. It is how governments do business, madam. They find their opponent's weakness and exploit it."

Cochran's prophetic words returned to haunt her. How had she missed the depravity lurking behind the official's piglet eyes? Did he even work for the government? Doubtful. She must consider everything he had told her up to this moment to be a lie, including Sebastian's involvement with the French.

Sebastian.

What a fool she had been. How could she have even for a moment thought he was a double agent. The man's honor was a solid as an oak.

"I'm eager to hear how you're going to obtain the list, Mrs. Ashcroft. Spare us no details."

At the use of the term "us," she remembered the others in the room. The sable-haired woman hovered near the door and the frightening man—Silas—kept vigil next to her chair.

At first glance, Silas appeared to be in his late fifties with his hunched shoulders, unsteady gait, and thinning brown hair. But on closer inspection, she noticed his eyes and mouth did not carry the deep grooves so common of that age. No, this drab man could not be more than a half-dozen years beyond her nine and twenty.

Sophie squirmed beneath Cochran's hold.

"Please allow my daughter to go upstairs," she pleaded once more. Cochran's hulking presence so near to her baby sent a shiver of debilitating dread through her. How in Heaven's name would she get them out of this?

He leaned forward, and his thick lips spoke near Sophie's temple. "Mrs. Ashcroft? We're waiting."

She unlocked her ankles and gripped her knees with shaking hands. What did he want from her? She had already searched every room where she thought Sebastian would keep private papers.

Cochran considered her for a moment, then lowered his mouth to Sophie's ear. "Your mother holds out hope that she has a choice in the matter. It's best to clear up such misconceptions at the onset." He straightened and spoke to his female companion. "Mrs. Clarke, stoke the fire. Our fine summer weather has taken a turn, especially during these cloudless afternoons. I don't want the ladies to catch a chill."

A flush of cold panic coated her palms. She glanced from Mrs. Clarke bending over the fire to Cochran's dispassionate gaze to Sophie's pale face and felt the stabilized world she had erected for her daughter break apart.

She pushed up from her chair, intending to go to Sophie, to offer what comfort she could, but Silas clamped a hand around her neck, forcing her back into her seat.

"It is best you stay seated, Mrs. Ashcroft," Cochran said.

"M-mama?" Sophie's voice cracked.

Silas's fingers tightened on her neck, making her wince. She stared into her daughter's uncertain eyes—a look so uncharacteristic of the imp whose escapades kept everyone in the household on guard—and a weighty helplessness held her immobile while her brave girl contorted her body to elude Cochran's despicable touch.

She balled her hands into painful knots as the weight

on her chest grew heavier. She pulled in a calming breath, one that barely registered, then forced a reassuring smile. "Do not fret, pumpkin. Mama will take care of everything. I promise."

While the lie burned in her throat, she watched as Sophie visibly relaxed, having no reason to believe her mother would fail. She never had before. But Catherine knew this time was different. A palpable evil had entered their home, one she was ill-equipped to fight.

Cochran directed his attention toward the pulsing coals. "You did well with the fire, Mrs. Clarke."

The woman averted her face.

Bending forward, he rubbed the backs of his fingers across Sophie's rounded cheek. "Can you feel the fire's warmth, *pumpkin?*"

Catherine's eyes welled with tears.

Sophie scrunched up her pert nose and leaned away from his caress. "It's hot."

"Is it?" His careless tone belied his concern. "Let's ask your mama. Do you think the fire's hot enough, Mrs. Ashcroft?"

Her throat closed around a useless scream. Besides Mary, who had nowhere to go, the servants had all gone home to spend time with their families, as they did every Tuesday afternoon. It was the only time she truly had Sophie all to herself. Even her mother had gone out to visit with friends. Had Cochran known they would be alone?

He must have. How else could he be so calm, so unconcerned?

She fought the urge to close her eyes, to wish this nightmare away. If anything happened to Sophie—

Swallowing hard, she cut the thought short and allowed her anger to build. She thought back to all the achingly lonely nights she had spent waiting for Geoffrey, all the times her daughter searched the drive for her father.

She thought about how she would kill these men for threatening her baby.

"I will do what needs to be done," she said.

Cochran eyes lifted to Silas before returned to her. "I am not convinced. Mrs. Clarke?"

The sable-haired woman stared at the fire, unmoving.

"Mrs. Clarke, need I remind you—"

"No, Mr. Cochran." The woman turned bleak eyes to the fire and bent to retrieve the red-tipped poker. She turned toward Sophie.

"No!" Catherine catapulted herself out of the chair.

Clawlike fingernails raked across her skin as Silas lost his grip. His other hand swept around, seizing the coil of hair pinned at the back of her head, yanking her to a painful halt. A cry of shock-pain escaped her throat and her body bowed backward.

"Let me go!" Keeping her burning gaze on the glowing poker, she made mad swipes at the hand entrenched in her hair. A couple of her nails connected with flesh, and her captor jerked hard in retaliation, sending her sprawling back into her seat. He did not release his hold.

"Leave my mama alone!" Sophie cried, fighting against Cochran's restraint. Tears streamed down her terrified face.

Unable to free herself, Catherine tightened her grip on her captor's wrist while she warned Cochran. "Leave her be, you brute." To her daughter, she said, "Sit still, pumpkin. Mama's fine."

She caught Cochran's eye. "I'll tear apart every room, ask questions, eavesdrop on conversations. I'll revisit his bedchamber. *Whatever* it takes." A mother's determination bolstered her tone. "I swear it."

Silence followed her declaration. She focused on Cochran and awaited his verdict with thundering ears. Her daughter's broken cries sliced through her heart yet strengthened her resolve.

Finally, Cochran nodded, releasing Sophie at the same time Catherine's captor withdrew his painful grip on her hair.

She barely had time to sit up before her daughter launched herself into her arms. She hugged Sophie's small, trembling body, keeping a cautious eye on her uninvited guests.

"It's time I formally introduce you to my lovely assistant." Cochran gestured to the woman. "Mrs. Clarke will join your household until you have completed your task."

"Whatever for?"

"Insurance, of course."

A gaoler.

Now that the woman no longer held the hot poker, she appeared stern and uncompromising.

"How am I to explain her presence?"

His gaze sketched over her daughter, who now fought Catherine's protective hold to see the other woman. "I'm sure you'll agree that your daughter could use a bit of refinement. Mrs. Clarke will make an excellent governess."

Sophie shook her head. "No, Mama. I don't want her."

A lump formed in her throat. He expected her to hand over her daughter to this woman? To this unsmiling creature who would no doubt report her every move and would do God knew what to her daughter?

"I see your apprehension, Mrs. Ashcroft. You've no need to worry. Mrs. Clarke is quite good with children." He smirked at the other woman. "Isn't that right, dear?"

"Yes, Mr. Cochran."

"You see, there's no call for concern."

She tried to reason with him one more time. "I can do this without your insurance."

"No doubt. Mrs. Clarke, take the girl to the nursery."

She tightened her hold around Sophie. Now that the immediate danger had passed, she did not want to lose sight of her daughter. As long as she could see Sophie, she could maintain the illusion of control.

Mrs. Clarke approached Catherine's chair and held out her hand. "Miss Sophie, come show me your toys."

Catherine stared at the woman's outstretched fingers, noted their slight tremble. The woman did too, and dropped her arm, fisting her hand.

Interesting.

But her daughter had already shied away, clutching Catherine's face between tiny hands that smelled like dirt and worms. "No, Mama," she pleaded, her eyes filling with tears. "I p-promise to behave. *I promise.*"

She could barely speak around the tears clawing at the inside of her throat. Resting her forehead against her daughter's, she squeezed her eyes shut.

Lord, give her strength.

Sophie pushed against Catherine's cheeks, cutting her prayer short. She bent to capture Catherine's gaze. "Please, Mama. I want to stay with you."

Managing a wobbly smile, she said, "I love you, pumpkin. I love you just the way you are. Never forget it. Now cover your ears." She waited for her daughter to comply before lifting her gaze to Mrs. Clarke. "You harm one hair on my daughter's head and you will come to regret it. Understood?"

A stark emotion crossed the woman's face before she gave Catherine a swift nod.

Drawing in a bracing breath, she eased her daughter's hands away from her ears. "You must go with Mrs. Clarke."

"*No.*" Sophie wrapped her amazingly strong arms around Catherine's neck. "No, I don't want to go."

She noticed Cochran's patience had come to an end. His message was clear—if she could not control her daughter, he would. And soon.

With a mother's gentle strength, she unwound Sophie's arms and set her back. "Sophia Adele Ashcroft," she said in her sternest voice. "Stop this nonsense at once."

"But, Mama—"

"Enough." Her heart broke with each harsh word. "You will go with Mrs. Clarke now, or you'll be forbidden to ride Guinevere for an entire month."

Her daughter's eyes widened in wounded horror, and the remaining pieces of Catherine's heart shattered.

Sophie adored her pony. The two were caught more than once tearing across the open field near the stables. To her daughter, a month without Guinevere would be like a month without sustenance.

Scrambling off her lap, Sophie stood before her with her arms locked at her side and her nostrils flaring with each angry breath. "You can't do that. Papa gave her to me."

Irritation abraded her nerves. She had done what she could to preserve Sophie's memory of her father, and to his credit, Geoffrey had never forgotten his daughter's birthday. Lavish gifts arrived on time every year to honor her birth—and to soften the sting of another missed celebration.

As a result, Sophie worshiped her father, and she would have it no other way. But her daughter's choice to invoke her father's so-called wishes against her cut deeper than her husband's abandonment had.

Cochran moved to stand next to Mrs. Clarke.

Hardening her resolve, Catherine sat forward in her chair and pointed toward the door. "Go. *Now*."

Her intelligent girl recognized her I'm-through-talking tone and ran from the room, leaving Mrs. Clarke to follow at a more sedate pace.

When the door closed, Cochran threw something onto her lap. She glanced down and recognized Sophie's lost figure, a kilted warrior holding a two-handed claymore.

Ice wrapped around her heart. How did he have this in his possession? Silas had not moved from his position behind her, so he could not have given the toy to him.

Which meant Cochran had been in Sophie's bedchamber.

"Finish what you started, Mrs. Ashcroft, or I will take more from your daughter than a mere toy."

TWENTY-SIX

Sebastian's bedchamber door closed behind a reluctant Danforth. After watching him succumb to the effects of a concussion, the viscount had not been keen on leaving. Sebastian had spent the last half hour convincing the agent that his efforts were better spent in London, tracking down their enemy, than playing nursemaid.

He propped his bare feet atop the sitting room's ottoman, unhappy to realize the laudanum the physician had prescribed was wearing off. Much to his relief, his nausea had dissipated; however, a dull throb continued to batter his brain, lower back, and behind his left knee.

His assailant had known what he was about. With three swift and violent strikes, he had incapacitated a seasoned agent, who knew a score of ways to kill a man—when not in his cups.

Tilting his head back, he gave in to the bone-deep weariness that had invaded his body. For someone who was rarely sick and needed little sleep, his current condition put him in a sour mood. That Catherine had not bothered to check on him all day had nothing to do with his present foul temper. Nothing at all.

He closed his eyes and the relief was instant. The candlelight glowed bright enough to be a nuisance, and he still had a difficult time focusing. Once the muscles in his face relaxed and the tautness in his shoulders eased, he allowed his mind to wander. Allowed it to seek a source of calm and tranquility. Most times when he performed this exercise, he would find himself standing at the bow of a fast-moving ship, heading toward the sunrise, the rejuvenating buff of a sea breeze sliding along his skin.

But not this time. This time, his mind moved inexorably to Catherine, to her mischievous eyes and honey-gold hair. To her berry-red lips and God-blessed figure he had yet to fully explore.

Last night, when he found her sitting on the hearth rug, brushing her hair and eating bits of cheese, a feeling of completion had overcome him. Images of them making love, sharing a steaming tub of water, and idling away hours on the balcony while admiring a moonless night drenched his mind.

He had wanted to make love to her so badly last night, but could not break free of the secrets he was sworn to keep. Caution had been his bedmate for many years and discretion had never let him down.

Even so, he had nearly given in to her plea for information. Had nearly laid out everything he knew of her husband. How brave he had been. How he had saved so many lives. How devastating Ashcroft's death had been for him.

But all those confessions would lead her to the Nexus, exposing his agents to unforeseen perils. Something he would never do while chief, and never allow her to do.

He prayed she had not become involved in his war with Latymer. In her single-minded attempt to seek justice for her husband's murder, she might have inadvertently stepped inside Latymer's web.

He had learned long ago that what lies within one's heart is often hidden behind the best defenses. But, as he told Danforth, he would rule nothing out. For all he knew, Latymer could have sent her to him in London. A fraud from day one.

Perhaps that was what motivated her to help him with estate matters. Observe him, make note of his weaknesses, draw out information—one kiss at a time. His body constricted against the thought. She had been dealing with his tenants long before Reeves's request.

His lungs released a shuddering breath, and the distinct urge for oblivion returned. He toyed with the idea of pouring himself a drink, then recalled his vulnerable state last night and pushed it away. He would not endanger those beneath his charge for a few hours of numbness. He eased up from his chair, stretching his back and testing his injured leg.

With more hobble than stride, he made his way over to the bank of high-ceiling windows and peeled back one of the drapes. He was grateful to see the onset of evening. Swirling hues of pink, orange, and yellow rode low on the horizon, bringing an otherwise dismal day to a gracious end.

He wondered how Catherine's meetings with the craftsmen had gone and if she had stopped by the McCarthys' to offer whatever solace she could. Regret weighed heavily on his mind. He should have been with her. Neither task was hers to bear alone.

A low knock sounded at the bedchamber door, then an

exchange of words ensued. Seconds later, his valet appeared in the sitting room doorway. "My lord," Parker said in a near whisper. "Mrs. Ashcroft is here to see you."

She came.

With his heart hammering inside his chest, he said, "Show her in."

Parker eyed his attire. "Sir, perhaps you'd like to avail yourself of a shirt and trousers first? Stockings and neck-cloth, too?"

"No need to whisper around me any longer, Parker. The pain is down to a tolerable ache."

"Very well, my lord." He hesitated, eyeing Sebastian's black silk banyan. "And the other?"

"This will do."

Parker made a pained expression and disappeared. The next several minutes seemed an eternity while he waited for Catherine to appear. Why had she chosen this moment to check on him? Why not hours ago when her cool palm could have soothed his splitting head?

He stretched his neck and rolled his shoulders. The exercise relieved some of his tension but failed to calm his heart.

Seconds ticked by, each holding a decade's worth of time. He longed to see her, yearned to feel her body pressed to his. Through the haze of his need, he recalled his promise to Danforth.

"I will keep my wits about me."

Notwithstanding his imminent departure back to London, he had to maintain a level of emotional distance until he either absolved her of any involvement with Latymer or confirmed a connection. *Yearning* and *longing* had no place in their dalliance.

The door closed in the outer chamber, and he drew in a

calming breath. His jaw ached from the pressure of his clenched teeth. The hint of a feminine silhouette approached the open doorway.

Within seconds, Catherine filled the frame. Beautiful, proud, tempting. Cautious.

"My lord." Her voice held a slight quaver. "Mrs. Fox said you were attacked by a thief last night. Is this true?"

He studied her shadowed face, unable to make out her features. "We have yet to determine if the man was a thief. Nothing appears stolen. But yes, I came upon a man in my study."

She moved farther into the sitting room. Something was wrong with her eyes and her features appeared drawn and hesitant. Without thinking, he limped toward her. "What's the matter?"

"You're injured." She rushed into the chamber. "How badly?"

"A bruise, nothing to worry over." He tilted her chin up. "Have you been crying?"

TWENTY-SEVEN

"Of course not." Catherine stepped away. She had hoped her bout of self-pity would not be evident by the time she arrived. Since she could not discuss the reason behind her puffy, gritty eyes, she redirected the conversation back to him. "Besides your leg, where else are you hurt?"

"I am well on the mend, Catherine. No need to concern yourself."

She studied the bandage near his temple. "The doctor was here?"

"Yes."

She scrutinized him more closely. He balanced his weight on his right foot and he seemed to be squinting, almost as if it pained him to look upon her. Beyond those two indicators of discomfort, she could detect nothing else.

"What are you doing here?" he asked.

Saving my daughter. "I came to check on you."

"When did you learn of my condition?"

"Earlier today."

"And you're only now checking on me?"

In truth, she had not planned on coming here tonight. But after learning he had been attacked, she had to see him. Had to make sure he was all right. "This morning, you didn't answer my knock. I thought you needed the rest. However, when I returned later, Lord Danforth said you were unwell and couldn't receive visitors. He said nothing about an altercation with an intruder, though."

"Danforth failed to mention your visit." Annoyance laced his words. "How did you come by the information?"

His tone carried an air of interrogation, making her feel as though she had done something wrong. Had Mrs. Fox told her more than she should? "If you didn't want your household to divulge the information, you should have informed them. I inquired about your recovery and was told about the attack." She held out a small tin. "Sophie made you biscuits to speed up your recovery."

By slow degrees, she watched the hardness in his features soften and the rigid set to his shoulders ease. If she did not know any better, she would suspect that he knew about Cochran's visit and subsequent demands. But he could not know. No one knew but Mary, and the maid would never betray her.

On some level, she regretted his transformation. Now that she did not have his cold inquisition on which to focus her attention, she became keenly aware of *him*.

With his disheveled hair, scruffy face, and loosely tied banyan, he looked disreputable and wholly desirable. She wished they had met under different circumstances, at a time when they could have explored this attraction they held for each other. But their association was caged within the walls of deception, with no way to break the barrier.

He prowled closer, his unwavering crystalline gaze on hers. She held her breath, unsure of his mood and unable to block the memory of her daughter's screams. She could do this. She could do whatever it took to secure the damned list, protect her daughter, and be rid of her gaolers. She could do this.

No matter how much it broke her heart.

His fingertips skimmed the curve of her cheek. "You have been crying. Why?"

She fought the compulsion to lean into his touch. "Meghan." The lie fell easily, too easily from her lips.

"Catherine. *Cat*." He clasped the back of her head, drawing her forward, into his chest. "I'm sorry you had to witness such barbarity. Such things are not for the eyes of innocents."

God help her, she sank into his comfort. Slid into his arms as if she had done it a thousand times before. No matter what Cochran had claimed, she did not believe Sebastian was capable of betraying his country. She suspected information he withheld about Geoffrey's murder had more to do with protecting people than with concealing it from her. She could not explain why she felt the way she did, but her belief in him was as strong as any forged steel.

The knowledge made what she had to do to save her daughter all the more difficult.

"Why kill her?" she asked, maintaining her pretense. "The babe's father could have disappeared and never returned." She burrowed her nose deeper into his silk wrap, absorbing his musky scent and banishing forever the stench of mud and death.

"Perhaps the father could not leave. Maybe he had a family and was afraid Meghan would reveal their secret. There could be any number of reasons. None of them acceptable."

His embrace tightened, and she reciprocated. Air hissed between his teeth, and he stiffened.

"What's wrong?"

"Nothing," he said through stiff lips.

"Liar." She tugged on the end of his sash, pulling the tie free.

He backed up, securing his wrap. "What are you about?"

"You have another injury you failed to mention."

"The doctor has already seen to it."

"What is *it*?"

He seemed to be weighing his options. No doubt considering whether to brush off her question with a vague response or put an end to this line of inquiry with the truth. From her perspective, the decision took much longer than it should have.

"A contusion," he admitted.

She frowned, not familiar with the term.

"Bruise," he clarified. "A rather unpleasant one."

"Is it the same on your leg?"

He nodded. "Thankfully, my assailant did not shatter my knee."

"Oh, Sebastian." She reached for his hand, and her chest clenched when his fingers grasped hers in return. "What else?"

He released a long, heavy sigh. "Concussion."

"Where?"

"Are you this motherly to everyone?"

"Only to those who insist nothing is wrong. Point, please." When he did nothing but narrow his gaze on her, she said, "Your attempt to stare me into submission won't work." She waved toward his head. "Where else did he bash you?"

Rather than point to the location, he grabbed her wrist and lifted her hand to his hair. He carefully guided her fingers through the soft strands until she reached a large bump three inches above his left ear.

She sucked in an astonished breath. "Goodness, my lord. Why are you not abed?"

He closed his eyes, seeming to take comfort from her caress, although she did not touch the painful lump again.

"Hearing you say my name is so much more preferable than 'my lord.'"

Heat rose into her cheeks. "Why do you always evade my questions?" Recalling his other injuries, she stepped around him, her fingers tracing down his nape.

"For the same reason you're keeping the true source of your tears from me." His luminous gaze followed her progress.

His wide shoulders filled her vision, and she once again experienced a sense of her own delicacy while standing next to him. With a feather-like touch, she skimmed her fingers down his back, circling the lower portion. "Is this where he hurt you?"

He swallowed. "Yes."

"May I see?"

"You might find more than an ugly patch of skin."

She hoped so. Retracing her path, she memorized each silk-draped sinew before gripping the neckline of his banyan. With her eyes riveted on her hands, she drew the shimmering cloth off his shoulders. Something desperate and raw raked along her every nerve ending, making her hands tremble and her breaths shake.

Once his upper arms were free, the silken wrap, secured by his sash, drooped over his bottom, revealing a six-inch-long black bruise that ran perpendicular to his spine. The visual evidence of the violence he had endured and suffered alone forced her pleasurable thoughts to the wayside. "Sweet Lord."

Further speech was impossible, for her throat had closed around that simple, inconsequential phrase.

"It's nothing," he said in a rough voice. "I hardly know it's there."

Fury replaced the ache in her heart. "Well, I know it's there." She reached around and freed the sash again. The length of cloth released, and his wrap melted in a pool of midnight silk at his feet.

Her heart hammered in her ears, nearly deafening in its ferocity. He was magnificent. Smooth angles and firm ridges. Taut skin and rippling muscles. Without moving a single inch, he stole her breath.

"Have your look, Catherine." His blue-gray eyes pulsed with fire. "Because in ten seconds, I'm going to show you why that was a dangerous decision."

His masculine perfection befuddled her mind so badly that it took her several precious seconds to work through his warning. When she finally did, she dropped to her knees and bent to inspect yet another injury. He stood with most of his weight on his right leg, his left leg cocked to provide a measure of balance but little else.

Similar to his lower back, a large bruise covered the underside of his knee. This one looked so much worse. Rather than a perfect outline of a geometrical shape, the bruise on his leg spread out in all angles like a slow-moving cancer. Her fingers hovered over the area, but she dared not touch. "What type of weapon causes this kind of damage?"

"Some type of cudgel, I suspect."

She sat back on her heels. "You're rather nonchalant about your attack. Does this sort of thing happen often?"

"Nine. Ten," he said, ignoring her question. "Time's up." The rich timbre of his voice held both promise and foreboding.

As he angled his body around, her eyes grew more and more round with every new inch revealed. *Magnificent.* All the adjectives she had used to describe his body thus far were like defining the Crown Jewels as a set of pretty baubles.

Pretty did not come close to describing his baubles.

He held out his hand. "Come with me."

She glanced from his hand to his smoldering eyes to the pulsing length of his erection. And there her attention remained, fixed on the delicate smoothness of his flesh straining to accommodate his building arousal. Engorged veins lined the underside of his staff, leading to a round, velvety tip that pointed toward his navel. From there, she followed a slender line of dark hair down to his thick base, which led back to pulsing veins and straining flesh.

In all her years of marriage to Geoffrey, he had never been so blatant, so confident with his bare form. Her mouth felt dry, and that's when she realized her jaw hung open. She closed her mouth so fast that her teeth clicked together.

He crouched down in front of her, the action causing him to wince. "I am inviting you into my bedchamber, Catherine. Do you accept, or must I persuade you?"

Could he hear her pounding heart? The rhythm vibrated through her entire body. What had started out as a seduction to save her daughter was progressing into far more dangerous territory. She could no longer feel the guilt or the shame, only the hunger. Terrible, exciting hunger. "Both?"

Bracing his hand on the floor, he leaned forward, sliding his nose alongside hers. The caress of his breath fanned over her lips, compelling hers to part. His kiss was warm and passion-filled, sending tingles to glorious places.

"Are you persuaded now?" His words were low, seductive.

Unable to open her eyes, she nodded. "Oh, yes."

"Look at me."

She blinked her eyes open, surprised by the heavy weight of her lids.

"Do you recall the terms of our *affaire?*"

A sharp ache pierced her chest. "Of course."

"Then you recall that I will be returning to London in a few days."

The ache spread to her throat. "You have nothing to worry about, Sebastian. I understand that our time together is ephemeral."

His eyes hardened for the briefest of seconds, then he blinked and their glowing intensity returned. She accepted his hand, and they strode into a connecting room. One hand sporting nothing but the perfection of his bare flesh and the other draped in mournful black linen. The contrast was startling and evocative.

The moment she stepped into his bedchamber, her senses sharpened. Candles flickered around the room—candlelight she did not recall seeing moments ago when Parker had let her in. The air was redolent with Sebastian's special scent.

She gathered in a long breath, savoring the delicate woodsy bouquet. The mix of musk and violet suited him much more than the popular than stronger fragrances like sandalwood or ambergris.

His thumb smoothed over the backs of her fingers. The tender caress reclaimed her attention as he guided her toward his massive, curtained bed. Like most things in this house, the earl's bed bespoke privilege, wealth, and an appalling flair for the vulgar. But in this instance, the ceil-ing-to-floor sapphire hangings, with their silver embroidered cuffs and their plush folds, compelled rather than repulsed.

He stopped near the side of the bed and cradled her flushed cheeks. Bending close, he kissed her forehead before skimming his mouth over hers. "I am going to do unspeakable things to you in that bed, Catherine," he breathed against her lips. "If you have thoughts of fleeing, now would be the time."

"The only place I wish to flee is deeper into your arms."

The pressure on her cheeks tightened infinitesimally, and his nostrils flared around a shuddering breath. "Then come, my sweet."

At his urging, she carefully curled her arms around his back, sliding her trembling hands up the satiny planes of his shoulders. He was so large. So solid and strong. Yet his hands explored her body with a gossamer touch, with a skill that left her aching for more.

She pressed closer, delighted and aroused by the evidence of his desire. Every inch pulsing against her stomach was for her, for want of her. The realization was exhilarating. Tormenting.

She should not want him so much. Every act between them was nothing more than a link to a greater betrayal. They both had secrets, underlying motives for igniting their passions. And he would soon be gone.

The knowledge that he would leave her behind, as her father and Geoffrey had done, sent a bolt of realism straight through her heart. That flash of insight was all she needed to start mentally erecting a familiar barrier, one designed to keep her heart intact and her sanity in place.

"Turn around, please," he whispered.

She swiveled around, and he worked on the fastenings of her gown. All the while, she continued building her protective wall, stone by stone. However, this particular barrier proved more challenging than past ones. The brush of his fingers along her back and the warmth of his lips pressed against her nape distracted her from her task.

Her gown sagged, then billowed to the floor. She evaluated her barrier and groaned. Large clumps of mortar dripped from the seams, and stones sat haphazardly within each row, leaving dangerous gaps. Cool air kissed her burning flesh, and she scrambled to hold up her quivering wall.

He skimmed his hands down her arms until their fingers laced together. "Relax," he said against her temple.

From his vantage point, he had full view of her nudity, especially when she tilted her head back to rest on his shoulder and arched her arms around until she could clasp her hands behind his neck. With her breasts jutting forward and her bottom snuggled against his rigid length, she felt both vulnerable and luxuriant. His hands caressed their way over her quavering stomach to her swollen, tender breasts. She closed her eyes and tracked his movements with her sense of touch alone.

"Beautiful." He closed his hand over her aching breast, adding the slightest bit of pressure to her ruched peak. A stab of need sliced through her body, lifting her to her toes.

"So responsive." He squeezed again, this time harder, compounding the torturous move by ravishing her mouth.

His tongue slid inside with a thoroughness that made her inner muscles clench. She wanted to hold on to this moment for as long as possible. She wanted to experience a man's need and have him assuage hers. She wanted to feel alive again.

Breaking the kiss, he threw back the covers and climbed into bed. He reclined against the mound of pillows, lifting one knee. A shiver raced along her bare flesh, having nothing to do with her state of undress and everything to do with his sultan-like pose. Rippling muscles, smoldering steel-gray eyes, raw desire. The erotic combination stole her breath.

"Take your hair down for me."

The breath she had been holding *whooshed* from her body. She was not used to such blatant commands. They made her feel uncertain and shy, beautiful and bold.

Straightening her spine, she lifted her hands to her hair and began pulling out pins. He followed the unfurling of every long lock with such intensity that her attempt to appear seductive and unhurried began to fray.

When she finally located the last pin, she breathed a sigh of relief as she swept her mass of blond hair over one shoulder. "Anything else, my lord?"

"A good deal more, I assure you, madam."

He lifted his hand in invitation, and she noticed it was no steadier than her own. She swallowed back the last of her trepidation and accepted his assistance. Once she had scaled the high bed, he shifted until the pillows cradled his neck and shoulders. He wanted her to mount him. Never had she assumed such a place of power with Geoffrey.

Perceptive as always, he noted her hesitation. "Do you mind? I'm afraid my knee won't hold up to the traditional way."

He radiated so much power and strength that one

could easily forget about his injuries. "Not at all. What of your head wound?"

"I will be careful."

Tugging on her hand, he guided her into position. She wanted to lower her feminine center against his erection, to feel his heat and need. But she kept her weight on her knees while she slid her palms down his arms to entwine her fingers with his. She pinned his hands above his head, taking in the surreal image of him beneath her, gazing up at her as if she were his entire world. Power surged through her, and she lowered her aching cleft until it rested on the warm strength of his erection.

Fire shot up her spine. Her back arched and inner muscles clenched. Closer. She needed to be closer. Needed to feel more of him.

Releasing his hands, she flattened her palms against his chest. She rubbed her slick flesh against his hardness, the exquisite friction making them both moan their approval. She increased the pressure and her pace, delighting in the sweet, piercing ache that stabbed through her every time her sensitive nub connected with his hardness.

"Do you like," she panted, "this?"

"Does day follow night?" he responded in a desire-clogged voice. "Kiss me."

She took his mouth with hers. The kiss turned feral. Exciting. Unlike anything she could have imagined.

His fingers dug into her hips, and she felt him at her entrance, probing, seeking, asking.

She adjusted her position, and he eased inside, filling her with a fullness that made her blood sing and her heart thunder. With her hands on his chest, she had the odd thought of how small they looked against the breadth of him.

He grasped her hips and lifted her high, to the point of nearly releasing him from her channel. Then he coaxed her to sink low once again. On and on it went, their languid pace increasing as the scent of desire flooded their senses.

"Come with me, Cat."

She closed her eyes and searched inward for the tiny spark that would ignite her release. But it remained stubbornly out of reach. Her legs quivered from her exertion, sweat dampened her brow. "I'm t-trying. Can't quite—"

"Hold on to me," he commanded.

With barely enough time to comply, she clung to his shoulders while her world upended itself until she stared up at the sapphire canopy above his bed. "Sebastian, your knee!"

"Forget it. Prop those beautiful legs up and meet me halfway."

Power surged inside her, and her hips flexed. She kissed his chest, his neck, his mouth, all the while meeting him with a confidence that surprised her. This is where she belonged, within the cage of his arms, beneath the power of his body. Here, she did not want to be strong, did not want to be in control. At least, not yet.

He hit the spark, and she lifted her hips, pressing closer and closer. No longer pumping a rhythm, only seeking repletion. Greedy in her purpose and not caring a whit.

The spark ignited, sending her into the beloved white light.

Their mingled cries of pleasure echoed through the chamber. Within seconds, silence settled around them. Their harsh breaths the only indication life existed after such a fierce loving.

All too soon, he peeled his body off hers, kissed his way down to her breast and drew her nipple into his mouth. His actions were languid, not meant to arouse, but simply enjoy. When he'd had his fill, he rolled onto his back, bringing her along.

She stiffened in his arms, afraid she would hurt him. "Perhaps it would be best if I did not crowd you."

"Perhaps," he said, keeping his eyes closed. "But I prefer that you stay right where you are."

Unwilling to argue about something she wanted anyway, she carefully molded her body around his and rested her head against his chest. She listened to the chaotic beating of his heart until it calmed to a normal rhythm.

And that's when the first tears gathered. She had come here to seduce the earl for a scrap of paper, while her daughter slept beneath a canopy of evil. There was no way to get through this intolerable situation without someone getting hurt, either physically or emotionally.

However, she tried not to fool herself where Sebastian was involved. *Affaires* were commonplace for him. Pleasurable while they lasted, but he likely gave them little thought once they ended.

After his breathing deepened and his hold slackened, she waited a full fifteen minutes before easing out of his bed and dressing. She wended her way down the broad staircase, bracing herself for the appearance of a wide-eyed servant. To appease Cochran, she would search the study again tonight and, tomorrow, the library. She pushed the study door open and held her breath. The room was empty. Dark.

She ran to Sebastian's desk and lifted the ink blotter. Had he added anymore names to the sheet of paper? Would she recognize anyone?

The list was gone.

"Blast," she whispered.

The realization that she would need a light to continue her search struck terror in her heart. She located one of those lovely Argand lamps on Sebastian's desk, but discarded the notion of lighting it.

From what she had read, they provided the same amount of illumination as six candles. So much light might would be visible beneath the door and draw the attention of anyone who might happen by. The flicker of one candle would serve her purposes.

But she could not locate a single taper anywhere. Going against her good sense, she lit the lamp. Golden light flooded the room, momentarily blinding her. She glanced at the crack beneath the door and rushed to retrieve a throw from the chaise longue to place in front of it.

The clock on the mantel mocked her with its incessant passage of time. Perspiration dampened her skin. She searched his desk, his bookshelves, and checked beneath every knick-knack in the room.

Nothing.

Recalling the hidden compartment in her writing box, she returned to his desk and bookshelves to poke, push, pull anything she could get her hands on.

Still nothing.

Frustration seethed beneath layers of fear and desperation. She whirled in a wild circle, seeking some other source for secreting away valuables.

Nothing, nothing, nothing.

She drew in a ragged breath, grappling with a sense of defeat and utter relief. Pulling herself together, she extinguished the lamp and replaced the throw on the chaise. She stood in the gloom-filled study, hesitating.

Her gaze lifted to the upstairs bedchamber, where a

handsome, complicated earl slept in a halo of repletion. Repletion she had given him.

Every well-loved muscle in her body urged her to return to his side, to the comfort of his arms. To steal a moment of peace for herself.

But no amount of loving could quiet the cry of a mother's blood. The inexplicable instinct to return to her daughter and ensure, with her own eyes, that she was safe.

Opening the tall paned doors that led out to the garden, she closed them behind her and made her way down to the stables to fetch Gypsy.

She did not sense the naked man standing in the upper story window, nor the pair of searing eyes following her.

She was too busy repairing the ruins of her wall.

TWENTY-EIGHT

"Still no sign of the list, daughter?"

Catherine finished entering the date of Mr. Tucker's repair on her schedule before answering her mother. Once the notation was made, she surveyed the meadow for their two gaolers from beneath the small tent Edward had erected for her and her mother.

Silas was nowhere to be found. A condition that made her more nervous than if he had been standing five feet away. She located Mrs. Clarke kneeling on a blanket out in the middle of the field, instructing Sophie on how to build a kite. With nothing more than a couple of sturdy sticks, yards of string, and silk from an old ball gown, her daughter was well on her way to flying her first kite.

Too bad the joyful moment was tainted by an undercurrent of fear.

She shook her head. "Two evenings of searching, and not a single treasonous note."

Her mother drew a long, red thread through a square of linen. "Have you searched Lord Somerton's rooms?"

"Not yet." She dropped her quill pen onto her

portable writing box. "Now that I've completed the lower level, his private chambers are next." She hated speaking of such things with her mother. Although the words were never uttered, Evelyn Shaw knew how her daughter spent her evenings. Thankfully, her mother understood the situation well enough not to cast judgment on Catherine's actions. "Last night, I found a half-composed letter on the writing desk in his bedchamber. From the few sentences I had time to read, the words were disjointed and illogical."

"Disjointed," her mother repeated. "Could it be a coded message, like Ashcroft's letters?"

"Perhaps." She stared at Sophie, standing now with the framework of a kite. "I'll copy it tonight, so that I might study it in more detail on the morrow. If I can't obtain the list of agents, Cochran might be appeased with an important message instead."

They sat in silence for a few minutes until Sophie's laughter broke into their musings.

"My granddaughter seems to be taking to her new governess."

"Yes." After the initial shock of their gaolers' invasion had passed, Sophie had gradually warmed up to her constant companion. Mrs. Clarke's kindness and inventiveness kept Sophie's mind occupied with games and an assortment of crafts, rather than on the disastrous way in which they were introduced. "In many ways, Mrs. Clarke is the perfect governess for Sophie."

Proving Cochran's contemptuous comment true. Why would a woman such as she align herself with so despicable a man? The question piqued her troublesome curiosity.

Then again, Mrs. Clarke might be pondering the same thing about her. Catherine's reasoning had been so clear only days ago, now she wondered how everything had gone so wrong.

Evelyn said, "I'm sorry you have this to deal with in addition to the loss of your father and husband."

"No need to fret on my account." She clasped her mother's cold hand in hers, forcing a light tone into her voice. "Although I would rather be in Brighton, basking in the sun and listening to the waves, my situation could be far worse. I could be consorting with a man ridden with gout, thrice my age, and who has a propensity for greasy foods."

An image of Silas skulking in her entrance hall surfaced. After her first evening with Sebastian, she had returned home before the sun had crested the horizon. Silas had emerged from a darkened corner, the play of shadows over his disturbing features making him appear more insidious than ever.

Every night thereafter followed the same routine. His only greeting: "Do you have it?"

And each time, she would shake her head and brace herself for his reprisal. Other than his lips thinning in displeasure, he had not reacted, simply stepped back and nodded toward the staircase. She had wasted no time in complying.

"Given that dreadful image," Evelyn said, interrupting her thoughts, "I shall view this situation in a more positive light, but I still prefer that you were not involved at all."

"Had I not drawn attention to myself and Geoffrey's letters, neither Lord Somerton nor Mr. Cochran would have given me a second's thought."

"Where do we go from here?"

"I must proceed with my search until I find something of value for Mr. Cochran. With any luck, the indecipherable missive I found will assuage his demands." She squeezed her mother's hand. "Can you continue watching over Sophie?"

"Of course. There's no need for you to ask."

"Thank you." She recalled Cochran's parting words. *Finish what you started, Mrs. Ashcroft, or I will take more from your daughter than a mere toy.* "Promise you will send for me the moment you believe something has gone amiss."

"Be at ease, daughter." Evelyn leaned forward and patted her hand. "I will not let you down in this."

The muscles in her throat constricted. "I never doubted it, Mother."

A whoop of laughter broke into their reverie. They looked up to find Sophie tearing across the meadow, her kite flying thirty feet above. Mrs. Clarke ran alongside, encouraging her with gentle instruction.

Jumping to her feet, she cheered on her daughter, whose giggles carried across the meadow. She glanced over at her mother, who had risen to join her. She wore the same proud smile and her hands were clasped together at her chest. They grinned at each other, then turned as one to shout encouraging words to their little girl.

TWENTY-NINE

Sebastian cursed his impatience, even while the heels of his boots tore into the graveled path leading to his stables. With hours to go before Catherine made her nightly appearance, he could no longer tolerate the sound of his own interminable pacing. He needed something to take his mind off the widow and her penchant for vacating his bed in the middle of the night.

For the past two evenings, they had indulged their carnal desires, and afterward, she would crawl from his bed and set about searching his home with a thoroughness that would put many of his agents to shame. After their first night together, when he was still suffering the effects of his beating and fell into a deep sleep, she had made the mistake of thinking he was not easily awakened.

But sleep was something he needed very little of and, as a result, it took him awhile to fall into slumber. Had she waited a little longer before deserting him, she might have pulled off the deception without his knowledge. But she had not, and he had been forced to follow her about the house as she combed through his personal items.

A movement by the paddock fence caught his eye. His steps slowed as he made out the form of a small child sitting atop the rail and watching his groomsman exercising Sebastian's prized white Arabian.

Sophie Ashcroft.

Closing his eyes, he counted to five. He could pretend he hadn't seen her and continue on to the stables, where he intended to muck out stalls, brush down horses, clean tack —anything—that would release the tension strumming through him.

When he opened his eyes, he noted her precarious perch and knew he couldn't walk away. Her mother would never forgive him if he allowed harm to come to the child. He would not analyze why he cared about the feelings of a woman who made passionate love to him one moment and deceived him the next.

Blowing out an exasperated breath, he headed for the horse-hungry imp. Even from this distance, he could make out her rapt expression. What he wouldn't do to feel such unreserved joy for something. Anything.

"Miss Sophie," he called.

She started, grabbing the rail for balance. Once she had recovered, she shoved a piece of paper into the pocket of her red pelisse before glancing over her shoulder with a guilty expression.

"Do you remember who I am, child?"

She nodded. "You're the Lord Earl."

Leaning his forearms against the fence, he followed Cira's progress. He shared the girl's fascination with the Arabian. Centuries of solid breeding had perfected the line. Although he was much too tall to ride the beauty, he appreciated the mare's trim lines and graceful maneuvers.

"In a manner of speaking, yes," he said with the same

patience as her mother. "I am an earl, but the proper way to address me is by using my title—Lord Somerton."

She wrinkled up her nose. "Lord Somerton."

His lips twitched. "Or you may call me Sebastian."

She perked up, but her gaze never veered from the Arabian. "Bastian."

He smiled, liking her version better. "That's right, Sophie." A few silent minutes passed while their gazes followed the white beauty as a groomsman led him around the paddock.

"Did you know Arabians are the oldest purebred horses in the world?" she asked with wonderment.

He did. But how did she? The child could not be more than six or seven. "I had heard something to that effect. What else can you tell me?"

She turned wide, expressive eyes on him. Her father's eyes. "King Sol-lom—"

"King Solomon," he offered.

"Have you heard this story?"

"I'm not sure. Why don't you tell me?"

"King Solomon housed *forty thousand* Arabians in his stable. Can you imagine? They'd fill your big barn."

"Indeed, they would. Yours, too."

"Holy horses!"

A laugh burst from his chest, alarming Cira and the groomsman and sending young Sophie into a gale of giggles. The intrepid child reminded him so much of Cora at her age that he felt an answering pang of longing for simpler times.

"Ohhhh, no," she whined. The abrupt shift from laughter to a child's pout surprised him. He glanced down and found her staring off into the distance, shrinking behind his shoulder.

He followed her gaze and noticed a feminine form headed their way. His heart stuttered for a moment, thinking Catherine had come to fetch her child. On closer inspection, the woman wore a light gray gown, rather than mourning black, and she had brown hair. Not his Catherine at all.

"Who is she?"

"My new governess, Mrs. Clarke."

"You don't like her?"

She shrugged her shoulders. "She's nice. This morning, she showed me how to build a kite."

"Impressive. How did it fly?"

"Really high. I ran out of string."

"Well done." Remembering the many times he had attempted to elude his tutor, he asked, "Are you hiding from Mrs. Clarke?"

"Not her." She slanted a glance toward her governess again. "Him."

He kept his pose casual while he scoured the area. The girl's tone carried a distinctive note of fear that could not be easily invented. "I see no one."

"He's there," she said. "He's always there. In the woods, behind Mrs. Clarke."

He peered beyond the governess, into the dense woodland. Still, he saw no one.

"Have you told your mother about him?"

Her eyes widened, as if she remembered something important. "Ahh, I'm going to be in so much trouble."

"Why is that?" He split his attention between the approaching governess and the tree line.

"Because I'm not supposed to tell anyone about him." Her voice lowered and she fidgeted with a ruffle on her dress. "Especially you."

Every muscle in his body hardened with fury. "How long have they been following you about?"

With her eyes downcast, she slid her hand into her pocket, and paper crackled.

He nudged her with his shoulder. "We're friends now, are we not?"

Her blond eyebrows squeezed together, considering.

"Did you hear of my invitation to visit my stables?"

She brightened, nodding. "Mama said I had to wait until my birthday on Saturday."

"That's correct. We must be friends, because I don't let just anyone into my stables."

"I feel the same way about Dragonthorpe. I asked Mama if I could show it to you, but she cried." Her lips pursed. "Not like that bad man made her cry. I think she misses my papa."

He stilled, trying to keep up with the girl's thought patterns. He had some experience with this particular malady from when Cora was young, but he was more than a little rusty. He tucked Dragonthorpe away, recalling Catherine's mention of the castle. However, ignoring Sophie's comment about Catherine missing her husband took a good deal more effort. He eventually managed it, as he knew he would.

"You miss your papa, too?"

Paper crackled again. "Sometimes."

"Do you have something there of his?"

Her eyes widened. "Oh, double trouble."

The moment didn't exactly call for humor, but the earnestness in the girl's voice tickled something deep inside. "A letter, perhaps?"

"Yes," she said in a small voice. "But it's all gibberish. You'd think Teddy wrote it instead of my papa."

Could she be carrying another letter of Ashcroft's? He tried to keep his excitement under control. If Sophie had somehow filched one of her father's coded messages, then Catherine hadn't held anything back. She had given him everything.

He stared down at the child's bent head, and a different sort of pressure squeezed his heart. Had she taken her father's letter in a bid to be closer to him? Instead of finding reassuring words of love, she had found nothing but a confusing string of nonsense. "After your party, I promise to help you read your papa's letter. How does that sound?" He would make sure Ashcroft's final words were a comfort to his only child.

"Mama might get upset."

"I'll take care of your mama. Agreed?"

"Yes, Bastian."

"Would you mind if I took a peek at it now?"

With obvious reluctance, she pulled a folded missive from her pocket and held it out for him.

"Thank you, Sophie." He scanned the contents, no better able to decipher them than Sophie. But toward the end a name stuck out—Frederick Cochran. The name struck a chord of familiarity, but nothing came immediately to mind.

"I shan't have any problems deciphering this tomorrow." Another name stood out in stark contrast to the rest—Abbingale Home. He frowned, not understanding the reference and having no context in which to figure it out. "May I keep this until tomorrow?"

"You won't forget to give it back?"

"No." He slid the missive into his coat pocket. "I won't forget. You have my word."

He glanced up to find the governess at the outer edge

of the paddock. He moved on to the bad man. The one who made Catherine cry. "How long has the man been following you, Sophie?"

"Which one—the bad man or the scary man?"

Ice crystals formed at the back of his neck. "Either one."

"Three or four days." She sent him a pleading look. "Please don't tell Mama."

"It's our secret."

"Which man made your mama cry?"

"Mr. Cochran."

He strove for calm, even though his heart rocked inside his chest. "Is Mr. Cochran the one hiding in the tree, Sophie?"

"No, that's the scary man."

He laid his hand on her arm, wishing he didn't have to interrogate the poor girl, but knowing it was the only way to help them. "What does the bad man look like?"

She shrugged. "Tall. Blond like Mama."

"Miss Sophie," the governess called. "It's time for you to come home now."

The little girl pulled so hard on her flounce that it separated from her dress.

"I won't allow anyone to harm you, Sophie."

"And Mama?"

His heart contracted. "I'll protect her, too."

The governess' strides quickened.

"Promise?" she whispered.

He suppressed his own sense of desperation. "You have my word."

She made to climb down the fence. "One more thing," he said, with a touch to her arm. "Your governess. When did she arrive?"

"The bad man brought her a few days ago."

With that pronouncement, she swung her legs over to the opposite side of the fence and jumped down, hurrying over to her apparent gaoler.

The woman took Sophie's hand, nodded at him, and returned the same way in which she had come.

The bad man brought her.

He dug his fingers into the railing to prevent himself from going after the little girl. Seeing her pixie face mottled with fear nearly broke his heart. Even now, her head hung low, dispirited.

"Sophie," he called.

She turned to face him. "Yes?"

"Don't forget our appointment on Saturday. Cira's itching to go for a ride."

Her mouth dropped open like a startled fish. "I get to ride her?" She turned wondering eyes on the Arabian.

"Indeed," he said, relieved to see her normal exuberance returned. "But not if you're late."

"I won't be. I'll come early, Bastian."

He smiled. "That's my girl."

Sophie skipped away, leaving her governess to follow along behind. His smile faded. Turning away from the stables, he made his way back up to the house, faster, more determined than when he had descended.

He had a great deal to do—missives to write, a widow to contemplate, and a bad man to kill.

THIRTY

The bed dipped behind him and a soft rustling followed, alerting Sebastian to Catherine's midnight escape. He tracked her progress about the room, with nothing more than his sense of hearing. She pulled out a drawer on his writing desk, and he detected the distinct slide of paper against paper. The drawer closed, and she moved away. Into the sitting room.

He maneuvered his naked body out of bed, drawing his banyan over his shoulders. At the entrance to the sitting room, he drew in a steadying breath. From this point forward, their association would change, likely for the worse.

Regret sliced through his heart. With Catherine, he had glimpsed what life outside the Nexus could be. And he had enjoyed it, immensely.

Bracing his hand against the door frame, he hesitated far longer than a seasoned intelligence agent should. He did not want to give her up, but the spy in him clawed at his restraints. No matter her reasons, she was here on behalf of his enemy. Her actions had placed his country—a country he had fought years to protect—at risk.

This he could not allow.

No matter the personal sacrifice.

Fortifying his mind, he swallowed back his deep yearning and leaned against the doorjamb, crossing his arms. Fully dressed, she bent over something he could not see. Then she dipped the nib of her pen into an inkwell.

"Writing me a farewell letter?" he asked.

A short, high-pitched scream burst from her throat, and she shot to her feet. With her back to her makeshift writing table, she faced him. "Pardon?"

He pushed away, moving toward her with predatory intent. "Farewell letter," he repeated. "The last few evenings you've abandoned my bed without so much as a kiss goodbye. I thought tonight you might be tarrying long enough to write me a note." His voice lowered to a dangerous level. "An explanation."

When her eyes widened at his close proximity, he pivoted to stalk around the table, trying to see what she had been writing. "Of course, I would have preferred a kiss to a missive."

Her color was high, and he could hear the painful rasping of her breathing. Sympathy caught in his chest for what he was about to do.

"Yes, of course." She snatched up the pages on the table. "How silly of me. I will keep your preference in mind next time."

Afraid she would rip the sheets to shreds, he grabbed her wrist. "No need to waste good paper, madam. Allow me to read what you've written so far."

With surprising strength, she wrenched free of his hold. "Um, no." Her movements became jerky and her gaze slashed across the room, reminding him of a caged animal. "I prefer your method of goodbye to mine."

Dropping all pretense, he asked, "Who sent you, Catherine?"

She sucked in a startled breath. "I don't know what you mean, sir."

"I think you do." He nodded toward the papers behind her back. "Give them to me."

Backing away, she shook her head. "It's nothing, really."

"You're not leaving this house until I see what you're hiding." He infused as much menace into his tone as possible. "Unless you would like for me to call the constable."

"Whatever for?"

"To report a theft, of course."

Looking more trapped than ever, she clutched the papers to her chest. "Please don't."

He gentled his voice. "You're giving me little choice."

"You don't understand."

"Then educate me. Explain to me why a widow with an impeccable reputation would risk an *affaire*. Tell me why you would betray my trust."

"I c-can't."

"Why? Who are you protecting?"

"Please, Sebastian." Tears filled her eyes. "I beg you. Pretend you never saw this. If you do this for me, I swear I'll not grace your doorstep again."

His chest heaved with his building anger. On one level, he stood before this beautiful woman, who had somehow woven a spell around his heart, angry and hurt. On another level, he observed the scene from a great distance. Disconnected and ruthless.

Betrayal, lies, and death were nothing new to him. He

had come to expect them all with every new mission. That did not stop him from struggling with the knowledge that she acted out of desperation, with an unfortunate side effect. Deceiving him.

Although he did not know the source, he understood her motivation and respected her for having the courage to do what needed doing. But still, her decision not to confide in him split open a wound that not even stitches could mend.

"Tempting, my dear. But, like you, I cannot." He flicked his fingers toward the papers. "I won't ask for them again. When it comes to physical strength, I win."

Unabated tears streamed down her face. Her silent torment was nearly his undoing. Had she wailed and screamed, he would have known how to deal with such theatrics. Desperate silence was another thing altogether.

Wanting nothing more than to end both their suffering, he stepped forward to remove the papers from her crushing grip.

"If you take th-these," she said around a sob, "they will kill her."

That stopped him. "Her?"

"Sophie."

"Who would dare threaten to harm your daughter?" When she said nothing, he demanded, "What madness have you embroiled yourself in?"

She clasped her hands over her ears, flattening the papers against her head. "I didn't mean to. Dear God, I would never knowingly place Sophie in danger. Never."

He stepped forward, aching to wrap his arms around her trembling body. "For what it's worth, I believe you."

"Do you? Given our circumstances, I'm not sure I'd believe me."

"I've been at this a long time. There's little I haven't seen or experienced."

Sadness stole around the edges of her fear. "How awful for you."

His throat grew taut, trapping his pithy retort. No one had ever taken the time to consider the personal anguish he had suffered by way of his position. Most thought him cold and ruthless—and they were right—but not until Catherine had anyone examined the reasons behind those qualities.

"Do you trust me, Cat?"

"No one is who they seem to be."

"Do you trust me?" he asked in a harsh, unsteady voice.

New tears slid along the path of the old ones. "I want to."

"But you don't."

"He said you and your band of traitors were responsible for Geoffrey's death."

Band of traitors. His fear for her grew tenfold. On her quest to rout a murderer, she had wandered into the midst of a brutal war. "He?" She said nothing. "Did he provide a name for this group?"

"Nexus."

Fury burned through his veins. His gaze dropped to her hands. "What do you think you have there?"

"Something that will save my daughter's life."

"Did you by chance purloin one of those items from the second drawer of my writing desk?"

A mixture of chagrin and alarm tumbled across her face.

"Is the letter written in a strange, indecipherable hand?"

"Yes," she whispered.

He sent her a pitying smile. "It's nothing more than a decoy."

"What do you mean, 'decoy'?"

"A coded message placed specifically for my enemy's redirection." He lowered his voice. "Who knew my enemy would be so beautiful and clever?"

The blood drained from her face. "This message means nothing?"

"Only if you're interested in the eating habits of hedgehogs."

"Oh, God." The pages drifted to the floor. "I've failed."

He glanced down at the discarded pages and noticed she had been copying the coded missive.

"*Sophie.*" She shot across the chamber.

He hooked his arm around her waist and drew her against his chest. "Where do you go?"

She clawed at his hand and kicked at his shins. "Stop it, Sebastian. I must get Sophie and my mother away from here."

"Catherine, enough." He subdued her flailing arms. "You cannot win a physical battle against me. Tell me who he is, so that I can protect you."

The fight went out of her as abruptly as it had begun. She sagged against him. "Why would you wish to help me after I seduced my way into your bed, only to betray you?"

That hurt. A piece of him had hoped she'd had more compelling reasons for sharing his bed. "Because I must take responsibility for my part in this debacle."

She swiveled her head around to meet his gaze. "In what way?"

"Promise you won't try to flee?" When she nodded, he eased his hold and guided her to one of the upholstered chairs. He did not sit, nor did he stand unmoving, as he was prone to do in situations of high tension. Instead, he paced. "I have much to repent for, Catherine. However, given the same set of circumstances, I would act the same."

Even bedding a blond-haired, lonely widow in over her head.

"Why do you feel the need to repent for your actions?"

"Because most noble acts have regrettable consequences."

"Geoffrey was a regrettable consequence?"

He nodded. "And I suspect Meghan McCarthy was as well."

"A-are you a traitor, Sebastian?"

Given the lengths he had gone to and the plans he had diverted to protect his country from a war-mongering upstart, her question was almost laughable, if it were not so damn painful.

"Is that what your friend told you?"

"He's not my friend."

"Then tell me his name." He recognized the stubborn set to her features before she ever said a word.

"I will, as soon as you answer my question."

"No."

She blinked. "Are you refusing to answer, or was that your answer?"

His lips twitched, despite the seriousness of the situation. "I'm not a traitor. Your turn."

Her features softened and the tautness of her body loosened.

"Frederick Cochran."

He nodded, expecting as much. However, the name he had hoped to hear from her lips was *Latymer*. "Tell me, are Cochran and John Chambers one and the same?"

She winced, glancing away. "Yes."

"Why the subterfuge?"

"I honestly don't know." She met his gaze. "Everything was happening so fast. I found myself in the midst of something terrible that I didn't fully comprehend, and I acted on instinct."

"Because you didn't trust me."

"I didn't trust anyone at that point."

He skimmed the backs of his fingers down her upper arm. "Do you trust me now?"

"How do I know you're not lying to me like Mr. Cochran?"

"You don't." He beat back his frustration. "In this, all I can offer you is my word and a reminder. Ashcroft was my friend. He trusted me." Her expression remained skeptical. "Have I ever threatened you? Made you or Sophie feel unsafe?"

"No. Never." She swiped the tears from her face. "I'm sorry, Sebastian. It's all just...too much."

He cupped her cheek, and she leaned into his touch. The simple action made him feel powerful in a way he never had before. More powerful than when he had obstructed an attempt on the Prime Minister's life and when he had saved a Russian princess from Napoleon's grasp.

"Trust me, Cat."

Fresh tears welled in her beautiful brown eyes. "Yes," she whispered.

His chest swelled, and her mouth drew his attention. He wanted to lap the words from her lips, know the taste of her belief. Instead, he focused on pulling every bit of information from her, because he had promised Sophie he would not tell her mama.

"Thank you. Can you tell me if Cochran is working alone?"

"I thought so until Tuesday. He brought a woman to act as Sophie's governess, and the frightening man we saw outside church on Sunday has become my shadow."

He remembered the skeletal creature. Sophie's scary man, no doubt.

"No one else?"

"No."

If Latymer was involved in this scheme, he was keeping to the background, allowing Cochran to take the lead on this mission. Such an elaborate ruse, for what? Latymer's goal did not appear to be Sebastian's death this time around. At least, not yet.

What would make Latymer go to such lengths? What did he value so much that he would turn his back on everything he believed in?

"At least not that I recall," she clarified. "With Cochran threatening to jab a hot poker into my daughter's eye if I didn't cooperate, I'm afraid my focus was somewhat narrowed."

"Bloody bastard." He saw the scene as clearly as if he were in the room. A precocious girl's smile transforming into a mask of terror. Then he saw Catherine—helpless, frightened, desperate to save her child. Desperate enough to betray her neighbor, whom Cochran accused of seditious behavior and murder. "They will come to regret that act of violence, Catherine. You have my word."

She drew in a deep, audible breath and lifted her head. "Perhaps now would be a good time to divulge the full extent of your relationship with Geoffrey."

Thanks to Cochran, she already knew more than was good for her about the Nexus. Which meant he would not be breaking any confidences or endangering anyone's life if he filled in the gaps.

The notion lifted an unbearable weight from his shoulders. Protecting his agents had always been a burden he had gladly carried and wholeheartedly accepted. But withholding the truth from Catherine had placed a far greater strain on his forbearance than he had realized.

"Perhaps you're right." His gaze fell on a decanter of amber liquid. "Care for a drink?"

"Would love one, thank you."

He moved to a small sideboard that held an assortment of liquor and poured two fingers in a tumbler. "Give it a try. Its numbing properties can be quite beneficial."

"You're not having any?"

He rested his forearms on the back of the chair opposite hers. "No."

She accepted his offering, gave it a delicate sniff before upending the glass.

"Catherine, be careful—"

Her eyes widened and her nose turned raspberry red, but she made it through the fiery drink with nothing more than a delicate cough. She handed her empty glass back to him. "Quite bracing."

"Indeed." He cocked his head to the side to assess the damage. "Another?"

She shook her head. "I believe I am sufficiently numbed."

Envy rolled through him. What he would not give to be relieved of the constant carousel of disturbing thoughts and images.

"About five years ago, your husband came to my attention. Many people in my circle spoke highly of him. They praised his intellect, his ambition, and his sense of morality.

I spent the next year gathering intelligence on him, checking his connections and finances, monitoring his political leanings, and evaluating his mental stamina."

"Mental stamina? How do you evaluate such a thing?"

He hesitated but could not come up with a valid reason not to elaborate. "By placing obstacles in his path, then observing his reactions."

"You can't be serious."

"Why is that? To be a successful Nexus agent, one must prove oneself capable of logical thought while under incredible pressure. Our agents are often alone in the field and must rely on their own wits to survive."

"Sounds insidious."

"Yet necessary."

"I shall have to take your word for it." She rubbed her hands down her skirts. "Geoffrey passed your test, I take it."

"More than passed it, he excelled at that particular stage of the recruitment process."

"How many stages are there to becoming an agent?"

Being able to discuss his work with her felt good. Oddly liberating and unexpectedly intimate. His gaze roamed the exquisite lines of her face. "As many as it takes for us to know."

THIRTY-ONE

Catherine caught Sebastian's slow perusal of her features and felt an answering jolt in her chest. She angled her body more fully toward him. "Until you know what?"

"That the individual is trustworthy." He pushed away from the chair and prowled around the side, his gaze locked with hers. "That he is English to the core." He stopped in front of her. "That he has a good chance of survival."

She swallowed back her trepidation. There was something about this side of him that intrigued her beyond bearing. His tactics were calculating, merciless. Some would even call them cold and unfeeling. But she saw also their brilliance and a deeper, more underlying quality that drove him to these brutal lengths. He cared—about England and his agents.

"What is it exactly that they must survive?"

"A power-hungry dictator who wishes the world to bow at his Corsican feet. At present, Napoleon Bonaparte's most desperate wish is to destroy France's longtime enemy, England."

"Surely such a thing isn't possible."

"With the right strategist, it's quite possible, I assure you."

"But how? England has the greatest military force in the world." At least, she thought so. She had to admit that she knew little about the security of her country, let alone anything beyond English borders.

"By closing the continent to British trade. He could destroy us without the mess of bloodshed."

"Dear God." Everything Cochran had told her was a lie. *Everything.*

The Nexus was organized to protect English shores against a French invasion, not to invite them in. And Geoffrey had been in league with the Nexus, not investigating them. Shame filled her heart.

"How could I have been so stupid?"

"There's nothing stupid about believing in the purity of another's heart. Unfortunately, there are those who would take advantage of such goodness."

She could barely breathe around the constriction in her throat. "When did Geoffrey become an agent?"

He stopped before her, and she felt the same sense of being overwhelmed as she did all those days ago in London. This time, however, she better understood the man behind the cool facade. Knew the hero within. The masked vulnerability without. He lowered himself in front of her.

"Sebastian, what of your knee?"

"All the pressure is on my good one. No need to worry, mama hen."

She sent him a cross look. "Geoffrey?"

"We discussed his inclusion during my last visit to Showbury."

Four years ago.

"During the Harrison house party?"

"Correct. How did you know?"

She shifted her attention to his shoulder. "A guess."

"A very good one." Bending forward, he gripped the arms of her chair. "What brought you to that conclusion?"

Her chest seemed to cave in, pressing against her lungs. No matter how she turned the words in her head, they still made her sound pathetic. But she would not hold back now, no matter how painful the revelation.

She forced her eyes up to meet his. "The house party was the last glimpse of the man I married. Afterwards, he changed, shifted into a near stranger. All the times I saw him between then and his death, he was nothing more than an actor playing a part."

The warmth that had been building behind his steel-gray eyes extinguished, and his supple lips compressed into a thin, resolute line. With one glance, she knew he regretted the consequences of his association with her husband and she also knew he would not apologize for them either. He was a man of action. Once he evaluated the situation and made a decision, he did not look back.

Instead of moving away, he pressed closer. "Do you miss him?"

"Would it matter if I did?"

"No." His eyes remained hard, but his voice grew rough. "But I would like to know, all the same."

"I stopped missing him a long time ago."

He brought his hand up to caress the line of her jaw. "Ashcroft served his country well. First as a messenger and, later, as an intelligence agent. He saved lives, helped avert disasters. He was a hero. Remember that, Catherine. And one day, when Sophie is older, tell her. Tell her how her father helped save England during its bleakest hour."

She knew from experience that such knowledge did not soothe the hurt of missed birthdays and holidays, of not witnessing a daughter's first big catch or her first gallop across the meadow. The Navy had been Catherine's father's life, his one passion above all else, even above his family. All his colorful medals and his crew's effusive praise had done nothing to mend the many breaks in her heart.

But she appreciated what Sebastian was trying to do. She folded her hand over his and kissed his palm, afraid to meet his gaze or express her gratitude. Because if she had done either one, he would have seen her fall in love with him.

Sensing her distress, he framed her cheek and claimed her mouth. His kiss was passionate, full of volatility. The bone-deep chill that had invaded her body began to thaw, warming beneath his sensual assault. For the briefest of seconds, he let her burrow beneath the iron casing protecting him from harm. Beneath the casing beat the noblest of hearts, the purest of intentions. Beneath the casing she found hope.

She pushed deeper, needing to learn more about this complicated man. But he discerned her attack and nudged her back, closing the small portal.

Lifting his head, he leveled his burning, resolute gaze on her. "What do they want?"

"Sebastian, I'm so sorry—"

He placed a finger across her mouth. "There's no need."

"But—"

The pad of his finger smoothed over her lower lip. "Answer me one question."

She nodded, and he drew his hand away. He said

nothing for several seconds, seeming to debate the merits of asking his question.

Then, "At any time, did you enjoy my touch?"

Her throat ached for the courage it took to ask such a question. She brushed the backs of her fingers along his unshaven jaw. "Every time, Sebastian. *Every* time."

Beneath her caress, a muscle jumped. She returned her hand to her lap, unwilling to reveal any more of her blossoming feelings. Despite their shared passion, he would leave. And she would be left alone again. This time, however, she knew better than to wait, for this man would not return.

He pressed a kiss to her forehead and rose. At the table carrying an array of spirits, he paused. His stillness disconcerted her. "Are you unwell?"

"I'm fine." When he turned back, he asked, "What does Cochran want?"

His expression, his tone, his stance—it was all reminiscent of the day she had visited him at his London town house. That meeting now felt as if it had taken place an eternity ago. She fought to hold back a violent shiver.

"A list," she said.

If she thought he was still before, she had been wrong. The man who faced her was hewn of solid marble, not a hair or muscle moved. All warmth was gone. "What sort of list?"

"The one cataloging all trait—agents of the Nexus."

Fury twisted his handsome face into a mask of hatred. He grasped something off the table and propelled it across the chamber. A monstrous shattering of crystal followed. "Bloody Reeves!"

Frowning, she asked, "Reeves?"

But his anger made him deaf to her query. He prowled

the length of the chamber, muttering recriminations and casting Reeves to the devil.

She rose and placed the chair between them. The chair would provide little in the way of protection, but the meager barrier gave her a sense of comfort all the same.

He stopped. "Who the hell is Cochran?"

She clenched her teeth. "Supposedly a friend of Geoffrey's. Someone who worked with my husband at the Foreign Office."

"When did Cochran first approach you?"

"In London. The afternoon following our meeting. He caught me outside Grillon's and offered his condolences."

"And a good deal more information, I suspect."

With his mask of indifference back in place, she could no longer read the true intent behind his words. "Yes."

"The Foreign Office official shared some of the sordid details about your husband's death, enough to cast me in a poor light." He lifted a brow in her direction.

She nodded.

"Then he ever so casually mentioned the government's investigation into my last mission, sending further suspicion in my direction."

She closed her eyes, feeling like the absolute gudgeon she was.

"After Cochran established his willingness to share sensitive information, he asked for a favor in return."

Nausea bubbled in the back of her throat. "All I wanted was the truth about my husband's death." She covered her mouth with her hand, certain she was about to be sick.

A large warm palm wrapped around her trembling fingers. He drew them to his lips, kissing their pads. "I'm sorry, Catherine. I should not have allowed my anger free rein. You are innocent in all this."

"My stupidity"—his hand tightened, cutting off her recrimination—"my naïveté knows no bounds, does it?"

"Don't fret." He pressed a gentling kiss upon her lips. "We have all succumbed to such ploys."

She swallowed, wanting more of his reassuring lips. "I find that hard to believe."

"Believe it." He released her hand and moved away. "Did Cochran ever mention a Lord Latymer?"

"Not that I recall."

He released a frustrated sigh. "Then I would like to know how Cochran found out about Reeves's directive that I provide a list of all my agents, including their true identities."

"Who is Reeves?"

"He's the new Superintendent of the Alien Office." He threw her an inquiring look. "Cochran explained the Alien Office's function?"

"Intelligence gathering?"

"Good enough. To my knowledge, no one knew about Reeves's order, besides myself and three of my trusted agents."

"Maybe they let it slip?"

"Absolutely not."

"Is there a list?"

His expression grew cold, dangerous. "I considered it, even wrote down a few names."

"Yet you destroyed the list."

"Time will tell if I made the right decision. But I will take my agents' identities to the grave."

She stared at him with something akin to awe. How does one contain such a noble heart behind a shroud of ice?

At great sacrifice to himself, he planned to disregard his superior's order and protect the men and women under his command. The same way he'd protected his young wards all those years ago. The same way he promised to protect her and Sophie now.

On the cusp of that realization, her awe faded and a new sentiment emerged.

Terror.

"If I don't bring Cochran the Nexus, he's going to kill my daughter."

A cold smile graced his lips. "Then let us give him the Nexus."

THIRTY-TWO

Saturday morning dawned bright, matching Sophie's winsome birthday smile. Her daughter's infectious exuberance swept through the household with a velocity that would rival the *ton*'s most determined gossip. By the time the festivities started, Catherine's entire staff was giddy with anticipation and Sophie was near bouncing off the walls.

Catherine did her best to put on a happy face, but she could not shake the terrible dread that hovered at the edge of her mind. Cochran still expected her to bring him the list. A list that didn't exist—and never would.

"The gathering is a smashing success, Mrs. Ashcroft." The vicar appeared next to her, juggling a heaping plate while following the children's sack race. "Creating a life-sized version of Castle Dragonthorpe was no small feat."

She agreed. A drawbridge made of burlap, a moat outlined by timbers, and trellises for turrets took a great deal of ingenuity, but all the effort had been worth her daughter's jubilation. "I'm glad you could come, Mr.

Foster. The day would not have been the same without you."

"Meghan McCarthy's violent death has shaken Showbury's residents. Some have gone so far as to whisper names for the missing father."

She raised an eyebrow. "And, therefore, the murderer?"

He nodded while wrestling a melon ball onto his fork. "This is a disturbing turn of events, but not surprising. In our grief, we believe the only way to set our loved one's soul to rest is by punishing those responsible."

She caught sight of the earl strolling along the perimeter—er, moat—of Castle Dragonthorpe's inner bailey. He projected calm and idleness. Few would recognize the occasional narrowing of his eyes or his preference for hovering near her daughter.

"But justice," the vicar continued, "is mankind's tool, not God's, for keeping peace and is society's attempt at soothing the hollow ache of those left behind."

Could the same philosophy be applied to her? Was her effort to track down Geoffrey's killer and bring the man to justice nothing more than an attempt to relieve the never-ending void of loneliness in her heart? Something she had lived with long before his death?

"Forgive me, Mrs. Ashcroft." His kind eyes roamed over her features. "This is not the place or time to discuss such a dreary topic. Today is about celebrating life and laughter."

She smiled, thankful to be quit of the subject, even though a shadow lingered in her thoughts. "Indeed, Mr. Foster." For what seemed like the thousandth time, her gaze sought out her daughter's location and found her playing quoits with Teddy. "How is your courtship going?"

The vicar's face reddened, then beamed with delight.

"Miss Walker has consented to a drive and picnic tomorrow after services."

She placed her hand on his sleeve. "That is good news."

"Thank you. I appreciate your kind counsel on the matter."

"Good morning, Vicar. Mrs. Ashcroft," a newcomer interrupted. "How do you fare today?"

She started. Sebastian's voice sounded inches from her ear. Lifting her gaze, she found him staring at her hand resting on Mr. Foster's arm. She eased her fingers away and clasped her hands together.

"I'm doing very well, my lord," the vicar said. "How goes the search for a new steward?"

"Slow, I'm afraid." He scanned the gathering. "If you know of a dependable gentleman with legitimate references and experience, please send him my way."

"As it happens, I heard from an old university chum yesterday. His employer passed on and the heir is a bit of a scoundrel, or so my friend tells me. Timms is now considering his options. You'll never meet a more honorable man. Such a shame, what's happening, but fortuitous, don't you think?"

"Sounds just the thing. Please have him come see me."

"Thank you, my lord. He'll be delighted—"

"My dear Vicar." Evelyn sailed into their midst. "I see you have cleared a spot on your plate. Come with me and I'll introduce you to Cook's famous lemon cheesecake."

He hesitated, clearly not interested in giving up his tête-à-tête with the earl.

"I promise you, sir," her mother coaxed. "You shall not be disappointed."

Pasting his vicar-smile on his face, he said, "Pardon, Mrs. Ashcroft. My lord. I will return in a moment."

"Please do." Catherine followed the duo until her mother began an animated conversation on—she squinted to make out the object of their attention—she knew not what.

Sebastian guided her away from her guests milling about. "You and the vicar were rather cozy."

She sent him a sidelong glance. "I've told you before, he's a dear friend."

"Dear enough to marry?" He must have regretted his query the moment it emerged, for he followed it with a rough command. "Forget it."

"That's not possible." Her daughter's laughter caught her attention. She watched Sophie's next throw and smiled when the shoe hit the iron hob. "Where is this line of questioning coming from, Sebastian?"

A full minute ticked by before he answered. "The vicar mentioned he was contemplating marriage during our ride the other day. I thought perhaps you were his chosen bride."

His jealousy should have irritated her, but instead, his gruff explanation charmed her. "The good vicar has his sights set on Miss Walker, and she on him. But neither have had the gumption to approach the other."

"I suppose you have been encouraging him to declare himself during your long drives?"

Fingers of heat spread into her cheeks. "Life's too short to spend it alone and unhappy."

She felt his searing gaze on her, but did not dare meet it. "How is that particular endeavor coming along?"

"They're going on a picnic tomorrow afternoon."

"What of you, Cat?"

His low, intimate tone pierced her heart. "I don't understand your question."

"What will you do once your mourning has ended? Will you seek a father for your daughter?"

"Eventually. I am wise enough to realize not all men are like my father and husband. Next time, I will choose more carefully."

"Indeed—" Something caught his eye over her shoulder. "Where is Sophie?"

"She's right over there." She swung around to where her daughter and Teddy were throwing quoits. Her eyes widened when she found nothing but two iron hobs sticking out of the ground and their discarded quoits. "Sebastian," she whispered. "They were playing there not but a minute ago."

"Stay calm," he warned. "There are many tempting items in your make-believe castle to draw their attention." He peered over her shoulder and flicked his index finger in a sharp circle. "Let us make a circuit of the area."

"Yes, of course." She accepted his arm. "Cochran would be a fool to attempt something while so many people are in attendance."

"Yet a crowd can provide the best cover. Or he could have Mrs. Clarke spirit Sophie away." He glanced down at her. "I mention this not to frighten you, but to keep you from becoming complacent. You must never, ever underestimate your enemy."

Her heart hammered within her chest. She did not like this spying business. Before this was all finished, she was quite certain her heart would never pound again.

They made a full circle around the crowd without one glimpse of a golden-red curls. Her trepidation grew. She had made Sophie promise to stay within sight today, an edict that had engendered a great many moans. Although her daughter liked to poke and prod the boundaries

Catherine set, she had never outright disobeyed her in this way.

When Sebastian finally drew them to a halt, the muscles in her throat ached from her effort to hold back the compulsive scream of her daughter's name. She peered up at him. "I will round up several of the adults to scour the area. I don't want to scare the children." The moment she made to pull away, he covered her hand.

"A moment." Rather than searching the area again with a thorough sweep of his gaze, his attention jumped from one point to the next.

"Sebastian, please." She pulled at her hand. "I cannot stand this inactivity."

He nodded at someone in the distance, and the tension faded from his taut features. "Come, I believe we missed a hiding spot."

Confused by his odd behavior, she accompanied him across the lawn without a word, although she chafed at his unhurried pace. He stopped next to the dessert table and pointed to a two-inch gap between tablecloths. "Your damsel in distress, madam."

She crouched down and peered into the gap. Sure enough, Sophie and the stable lad, Teddy, sat beneath the table, alternately stuffing chocolate puffs into their mouths and staging battles with pieces from her daughter's Dragonthorpe collection.

"Sophia Adele, may I see you for a moment?"

Round blue eyes peered through the opening.

Catherine crooked her finger.

"Don't kill my gargoyle while I'm gone, Teddy. I'll be vexed." Her daughter scampered out from beneath the table, brushing an incriminating crumb from her lavender skirts. The half-mourning color was a small concession for her party. "Yes, Mama?"

She grabbed her daughter's hand and led her away from the guests. "Did you not promise to stay within sight?"

Sophie glanced back at the table.

"I shall have your full attention, young lady." She waited until her daughter's gaze returned to hers. "Did I not tell you, if you can't see me, I can't see you?"

"But, Mama, I could see you." She indicated the space between the tablecloths, where Teddy now watched her daughter's scolding with rapt attention. "I saw you chatting with the vicar and strolling with the earl."

Catherine blinked, unable to think of a response to her daughter's six-, or rather, seven-year-old logic. "Do you know the scare you gave me?"

"I'm sorry, Mama." Sophie turned her doleful blue eyes on her. "Please don't be upset."

Cupping the back of her daughter's head, she kissed the vixen's forehead. "I'm not, but allow me to clarify my statement. We must *both* be able to see each other."

Sophie nodded, her gaze going back to the table again.

"None of that, dear. You have many guests to attend. All of your time cannot be spent with Teddy, no matter how tempting."

"Do you think the earl would mind if Teddy came along to see his horses?"

She glanced back to find Sebastian encouraging the boy from beneath the table. "There's only one way to find out, and that's to ask." She held out her hand when Sophie started to rush over to her two favorite men. "Make your request like a young lady, title and all."

Her daughter smiled. "Thank you, Mama."

She took off, but immediately slowed her breakneck pace to a more sedate stroll. Well, almost sedate. She looked the epitome of sweetness from the waist up. However, her feet were throwing up patches of grass in her wake.

Stopping before Sebastian, Sophie executed a perfect curtsy. "Good afternoon, Lord Somerton. Are you enjoying my birthday celebration?"

He bowed. "Indeed, I am."

She waved her hand toward her friend. "I see you've met Teddy. Did he tell you about his mama?"

Sebastian glanced at Catherine, a glint in his eyes. "I'm afraid not."

Sophie sent her friend a sympathetic look. "His mama is terribly ill."

"I'm sorry to hear that, Teddy."

The stable lad's face flamed. "Thank you, sir."

"He loves horses." Her daughter bent at the waist until Sebastian's attention shifted back to her. "The only horses he sees all day are Guinevere and Gypsy. Sweet creatures, but they cannot compare to a *whole barn full* of horses." She rose up on her toes as if to punctuate her statement, an expectant look lighting her cherub face.

"Hmm." Sebastian rubbed his jaw. "As it happens, I have a whole barn full of horses."

Sophie clasped her hands together, looking from Sebastian to Teddy. "I know."

In a conspiratorial whisper, Sebastian asked, "Do you think your friend would like to join us later this afternoon?"

Her daughter let out an excited squeak. "Teddy, the earl has invited you to see his horses. Maybe he'll let you ride Cira, too."

Catherine raised an eyebrow, but Sebastian kept his attention on the boy.

Teddy smiled, revealing the beginnings of a new tooth coming in. "Thank you, m'lord."

"Oh, dear me." Sebastian laid an exaggerated hand to his chest, a look of consternation on his handsome face.

Sophie and Teddy shared a worried glance. "What's wrong, earl?" she asked.

"I just recalled something very important. Something that might change your mind about visiting my stables."

Sophie slipped her hand into Sebastian's. "Don't worry, sir. Teddy and I will want to see your stables, no matter what."

"Truly?" He looked between two pairs of earnest eyes. "Even if I don't have a brown horse?"

Her daughter frowned, and Teddy looked bewildered. Catherine covered her mouth to hide her smile.

Then Sophie noticed Sebastian's lips twitch. "Oh, Bastian. Horses are nothing to joke about."

"Sophie," Catherine scolded. "You must not be so informal with his lordship."

"I gave her leave to do so." He sent her daughter a gentle smile. "Didn't I, sprite?"

She giggled. "Yes, Bastian. If I'm a sprite, does that make Teddy a brownie?"

Sebastian, bless him, tousled poor Teddy's hair. "What do you say, lad? Would you like to be a brownie to Miss Sophie's sprite?"

He gave them another gap-toothed grin. "Brownies like barns, don't they, sir?"

"Indeed, they do."

"Then I shall be a brownie."

"And I a sprite."

"And I Bastian."

Three pairs of eyes turned toward Catherine. "What?"

"What shall we call you?" Sophie asked, bouncing with excitement.

"Um...Mama?"

Sophie groaned, Teddy ducked, and Sebastian smiled.

"Let us give your mother's nickname some thought, shall we?" Sebastian suggested. "In the meantime, I believe sprite has a few guests she needs to greet." He glanced at Catherine for confirmation.

"Off you go," she said.

"Come on, Teddy," Sophie said. "Let's see who we can get to bob for oranges."

"Oranges don't float," he protested.

"Precisely, you silly brownie!"

Catherine shook her head, enjoying Sophie's boundless good cheer.

"She is a marvel," Sebastian said.

"Yes." Catherine peered up at him. "You're very patient with her, *Bastian*."

A tinge of color darkened his cheeks, and her unsteady wall crumbled to the ground.

"Years ago, when my wards were young and grieving over the loss of their parents, I made many mistakes." He met her gaze. "Not knowing if I would be alive or dead from one day to the next, I taught them skills that might one day save their lives, and I ensured they never had to be concerned about finances."

"Where is the fault in your actions, sir?"

"I kept them at arm's length, praising them rarely and hugging them never." He released a shaky breath. "I told myself it was for their own good. They would never feel the devastating loss of a parent again."

"In your own way, you were trying to protect them. No matter how hard we try to do right by our children, we will inevitably get it wrong at times. Take my current circumstances, for instance."

As if they read each other's mind, their gazes sought out Sophie.

"Yes, well," he said. "I lied. To myself. You see, before joining the Alien Office, I wanted a wife and family. Desperately. But after my mentor's and his wife's brutal murders, I suppressed the need. Keeping the two young deBeaus at a distance was as much for my protection as theirs. In the end, I fell in love with the little terrors anyway. Too bad they will never know."

"Pardon, m'lord. Ma'am."

A maid with short-cropped mahogany hair and a scarred left cheek held out a tray of oysters nestled in scallop shells. Catherine did not recognize the maid, but she had a vague memory of her mother saying something about hiring additional servants to help out with the festivities. With her mind so wrapped up in protecting Sophie and finding nonexistent lists, she had readily left the issue of event staffing to her mother.

The maid nodded at the tray. "Care for one?"

Sebastian stiffened. "No, thank you."

"Are you sure, sir? I hear they're a right treat."

"Quite. Sure."

"What about your missus? She might like—"

A nasty shade of red suffused Sebastian's features.

Catherine interrupted, reaching for a shell. "Thank you..."

"Belle, ma'am," she said with a curtsy.

"Belle, I should like one." Something about the interplay between Sebastian and the maid seemed off. She could not quite put her finger on it. His warning tone, her direct look. The stiffness in his shoulders, the twinkle in her eyes. It all held an undercurrent of familiarity that would normally only be attained through years of acquaintance. Not seconds of discussion. "My mother is quite fond of these. Please see if she would like one."

"Yes, ma'am." Belle curtsied again. "Sir."

The moment the maid turned away, Sebastian's eyes narrowed on the young woman's back.

"Do you know her?" She opened her mouth and let the oyster slide inside.

His eyes snapped to hers. "Why do you ask?"

She swallowed. "You appear *disturbed*."

"She interrupted a private conversation. I'm annoyed, not disturbed."

Catherine considered the maid as she held out the tray to Evelyn. Belle's chin remained high and her gaze never lowered. *Bold girl.* "My apologies. Mother must have hired additional staff for today."

"Your apology is unnecessary, I assure you." He scanned the crowd. "Do you see other unfamiliar staff?"

"Besides Belle, I've noticed two other unfamiliar maids and a couple new footmen."

"Care to point them out?"

Something in his tone caused wariness to creep into her heart. "Is there something I need to be concerned about?"

"Not at all. I'm simply eliminating potential threats."

Threats.

Her hand lifted to her chest as her gaze sought out Sophie. She found her bent over with laughter as Teddy lifted his drenched head from the barrel. An orange in his mouth.

"I'm sorry, Catherine," Sebastian said in a low voice. "I didn't mean to alarm you. Sophie is safe."

"My daughter won't be safe until this business with Frederick Cochran is resolved."

A warm hand rested on her lower back. "She's safe. I swear it."

"I hope you're right."

He removed his hand, and she immediately mourned its absence. "You were going to point out the unfamiliar servants," he prompted.

Relieved to have a task that would take her mind off thoughts of Cochran, she nodded toward an older maid weaving through the guests. "The buxom maid striding past my mother."

"Who else?"

"The distinguished footman with a queue helping Belle fill her tray with more delicacies."

He followed her direction and his lips thinned. "Go on."

"Near the bevy of young misses is a roguish footman with black-as-night hair eyeing Miranda Walker." The gentleman glanced in their direction before turning back to his duties.

The earl nudged her in the opposite direction. "Any other foreign faces?"

"Only the tall maid, with the black hair and spectacles."

He stopped and performed a surreptitious scan. "I don't see a maid matching that description."

"I don't see her now, either. But earlier, she appeared to be taking care of refreshments and cleaning away dirty dishes." An awful thought struck her. "What if my mother didn't hire them? Maybe they do work for Cochran. It wouldn't be the first time he's disrupted my household by bringing in his people."

"Doubtful." He resumed their stroll, halting a few feet behind the vicar and her mother. "You concentrate on making Sophie happy. I'll look into the matter of the servants."

"But—"

"Trust me. I might be a failure in the area of finer feelings. But when it comes to protecting those under my charge, I'm unmatched."

Emotion gripped her chest, and she wanted nothing more than to kiss the man silly. She settled for a hand on his sleeve. "I haven't found you lacking in either pursuit, Sebastian." Something feral and very male entered his expression.

She retreated with a pat to his arm. "Very well, my lord. See to the mysterious servants and I'll take care of my daughter."

His heavy-lidded gaze did not budge from her face for several heart-pounding seconds. She worried he would do something embarrassing—and highly enjoyable—like kiss her.

Then he drew back a step and inclined his head. "Until later."

She forced her gaze to sweep over her guests, rather than follow Sebastian's progress. Had she done otherwise, she would not have been able to mask the yearning burning in her soul.

THIRTY-THREE

Arm in arm, Catherine and Sophie strolled down the path leading from the barn to the house. Dusk was on the horizon, signaling the end to a memorable day. She glanced down at her daughter's bent head. "What's the matter, dear?"

Sophie shrugged her narrow shoulders. "I wish Teddy didn't have to do chores."

"Me, too, sweetheart." She hugged her little girl closer. "But that's the deal he struck with Carson so he could spend time with you today. He made a choice, one he seemed more than content with."

"I suppose so."

They entered the house and made their way to the nursery. "It was kind of you to include him on your tour of Lord Somerton's stables."

"Bastian's horses were grand, weren't they, Mama?"

"Very grand."

"Did you see me ride Cira?"

"Indeed, I did. You were quite accomplished, young lady."

Sophie beamed. "I thought about asking Eloisa Walker, but she would have complained about the smell the whole time."

"Then it is good you didn't extend an invitation."

"She might be miffed at me."

"I'm sure you will have no problem coaxing her out of her pout." She pushed open the nursery door and found Mrs. Clarke pacing inside.

The governess swung around, her eyes red-rimmed and her hair askew.

Oblivious, Sophie ran to her faux governess. "Mrs. Clarke, you should have joined us. So many lovely horses."

The governess rested her hand on Sophie's shoulder. "I'm sorry I missed your outing. Sounds like you had an exciting time."

Sophie's smile diminished. She reached up to trace a fingertip over Mrs. Clarke's blotchy cheek. "Does your head still hurt?"

Fresh tears wobbled in the woman's eyes. "Somewhat. Thank you for asking." She grasped Sophie's hand in both of hers, kissing her fingertips. "Now we must wash the barn from you."

Her daughter groaned.

"Perhaps we can hold off until tomorrow morning, Mrs. Clarke," Catherine suggested.

Sophie turned wide, hopeful eyes on her governess.

"As you wish, ma'am." To Sophie she said, "I have your nightclothes laid out in the other room. Let us get you ready for bed."

"Sophie," Catherine said, "get started without Mrs. Clarke. I need to speak with her for a moment."

Her daughter tore across the chamber and flung herself

into Catherine's arms. "Thank you for the best birthday ever."

Tears stung the back of her eyes. "You're welcome, pumpkin." She kissed her nose. "Now off with you."

Sophie skipped from the room, leaving two teary-eyed women behind.

"Why are you here?" she asked the governess in a quiet voice.

"To watch over your daughter."

"Yes." She clasped her hands together. "That's why Cochran brought you here. What I want to know is why *you* are here."

A haunted expression froze the governess's features. "I don't know what you're talking about."

Catherine shuffled closer. "Don't you?"

The governess shook her head, her lips firming to stop their trembling.

Closer still. "I recognize a mother's fear."

Mrs. Clarke's eyes closed briefly. When they opened again, bleakness penetrated their depths. "Please don't."

"Why? There is no one to hear."

A maniacal laugh burst from her lips. "There's *always* someone to hear, Mrs. Ashcroft. Never doubt it." She threw off her grief as if it were a cumbersome mantle. "Now, if you'll excuse me. I must attend your daughter." With that pronouncement, the woman marched into the next chamber.

Catherine's gaze cast about the nursery, recalling Sebastian's warning never to underestimate her enemy. Feeling heartsick, she left her enemy behind to tend her daughter. Two doors from her bedchamber, she rounded the corner and came to an abrupt halt.

In the middle of the dimly lit corridor stood Silas,

looking more tattered than normal, with his neckcloth missing and an unflattering amount of flesh showing. The area around his mouth glistened in a way that turned her stomach, and she could see he was holding something behind his back.

"Have you anything for my master?"

Why was he asking now rather than waiting until she returned later this evening? Much about Silas tonight seemed stranger than normal. Thank goodness, she and Sebastian had been able to sneak away for a little while to discuss their next steps while Bellamere's stablemaster fielded Sophie's and Teddy's many questions.

Recalling Sebastian's instructions, she said, "This afternoon, I found what looked like a catalog of names and locations, but everything appeared to be in some type of code."

"How many traitors are on the list?"

Her heart froze in her chest. They had not discussed numbers. "I didn't count them."

His head tilted to the side and he seemed to be playing with something in his teeth. "What is your best guess, madam?"

What would be a believable number? One that would not be laughable or too extraordinary, but large enough to give Cochran pause? She released a slow breath. "If I had to guess, I would say between twenty and twenty-five."

He stared at her, unblinking, for several bone-racking seconds. "When can you make delivery?"

Relief straightened her spine. "Within the next couple days, I suspect."

"Not sooner?"

"I don't see how. The list is in his lordship's bedchamber. It's difficult to copy something so well hidden when I'm rarely left alone."

"Then don't copy it. Bring the original."

The longer they spoke, the more agitated he became. In a level voice, she said, "Mr. Cochran's instructions were quite clear, sir. I'm not to arouse Lord Somerton's suspicions. If I take the list and he's still cataloging agents, he'll warn every member of the Nexus."

As if Silas weren't peculiar-looking enough, his right eye twitched when angered.

"Are we finished here, Mr. Silas?"

The twitching grew worse. He nodded but did not move out of her path. And his hand remained half hidden behind his back.

She lifted her chin and strode forward. "Good night, Mr. Silas."

His arm swung out, and he held a large, cudgel-like weapon in his hand. She gasped, ducking beneath the cover of her arms, and waited.

Nothing happened.

Then came a disgusting sucking noise. Easing up from her crouched position, she realized the sound was coming from his mouth. He was ripping chunks of meat off a large bone with his jagged teeth. Juices from the succulent piece dripped down his chin and landed on his bare chest.

Bile shot into the back of her throat.

"Your reflexes are much better than the earl's." He cocked his head to the side. "And you didn't wail like the Irish girl."

She pressed her back against the wall as the world beneath her feet began to shake. "You're the one?"

It was then Silas did something truly terrifying.

He smiled.

An awful smile, filled with bits of meat and rotting teeth.

Evil.

"The spymaster interrupted my search."

"W-what were you looking for?"

"The same as you, madam."

"What of Meghan McCarthy?"

"She had become burdensome to my master." He jerked his head toward the empty corridor. "Time for you to prepare for your visit with his lordship."

The conversation concluded, and she was glad of it, though she had a hundred more questions she wished to ask. Once she had scooted clear of her gaoler, she ran the short distance and slammed her bedchamber door shut. She knew he would follow. Knew he would eventually bed down outside her door. The hour she sought her bed might change from night to night, but Silas's constant guard never faltered.

They had killed Meghan. Did that mean Cochran was the father? It must, but how? He had only arrived a few days ago.

How long had he been watching her? Waiting for Geoffrey to make an appearance? Perhaps his letters were warning Sebastian of Cochran's perfidy. Good Lord, could this situation get any more complicated and dangerous?

She only hoped that the seed she had planted took root. Had it burrowed deep into Silas's fertile mind yet? Could he even now be making his way to Bellamere to steal the nonexistent list of agents? She fought to control her fear for Sebastian. Would he be ready for Cochran's miscreant?

The thought of something happening to Sebastian scorched her soul. So many depended upon him, and England's safety revolved around his continued leadership of a little-known group of spies. Moreover, she would miss him.

She drew in a deep breath and transformed her fear into faith. He was England's greatest spymaster, a man sworn to protect his countrymen and one who had promised to keep her and Sophie safe. A villainous official and a puny footpad would be no match for his lethal mind.

Squaring her shoulders, she clicked the fragile door lock in place, knowing it provided minimal protection. She strode to her dressing table and peered in the looking glass at her hair. The wind had not been kind.

She located the painted porcelain dish that held her stash of pins. And that's when she noticed the letter. Her name was not written on the front, nor did it contain an address. But the missive sat propped between a bottle of lotion and a tin of powder. She glanced around the chamber. The room was quiet, almost as if it held its breath, waiting for her to assuage her curiosity.

A heavy blanket of dread bore down on her as she reached for the scrap of paper. Unfolding the note, she read the neat but hastily written message. By the time she reached the end, the words were hidden behind a veil of tears and the pressure around her chest threatened to suffocate her.

"Sebastian."

THIRTY-FOUR

Catherine peered down at the anonymous letter again, her tears making the feminine handwriting blurry and incomprehensible.

My dear Mrs. Ashcroft,

I risk discovery to bring you the truth about Lord Somerton's care of my brother Ethan and myself. Not only did the earl offer shelter to two grief-stricken orphans, who were no relation to him, he gave us a home, one complete with all the comforts a child could want and all the parental devotion a child might need.

Never once in all the years I lived beneath his guardianship did I doubt his love for me. There are many ways to love another, and all do not require a confession of emotion. Love is in the heart, and I see it shining in his for you.

If you feel the same, which I believe you do, seize this moment. He will never give you a day where you doubt his affection, for his is the truest of hearts.

> *Warmly, and your new admirer,*
> *Cora-belle*

PS—Lord Somerton can, at times, be rather mulish in his protection of those he loves. Sometimes that noble quality can lead to sacrificial decisions. If you need suggestions on how best to knock some sense into him, I am at your service.

Lord Somerton's ward, or rather former ward, was here. And sometime during the festivities, she had invaded Catherine's private quarters and used her personal stock of paper to write a devastating letter.

With trembling fingers, she set Cora's note down and wondered how her life had become so complicated so fast. Her love for Sebastian grew with every encounter, and not even his alleged involvement in Geoffrey's death had stopped her from plunging in over her head.

How had she managed to attach her affections to a man even more obsessed with his cause than either her father or her husband?

A low knock sounded, and she hastily wiped her eyes and tucked the missive away. At the door, she asked, "Yes?"

"May I come in, daughter?"

She should feign weariness and send her mother away. After her encounter with Silas, she was in no mood for company. But a part of her was still a girl in need of her mother's comfort. She could not ever remember needing it more than she did at this moment.

Patting her cheeks and hair, she ran her hands down the front of her dress before unlocking the door. Brown eyes, not dissimilar from her own, rounded at the sight of her daughter's ravaged face. Evelyn rushed forward, slamming the door closed behind her and enfolding Catherine in her arms.

"Oh, daughter," Evelyn whispered. "All will be set to rights."

The warmth, the security, and the familiar scent of gardenias in her mother's embrace propelled Catherine back to her adolescence. The traitorous tears returned. "It's too much."

"No, it's not." Evelyn clasped her tighter. "You have a strong spirit, one that will see you through this and many more challenges in the years to come. Don't give in to the fear. Sup from it, draw strength from it. Then vanquish it."

She pulled away, swiping at her face. "Silas admitted to attacking Lord Somerton and killing Meghan McCarthy."

"Dear God."

"There's so much at stake, Mother. One wrong word or one erroneous act, and I could lose my daughter and mother and the man I—" The damning words stuck to the back of her throat.

Keen-witted woman that she was, Evelyn offered, "The man you love?"

Closing her eyes, she fought back a wave of complicated emotions. "Caught in my own tangled web." She drew in a deep breath and stepped away as an unaccountable chill settled in her bones.

"Don't be so harsh on yourself," Evelyn admonished. "Given the circumstances, you were left with few choices. As for you falling in love with Lord Somerton," she propped her hands on her hips, "many a male neighbor and traveler has tried to seduce you into their beds over the last few years, with no success. I suspect there's something rather special about him, or you would have sent him to the devil with all the rest."

Using her fingertips, she placed pressure on each throbbing temple. "For years, I viewed Lord Somerton as a cold, reclusive man with little interest in his country estate."

"And now?"

"Now, I see that he is everything I was certain he wasn't." She thought of his kindnesses toward Sophie, his sense of urgency with the repairs, and his unwavering determination to find Meghan McCarthy. And there was the way he had ripped away her loneliness with a single, passionate kiss.

"I will never go back to my former half-life." She wrapped her arms around her middle. "For years, I wondered what horrible thing I had done or had not done that caused Sophie to lose her father. All those worries and recriminations were for nothing. I suffered years of useless guilt. Never again."

She halted her monologue long enough to draw in a calming breath. "This might sound selfish, but I'm beyond caring. I want a gentleman who will put me—and my daughter—above all else. Someone who will love me and stay by my side, no matter how badly I vex him."

Evelyn's smile was a mixture of pride and sorrow. "As you should, daughter."

She didn't know how to ease her mother's past regrets. "Mother, we must all begin anew." Catherine squeezed the other woman's hand. "Let us put the past to rest."

"Yes," Evelyn said. "Yes, I do believe you're right." With her normal fortitude, her mother collected herself. "The seed is planted?"

"I believe so."

Silas's unusual behavior and Mrs. Clarke's tear-stained face made Catherine uneasy. "I'm so torn. I need to convey

Silas's confession to Lord Somerton, but I also wonder if I should forgo visiting him tonight."

"Why is that, dear?"

"Our unwanted guests appear out of sorts, don't you think?"

"Not any more than normal, but I haven't seen either one since before you left for Bellamere's stables." Her mother glanced at the closed door. "If you stay, you take the risk of agitating Silas. He doesn't seem the type one should provoke."

Catherine recalled the man's twitching eye, awful smile, and vile confessions and decided her mother was correct. "I suppose, though my stomach is not happy about it."

THIRTY-FIVE

"You can't be serious, Chief," Lord Danforth said. "She picked everyone out?"

Sebastian stared into the empty fire grate, not looking up at the small group of Nexus agents assembled in the drawing room. Had he done so, the mixture of irritation and pride lighting his eyes would have confused them all.

"Everyone but you and Bingham, and that's only because you were both walking the perimeter." Many years ago, he had hired Bingham, along with Dinks and Jack, to watch over Cora while she was on assignment in France. Bingham acted the coachman, Jack the footman, and Dinks the lady's maid. The quartet had become close, each protecting the others like beloved family members.

"No one ever pays attention to servants," Danforth grumbled.

"I have come to realize Mrs. Ashcroft isn't like most people."

His statement was met with a thick fog of silence. He glanced up then and found four pairs of fascinated eyes on him. Danforth looked more appalled, Lord Helsford stared without expression, Cora appeared on the verge of happy tears, and Dinks chortled until she snorted.

"I'm doomed." Danforth groaned and slumped back in his chair.

Cora sent her brother a sharp look. "What are you nattering on about?"

"If a woman can steal the chief's heart," Danforth nodded toward Sebastian, "there is no hope for my continued bachelorhood."

"Ethan!" Cora scolded.

Sebastian's muscles coiled into bands of steel. Although Danforth had a tendency to blurt out whatever was on his mind, inappropriately so at times, the man's instincts tended toward genius. Which, in this particular case, did not bode well for Sebastian. "I assure you, my heart is where it should be."

He resumed their former discussion. "In addition to identifying each of you, Mrs. Ashcroft noted an unfamiliar tall, black-haired woman. Anyone else notice her?"

Danforth perked up. "Black hair, you say?"

Nodding, he asked, "What do you know?"

"Nothing for certain." The viscount's gaze turned inward. "But that description matches the maid who helped nurse me back to good health." His brow clenched together. "Except the tall part. That's not how I would describe her."

"You were also flat on your back," Helsford said, "with a concussion and a number of other injuries hampering your judgment."

"True."

"Let us set aside the black-haired maid for now," Sebastian said. "Catherine will be here soon, and I think it best to keep your presence a secret for a while."

"Are you sure?" Cora asked. "She might like knowing help has arrived."

"You're no doubt correct," he said. "But she's not accustomed to prevarication. Ignorance will protect her while interacting with her gaolers."

Danforth interjected, "What next? Track down Cochran, or wait for him to come to us?"

"Find him. He's somewhere close. The three of you, go into the village and ask around."

"Guy and Ethan can interrogate the villagers without me," Cora said. "I should like to stay here and keep watch."

"I don't need you underfoot." *Or nosing into my* affaire *with Catherine.*

"You won't even know I'm here."

"Why *are* you here? You should be home, recovering from your injuries."

"Amen," Helsford said.

After surviving two weeks of torture in a French dungeon, she had returned to England only to be betrayed by one of her own countrymen. With Latymer's aid, her French tormentor had stalked, kidnapped, and stabbed her before she and Guy, working in unison, sent the bastard to hell.

"My body is fully recovered," she said.

"And what of your mind?"

The light in her blue-green eyes dimmed, and he braced himself against the answering rip inside his chest. He did not like hurting her, but he would move entire mountains if that was what it took to keep her safe.

"My mind is as sound as anyone's in this room." She lifted her chin. "What I need—what we all need—is to find Cochran and figure out who he's in league with."

Knowing further discussion would be a waste of breath

and time, he turned to Helsford. "You delivered my message to Reeves?"

"I had to leave it with his clerk, Bradford. The superintendent is attending a family crisis at the moment. Bradford expected him to return this afternoon."

"Very well. Report back here tomorrow morning."

As they began filing out of the drawing room, Sebastian halted Danforth. "Stay in Showbury."

The younger man's face hardened. "I learned my lesson well last time, Chief. I will be where you tell me to be." He strode from the room.

Helsford bent to kiss Cora's temple. "Don't do anything foolish—"

She leveled her blue-green eyes on her betrothed, retribution in their depths.

"Until I return," he finished.

She waved her hand toward the door. "Go play nursemaid to my brother, while the chief and I develop a plan to bring down our enemy."

A feminine snort sounded from the back of the room.

Helsford winked at the buxom lady's maid. "Behave."

Dinks laughed. "I'll work on it, my lord." She sobered. "Watch over that young hothead for us."

"I'll make sure Jack returns in one piece."

"And that shite-scooping mongrel," Dinks muttered. "Watch over him, too."

Helsford shared a look with Cora. "Is that your way of asking me to give Bingham a kiss for you?"

The maid's face heated. "Bah!" She stomped away.

"Do you think they'll ever declare their feelings for one another?" Helsford asked.

"No," Cora said, smiling. "They're having too much fun tormenting each other."

Helsford nodded, then turned to Sebastian. "I'll send word of any developments." After one last long look at his intended, he followed in Danforth's wake.

A prickle along his neck warned Sebastian that he had become the focus of determined feminine attention. He glanced longingly after the other two men.

"Do you love her?" Cora asked in a soft voice.

Having no intention of answering her question—for he did not know the answer—he sent her a withering glare.

"If you do," she said, impervious to his warning, "don't lose her to this cause. One lifetime is not enough."

She would know. Of all his agents, Cora would be most familiar with that particular sentiment. "In case you have forgotten, she is newly widowed and not in a position, nor I doubt inclined, to accept the suit of another man." He speared the crystal decanters a glance.

"Then wait for her."

"I have not acted the gentleman with her."

"Start over, then. Court her as you would any potential wife."

Wife. The word caressed the rough edges of his soul. "We are too far beyond courtship."

A charged silence followed his statement, and the two women share a glance.

"There's nothing for it then, my lord." Dinks smacked her thigh and marched over to block his view of the decanters filled with amber temptation. "You must seduce her. To do that, you're going to need all your wits."

"You go too far, Dinks."

She braced her hands on broad hips. "You can give me the boot after you woo your lady. Until then..." The maid widened her stance, and her gaze became even more defiant.

"Dinks is right." Cora broke into the pair's visual duel. "Keep Mrs. Ashcroft in bed until she promises you forever. From the looks she was casting your way today, I would say she's already halfway—if not entirely—in love with you."

He tunneled his fingers through his hair. "Even if that were true, she wouldn't have me."

"Why on earth would you say such a thing?"

"Because her marriage with Ashcroft was nothing short of disastrous, and any union with me would be ten times worse. Not only that, anyone associated with me becomes a target, or worse, leverage." He caught her gaze. "As you well know."

"Dinks," Cora said, "would you give us a moment?"

"Certainly." The lady's maid sent Sebastian a warning glare before hastening from the room.

"She does understand that I pay her wages, right?" he asked.

"Dinks is worried about you. As am I."

"The maid has an interesting way of showing her concern." He moved to the opposite side of the room from the brandy.

"More than likely, our enemy has already discerned your affection for Mrs. Ashcroft. There's no better place for her than by your side."

"Where did you learn to be so ruthless?"

"I was mentored by the very best."

He sighed. "Let us focus our attention on how we will keep the Ashcroft ladies safe until this is all over, shall we?"

"What will you do? When this is over?"

"Return to London."

"What of Mrs. Ashcroft?"

Her intrusive questions made him think about things he had no wish to think about. Catherine and he had an agreement to end their *affaire* once he returned to the city. Nothing had changed to alter their plans.

Nothing.

"I suspect she will continue on as before." His stomach cramped into a tight ball.

"Have you never considered giving up the Nexus?"

Every day since returning to Bellamere. "Why would I surrender my only sense of purpose?"

"You don't mean that."

"Why wouldn't I?" The words emerged harsh. "I have no other interests, no hobbies or expensive peccadillos. I live, eat, breathe, sleep this fight against Napoleon's domination. Someone with my specialized talents is of little use anywhere else."

"I disagree, sir." She rose from her seat. "I have always known you were meant to be more than a mentor or guardian or even a chief of the Nexus."

"There's nothing more for me."

"The greatest role of your life still awaits." She gazed upon him with gentle, loving eyes. "That of husband and father."

THIRTY-SIX

Catherine rubbed the growing ache in her stomach. It was stronger now, verging on nausea. At first, she thought the unpleasant sensation was nothing more than nerves. After all, a country mother could only handle so much deceit, death, and threat before falling victim to such feminine frailty.

But she was not experiencing a bout of anxiety. No, these symptoms were darker, graver. They bespoke foreboding and danger. *Death*. The warning flashed through her mind, sharp and clear.

She buried her nose in the thin layer of linen covering Sebastian's chest and inhaled. His familiar scent, his silent strength, and his willingness to just hold her for the last hour had done nothing to assuage the dread crawling in her stomach.

"I'm sorry," she said, "but I must return home." Unfolding her body, she rose from his lap. "I cannot shake this feeling that something's wrong."

The moment she had arrived, she'd conveyed her conversation with Silas to Sebastian. Although disturbed

by the news, he had not been surprised by her gaoler's revelations.

He pushed out of the cushioned high-back chair to
stand beside her. "I have men watching over your family."
He slid a large, warm hand around the side of her neck, his
thumb smoothed across her cheek.

"The last time I experienced this kind of unrelenting
anxiety, I found Sophie stuck in a tree with a feral dog
prowling beneath."

His other hand came up to frame her face before giving
her a long, slow, achingly tender kiss. A kiss that wove soft
fingers of longing into the midst of her fear.

Lifting his head, he said, "Then it is a sensation not to
be ignored." He moved away and began tucking in the tail
of his shirt.

"What are you doing?"

"Coming with you."

"I thought we were to carry on as before—at least for
another day or two."

He grasped her hand and towed her from his bedchamber. "It's always best not to draw undue attention, that's
true. However, your gaolers cannot fault me for seeing you
home."

Fifteen minutes later, they guided their horses down
the path connecting their two properties. With unerring
accuracy, he led them along the same route she had taken
since the onset of their *affaire*. He even selected the narrow
deer path she preferred, rather than forging down the
wider track that skimmed along the edge of a thirty-foot
ridge.

In the daytime, she enjoyed the view such a path
provided. At night, she liked something a little more stable.

"Have you been following me home?"

"What gave you that impression?"

Did the man never provide a direct answer? "Your familiarity with a route others would pass by without notice."

"I might have ventured along this path a time or two."

She narrowed her eyes on his back. "Still don't trust me with your secrets, my lord?"

He threw her a heavy-lidded glance over his shoulder. "The same could be said of you."

"What do you mean? I have told you every detail of Cochran's plan—at least, what I know of it."

He whipped his big, black horse about, making Gypsy toss her head in annoyance. "I'm not speaking of Cochran's plan." His heated eyes caressed her features with a thoroughness that left her breathless and exposed.

She lowered her gaze to Gypsy's mane, afraid he saw too much. "Pray enlighten me, sir."

Silence reigned through the dense woodland for several uncomfortable seconds. Then he said, "Some secrets are best left unrevealed, don't you think? Enlightenment can sometimes complicate an uncomplicated situation."

He definitely saw too much. The back of her throat ached with unshed tears. Had she really allowed herself to hope? To think that their time together had burrowed beneath his skin and taken hold of his heart, as it had hers?

Stupid, stupid, lonely widow.

"Wise as always, my lord." She squared her shoulders and met his gaze. "Perhaps we should carry on."

He hesitated but a moment before turning toward Winter's Hollow again. If his pace was somewhat faster than before, she dared not remark upon it. One reminder of their agreement in a five-minute time span was more than enough.

They spent the rest of their journey in contemplative silence, a circumstance both painful and welcome. Once they reached the edge of her garden, they dismounted and tied off the horses. Grasping her hand, he led her along the garden wall, pausing several times to listen. He circled around to the east side of the manor. All the while, his gaze never stopped moving, never stopped searching. The closer he maneuvered them to their destination, the more focused he became.

Rather than continuing on to the front entrance, he stopped at the corner, pressing them up against the rough stone of the manor.

"What's wrong?" she whispered.

He squeezed her hand in warning, then peered around the corner. When he shifted back, he said in a calm, too calm, voice, "My men are not at their posts."

Sophie.

The dread she had been carrying intensified to a crushing degree. She should have listened to her instincts, not languished in the comfort of Sebastian's arms.

When she pushed away from the stone wall, he dragged her back and placed a finger against her mouth. She stilled, understanding they were no longer alone.

He searched the curtain of darkness around them. The moment stretched.

A bird twittered, and his grip on her softened.

In a voice barely above a whisper, he said, "Raven, to me."

A young woman wearing silken breeches emerged from the curtain of darkness and stopped beside them. "Chief. Mrs. Ashcroft."

Without conscious thought, Catherine leaned into Sebastian's body. The scar curving around the woman's left cheek triggered a vague memory, but her mind wanted to focus on nothing but getting to Sophie and her mother.

"The others are not where they should be," he said.

Cora nodded. "Something didn't feel right, so I've been making my way around to check on Jack and Bingham. I discovered two dead guards so far."

"Sebastian, please," she said. "I must check on Sophie."

"Catherine," he said. "This is my former ward and best agent, Cora. She will accompany you inside while I check on things out here. You may trust her as you trust me."

Everything came together in a flash of images. The maid serving oysters, the servants she did not recognize at her daughter's party, the heart-wrenching note scribed by Cora-belle.

The Nexus had come.

To Cora, he said, "One of her gaolers might be awaiting you just inside, though I doubt it. Dispose of him if you must. However, your mission is to locate the child and grandmother."

"Yes, sir."

"If I don't return in ten minutes, go to Helsford and get the women to safety. Understood?"

The younger woman's lips compressed, but she nodded her agreement.

His thumb swiped over the ridges of Catherine's knuckles before nudging her out of the shadows. "Go."

"But—"

"Go, Cat," he said in a firm but not unkind tone. "Listen to Cora."

"Come, Mrs. Ashcroft," the agent said. "Let us make sure your family is well."

The landscape of her world shifted and tilted in so many directions and with such velocity that she found herself following a stranger, who wore a contraption around her midsection housing an assortment of lethal weaponry, without complaint. Accustomed to making her own decisions, she would have found her current dilemma laughable if it was not all so terrifying.

Before rounding the corner, she glanced back to find Sebastian's eyes on her. The situation was reminiscent of their time in the woods while searching for Meghan McCarthy. A shiver tracked down her spine.

Drawing in a deep breath, she followed *Raven* into the unknown.

LATER, Catherine would not recall her flight from the ground floor to the third-floor nursery. Silas's absence at the door combined with Sebastian's missing men confirmed the sensations she'd been battling all evening.

Sophie was in danger, and she had not been here to protect her baby girl.

Somewhere along the way their panicked flight roused her mother, who was now trailing in their wake. Once they reached the nursery's closed door, Cora motioned for Catherine and her mother to move aside. The agent drew a wicked knife from the intriguing sash around her middle. She turned the handle and stepped back, using her fingertips to slowly open the door.

Cora raised a staying finger to them before slipping into the too-silent room. Catherine had no intention of lingering in the corridor while the other woman put her life in danger.

She inched her body around the open doorway, and Evelyn's shoulder bumped into hers. The two of them stood side by side, shaking with fear but determined to save their girl, the one who brought sunshine into their lives each and every day.

Castle Dragonthorpe yawned before them, occupying half the common room. The other half consisted of a school desk, a small bookcase, and an assortment of more feminine toys littering the floor. Two doors framed the common room, the right one an entrance to her daughter's bedchamber and the left one spilling into the nurse's small chamber, which was currently occupied by Sophie's faux governess.

Cora was nowhere in sight.

Foregoing the nurse's chamber, she veered right, her mother at her heels.

"Mrs. Ashcroft," Cora yelled from Sophie's room. "Come quickly."

Blood fired through her veins. She barreled across the short distance and skidded to a halt inside her daughter's bedchamber. "What?"

An answer was unnecessary, for the pool of blood at her daughter's bedside said it all. Terror gurgled up into the back of her throat, and she released it in one long never-ending breath.

THIRTY-SEVEN

Sebastian stilled. His gaze slashed to the manor's third floor.

"Bring Danforth and Helsford now." He didn't wait for Jack's acknowledgment before turning toward the house. Toward Catherine's terror-filled scream.

He made his way to a side entrance and tore up the servants' stairs, his heart thundering with every step. What had he been thinking, to let her out of his sight? He should have been the one to accompany her inside and allowed Cora to continue her circuit.

Cochran had seen through their plan and made his play. He hoped to God it didn't destroy them all.

Following the voices, he ran toward the nursery, his heart shrinking in fear with each pounding step. He dashed toward Sophie's bedchamber, then came to an abrupt halt.

"S-sorry." Mrs. Clarke fumbled for Catherine's hand. "Had no choice—" A wet, rattling cough seized her and spittle, thick with blood, sprayed the floor and splattered their clasped hands. "My son." Her voice grew weaker and a single tear curled over her nose. *"Giles."*

"Mrs. Clarke," Catherine pleaded, "where are they taking my daughter?"

"My son. Find him. London boys' home." She coughed again.

"Mrs. Clarke, please—"

"The bleeding won't stop," Evelyn said, pressing what looked like a bed sheet against the injured woman's stomach. "You must try not to cough, Mrs. Clarke."

More tears streamed over the bridge of the governess's nose. "Tell Giles I l-love him, tell him I wanted to do what was right—" Another wave of coughing, this one far worse than the last, halted her confession. When she finished, she could barely lift her eyelids. "His father—danger..." Her dying body sagged onto the floor like an inflammable air balloon losing its heat. The dead woman's grip on Catherine's hand loosened.

"Catherine," he said.

She lifted tear-drenched eyes to his. "They took Sophie."

"I'll find her. I swear it, love."

She jerked out of his arms.

"Catherine—"

"Please don't," she whispered.

Evelyn moved between them. "I found this beside Mrs. Clarke's body."

He tore his gaze away from Catherine's quaking back to peer down at a blood-spotted letter she offered. Taking it, he suggested, "Let us remove to somewhere more comfortable, shall we?"

Once they had all filed into the drawing room, Catherine asked, "What does Cochran's letter say?"

"He wants an exchange."

"What sort of an exchange?"

Tension rippled along the muscles in his shoulders. He did not want to hurt or frighten her any more than she already was, but he could see no other way around telling her the truth.

Sensing what was to come, Evelyn stepped to her daughter's side and wrapped an arm around her waist.

"Sebastian," Catherine said. "What does Cochran want? The list of agents?"

He nodded. "In exchange for your daughter's life."

"Dear God." She turned into her mother's embrace.

His jaw clenched, wanting to be the one she sought for comfort. But after his insensitive remark on the path, he understood why she would not want to invest any more emotion into an *affaire* with an end date. *"Bloody stupid bastard,"* he said beneath his breath.

Evelyn asked, "Does Cochran's letter say anything else?"

"For us to stay put, that he will send more instructions, and to keep the authorities out of it."

Evelyn raised a brow. "Is that all?"

"I cannot wait so long," Catherine said, swiping at her cheeks.

"What are you planning, daughter?"

"I'm going after Sophie."

"Don't be ridiculous—"

"No, you're not," Sebastian said.

Determined brown eyes met his. "You cannot stop me."

If she only knew the many ways he could stop her, she would run from the chamber and never look back. "Very well, Catherine. But we ride hard and we ride fast. With any luck, Cochran's using a carriage, thinking he had hours before anyone would notice your daughter's absence."

"I'll come with you," Evelyn said.

"It would be better if you stayed here," Catherine said. "There are injured men—and worse—outside. One of Sebastian's agents, Cora, is assessing the damage. She might need your aid until the doctor arrives."

"I'll prepare some bandages."

"Lords Helsford and Danforth should be arriving soon," Sebastian said. "If you could point them in our direction—"

"Of course, my lord."

Satisfied nothing more could be done here, he strode away, grasping Catherine's hand on his way by.

THIRTY-EIGHT

Teddy closed the barn door, exhausted to the bone. Guinevere and Gypsy had made a right mess out of their stalls while he was away. And if that wasn't enough, one of the sheep had wedged its head in between the rungs of an old cartwheel, forcing him to chase the bleating animal all around the barnyard. He hadn't been gentle when he popped the wheel off the blighter's head.

Lifting his arms high above his shoulders, he stretched his aching muscles before turning toward the dark, shadow-ridden lane. He didn't care much for this part, although given the same choice—play with Sophie Ashcroft or finish his chores on time—he would make the same decision again. Being the focus of her pretty smile all day was worth every hair-raising step he was about to take.

Not for the first time, he regretted his family's *reduced circumstances*, as his mother liked to call their lack of funds. According to his parents, they once lived in a grand house like Winter's Hollow and had scads of servants seeing to their every need. He recalled only small glimpses of their former life, yet it was enough to make him yearn for more than their single-room cottage and meager table fare.

Especially now that his mama was sick. Money would pay for a doctor and medicine to make her better. Money would allow them to hire servants to see to her comfort while he and Papa were at work. Money would mean he could go home tonight and melt into a plump, warm bed, rather than having to fix dinner for his papa and care for his mama.

Night sounds closed in around him, growing louder with every meter he distanced himself from the barn. The sunny day had given way to a partly cloudy night and, at times, he could barely see the hard-packed road beneath his feet.

Hunching his shoulders, he shoved his hands in his pockets and wrapped his fingers around the carved wooden figure. He still couldn't believe Sophie had given him a piece of Dragonthorpe.

An animal screeched in the trees far above him. He gripped the figure tighter and picked up his pace, not daring to look left or right for fear of encountering a pair of bright eyes in the shadows.

Had it not been for the distinctive jingle of a horse's harness, he might have toddled right into the back of the motionless carriage. As it was, he'd stopped not six feet away. Fear flashed like a frigid breeze across his flesh before plunging beneath the surface to lock around his pounding heart.

Some instinct urged him to hide. Ducking low, he scrabbled into the knee-high weeds along the side of the lane and crouched there. From this position, he could make out the carriage's black-as-night panels and carved trimmings. Four matching bay horses stood quietly at the lead. Their driver faced forward in the same state of readiness.

Readiness for what?

He glanced down the lane, in the direction he had just come, but the lack of moonlight prevented him from making anything out. The silent wait did funny things to his body.

Sweat slicked down his back and his stomach gurgled. With each passing second, the gurgling grew in intensity, an unpleasant sensation that would normally have sent him running for the nearest privy. But he dared not move, even though he was in danger of soiling himself. Something didn't feel right about the carriage sitting on the dark lane, with no lamplight.

With Sophie's papa gone, there was no one to protect her but him. Not for the first time, he wondered about the new people staying at her house. People she refused to talk about but always watched with a wary eye. No one knew them, and they seemed to just show up one day. When he'd asked Carson about them, the groomsman told him to mind the shite and not the goings-on at the big house.

The feeling in his stomach grew worse, making him squirm while his face flushed with heat. When he was on the verge of rushing into the woods, the air around him stirred and a hint of foul odor assaulted his senses. Out of the darkness emerged the most hideous creature, one he'd encountered several times in the last sennight.

Silas.

Teddy's eyes narrowed. The skeletal man's body looked larger than normal, misshapen. He hunkered down as the man drew near. The large, deformed lump at his shoulder materialized into a body.

Sophie's body.

She dangled over the man's shoulder, unmoving. She did not struggle or scream or curse her captor to perdition. She simply hung there.

Was she dead?

Anger and sadness and confusion nearly sent him barreling into the wicked man, but Silas tapped the carriage door and all thoughts of pummeling the man disappeared.

The carriage's window curtain parted, and a man said, "I see the governess held up her end of the bargain."

"Yes, sir."

"And the governess?"

"Taken care of, as you instructed."

"My message?"

"Delivered."

"Very good, Silas." The carriage door opened. "Place the girl on the bench and let us be off."

After Silas completed his task, he shut the door and climbed up into the driver's box. Once he was settled, the coachman flicked the reins and the horses lurched forward.

Teddy rose from his crouched position and glanced toward Winter's Hollow. No sounds of rescue reached him. Swinging his gaze back to Sophie, his knees almost buckled when the ambling carriage disappeared behind a wall of impenetrable black.

With one last look toward the big house, he took off and he did not slow until his fingertips touched the metal rail of the carriage's luggage boot. Having climbed rickety ladders all his life, it took little effort for him to maneuver himself onto the small ledge.

He folded his arms around his raised knees and winced when he felt something sharp prick his hip. Reaching into his pocket, he pulled out the wooden archer Sophie had given him. The carved piece stood with his legs splayed, one hand holding a bow and the other drawing back an arrow. He had been drawn to this figure from the first moment he saw it standing atop Dragonthorpe's parapet, a brave soldier protecting his princess with nothing more than a bit of iron and willow.

At the crossroads, the carriage veered toward London, and he squeezed his eyes shut, burying his face into his upraised knees. He prayed his mama and papa would be all right without him. And he prayed his aim would be true when it came time to save the princess.

THIRTY-NINE

"Whoa!" the driver yelled.

Teddy had enough of a warning to brace himself before the front of the carriage bucked high into the air and came crashing back to the ground. Horses screamed, wood splintered, men cursed. Teddy rubbed his bruised bottom.

The carriage door flew open. "What the hell happened?"

"Pardon, Mr. Cochran," the driver said. "A large branch in the road. With this godforsaken blackness, I didn't see it in time."

Teddy heard a loud click.

"Silas, take a look."

"Yes, sir."

Bracing his feet wide, Teddy levered himself up enough to peer through the small window at the back of the passenger compartment. Inside, he found the shadowy silhouette of Sophie sprawled on the far seat, still in her nightdress. She appeared unharmed, but tousled.

The carriage tilted to the side and the door closed

softly. Teddy ducked back down, holding on to Sophie's wooden archer with all his might. A scuffling noise to his left made his ears perk up.

"Put your weapon down, Mr. Cochran," a new voice said. "We have your man."

The newcomer's statement caused a moment of silence. Then Cochran demanded, "Who's there? Show yourself."

"Name's Declan McCarthy. Now drop your pistol and stand clear of the carriage."

Teddy's eyes rounded. What was Meghan's papa doing out here?

"McCarthy," Cochran mused. "Little Meghan's father, I presume?"

"That's right, you bastard. You'll pay for what you did to my wee Meghan."

While Mr. McCarthy spoke, Teddy followed the path of the man's voice, which seemed to be moving closer to Cochran's side of the carriage. The carpenter wanted to kill the man who'd kidnapped Sophie. Did he even know she was inside? If he shot at Cochran, he might miss and hit Sophie. Teddy rubbed his aching chest.

Then the soft thud of hooves against hard-packed earth caught his attention. He shifted around and the painful beating of his heart stopped cold. At the side of the road, he spotted a phantom in a long black cape astride an even blacker horse. The rider edged closer, and Teddy pressed his back into the paneling, his eyes growing larger the closer the phantom came. The rider halted and lifted one gloved finger to his lips in an age-old signal for silence. At least, Teddy assumed it was the phantom's mouth. The large cowl hid the rider's face, revealing nothing but a dark, gaping maw.

"Come now, McCarthy," Mr. Cochran said. "Don't the Irish reproduce like vermin? Surely, you have another child to take the chit's place."

Teddy could hear more clicking of metal coming from the passenger compartment. The phantom's presence kept him rooted in place.

"The only vermin here is you," Mr. McCarthy roared. "Why did you have to kill her? You could have gone away and never returned."

"And allow the baggage to snivel my name into Mrs. Ashcroft's ears?" Mr. Cochran's voice turned cold. "You should thank me. Now, there's two less peasant mouths for you to feed."

"*Bastard!*" Mr. McCarthy roared. "She wasn't a peasant. She was my daughter!"

"McCarthy, no," someone cautioned.

Teddy recognized the butcher's voice, but he didn't dare take his eyes off the phantom rider.

"Yes, calm yourself," Mr. Cochran said, unruffled.

"I won't tell you again," Mr. McCarthy said between harsh breaths. "Drop your weapon and step away from the carriage."

"Tell me one thing first."

Teddy swiveled around when he heard another noise, this time closer. Two men in ragged clothing were inching their way toward the carriage. With their dirty faces, they were near invisible. But Teddy saw them. One was serious and intent. The other flashed Teddy a white smile followed with a wink.

"What?" Mr. McCarthy demanded.

"A simple matter of clarification," Mr. Cochran said. "How did you know I would be on this road at this time?"

"I received a note from someone named Specter. The

message said my Meghan's murderer would be fleeing back to London tonight. Seems my new friend was right."

Teddy glanced at the caped rider.

"I see," Mr. Cochran said. "You placed a great deal of faith in a stranger's note."

"Saw no harm in checking things out. Time for conversing is over."

A shot exploded from inside the carriage, and Teddy covered his head with his arms. The carriage door wrenched open.

"Stay back," Mr. Cochran warned, "or I'll kill the girl."

No longer silent, the night came alive. Masculine voices from all directions hissed curses upon Cochran's head. Teddy peeked over his arms in time to see the phantom motioning instructions to the two men before melting into the shadows.

Teddy got to his knees but froze when Mr. Cochran backed into view. He held Sophie against him, her arms and legs dangling like a doll's and her head rocking back and forth. Sweat bubbled on his brow and skated down his sides. Another step back and Mr. Cochran would find his hiding place. He glanced at the two ragged men drawing closer.

"Put the Ashcroft girl down," Mr. McCarthy demanded. "You've no call to bring her into this."

"I think having her at my side evens things out nicely." Mr. Cochran whirled around, baring his back to Teddy.

But not before Teddy saw Sophie's eyes flutter open. Heartened, he gripped his wooden archer tighter and prayed for a heroic plan to come to mind. Nothing surfaced, for his mind was too frozen with fear. If all went wrong, he could lose his friend. His brow scrunched into an angry vee. He couldn't let that happen.

In the distance, Teddy heard what sounded like a steady roll of thunder. Mr. Cochran heard it, too, and glanced up the road. For an instant, fear slackened the gentleman's features before they transformed into a slab of hatred.

"I require a horse." Mr. Cochran faced his unseen foes. "Now."

Feet waded through the nearby tall grasses. When Mr. McCarthy spoke next, his voice seemed to be within reaching distance.

"You'll have it," Mr. McCarthy said. "Let the girl go."

Sophie spotted Teddy then, and he glimpsed her determination, the fire burning in her blue eyes. A new terror gripped him as the thunder grew louder.

"Bring the horse, and I'll deposit her a mile down the road."

No! Teddy held his breath while waiting for the carpenter's answer. Mr. Cochran would take off on that horse with Sophie and he would never see her again.

Getting his feet underneath him, Teddy waited for Mr. Cochran to turn toward the thunder, which seemed to be right on them now. The two ragged young men were shaking their heads and waving him off. Teddy ignored them, catapulting himself onto the scoundrel's back and slammed the archer's wooden arrow into the man's neck.

The man's grip on Sophie to loosened, and she squiggled down far enough to sink her teeth into her captor's arm. A roar ripped from Mr. Cochran's injured throat.

She dropped to the ground, and Teddy went sailing through the air. His head struck the road, sending shards of pain through his skull.

A woman screamed and a man yelled right before a large black horse trampled his prone body.

FORTY

"*Teddy!*" Catherine yelled.

The stable lad had launched himself onto the back of a grown man, who would as soon kill the boy as look at him. Infuriated and writhing in pain, Cochran had dropped Sophie and wrenched the boy off his back, throwing him across the road like a bucket of yesterday's slop.

Right into their path.

"Watch out," Sebastian warned.

Out of nowhere, a big black horse appeared, carrying a cloaked figure. The rider maneuvered his mount over the stable lad, shielding him from their approach.

Sebastian jerked his horse to the right and Catherine pulled Gypsy's reins to the left. The three men behind followed suit.

"Danforth, to Catherine. Jack, the boy," Sebastian directed, after they cleared that particular danger. Helsford followed Sebastian into the fray.

Catherine scrambled off her horse and stood paralyzed as she watched Sebastian dismount and draw a pistol from the back of his waistband. Her heart soared when she spotted Sophie on the ground, evading Cochran as he attempted to recapture her.

She wasn't dead. Thank God, her little girl was alive and kicking at Cochran with all of her might.

From a distance, she heard Lord Danforth calling her, but she couldn't obey his entreaty for her to come away. The two people she loved most in the world were fighting for their lives.

"Cochran, stand down," Sebastian said, leveling the pistol at his head.

Sophie launched herself at Cochran. The impact forced Cochran to lose his grip and his pistol fell to the ground.

"You killed Teddy, you beast!" Sophie cried, fighting like a wildcat. "How could you?"

Catherine was equal parts proud and terrified. She wrenched free of Danforth's hold and ran forward.

"*Get back, Catherine.*" Sebastian's harsh command stopped her in her tracks. Vengeance blazed in his eyes blazed, freezing her heart.

From behind the battling duo emerged Declan McCarthy and several men from the village, including the vicar, who ran over to assist Jack with Teddy. Two of the men held Silas between them.

With her daughter acting the she-cat, Cochran appeared almost relieved when Sebastian stowed his pistol to pluck Sophie off her cursing and bleeding captor. Her sweet girl continued to scratch at the air, determined to do the man more damage.

McCarthy sank a fist into Cochran's stomach, then kneed him in the face when the man bent forward. He knocked the murderer to the ground and forced his arms behind his back. Lord Helsford pulled a length of rope from his saddle and tied Cochran's wrists and ankles.

With both men subdued, Catherine ran forward. Even though Sebastian tried to shelter Sophie's curious eyes from McCarthy's attack on Cochran, her daughter had observed far too much.

"Sophie." She held out her arms. "Come to Mama."

Fierce blue eyes turned her way. From one second to the next, the fight went out of her daughter and her eyes filled with tears. "Mama."

Sebastian handed her daughter over, and her eyes burned with tears when the girl's small frame began to quake. "I have you now, pumpkin. Everything's fine."

She smoothed a hand over Sophie's back in wide, calming circles. Sebastian dipped his head until he stood face-to-face with her daughter. "Brave little sprite, why the tears? You vanquished the enemy with nary a bruise."

Sophie reared back and settled liquid blue eyes on him. An instant later, she wrapped her thin arms around his neck. "Bastian, you saved me."

With Sophie half in Catherine's arms and half in Sebastian's arms, he stood awkwardly for a few seconds before finally giving in and embracing them both. Catherine closed her eyes and absorbed the moment. It was likely the last hug she would ever receive from him.

"Ah, that's so precious, Somerton," Cochran spat. "Weren't you supposed to protect the Ashcroft ladies, rather than seduce them?"

The muscles in Sebastian's arm rippled against her waist a moment before his hold loosened and slipped away.

FORTY-ONE

Sebastian ignored the ice raking down his spine long enough to finish his conversation with Sophie. "No, sprite." He disentangled himself from the girl's tight hold around his neck. "Your brownie friend must take all the credit for your rescue."

"But Teddy's d-dead." A fresh set of tears leaked from her eyes.

"Miss Sophie," Declan McCarthy said.

She peered over her shoulder at the carpenter.

"I believe this belongs to your brave knight." He held out a carved figure of a man holding a bow and arrow.

She accepted the piece. "I gave this to him." She glanced up at McCarthy, her pride evident. "Did you see Teddy jab the arrow into the bad man's neck?"

"Yes, miss," McCarthy said. "He's a courageous lad. You must be a very good friend."

"Mama," Sophie said. "I have to see Teddy."

Sebastian glanced over to where a small group had formed around the boy. The incredible pressure around his chest eased when Teddy wobbled into a sitting position.

He touched the girl's shoulder and nodded toward the stable boy. "Your brave knight rises, my lady."

Sophie's eyes widened at the sight of her friend. "Let me go, Mama." She scrabbled out of her mother's arms.

"Be careful with him, dear," Catherine warned, following her daughter at a more sedate pace. "He's injured."

"I will, Mama."

Catherine walked away, not sparing him another glance. What was going on in that beautiful mind of hers?"

"Woman trouble, Somerton?" Cochran taunted.

He set aside Catherine's withdrawal and focused on cleaning up the mess Cochran had created.

The cloaked savior had disappeared, as had the two young men who were approaching the carriage as Sebastian stormed into the fray. Were the three working in tandem? Or was something else afoot, altogether?

Declan McCarthy approached him. His normally wary eyes burned with purpose. "I'll take care of that mewling coward who killed my Meghan."

"You know?"

"Aye, m'lord. I received a note that the men who killed my girl were fleeing tonight. The murdering bastard admitted his crime right before you arrived." His hand balled into a fist. "Time to make him suffer."

Understanding the man's pain, he gentled his voice. "I can't let you do that."

"Don't try to stop me, m'lord."

Cochran laughed. "Get in line, Irish. Somerton's not going to let a dead girl stand in the way of protecting his precious Nexus."

"*Quiet.*" Helsford ground the heel of his boot into the traitor's back.

"Danforth. Mr. Foster," Sebastian called.

The agent and vicar were at his side in an instant. "Yes, sir?"

"How's our intrepid hero?"

"Teddy will be fine," the vicar said. "The lump on his head will cause him some pain for a while."

"Danforth, secure that carriage for Catherine and the children. And we need the men from the village out of here. Now." To the vicar, he said, "Usher the men back to Showbury and make sure they get plenty to eat and drink."

"Will do, sir." The vicar strode off.

Sebastian faced the angry carpenter.

McCarthy's green eyes burned with a mixture of grief and hatred. "I'll have justice for my Meghan and her wee babe."

"Yes, you will, but not until after I extract some information."

"For this Nexus?" McCarthy's lip curled in disgust.

"No." The lie fell smoothly from his lips. "Cochran speaks only to confuse you. His one hope of surviving this situation is to pit us against each other and only then might he have a chance at escaping."

He laid a hand on the carpenter's massive shoulder. "McCarthy, I need the carriage free and operable. Can you and the other men make that happen? I want to get Mrs. Ashcroft and the children away from this place." And he wanted to give the man something else to focus on.

McCarthy tore his murderous gaze away from Cochran. "For Mrs. Ashcroft. She's been nothing but kind to me and mine."

Once the men readied the carriage, Catherine bundled the two children inside. She and Danforth engaged in a short, heated exchange that resulted in the viscount throwing his arms up and grumbling something about stubborn women.

Mr. Foster climbed into the driver's box, ushering Cochran's coachman into the hands of the villagers. The carriage lurched forward, escorted by an unhappy McCarthy, the rest of the villagers, and Jack riding at the back.

Catherine stood at the side of the road, watching the conveyance lumber out of sight.

"Mr. Foster, wait." Sebastian rushed forward, but the vicar ignored his command and continued on toward Showbury. "What are you doing, Catherine?"

"What does it look like?" she asked in a calm voice. "I'm staying."

Warmth seeped into his heart, followed quickly by an ungovernable fear for her safety. "It's too dangerous."

"For you, as well."

"This could become unpleasant, Catherine. I don't want you exposed to this." Nor did he want her to witness his darker side, the one most detested for its ruthlessness.

"I'm not leaving you." She cleared her throat. "I mean, I'm not leaving you here to sort out Geoffrey's mess."

I'm not leaving you. A wild instinct, ominous and possessive, took hold of him, overwhelming in its strength.

"Chief, perhaps we should finish this," Helsford said.

"The carriage is gone, and I don't see Gypsy," she said. "I'm not walking back alone."

"Dammit, Catherine. You have no business here."

Malice laced her tone as she stared at Cochran. "He threatened my baby girl. I have as much right to be here as the rest of you."

She had placed him in an untenable situation. How

could he protect her *and* conduct a thorough interrogation of his prisoner?

Cochran laughed. "What's the matter, Somerton? Afraid your mistress won't like what she sees?"

Sebastian pointed toward the horses. "Stand over there, Catherine. Don't go near either prisoner, no matter what. Understood?"

"Yes, *Chief.*"

Inwardly, he flinched, but waited for her to comply before heading back to the circle of men. "Pick him up."

Helsford pulled Cochran to his feet. With his wrists and ankles bound by the same rope, the prisoner hobbled about until he gained his balance.

"Tell me who you're working for," Sebastian said.

Cochran smiled. "Why would I need to take orders from anyone?"

"Because you're not intelligent enough to mastermind this elaborate a plan."

Cochran's gaze sliced to Silas, who stood passively in Danforth's grip. "Intelligent enough to locate and silence your nosey agent."

Catherine's sharp intake of breath speared through their circle.

"Was it Latymer?" Danforth demanded.

Cochran's gaze landed on Silas again. He said nothing.

Sebastian nodded to Helsford, who knocked Cochran's feet out from underneath him. With his hands bound behind him, the prisoner landed on his face. Helsford grabbed the rope connecting Cochran's hands to his feet and set a boot to the middle of the man's back. He pulled on the rope like a bowstring, wrenching the prisoner's arms and legs into an unnatural angle. Cochran cried out.

"I believe Lord Danforth asked you a question," Sebastian said.

"Go to hell," Cochran said through gritted teeth.

The rope tautened.

"Care to try again?"

"*Yes*," Cochran ground out. "I reported to Latymer."

"What was your agreement with him?"

"To retrieve a list of your agents."

"In exchange for?"

More silence.

The rope tautened.

"Latymer discrediting you," Cochran gasped. "I've answered your questions. Now call off your dog."

"How would you benefit from my disgrace?"

Cochran glared up at him. "I would have taken your place."

Danforth barked out a laugh. "You? As Chief?"

"If not for someone named Specter meddling in my affairs, I would have been the new chief of the Nexus by tomorrow's end. Some of the greatest minds in England would have been at my disposal."

"Get him up," Sebastian ordered. "What made you think Reeves would appoint you as chief, rather than one of my agents?"

"Latymer still has powerful friends in the Foreign Office," Cochran said.

In a lightning-swift maneuver, one Sebastian had never witnessed before, Silas somersaulted out of his captors' grip and snatched a pistol from Danforth's waistband. Using his weapon, he motioned for a fuming Danforth to step back, then leveled the barrel at Sebastian. The man's features transformed into what on anyone else's face would be described as gleeful, but on Silas's, the expression was altogether more disturbing.

"*No!*" Catherine ran toward them, her fiery gaze on Silas.

"*Catherine, stop!*"

She halted. Her anguished gaze slashed between him and Silas.

He had wanted to know what it would feel like to have a champion in a wife. Now he knew. Even though they had not said the vows that would tie them together for a lifetime, they were bound, heart to heart, in this life and the next.

He poured every ounce of the love he felt for her into three little words. "You promised, remember?"

Tears filled her eyes. "Sebastian."

"Stay put, love." His hand inched toward his weapon.

Silas tsked. "Kindly raise your hands, my lord."

He weighed his options. With Silas's weapon pointed at his chest, he wouldn't be able to reach his weapon before the other man's bullet carved a hole in his chest. He could give Danforth the nod to rush Silas, but with Catherine so close the weapon could discharge in her direction. He gladly would die a thousand times if that's what it took to keep her safe.

He lifted his arms in the air.

Catherine rushed forward. "*S-sebastian.*"

"Stay, Mrs. Ashcroft," Silas warned.

She halted again. Her eyes met Sebastian's.

He produced a smile. "Do as he says, Cat."

"Silas," Cochran interrupted. "Come remove these bindings."

"In a moment, sir."

"What do you mean 'in a moment'?" Cochran tried to wrench free of Helsford's hold.

Silas's watery eyes settled back on Sebastian. "I am saddened by this turn of events," he said in perfect French. "The widow has been a worthy adversary, as have you. We shall meet again."

Before Sebastian could work through the man's cryptic remark, Silas swept his weapon toward Helsford and fired.

"No—" Sebastian dove toward his agent in a futile attempt to block the bullet, but it was not Helsford's body that bucked against the impact.

Cochran's head jolted back and his body froze for an instant before melting in Helsford's arms. His head rolled forward, revealing the bullet's entrance, his death told by a single line of scarlet tracking down his forehead.

With a fluid sweep of his arm, Sebastian grabbed his gun, twisted his body around to face Cochran's killer and pulled the trigger. His bullet cleaved into Silas's chest at the same time another lead ball from behind blasted into the man's back.

"Get down!" Sebastian yelled as he dove to the ground. "Helsford, to Catherine."

He didn't have to look to make sure his agent followed his direction—the man was trained to do so without question. Silas's body collapsed in a heap, dead before his face hit the hard-packed road.

"Who's there?" Sebastian searched from one corner of the darkness to the next. "Show yourself."

"It would be my pleasure, Lord Somerton," a new voice said. "As soon as you drop your weapons."

"I'll have your name first, sir."

"Reeves. John Reeves, Superintendent of the Alien Office."

FORTY-TWO

"If you three women don't stop pacing," Lord Danforth grumbled from his location near one of tall windows in Sebastian's study, "you're going to give me a megrim."

Catherine halted behind a burgundy damask chair, clutching the back with her cold, clammy hands. Cora and Dinks continued their assault on the expensive carpet, pausing only long enough to throw his lordship a leave-me-be look.

"No sign of them yet?" Catherine would never forget the steel coating Sebastian's blue-gray eyes when he forced her to return with the viscount while he and Helsford dealt with Reeves and the aftermath of Cochran's failed abduction.

Danforth sighed, having fielded the same question no less than a dozen times since they had returned to Bellamere an hour ago. "They could be coming down the drive right now, for all I know. This blasted darkness has been both a blessing and a damned curse."

"If you don't mind, Miss Cora," Dinks said, "I'll look in

on the wee ones. This waiting has my nerves stretched thin."

"Of course," she said. "Why don't you make sure Bingham is still abed? I caught him trying to limp off toward the stables not long after we arrived."

The maid's eyes narrowed toward the open door. "Did he, now?"

"Thank you, Dinks," Catherine said. "I doubt Mother has left the children's side, but I'm sure she's curious if there have been any new developments."

Dinks picked up the tea tray and turned to leave. "I'll have a fresh pot brought around."

Catherine noted Cora's sly smile. "Something amusing, Miss deBeau?"

"Do call me Cora. I detest such formality amongst friends."

Glancing between brother and sister, Catherine said, "We are friends?"

The other woman lifted a mahogany brow. "Are you finished plotting against Somerton?"

Danforth paused in his surveillance of the front drive to await her answer.

Heat rushed into Catherine's cheeks. "I hold no ill will toward Lord Somerton. I did what I had to do in order to save my daughter." She strengthened her voice. "And I would do it again."

Brother and sister shared a satisfied look, then two sets of blue-green eyes settled on her. Cora said, "You will make a nice addition to our circle."

Catherine's nails scored the tight weave of the uphol-stered chair. "It is kind of you to say so. But in a few days, the lot of you will return to London, and I will settle back into country life here in Showbury."

Danforth made a choking sound and pivoted back to the window. Cora scowled at her brother. "Why don't you head down the lane to meet the others?"

"Believe me, sister, I would like nothing better, given the new direction of this conversation. Not sure why I was relegated to women-sitting, rather than Helsford. All the same, I prefer my head attached to my shoulders."

Catherine frowned. "What do you mean, sir?"

Cora answered, "He means Somerton will lop it off if he leaves us—or rather you—unattended."

A soft knock drew their attention to the open door. Mrs. Fox said, "Pardon the interruption. I have a warm pot of tea."

"Come in—" Cora said.

"Please bring it in—" Catherine said at the same time.

Catherine's gaze cut to Sebastian's former ward, and a fresh wave of humiliation burned its way up her neck and into her cheeks. "My apologies, I forgot myself."

Cora smiled. "Mrs. Fox, please set the tea tray on the table next to Mrs. Ashcroft. She can do the honors." After the housekeeper withdrew, she nodded toward the tea. "I hope you don't mind."

"Not at all." Catherine appreciated the distraction. It would give her something to do with her hands besides worrying a hole in the chair's upholstery.

"None for me." Danforth strode toward the sideboard. "I will raid Somerton's stash."

Catherine lifted her gaze to Cora. "Sugar?"

"No, thank you. A spot of cream only."

Once they had their respective drinks, she and Cora perched on matching chairs while Danforth kept watch.

"Catherine," Cora said after a short silence. "Your life

in Showbury will be much altered now. Surely, you realize that."

"I have no doubt the events of the last fortnight will haunt my thoughts for some time, but I don't see how that fact will affect my living here."

A low groan sounded from the window. "Ladies, I am going to walk the perimeter." Danforth lanced his sister with a severe look. "Stay put, or I will haunt you—headless and all."

"You ceased intimidating me when I was twelve, brother. Save your threats for your elusive cloaked savior."

His lips thinned. "Can you not do as I ask just this once?"

Cora laughed. "This coming from the King of Rogues? From a man who takes the solitary path more often than not?"

From the thunderous look on the viscount's face, Catherine thought he might do his sister bodily harm. Instead, he jabbed his finger in the air. "You're Helsford's problem now." Then he stormed from the room.

"Rather lacking, as comebacks go, wouldn't you say?" Cora asked in an amused voice.

"Should he be left to his own devices?"

"Do not let our sparring upset you. It's our way." She set her teacup down. "Do you love him? Somerton, I mean."

Catherine could do little more than stare. Like Sebastian, Cora dipped and swayed from one topic to the next, making it impossible to anticipate the woman's next question.

"You think me too bold?" Cora asked. "I don't blame you. It is no one's business but your own."

"Thank you."

"I ask only because I want for Somerton what I have with Lord Helsford. Guy. As agents, we've devoted our lives to this fight against Napoleon, never taking for ourselves. Somerton more so than the rest of us. Until now, I never knew the sacrifice mattered to him."

Shock jolted her heart into an uncomfortable rhythm. "Surely, you're not suggesting that Lord Somerton holds any meaningful affection for me." Then she recalled the fleeting expression that had crossed his face when he thought Silas was about to kill him. A lump formed in the back of her throat.

"You are surprised by the notion?"

"I am *appalled* by the notion."

That stiffened the younger woman's back. "I can't think why you would be."

Her unease with their conversation grew with each word uttered. "Did Lord Somerton explain the *full* nature of our association?"

Intelligence gleamed behind the woman's sharp gaze as she assessed Catherine's words. Then the sharpness softened into comprehension and, even worse, empathy.

"Believe me, when I tell you," Cora said, "if there is one man in all of England who would understand your motives, it is Somerton. He might even be more drawn to you because of your warrior instincts."

"You do not understand. I deceived him in the worst possible way."

"Did he not deceive you by keeping the manner of your husband's death to himself?"

Catherine stood. "It's not the same. I made love to him to obtain a list!"

"Of suspected traitors?"

Catherine turned her burning eyes on her.

"To save your daughter?"

Her breathing became more difficult.

"Do you not think England's greatest spymaster would do the same in your stead?" Cora rose and moved to stand in front of her. "No need to answer, for I will. He would. That, and a whole lot worse."

"Our association has been built on suspicion and betrayal. A poor beginning."

"One does not *make love* to obtain information," Cora pointed out. "One does something altogether less pleasurable."

"You sound as if you speak from experience." Not for the first time, Catherine wondered how the agent had come by the scar on her cheek.

"I do." A shadow crossed the other woman's face. "And that experience tells me the two of you have much more to build on than the awful circumstances that brought you together."

A disturbance from the entry hall caught their attention, and they grappled for each other's hands as they rushed to the door. But when she tried to open it, Cora placed her palm against the oak panel and turned to her. "Give him a chance to love you."

The pressure around Catherine's chest tightened, and her pulse roared in her ears. Overcoming the reason that brought them together was only one of their many hurdles, the biggest being Sebastian's role with the Nexus. That role would take him away from her for long periods of time, during which she would constantly worry for his return.

Constantly be waiting.

She couldn't live that way again.

She turned the latch, prompting Cora to remove her hand. At the far end of the corridor, Sebastian, along with

Lords Helsford and Danforth and Superintendent Reeves, hovered in the entry hall, looking disheveled and dangerous. The sight of Sebastian sent a tide of relief through her body, and she released a *whoosh* of air.

Give him a chance to love you.

As if he sensed her presence, his eyes met hers. Something primitive stole across his handsome features, and he stepped forward as if pulled by the strength of her gaze. Cora squeezed past her and headed straight for her betrothed. The small disruption was enough to sever her visual bond with the earl.

When he retreated beneath the guise of cold civility he wore so splendidly, she smiled inwardly, lifted a battered brick, and began rebuilding her wall.

FORTY-THREE

ebastian's heart nearly exploded with relief to find Catherine hale and looking more beautiful than anyone had a right to after such a harrowing experience.

Confronted with losing her daughter, she had exhibited great courage—and foolishness—in running Cochran to ground. Thank God, the children had been clear of the area when the shooting began. As for Catherine, he could only be grateful that she had listened to him when it counted most.

If something had happened to her and Sophie...

An image of his mentor's wife's dead body flooded his vision. The horror the man must have faced, watching his wife die, haunted Sebastian every time he gazed upon Catherine. Knowing one's wife was about to be murdered and being helpless to do anything to stop it was a nightmare Sebastian had sworn he would never experience.

But he'd come close tonight. Not with a wife, but with a little girl who had somehow attached herself to his heart. As had her mother.

Ice crackled, fusing together, inch by inch, until it slowly encased him inside a protective shell. Only he knew, far too well, that one kiss from Catherine would shatter the fragile barrier, leaving him exposed to a crushing torment.

She must have sensed his withdrawal, for her expression molded itself into one of indifference. Clasping her hands at her waist, she retreated to the study.

"Let us remove to someplace more comfortable," Cora said, clinging to Helsford.

Sebastian followed behind Danforth, Reeves, and the inseparable couple, mentally preparing himself for the next few hours. They had much to discuss and, unfortunately, he would have to pretend that he did not wish to whisk Catherine away to a private chamber.

Not thinking, he strode to the side table holding an assortment of crystal decanters. He poured brandy for the men and sherry for the women. When he made to tip back his first glass, he caught Catherine's concerned look out of the corner of his eye before she hastily averted her attention.

Something unpleasant swelled in his gut. The sensation grew worse when his nose caught its first whiff of the amber liquid's rustic fruity blend, followed swiftly by the sharp sting of alcohol. Lowering his hand, he set the untouched drink down and took up a familiar position near the fireplace.

"Superintendent Reeves," Cora said, "what brings you to Showbury? At such a propitious moment?"

If the Foreign Office official was bothered by Cora's suspicious tone, he did not show it. "Lord Somerton's letter."

Everyone focused their considerable attention on him. "At no time did our evidence point to Reeves, even though he was the logical choice. But I knew Cochran was getting his information from within the Foreign Office, so I took a leap of faith."

"After a few inquiries and several threats," Reeves said, "I found Cochran's source. My clerk, Bradford. A man I trusted."

"Does Cochran even work at the Foreign Office, sir?" Catherine asked.

"Yes, ma'am. He's a minor clerk to the under-secretary of the Foreign Office. In Bradford's defense, he did not realize the information he confided to Cochran was being used for such ill purpose. The man's ambitious nature led him to risky choices. I daresay he hoped Cochran would provide a suitable reference when the time came."

"And the investigation against Lord Somerton?" Helsford asked.

"Dropped."

The room's occupants breathed a collective sigh of relief. Catherine ducked her head and closed her eyes. Sebastian watched her mouth move over silent words.

Tearing his gaze away, he said, "Thank you, sir."

"It is I who should thank you. Although you were not fond of my decision to place you on leave, you appeared to understand." He surveyed the room at large. "And my apologies to all of you—especially Mrs. Ashcroft and her family—for the role my clerk played in this injurious plot. You cannot know how aggrieved I am at your suffering."

"Thank you, Mr. Reeves," she said. "But you are not to blame. If anyone owes us an apology, it is Frederick Cochran, and he is dead. So, we will pick up the pieces of our lives and carry on, good sir."

"You are too gracious, I assure you, ma'am," Reeves said, with a bow. "But I thank you, all the same."

"Three dead bodies in a small village like Showbury are bound to attract some notice." Danforth sank deeper into his chair. "Not good for the Nexus."

"Leave the bodies to me," Sebastian said.

"As I do not fully comprehend what 'leave the bodies to me' means," Catherine said, "I would like to make arrangements for Mrs. Clarke to have a proper burial."

He frowned. "You wish to look after a woman in league with the man who threatened your daughter's life?"

"I do."

"Care to expound, madam?"

"She was a mother."

"I take it the two of you found something in common."

"Before she died, she spoke of her son, Giles." She stared down at her hands for a moment, struggling with emotion. When she raised her head, her eyes were full of empathy. "He's in London, at a boys' home somewhere, to ensure his mother's cooperation. Mrs. Clarke did what she had to do to protect him."

As she had with her daughter, as he would with her and Sophie.

"We'll find the boy," he assured her, recalling the name *Abbingale Home* from Ashcroft's missing letter. His gaze settled on Danforth, who nodded his understanding. If anyone could find the missing link they needed to locate Latymer, it was Danforth.

He directed his next comment to the superintendent. "Near the end, Silas spoke fluent French."

"Perhaps others besides the Frenchman Valère have been working Latymer's marionette strings," Reeves said.

Helsford, who stood behind Cora, smoothed his hand over her short-cropped hair. She grasped his fingers and kissed their tips.

The sight sent an answering pang of longing through Sebastian. When he glanced at Catherine, he found her watching the couple's display of affection as well.

"Where do we go from here?" Danforth asked.

He rubbed his temple, feeling the events of the day depleting his strength. "You can begin making inquiries into Giles Clarke's whereabouts. Start with Abbingale Home." He dropped his hand. "Helsford, see if your informant can track down Latymer."

"What of me?" Cora asked.

"You are on leave until after the first of the year."

"What?"

"If you push me," he said in the hardest voice he could muster, "I will make it permanent."

Cora's body vibrated with anger, but she said nothing.

"Enjoy your respite, runt," her brother said. "Go home and play with that thing you call a kitten. If that doesn't excite you enough, I should like to have a nephew. Or a niece, if you must."

"Ethan," Cora attempted to rise, but Helsford grabbed her shoulders, "do you recall our conversation about your head getting lopped off?"

Danforth held a large bolster across his body like a shield. "No need for violence, sister. Just trying to offer you my support."

Helsford broke in. "Shall we report back to you here? Or London?"

The silence that pervaded the study rubbed his nerves raw, as did the avid stares of everyone in the room. Everyone but one, that was. Catherine's disinterest cut him more deeply than any enemy blade.

"London," he said. "It is past time for my return."

"Well," Catherine said, rising. "Since there is nothing

left for me to do here, I shall collect Sophie and be off. My mother must be frantic with worry."

His stomach knotted, yet he could not bring himself to dissuade her. "I sent a note the moment we returned."

The stiff line of her shoulders eased. "Thank you, my lord."

"Catherine, you must stay the night." Cora sent Sebastian a cross look. "We cannot be certain the danger has passed."

"For me, it has. Cochran and Silas are dead, and Lord Somerton is aware of my ruse. My unique services are of no further use to anyone. Now, if you'll excuse me—"

"Bastian! You're back." A whirlwind of fluttering furbelows and bouncing curls charged into the room and slammed into him. Thin arms enfolded his middle, and Sophie buried her face into the soft fabric of his waistcoat.

Stunned by the child's enthusiastic greeting, he stood rigidly in the center of the study, with his arms aloft. He glanced at Catherine for guidance and found her eyes misted with tears. When she lifted her watery gaze up to his, his heart ripped in half.

Sophie peered up at him. "What took you so long, Bastian? Ethan said you would be along soon, but that was *hours* ago."

He rested a hand on top of her head. "Ethan, is it?"

She gave him a broad grin, one that conveyed she already knew how to wrap a man around her little finger. Then her smile dimmed. "Did you take the bad men to the con-*stable*?"

"Constable, pumpkin."

"Didn't I say that, Mama?"

He crouched down. "You don't ever have to worry about the bad men again."

She leaned into him and toyed with his collar. "Do you promise?"

He tapped his finger beneath her chin. "Promise."

"Brilliant! I told Mama you would always protect us." Her voice lowered into a stage whisper. "She was crying when she returned, and I wanted to make her feel better."

"You were quite right to do so."

She shook her head and tears cracked her voice. "She cried harder, Bastian."

He clenched his teeth so tight that he was certain they would shatter from the pressure. He fought to keep his attention centered on Sophie and not her mother, because if he saw the truth of the girl's words on her mother's face his control would crumble to the ground. "We will have to convince her, won't we?"

Sophie's head bobbed. In a normal voice, she proclaimed, "Teddy has a big bump on his head."

He blinked at her change of topic. "A badge of courage."

"When my head hurts, Guinevere always makes it feel better." Her gaze turned earnest. "Imagine what a whole stable full of horses could do for Teddy's pain."

He chuckled. "Indeed, sprite. You should talk to Lord Danforth about visiting them tomorrow morning. He loves showing off my stables." In typical Danforth fashion, he was more interested in the swirling contents of his glass than the poignant conversation. "Isn't that right, *Ethan?*"

"What?" The viscount snapped to attention. "Uh, yes. That's correct."

"Oh, Ethan!" Sophie skipped across the room and crawled up into Danforth's lap. "Teddy will be so happy."

From the look on Danforth's face, one would think that an enormous spider was crawling across his legs. Slouched down in his chair, Danforth was nose-to-nose with the girl as she nattered on about all the horses she'd seen earlier that day. The viscount sent Sebastian a distressed look, making it impossible for Sebastian to contain his smile.

He gave in to the impulse to look at Catherine. The smile she gave him was warm and appreciative, but coated with a brittle edge. She would survive this just as she had survived her father's death and her husband's murder, a village full of opportunistic shopkeepers, and matrons who sought to place Ashcroft's abandonment on her shoulders.

She would survive the end of their *affaire,* as would he. One minute at a time, one day at a time, one month at a time. Because surviving was what they both did, no matter the personal sacrifice.

"Sophie." Catherine held out her hand. "Allow Lord Danforth to catch his breath. It's time for us to go."

Cora stepped forward. "Please reconsider, Catherine. There's plenty of room."

"I don't think it's a good idea—"

"Cora's right," he heard himself say. "You're welcome to stay. The cloud cover remains thick, making for a treacherous journey."

Sophie vibrated with excitement. "Oh, please, Mama. Can we stay with Bastian?"

Catherine's face softened. "Would you like that?"

"Yes!"

"Very well, but it's time for you to go to bed. You've had a busy day."

Sophie nodded her agreement. "I'll get lots of sleep, so Ethan and I can help Jasper feed the horses in the morning.

Danforth groaned and murmured, "God, help me."

FORTY-FOUR

In her borrowed dressing gown, Catherine paced the length of her bedchamber, knowing she would enjoy little sleep while beneath Sebastian's roof. She had made a mistake in accepting his invitation to stay. Such temptation so close at hand was far stronger than her meager will. She wanted one more night in his embrace, one more evening where she felt womanly and strong and cherished.

One more evening to love him.

Her head fell back, and she stared at the ceiling. How? How had she managed to fall in love with a man burdened with every trait she despised? Why couldn't she have fallen for a nice gentleman like Mr. Foster?

Someone who would spend his entire life in one place. Someone who was gentle and predictable and...*boring*.

She released a huge sigh while taking in the rose-and-lemon furnishings of her bedchamber. It was so different from the countess's cream-and-gold silk-draped chamber. And a good deal safer.

But the more modest-sized room made her feel caged

and restless. She strode to the door leading out to a small balcony and thrust it open. A gentle summer breeze whipped through her loose hair and caressed her burning cheeks. The air was redolent with the lush scent of roses.

The clouds had finally moved on, leaving behind an ebony sky sprinkled with diamonds. Two hours ago, one would never have known such perfection rode above the thick veil of evil. Meghan McCarthy's youthful face surfaced in her mind's eye, and she clenched her teeth against the sadness. Through no fault of her own, the young woman had become embroiled in the machinations of ambitious, greedy men.

Sebastian and the others had speculated that a disguised Cochran had made secret trips into Showbury, looking for clues to Geoffrey's whereabouts and learning the landscape. Somewhere along the way, Meghan had caught Cochran's eye.

Leaning against the iron railing, she absorbed the innocence of Sebastian's moon-kissed gardens and admired every perfectly placed hedge, blooming flower, and gnarled limb. When she reached the sunken garden, a man emerged from beneath the canopy of a small, multi-stemmed tree, his face uplifted, his gaze fixed on her.

Sebastian.

Catherine's fingers curled around the top railing, the metal cool and solid.

The intensity of the moment reminded her of the moment on the road, when she was certain Silas would pull the trigger and kill the love of her life right then, right there. She'd almost lost him.

Her heart thumped an erratic tattoo in her ears, but not loud enough to drown out the single word echoing in her mind.

Go. Go. Go!

Not stopping to think or to consider the consequences, she swung around and rushed through the bedchamber, having no care for her dishabille and bare feet. She stormed through the mansion as if outrunning logic and good sense. She ran until her lungs heaved and her muscles ached. She ran until she came face-to-face with her heaven and her hell.

"Sebastian."

He gave her no time to catch her breath. He framed her face in the cradle of his hands and closed his mouth over hers. She curled her arms around his back and met his fierceness with a passion that bordered on desperation. He tasted of warmed sugar and of tea and mint. He tasted of home.

She broke off for a much-needed breath. "Sebastian."

"Mmm-hmm." His magical lips continued their assault down her throat.

"I don't want you to go."

He froze, and she winced. Where had those words come from? She had intended to beg him to make love to her, not put them both in an untenable situation. "I'm sorry. I-I shouldn't have said—"

Sebastian curled his finger beneath her chin and nudged her face up. "It occurs to me that this is Saturday."

What an odd thing to say when she'd just made a fool of herself. "What of it?"

"That's four days until Wednesday."

"Now that we have established that you know the days of the week and their proper placement, perhaps you could tell me why that's important *now*."

"The timing is important, my impatient one, because it means I'm not going anywhere for four days."

"But you told Lord Helsford to report to you in London."

"Which he can do...after Wednesday."

Vexing man. "I don't understand the significance of this time frame."

"You wound me, madam. The end date of our *affaire* approaches. Does that fact not hold some importance in your heart?"

She studied his tender expression and the playful curve to his mouth. Something had changed in him during the short time they had been apart. Something significant.

"What are you about, sir?"

His lips twitched. "Whatever can you mean, dear lady? The notion that you may have forgotten our pleasurable arrangement calls for some distress on my part, don't you think?"

Her eyes narrowed in warning. "I have not forgotten our arrangement, as you well know. Hearing that you intend to stay for a while longer pleases me a great deal. But I wonder for what purpose?"

The playful amusement left his face. "For the pleasure of each other's company, of course."

"That reason is no longer enough." Her admission hovered in the air between them. They had been through too much, tiptoed around too many issues not to speak plainly now. "I have gone and complicated this situation even more by falling in love with you."

"Catherine, I—"

She set a finger over his lips. "I know you care for me, Sebastian. And I also understand intimate relations amongst your set are commonplace. That our time together was nothing more than a pleasant diversion for you during your banishment."

He pulled her finger away. "I admit that was the case in the beginning."

"I'm not casting judgment. Lord knows I have no right to after what I've done."

He skimmed the side of his finger along her temple. "You are a mother. You did what you had to."

"Perhaps," she said. "Perhaps not. One always has options."

"Does that mean you wanted to share my bed?"

For far longer than you shall ever know, my dear sweet lord. "You sound surprised."

"Relieved, more like. A man is no different from a woman in this regard. We want to be desired for ourselves and not for what one can gain from an association with us."

The vulnerable quality to his statement made her throat ache. "My point in all this is to release you from our arrangement."

His countenance darkened. "What if I don't wish to be released?"

"Sebastian, it would not be wise for you to stay." She squeezed his hand. "Surely, you see that."

"I don't."

She pushed out of his arms and paced away. The stubborn man was going to make her splay open her soul in all its foolish glory. "If you leave now, there's a slight chance that I might survive this *affaire.*" She raised her tear-drenched gaze to his. "Stay, and I am l-lost."

"Cat," he said thickly, taking a step toward her.

Unable to speak, she shook her head. One touch from him and she would gladly plunge into an abyss of heartache.

"Will you answer one question?" he asked.

She moistened her dry lips. "Of course."

"If I resigned my position as chief, would you have me?"

Her heart fluttered. "Have you?"

"As a husband?"

"You would do that?" she asked, startled. "Give up the Nexus—for me?"

"Without hesitation."

"But why? Why would you give up a cause that you have devoted your life to?" Her eyes narrowed. "I hope not because of some bothersome gentleman's code. My honor does not need protecting."

"No." The rich timbre of his voice prickled her skin. "Nothing so inconvenient as protecting your honor."

"Then why?"

"Because I love you and want nothing more than to spend the rest of my days with you and your managing daughter."

The tears spilled over her lids and streamed down her cheeks. "Truly?"

He smiled. "Truly."

"I deceived you in the worst possible way."

"Not the worst way, Catherine. Believe me." He smoothed his thumb over her damp cheek. "You exhibited great courage during a dangerous situation. A quality to be admired, not judged."

"Cora knows you well."

"Does she?"

She slid her hand up his chest. "I didn't dare believe her when she said you'd understand why I did what I did."

"I hadn't realized my agent had become a damned matchmaker."

"She wants you to have what she and Lord Helsford have."

"You may spare me the Raven's wisdom. I shall have to put up with her gloating looks for years as it is."

She toyed with a pleat on the shoulder of his shirt-sleeves. "Sebastian, I don't want you to give up the Nexus. They need you. As does England."

The muscle beneath her fingers stiffened. "My position requires me to be away for long periods of time and often without notice."

Past hurts crowded into her mind. "I won't lie and say that condition won't be difficult. A few assurances on your part might be necessary."

"What sort of assurances?"

She tried twice to force the words out, but they clung to the back of her throat.

He combed his fingers through her hair, soothing her like one would a distressed animal. "Don't lose your nerve now, my love." The tenderness in his voice made her eyes sting.

"That you'll always put us—Sophie and me—first."

"Done."

She raised a brow. "Just like that?"

"Perhaps you need something more tangible?"

She could do nothing but stare at him like a young miss right out of the schoolroom.

"Reeves offered me the undersuperintendent position." He fanned her hair over her shoulders. "I would be required to stay in London—no jaunts to the continent, no covert missions. My responsibilities would include coordinating the Nexus's efforts with those of the Foreign and Home Offices."

"Does this position interest you?" She tried to keep the budding hope from her tone.

"Oh, yes." He kissed her cheek, the corner of her mouth. "It would allow me to get started."

Her breaths came in short bursts. "Started on what?"

"A family."

Warmth encased her heart. "I believe such a task requires a wife."

"Indeed, it does." He whispered the words near her ear a moment before his lips closed around her earlobe.

Tingles raced down her spine, and she arched her lower body into his hardness.

"I believe one will become available next summer, after a certain mourning period has elapsed."

He worshipped her throat with slow, openmouthed kisses. Stopping only long enough to say, "Perfect. I have much to settle in the intervening months."

"Like locating Lord Latymer?"

"Yes." He trailed his tongue along her collarbone. "Before this incident, he was nothing more than a French pawn, for reasons I still don't understand. Now he's an active participant, which makes him a great deal more dangerous."

"Who will replace you as chief?"

"A good question." He slid her gown off one shoulder. "Helsford, Cora, and Danforth are the most experienced of my agents. All three are trustworthy, intelligent, and strong. However, choosing between the three of them would be like selecting my favorite place on your body to kiss." His lips skimmed the top of her breast. "Impossible."

"Whatever choice you make will be the right one." She arched her back, giving him greater access to her breast. "You will visit us often?"

"No."

"No?" Her head jerked up.

He kissed her nose. "I will have no need to visit, because you and Sophie will be with me."

"In London?"

"Yes, or Bellamere. Or Winter's Hollow. We can divide our time between the city and the country. But no matter where we settle, we'll be together. So much so, you will become sick of me and beg a reprieve."

She snaked her arms around his neck, happier than she'd been in years. More complete. "Never, my lord."

"That's what I was hoping you would say." He bent to whisper in her ear. "Have I ever told you about the delights to be found in this particular section of the garden?"

He backed her into the shadows until the ground beneath their feet softened and the sweet scent of freshly shorn grass reached her nose. Then slowly, inexorably, he lowered her to the velvety carpet and proceeded to show her how a spymaster loves his lady.

Above all else.

～

Thank you for reading *A Lady's Temptation*!

A LADY'S SECRET, Book 3 and Lord Danforth's story, is now available!

Next in Series:

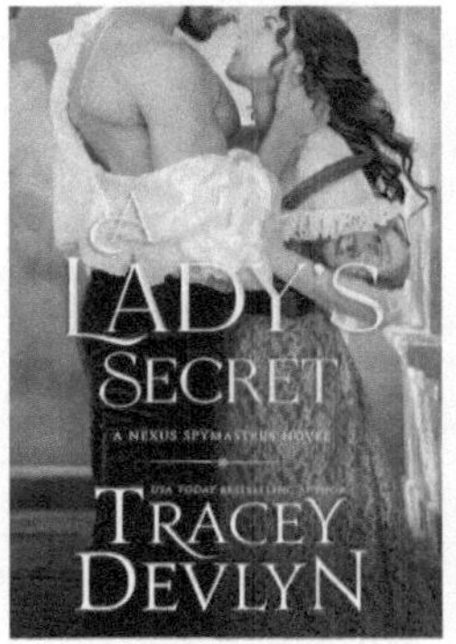

A mysterious proprietress investigates a home for boys while fighting her desire for a boudoir spy who could cost her everything.

A LADY'S SECRET

BY TRACEY DEVLYN

Enjoy an excerpt from *A **Lady's** Secret*, Book 3 in my
Nexus Spymasters series:

Ethan deBeau, Viscount Danforth, hated being a
drunkard.

The occupation enjoyed none of the creature
comforts to which he was accustomed. Indeed, for the past
hour, he had been forced to lounge on the hard ground,
propped against a gnarled tree, in too-tight clothes that
reeked of unwashed flesh and stale liquor. And if that
weren't enough, his surveillance position was directly
above a rather active anthill.

Once Lord Somerton appointed him Chief of the
Nexus, he would never again have to fend off insects, sit
on the ground, or seduce secrets from unsuspecting
women.

Of course, not being in the field meant long hours
behind a desk, reading mounds of reports, and attending

meeting after meeting. He wasn't sure which would be worse—the ants or the paperwork.

One niggling thought caused his pulse to jump. *Who was his competition?* The Nexus was so shrouded in secrecy that one secret service agent could be dancing with another and not even know it.

He knew the identities of only two agents—his sister Cora deBeau and best friend Guy Trevelyan. Others he suspected, but it wasn't as though he could insert the question into a conversation.

What would he say? *Hello, I'm an agent with the Nexus. Are you?*

A larger, more inquisitive ant took advantage of Ethan's moment of inattention to race up his inner thigh, heading straight for his groin. He flicked it off, the movement jarring his too-large pilfered hat, so that it now blocked his view of the boys' home.

With the jerky movement of the inebriated, he swiped his hand across his forehead and pushed it back into position. Just in time to see a child emerge from the lower-level servant's entrance of the Abbingale Home for Displaced and Gifted Boys, also known as the Home or Abbingale. The boy, perhaps seven or eight years old, scrambled up the stairs to street level, then took off.

Ethan raised a half-empty bottle of gin to his lips while he followed the boy's zigzag progress down White Horse Lane. Once the child disappeared into the crowd, Ethan turned back to the boys' home and continued to mentally catalog every rippling curtain, passing silhouette, and inquiring vendor. He noted anything and everything of possible interest and would sort through the morass tonight.

As soon as he understood Abbingale's daily operation,

he would make plans to penetrate the home, search for Giles Clarke, and extract the boy. He had never heard of the child until a sennight ago, when a dying Lydia Clarke had begged the Nexus to rescue her son. And so they would, even though settling domestic issues was not one of the agency's objectives.

The Nexus's main purpose was more far-reaching. Some would say more important than saving a single child.

Operating under the auspice of the Alien Office, a little-known section of the Foreign Office, Nexus secret service agents worked tirelessly to prevent Napoleon Bonaparte from breaching England's shores.

For now, he would see to the boy's safety—assuming he was inside Abbingale—then turn his attention to discovering why a murdered Nexus agent would mention Abbingale Home in his last coded messages.

A black carriage, with a driver in front and two footmen hanging onto the back, rolled to a halt outside the boys' home. Ethan's senses perked up, even while his body slouched farther into its uncomfortable pose.

The footmen jumped down, one running to help his employer alight and the other to rap on the Home's door.

Through the carriage window, he glimpsed two feminine profiles before their shadowy figures slipped out of sight. They reappeared a few seconds later, ascending the front steps. The women were opposites in every way.

One stood several inches above the other, with dark hair, square shoulders, and clothes stylish enough to grace any *ton* drawing room, while the shorter blond wore more sedate clothing and clutched a notebook to her chest.

The entrance door swung open, and the women strode inside.

His interest shifted to the bewigged footmen, who

appeared, from this distance, to be a perfectly matched pair. Handsome, too. *Bravo*, he thought.

Accomplishing such a difficult feat assured their mistress a place of envy amongst the hostesses of her set. Why the wealthy put so much stock into something of so little consequence, he didn't know. But then again, he had once spent an entire sennight searching for a matching pair of bays to complement his new phaeton.

When the footmen put their heads together in conversation, Ethan slung his knapsack over his shoulder and rolled to his feet. He drew hard on his gin bottle before toddling across the cobbles toward them in an uneven line. The more clean-shaven of the two footmen noticed his approach and eyed him like one would a rabid animal.

Ethan stubbed his toe on a nonexistent stone, making a big show of catching his balance. "Damn me, who put that there?" He glanced around while grumbling to himself and scratching the back of his head.

The eagle-eyed footman finally decided Ethan posed no threat and rejoined his companion. After a couple more tottering steps, he came within hearing distance.

"My bones hurt," the stubble-faced footman said.

His partner sent him a sharp glance. "How long?"

"Not quite sure," stubble man said. "You know how it is."

"Make a guess."

"No need to get testy, Mac. The pain started gradual-like. Sometimes it's there for a while before my brain registers the discomfort."

Eagle-eyed Mac sighed. "When did you first notice your bones, Mick?"

"When we were leaving the agency."

Mac glanced up at the Abbingale's facade. "You should have told me before now, dammit."

Ethan veered around the two men and stumbled up onto the foot pavement, belting back a drink and swaying to the side.

"What?" Mick asked. "You think you could have stopped her?"

"That's not the point. I could have warned her to stay alert."

"Do you even realize what you're saying? Have you ever known Miss Hunt—"

"*Shhh.*"

"Right." Mick glanced around. "Have you ever known her to go into a situation with blinders on? Get your head out of your heart, brother."

"My head is exactly where it needs to be," Mac said in a lethal tone. "As will be my fist, if you don't shut your trap."

"There's nothing that can come of it. You'd be better off paying more attention to the looks Amelia keeps giving you."

"Amelia, is it?"

Mick's mouth curled into a roguish smile. "Since you seem inclined to let another snap her up, I decided it should be me. I've become quite friendly with the wee assistant. Sweet thing."

Mac stepped forward. "Keep your filthy hands off Mrs. Cartwright."

"You can't have them both."

Hoping the footmen would continue their conversation, Ethan plopped down on Abbingale's steps and curled up into a nap-worthy ball. His new position shook things up a bit, causing him to burp loudly. Gin fumes stung his nostrils.

The two brothers on the verge of a nice bout of fisticuffs turned to him. Both had the same rugged features highlighted by the lightest blue eyes he'd ever seen. They were indeed perfectly matched.

Twins.

"Here now." Mick grabbed his arm. "You can't bed down there."

He knocked the other man's hand away. "I'll cut ye heart out if ye try to steal me medicine again."

"Medicine." Mac snorted in disgust. "We don't want your damned gin." He moved to the other side.

Strong hands clasped him by his upper arms and yanked him into a standing position.

"Good God, man," Mick said. "Are you drinking your spirits or bathing in them?"

"Let me go, ye bleeders. Ye got no cause to send me on me way."

"That's where you're wrong," Mac said.

"Can't have you blocking our mistress's way when she comes out," Mick said. "Besides, don't want you scaring any of the children."

They half-dragged, half-carried him several feet away before propping him up against the building next door.

"Too fine a lady to walk around?" he mumbled, checking to make sure he still had his knapsack.

"The very finest," Mac said.

Mick tugged on his coat at various places, presumably to make him more presentable. "Sober up first, my friend," he said with a pat to Ethan's shoulder.

He frowned, not understanding the footman's advice. "First for what?"

But the stubble-faced footman only winked at him before they resumed their positions near the carriage.

Beneath the rim of his hat, he studied the twins, marveling at their firm, yet respectful care of him. They obviously held their mistress—Miss Hunt—in high regard. Every time they spoke of her, their voices took on a reverent tone.

Abbingale's entrance door opened, and the estimable Miss Hunt and her assistant swept through the opening.

Halfway down the steps, Miss Hunt gave her footmen a hard shake of her pretty head. The action struck a discordant note with him, but he was at a loss as to say why.

From his new vantage point, he affirmed his earlier assessment of the lady and developed some new ones.

High cheekbones, black eyebrows above emerald eyes, and a strong, yet feminine jawline made her an intriguing contrast to many of England's delicate, oval-faced beauties. The high-necked gown and pelisse did nothing to obscure the elegant quality of her statuesque frame. She not only walked with a confident stride, she held a man's eye with no timidity.

Like she was doing with him right now.

Recognition struck him hard in the chest. His path had crossed with hers once before. *But where?* The answer danced just out of range, then disappeared altogether.

The woman raised a brow, and he realized he'd been staring. Cursing beneath his breath, he blinked owlishly. "Ye gents didn't tell me yer lady was so buxom. I wouldn't have been so easily removed." He produced a belch for good measure.

She slashed another glance at her eagle-eyed footman, who shrugged his shoulders. "Come along, Mrs. Cartwright."

The assistant nodded, and the women started down the steps.

"Mrs. Henshaw, your gloves." An older woman emerged from Abbingale's entrance door, holding out a pair of kidskin gloves to...*Miss Hunt.*

His gaze sharpened as Miss Hunt's hard features transformed into a vapid expression he'd seen a hundred times in ballrooms across London.

"Oh, dear me," Miss Hunt tittered. "I would have been quite distraught without my favorite pair of kids."

He cast a brief glance to the footmen standing at the bottom of the steps. Mac's stony expression revealed nothing, as usual; however, his brother seemed to be holding back a smile.

"Thank you." Miss Hunt's assistant accepted the gloves from the older woman and handed them to her mistress.

Miss Hunt clasped her kids to her chest and flashed a brilliant smile at the older woman. "Good day, Mrs. Drummond. I shall return soon."

Twirling about, Miss Hunt led the way to the carriage. Once the women were settled inside, Mac secured the steps and closed the door. Within seconds, the carriage lurched forward and the footmen jumped onto the rear.

As they passed, Mick gave Ethan a jaunty salute.

Ethan swiped his nose.

The footman laughed.

After following the carriage's progress for a while, he glanced back at the Home. What he saw there surprised him. The older woman—Mrs. Drummond—watched Miss Hunt's conveyance roll away with something akin to hatred sparkling in her eyes.

What was going on?

A footman in love with two women, a well-dressed lady

whose business at the boys' home upset the staff? A lady who also answered to two different names? What did her footmen need to warn her about?

Any other mission, he would dismiss the incident and refocus on his original assignment. But his ultimate target was more than likely linked to this place, which meant he had to follow every possible trail. Besides, he wanted to know where he'd come across Miss Hunt before.

Something about her features had sparked an air of familiarity, one he was compelled to connect with again.

He turned to gauge the carriage's location and cringed at how far it had traveled. Time to go. He would return to Abbingale tomorrow.

Careful not to break his cover, he took another drink of his gin and got to his feet, readjusting his knapsack over his shoulder. The older woman's malevolent gaze shot to his location, and he raised his near-empty bottle in her direction.

The woman squared her shoulders and sniffed the air as if she'd caught scent of something offensive before pivoting to reenter the boys' home. She shut the door with ominous finality.

Feeling a sense of urgency now, he wove his way down the foot pavement, stopping occasionally to scratch an inappropriate area or to cough up a disturbing amount of phlegm. A few minutes later, he straightened his spine, tossed his bottle in a bush, and laid his tattered coat across a bedraggled woman curled up beneath a lamppost.

He quickened his step. When Miss Hunt's carriage turned a corner, he changed his stride to a full-out run.

His hat flew off, and he tightened his grip on his knapsack's strap. Rounding the corner, he came to an abrupt and jarring halt. Miss Hunt's carriage sat idle in the lane, waiting for traffic to clear.

He searched for a doorway, a cart, a building, anything large enough to hide his big frame. He started for a nearby alleyway when the sound of his name stopped him cold.

"Danforth," an incredulous voice said, "is that you, old boy?"

Equal parts relieved and frustrated, he considered ignoring the Marquess of Shevington. The gentleman's slurred words were a testament to too much drink and not enough sleep. Knowing Shev, he probably hadn't slept at all and would likely not even recall hailing Ethan ten minutes from now.

He chanced a look at Miss Hunt's conveyance, and found her footmen's attention on the clog of carriages ahead and not the scene unfolding behind.

Decision made, he finger-combed his hair before facing the marquess's squinting countenance.

"Good God, it is you," the marquess said, hanging his head out the open carriage window. "What in blazes are you doing here, dressed like that?"

Striding forward, Ethan opened the carriage door and bounded inside. "Morning, Shev." Instead of taking the open, back-facing seat, he squeezed in next to his old school chum. "Be a good man and tell your driver to follow the carriage with the green livery."

The marquess dug out his handkerchief, flicked it open, and used it to cover his nose. "My word." The linen muffled his words. "Someone must have tried to drown your aristocratic hide in a vat of Blue Ruin. Either that, or you're harboring a dead animal upon your person." He moved to sit on the opposite side of the carriage. "Tell me you did not leave the lush confines of Madame Rousseau's last night for," he waved a hand toward Ethan's attire, "this."

Ethan began digging items out of his knapsack and tossing them onto the bench next to his friend. "You had disappeared into the depths of the Pearl and Ruby Room, so I had to make my own way home."

"You're blaming me for your current dishabille?"

"In a word, yes." Opening the door, he checked Miss Hunt's location and gave Shev's driver instructions to follow. Before sitting back, he drew the window curtain closed, leaving a small opening.

"Are you absconding with my carriage?" Shev asked, sounding more intrigued than put out.

The vehicle lurched into motion. "For a little while."

He and the marquess had been in each other's pockets since before either could speak an intelligible word. Shev knew nothing of his life with the Nexus, and Ethan went to great pains to keep it that way. Even though Shev had come across his friend in some odd situations—such as now—the marquess always seemed content with his less-than-descriptive explanations.

Lifting the tail end of his shirtsleeve, Ethan ripped off the foul-smelling coarse garment and rubbed his hands over his chafed skin.

"What, may I ask, are you doing?" Shev drawled.

He grabbed a clean shirt from the stash of clothes he'd pulled from his knapsack. "Your eyesight can't be that bad, old man." Soft linen cascaded over his bare torso, soothing his abraded flesh. He began working on the fastenings of his filthy breeches.

"Really, Danforth, must you do that now?" The marquess peeled back the curtain to peer outside. "What if we're set upon by highwaymen and they thrust open the door to find you in your smalls? Do you know what that will do to my reputation and my chances of continuing on with my dissolute existence?"

Ethan pushed his breeches down and removed his stockings. "Have you always had such dramatic inclinations?"

The marquess sniffed and turned away from the window. "Protecting one's reputation is a constant struggle."

"You must be very busy." He drew on fresh stockings.

"I suppose if I ask about your activities, you'll tell me to get buggered."

"You suppose correctly."

"Why do I bother being your friend if everything is a secret?"

"Because of my charming wit?"

Shev snorted. "Please alert me when either your charm or your wit appears. I'd like to make a note of the occasion."

"Continue along this same vein, and I'll be forced to remove my smalls, too."

"Good God, Danforth." Shev leaned away. "No need to threaten me with blindness."

Ethan sent his friend a quelling glance while he jabbed his feet into his breeches, arched off the bench enough to draw his buckskins about his waist, and fastened the front placard.

He tackled his neckcloth, tying it into a simple knot, before pulling on a buff-colored waistcoat shot with silver thread. His exertions left a fine line of moisture along his hairline, which he used to help bring some order to his tousled hair.

Spreading his arms wide, he asked, "How do I look?"

The marquess appraised his appearance with a discerning eye. "Like a degenerate viscount?"

"Perfect."

The carriage jolted to a halt, and a liveried footman approached the window. "What would you like the coachman to do, my lord? The carriage stopped outside Fifty-seven Mansell."

Shev sent Ethan a this-is-your-adventure-not-mine look.

He said, "Drive by slowly, but not so slow as to draw attention."

"Yes, sir."

Seconds later, the slap of reins and the jangle of tack reached Ethan's ears before the carriage rolled forward at a sedate pace. Anticipation curled around his insides, gliding over each organ with aching slowness, squeezing gently, inexorably.

Number 57 stood at the edge of a long row of town houses. The building's edifice looked as though it had received special care in the last few years, with new windows and a refurbished limestone portico supported by Ionic pillars. Flowers flourished in tall earthenware urns placed on each side of the entrance.

Above the door swung a sign. He squinted to make out the words.

"Hunt Agency," Shev said near his ear before plopping back in his seat. "Charming. Are you going to finally hire a valet instead of depending on your poor butler for such duties?"

Once they had passed, he sat back. "You're familiar with the agency?"

"Most households are." Shev sent him a pointed look. "It's only the most prominent staffing agency in London.

Operated by the iron will and hand of Miss Sydney Hunt. I'm sure your housekeeper can provide more detail." His eyes narrowed. "What is your interest in the proprietress of the Hunt Agency?"

"Curiosity, nothing more."

The marquess released a long sigh. "There's always something more with you, Danforth. Are you quite finished with your clandestine activities? I need to be rid of you, so that I might go home and sleep the day away." He glanced out the carriage window, his head tilted in a way to suggest he was noting the blue sky and bright sunshine. "It's far too cheerful-looking for one of my disposition."

Chuckling, he said, "I don't recall you being so querulous in the morning."

"And I don't recall ever having my carriage and person seized before."

"I'm glad to be your first." He draped an arm over the back of the seat, propped a booted foot next to the marquess, and waved his hand in the air. "You may proceed in getting rid of me."

He thought his friend mumbled "Thank God" beneath his breath before barking out orders to his driver.

Would Miss Hunt complicate his mission to find Giles Clarke? Why was she poking around his boys' home, using an alias and acting the featherbrain? Once he figured out their prior connection, he would coax the answers to his questions from the lovely Miss Hunt. Of this, he had no doubt. Because that's what the Nexus paid him to do.

Seduce information from the most beautiful women in the world.

Anticipation unfurled in his chest, the sensation shocking due to its scarcity. How long had it been since he'd looked forward to such an assignment?

Years.

He rubbed his palm over his tight chest, over his thundering heart.

The corners of his mouth lifted into a predatory smile.

Find out what happens next and order
A LADY'S SECRET

DID YOU ENJOY A LADY'S TEMPTATION?

Please consider leaving a short review on the site where you purchased the book, asking your local library to carry it, and/or gushing about it to a friend.

Reader recommendations are so important!

They help other readers find amazing, new-to-them books, which allows authors (like me!) to write more adventures. A win-win for everyone.

Many, many thanks! Your support and encouragement means the world to me.

ACKNOWLEDGMENTS

In addition to the original acknowledgments below, I would also like to thank Martha Trachtenberg for helping me breathe new life into this remastered edition of *A Lady's Temptation*, Elizabeth Mackey for designing an incredible cover, and Sandy Modesitt for catching those pesky typos.

~

A huge thanks to my amazing editor, Deb Werksman, and my patient agent, Donald Maass, for believing in my stories and me and for helping me make them shine.

Much love to my husband, Tim. You are my rock, my love, and my sunshine. Thanks for enduring the rigors of my sophomore book and for keeping me supplied with Slim Jims, Starbucks, and pasta puttanesca. I can't wait to climb more mountains with you.

Sending a shout-out to my awesome publicist, Beth Pehlke. Thanks for all your support and for making my releases seamless and fun. Heartfelt thanks to the rest of the Sourcebooks team—Skye Agnew, Susie Benton, Cat Clyne, and my incredible cover designer, Aleta Rafton. A special thanks to Danielle Jackson.

Big hugs to my critique partners Adrienne Giordano, Kelsey Browning, Theresa Stevens, and Tara Kingston.

You are the best, most amazing buds a girl could have. Thanks for always being there for me.

This acknowledgment would not be complete if I did not express my gratitude to my friend and fellow author Dyanne Davis. Enormous thanks to you (and Bill!) for spotlighting local writers at Bolingbrook Community Television. It's always a pleasure to be your guest. You're an incredible advocate for the romance genre and to writers at every level.

And to readers, librarians, and booksellers everywhere —thank you, thank you, thank you!!

ABOUT TRACEY DEVLYN

Tracey Devlyn is a *USA Today* bestselling author of historical and contemporary suspense, which often contains elements of mystery, romance, and environmental crime. Despite the thrilling, emotional ride she crafts for her readers, Tracey enjoys an annoyingly normal lifestyle with her husband and rescue dogs at her home in the mountains of North Carolina.

For access to exclusive content, new release notifications, special promotions, and behind-the-scenes peeks, join Tracey's VIP Reader List at https://TraceyDevlyn.com/Contact.

www.TraceyDevlyn.com
tracey@traceydevlyn.com

www.ingramcontent.com/pod-product-compliance
Lightning Source LLC
Chambersburg PA
CBHW030957190726
48285CB00004BB/1355